The Dying Season

The Dying Season

A Bruno,
Chief of Police
Novel

Martin Walker

W F HOWES LTD

This large print edition published in 2015 by
W F Howes Ltd
Unit 4, Rearsby Business Park, Gaddesby Lane,
Rearsby, Leicester LE7 4YH

1 3 5 7 9 10 8 6 4 2

First published in the United Kingdom in 2015
by Quercus Publishing Ltd

A CIP catalogue record for this book is available
from the British Library

ISBN 978 1 51000 537 2

Typeset by Palimpsest Book Production Limited,
Falkirk, Stirlingshire

Printed and bound in Great Britain
by TJ International Ltd, Padstow, Cornwall

MIX
Paper from
responsible sources
FSC® C013056

This book is dedicated to three wonderful women: Micheline Morissonneau, of Périgord Tourisme, Marie-Pierre Tamagnon and Anne Lataste, both of Vins de Bergerac, for all their unfailing help, support and friendship. I would not have learned half as much about the charms of our lovely region without them.

CHAPTER 1

B enoît Courrèges, chief of police of the small French town of St Denis and known to everyone as Bruno, had been looking forward to this day so much that he'd never considered the possibility that it might end in tragedy. The prospect of meeting his boyhood hero, of being invited into the home and shaking the hand of one of the most illustrious sons of France, had awed him. And Bruno was not easily awed.

Bruno had followed the career of the Patriarch since as a boy he had read of his exploits in a much-thumbed copy of *Paris Match* in a dentist's waiting room. He had devoured the article and dreamed of starting a scrapbook, but lacked access to the magazines and newspapers he would require. Instead he made do with libraries, first at his church orphanage and later, when he'd been taken into the household of his aunt, at the public library in Bergerac. The images had remained in his head: his hero silhouetted against camouflaged fighter planes in the snow; wearing shorts and a heavy side arm in some desert; drinking toasts in some ornate palace or grand salon. His favourite was

1

the one that showed the pilot, his helmet just removed and his hair tousled, waving from his cockpit to a cheering crowd of mechanics and airmen after he'd become the first Frenchman to break the sound barrier.

Now the great moment had arrived and Bruno could not help but smile at his own excitement. Bruno had worn uniform himself, knew the chaos of orders and counter-orders and all the messy friction of war. He knew, as only a veteran can, that the public image of the Patriarch must conceal flaws, fiascos and botched operations. He should have grown out of this hero worship by now. But some stubborn, glowing core remained of that boyhood devotion he had felt to a man he thought of as France's last hero.

As he waited in the receiving line to shake his hero's hand, Bruno knew that he'd never attended an event so lavish nor so exclusive. The chateau was not large, just three storeys and four sets of windows on each side of the imposing double-doors of the entrance. But its proportions were perfect and it had been lovingly restored. And while the adjoining tower with its stubby battlements was medieval, the chateau embodied the discreet elegance of the eighteenth century. The string quartet on the broad terrace overlooking the formal gardens was playing the 'Autumn' movement from Vivaldi's *Four Seasons*, a piece which perfectly suited the surroundings. Bruno could imagine the Fragonard paintings of perfectly posed maidens that should grace its rooms.

Below the terrace, at least a hundred people were sipping champagne as they chatted and strolled in the gardens. The sound of women's laughter made a perfect backdrop to the music. Around him, almost as many guests again were mingling, picking glasses from the trays offered by the waiters dressed in air force uniform. He heard snatches of conversation in English, German, Russian and Arabic, and picked out at least a dozen different national uniforms. He recognized politicians from Paris, Toulouse and Bordeaux, mostly conservatives, but with a scattering of socialist mayors and ministers from the government in Paris.

All the male guests without exception seemed to defer to a stunningly attractive blonde woman whom Bruno had just met, the Patriarch's daughter-in-law, Madeleine, who was acting as his hostess. Earlier, she had given Bruno a cool smile of welcome and raked him with a glance while shaking his hand in a practised way that moved him on to her husband, next in the receiving line.

Beyond the formal gardens of the chateau, the fields to the right sloped away to the River Dordogne and the grazing Charolais cattle looked as if they had been carefully positioned in place. To the left, between two ridges that were covered in trees turning gold and red, a lazy curve of the River Vézère glinted in the autumnal sun. Even the weather, Bruno thought, would not dare to spoil the ninetieth birthday of such a distinguished son of France.

'This must be one of the finest views in the country,' said the elderly woman known as the Red Countess, looking up at him from her wheelchair. 'That church spire on one side of the river and the ruined castle on the other make it almost perfect. Marco bought this place for a song, you know. I was with him when he first saw it and decided to buy it. I think it helped that my own chateau was close by.' She paused, smiling.

'Where did you meet him, *grand'mère*?' asked Marie-Françoise, the Countess's American-born heiress. She was looking fresh and enchanting in a simple dress of heavy blue silk that matched her eyes. Her French, once halting but improved by her time at university in Bordeaux, was now fluent.

'I met him in Moscow, where he was a star. It was the Kremlin reception after Stalin's funeral, and Marco looked magnificent in full dress uniform. The only medal he wore was his Hero of the Soviet Union. Everybody knew him, of course. Our Ambassador was rather put out that Marco was given precedence over him. Khrushchev came up to embrace him. Apparently they'd met somewhere on the Ukraine front after the Battle of Stalingrad.'

She looked up at her great-granddaughter and gave a gleeful smile that made her look younger than her years. 'I'll never forget those frosty glances from the other women present when Marco came up to give me his arm. *Mon Dieu*, he was a handsome beast. He still is, in his way.'

Bruno followed her gaze to the double doors leading from the terrace into the chateau where the man known across France as the Patriarch was still receiving his guests. He stood erect in his beautifully cut suit of navy blue, the red of his tie matching the discreet silk in his lapel that marked him as one of the Légion d'Honneur. His back was as straight as a ruler and his thick white hair fell in curls onto his collar. His jaw was still as firm as his handshake, and his sharp brown eyes missed nothing. They had looked curiously at Bruno when he'd first appeared, pushing the wheelchair. But once Bruno was introduced by the Red Countess as the local policeman who had saved her life, the eyes had crinkled into warm appreciation.

'That is the magic of this woman,' he'd said, in the voice of a much younger man, and he'd bent to kiss her hand. 'She always finds a knight errant when she needs one.'

Colonel Jean-Marc Desaix was known to his fellow airmen and the women he had loved as Marco. But to the rest of France he was simply the Patriarch, a war hero in two countries, recipient of the Grand Cross of the Légion d'Honneur and the gold star and red ribbon of a Hero of the Soviet Union. The first had been presented by his friend Charles de Gaulle, and the second by Stalin himself at a glittering ceremony in the Kremlin.

Like most French boys, Bruno knew that the Normandie Niemen squadron of French pilots flying Soviet-built Yak fighters had shot down more enemy aircraft than any other French unit. And it had been the second-highest scoring squadron in all the Red Air Force, shooting down 273 enemy planes. Twenty-two of them had been downed by Marco Desaix, then a dashing young man whose bold good looks featured constantly in Soviet newsreels and newspapers. For occupied France, hearing of his exploits over the BBC, Marco became a hero at a time when France had sore need of such warriors.

Bruno had read it all in one of the tattered books in the orphanage library. He'd thrilled to the exotic names of the young fighter pilot's postings in Syria and Persia and tried to imagine the long train journey from desert heat to Russian cold. To this day he remembered that the French fighters shot down their first enemy, a Focke-Wulf fighter, on 5 April, 1943. By the end of the summer, they had shot down seventy more, and were down to six surviving pilots. But they had won more than just their dogfights. Claiming that these men were rebels and traitors to their Vichy-run homeland, the Nazi Field Marshal Wilhelm Keitel ordered that any captured French pilot should be shot out of hand and their families back home in France should be arrested and despatched to concentration camps.

Bruno had vowed to become a pilot, like his hero, until an overworked teacher in his overcrowded school told him brusquely that his poor scores in maths and physics ruled out any prospect of him being accepted by the French Air Force. As the next best thing, Bruno volunteered to join the French Army before his seventeenth birthday. But he could still read about the adventurous career of Marco Desaix. He had returned to France in 1945, leading the flight of forty Yak fighters that Stalin had decided the Normandie-Niemen pilots could fly home to join the reborn French Air Force.

Then in 1948, with discreet official backing, Marco volunteered to fly for the infant state of Israel. He found himself flying a Messerschmitt fighter donated by the Czech Government and became an ace all over again. Back in France, he joined Dassault Aviation as a test pilot and became the first French pilot to break the sound barrier. Marco then helped Dassault sell its Mystère and Mirage jet fighters, which became the core of the new Israeli Air Force, and launched his next career as a businessman, becoming a director of Dassault and later of Air France and Airbus. Finally, in tribute to a long and patriotic career, he had been elected to the Senate.

It was an epic life that Bruno knew by heart and so the invitation to attend the Patriarch's ninetieth birthday celebration at his chateau had thrilled him beyond measure. He knew he'd not been invited on his own account but was there as escort to the Red Countess, as a man who could be relied on to manage a wheelchair and its fragile passenger.

CHAPTER 2

Among the guests in the garden, Bruno saw only a handful of people he knew. The Mayor and Dr Gelletreau from St Denis were chatting with Hubert, who owned the town's celebrated wine *cave*, and the stylish Clothilde Daunier, curator of the national museum of prehistory at Les Eyzies and a scholar with an international reputation. Beyond them, he saw his friend Jack Crimson, a supposedly retired British spymaster who had a house outside St Denis, chatting with the French Foreign Minister.

Beside Crimson, looking very fine with her red-bronze hair piled high, Bruno spotted Pamela, the woman who had been his lover for the past year, although he wondered increasingly how long their affair would continue. She'd been delighted when Crimson had asked her to accompany him to the Patriarch's birthday, the event of the season. She had courteously asked Bruno if he approved. Of course, he had said, stilling the twinge of jealousy that lasted until the Countess had called to ask him to escort her and her great-granddaughter. Pamela caught his eye and feeling obliged to stay in attendance on the Countess, Bruno waved and beckoned her to come and join them on the terrace. To his surprise, Pamela shrugged coolly in return and turned back to give Crimson her renewed attention.

'Who was that?' the Countess asked.

'A friend,' said Bruno, and changed the subject, asking about the Patriarch's family. The Countess evidently knew them well. His son, Victor, also a former pilot who now ran the family vineyard, and his wife, Madeleine, had each embraced her in the receiving line. Victor must have been around sixty, Bruno calculated, but his vivacious wife seemed much younger. Bruno would have guessed her to be in her early thirties. So he was startled when their daughter, Chantal, approached and hugged Marie-Françoise, whom she knew from university. Chantal must be around twenty so that made her mother closer to forty, Bruno's own age.

As Chantal greeted the Countess and Bruno, her mother suddenly appeared. Placing an elegant hand on the shoulder of each of the young women she posed, briefly cocking an eyebrow at Bruno, before saying to the Countess, 'Marie-Françoise looks so like those famous photos of you when you were her age. You must be very proud of her.'

'At my age, it's privilege enough just to see your great-grandchild, let alone to watch her beauty grow,' the Countess replied. 'And Marco tells me he can hardly wait for one of your children to make him a great-grandpapa.'

'Don't listen to her, *chérie*,' Madeleine said to her daughter, with a laugh that didn't sound quite as carefree as she'd intended. 'I'm in no hurry for you to make me a grandmother, nor your brother.' She gave Bruno an appraising glance. 'So this is the local policeman who saved you from your awful sister.'

'He saved me, too, in the cave,' said Marie-Françoise. 'I'll never forget it, the gunfire in that enclosed place.'

Bruno remembered the stricken look of the girl, her face bloody and her mouth staved in from where she'd been hit with a gun butt. There was no sign of her injuries now and her teeth looked as perfect as expensive dentistry could make them.

'Both of you must come to lunch at the vineyard and tell us all about that time in the cave. I never really heard the whole story,' said Chantal.

'Good idea, maybe when Grandpa comes. I know he'd like to hear it, too,' said Madeleine. 'And you must come, too, Hortense,' she said to the Countess. 'You know how Grandpa loves to see you. I'll call to confirm the date.'

Bruno felt Madeleine's eyes stay on him as her daughter asked the Countess if she might take Marie-Françoise away to join some of the other younger guests in the garden. He watched as the three women left. From the rear, they looked identical, slim-hipped, long-legged and elegant, each moving with the same, assured grace.

'There's a very pleasant woman whom you ought

to meet, Marco's daughter by his Israeli wife,' said the Countess when Bruno enquired about the non-French family members. 'Marco had just divorced her when we met, but their daughter, Raquelle, has lived here in the Périgord for forty years. She's always been a favourite of mine; she's one of the artists who did the reconstruction of the Lascaux cave. Then there's Yevgeny, Marco's son by a Russian woman in wartime. I first met Yevgeny in Moscow when he was a little boy – and here he is.'

A big-boned bear of a man in his sixties with grey hair tumbling to his shoulders had suddenly appeared before the wheelchair. He bent to kiss the Countess soundly and sat back on his heels to admire her.

'They told me you were bedridden,' he said, in strongly accented French. 'I'm so glad they were wrong.'

'Much exaggerated and it was all the fault of my dreadful sister and her crooked grandson,' she said. 'You can thank this young man standing here for rescuing me.' She gestured at Bruno and Yevgeny rose to shake hands. 'You were what, seven or eight when I first laid eyes on you?' she went on.

'Eight. I'd never seen anything in Moscow like you, all dressed in Dior and with your long cigarette holder, you were like something from films,' Yevgeny said, smiling. 'You gave me French chocolates. You know, I've been in love with you ever since.'

'From what I hear, Yevgeny, you say that to a lot of women! But is it true that you're living here now?'

'Yes, I have a house near Siorac with glorious light and a big barn that serves as my gallery. You must come and see my latest paintings.' He turned to Bruno and said, 'I did a series of portraits of the Countess, all called *Parizhanka*, the woman from Paris. The first ones were from my boyhood memory, but then she started coming to Moscow again and I could paint her from the life.'

'It's all a long time ago,' the Countess said. As he shook hands with the big Russian and murmured the usual courtesies, Bruno was doing the sums in his head. If Yevgeny had been eight when Stalin died, he'd have been born in 1944 or 1945. The Israeli daughter, Raquelle, had been born and Marco and her mother had divorced by the time he met the Countess in 1953, so Yevgeny's half-sister would be just a few years younger. And then there was Marco's third child, Victor, the one who ran the vineyard. Three children by different mothers, all three gathered here for their father's birthday and all living nearby.

It said a lot for the old man that he remained that close to his children and even more that they wanted to be near him. Or maybe the attraction lay in the eventual inheritance, Bruno thought, looking around at the chateau with its well-kept grounds. The Patriarch was usually described as a wealthy businessman and he must have made

13

money from his directorships. The family vineyard in the hills above Lalinde was respected, mostly producing Bergerac reds and whites with a small and separate vineyard in Monbazillac, but it was hardly a gold mine. Bruno knew the old saying that the way to make a small fortune in wine was to start with a large one.

As they waited in the Patriarch's receiving line, there had been time to study the array of photos that lined the hallway. He was posed with each of the presidents of France, with two American presidents, with Stalin and Khrushchev, Brezhnev and Gorbachev, Yeltsin, Putin and Deng Xiao Ping. Alongside these were other photos of him with popes, German chancellors, British prime ministers, assorted generals, astronauts, film stars and opera singers. The Countess had preened at a photo of her younger self with the Patriarch at a Cannes Film Festival in the fifties. The young Brigitte Bardot had also been in the photo, but the Patriarch only had eyes for the Countess.

Suddenly the sound of a glass breaking shattered the civilized atmosphere. A small altercation seemed to take place just below their place on the terrace, with raised voices and a swirl of people. An older man who looked drunk was pulling Chantal by the arm and she was telling him to let go, assisted by Marie-Françoise. Although staggering and with glazed eyes, the man was impeccably dressed in a double-breasted suit with the red ribbon of the Légion d'Honneur

14

in his buttonhole. A once-handsome man running fast to seed, his thick grey hair was falling over his forehead.

Victor, the Patriarch's youngest son, appeared through the guests, Dr Gelletreau at his side. The St Denis parish priest, Father Sentout, seemed to come from nowhere with a good-looking young man who bore a more than passing resemblance to the Patriarch.

Before Bruno could push his way to the steps to join the rescue party, they'd managed between them to separate the drunken man from Chantal. Then they were joined by a new figure, a large and burly man dressed in a tweed jacket and flat cap and wearing boots and gaiters that gave him the look of an old-fashioned gamekeeper. He put his arms around the drunk, lifted him bodily and then carried him away and round the side of the terrace to the old medieval stone tower. The other men followed, except for the young man, who remained with Chantal. She sank gratefully into his arms but seemed none the worse for the incident.

The buzz of conversation had silenced for a moment as people turned and craned their necks to see the cause of the flurry. But the string quartet continued to saw away at their instruments, there was nothing more to see and the babble of voices was quickly resumed.

'Who were those young men?' Bruno asked.

'I don't know the big one; he looked like some kind of servant. The handsome young man is

Raoul, Victor's son, Marco's grandson. He's here to learn the family business before going to business school in America. Marco thinks his grandson will make a fine match for Marie-Françoise. I rather agree, so we're arranging for them to see a fair amount of one another. It would be a very suitable marriage for both families.'

Was that how these things were managed? Bruno was surprised, assuming that the days of arranged marriages were long gone. But when it came to countesses and chateaux, perhaps the old ways continued. The Patriarch's money and the Countess's estates and titles would make quite a combination.

'Were you never tempted to marry the Patriarch yourself?' he asked her.

She looked up at him, amused. 'There are men you marry, for the family's sake, and men you take to bed, for your own. I'm not sure it makes sense to confuse the two.'

'And who was the drunk pulling at Chantal?'

'That was Gilbert, an old friend of the family,' she explained. 'One of those young daredevils who dreamed of following in Marco's footsteps. He never got over the fact that there were no wars for him to win fame and glory.'

She told him that Gilbert had become friends with Victor when they were cadets together at the French Air Force Academy at Salon-de-Provence and then went on to serve in the same squadron as fighter pilots. When Victor left to join Air France,

Gilbert remained in uniform and became an air attaché at the French Embassy in Moscow, where there had been some kind of scandal. The Countess didn't know the details. Dashing and charming but always a heavy drinker, Gilbert was now a barely functioning alcoholic, with a trail of affairs, debts and failed marriages behind him. For old time's sake, Victor let him live in a small house on the family estate where he was nominally employed to catalogue the Patriarch's archives.

Bruno left to get a plate of canapés for the Countess, whose wheelchair had a folding table attached from which she could eat. When he returned, balancing two glasses of champagne and two plates, she was in conversation with an elegantly dressed white-haired woman. She had one bold lock of coal-black hair running back from her forehead and the Patriarch's warm brown eyes.

'Meet Raquelle, the Patriarch's daughter,' the Countess said. 'I've told her all about you and she can have my glass of champagne. I'll go onto the white wine.'

Bruno shook hands and told Raquelle he admired the copy of the Lascaux cave she had worked on and asked about her new venture.

'It's at Le Thot, the park where they are trying to breed historic animals,' Raquelle replied, in a deep, attractive voice. 'We're upgrading it now with virtual reality and animatronics, lifelike mammoths and aurochs that we designed on computers. Some of the family are coming to lunch next week to see our progress. Perhaps you might like to come along?' She handed him a business card with an image of some wild-looking men in furs brandishing spears and stones as they surrounded a trapped mammoth. Her phone number, address and email were on the reverse side.

The insistent sound of a spoon being tapped on a glass heralded a speech. The string quartet had stopped playing and the Patriarch had advanced to the edge of the balcony, his arms held up for silence.

'Excellencies, generals, friends, you know I never give speeches, far less long ones,' he said, pausing for the laughter. 'So I simply thank you all for coming here to my native Périgord to celebrate my ninetieth birthday and I hope you will all return in ten years time for the big one. I'll be here if you will.' There was more laughter and scattered cheers.

'And now, if today's Armée de l'Air is half as punctual as we were in my day, you might want to protect your ears. I only wish I were flying one myself.' He gazed to the west and pointed.

Bruno became aware of a distant growl growing steadily louder and then saw the sun glinting on wings. Then with a monstrous howl that seemed to shake every bone in Bruno's body, three Rafales swept overhead, unbelievably low and impossibly fast. France's latest jet fighters, worth a hundred million euros each and capable of twice the speed of sound, they lit their afterburners and soared into a vertical climb. Plumes of red, white and blue smoke spilled from their tails in salute as they rose in formation and then spread apart. Somewhere over Sarlat they turned and came diving back in line astern, each warplane performing a victory roll as they passed over the Patriarch's head.

'*Mon Dieu*, I loved that,' said the Patriarch as the roar of the jets faded. 'My thanks to my friend the Minister of Defence and to General Dufort for that wonderful demonstration, and to the memory of my revered old boss, Marcel Dassault, who has given France so many magnificent aeroplanes. My thanks to all of you who are French taxpayers, who paid for that splendid birthday gift. And now, enjoy the rest of the party.'

The Countess was wilting, and Chantal said she'd bring Marie-Françoise home later. So the old lady made her farewells and Bruno wheeled her back through the house, out to her car and drove her home. It had been a remarkable day, he reflected; his boyhood admiration had not been in the least dented by the reality of meeting the Patriarch. And he'd been invited to lunch by Raquelle, and to another at the vineyard, where he'd be able to see more of the great man and maybe hear some of his stories. He saw the Countess installed safely back in her chateau and drove home to walk his dog, feed his chickens and tend his vegetable garden. And with his thoughts returning to the coolness Pamela had displayed, Bruno knew nothing of the drama that was unfolding in the house that had just echoed to the roar of the Rafales' fly-past.

CHAPTER 3

Just after dawn the next morning, Bruno had begun sharing his breakfast with his basset hound, Balzac, when the Mayor phoned. He sounded subdued and shaken as he told Bruno he was calling from the Patriarch's chateau, where there had been a death. Startled, Bruno paused before voicing his immediate concern for the Patriarch himself, but the Mayor rang off before Bruno could ask for any details. That was odd, Bruno thought, as he changed into his police uniform and headed off in his police van. He was usually informed of deaths by the emergency services, or by a doctor or by a priest. As a municipal policeman, Bruno was an employee of the town of St Denis, which meant that the Mayor was his boss. This was the first time he'd been summoned to a death scene by the man who'd hired him and Bruno wondered what the Mayor was doing at the Patriarch's place so early.

The chateau felt different in the early-morning light, sombre rather than joyous without the animation brought by the previous day's throng of fashionably dressed people. Bruno parked, and

21

seeing no signs of life at the front of the building he walked around to the terrace, calling to ask if anyone was there. Just as he was beginning to wonder if his summons were some bizarre joke, the Mayor came out to greet him with a handshake.

'You'll just have to take care of a few formalities,' he said, steering Bruno indoors. 'Dr Gelletreau has already signed the death certificate.'

The dead man was in a large, semicircular room in the base of the old medieval tower, which seemed to be used mainly to store garden furniture and tools. The body rested on a lounger of tubular steel and canvas that would have looked more at home beside a swimming pool. The room stank of booze and vomit and seemed full of people when Bruno arrived, although it was almost too dark to see. A single narrow window slit and the open door that led to the chateau provided the only light. As his eyes grew accustomed to the gloom, Bruno made out Victor and Madeleine standing hand in hand beside the lounger. Victor had his other hand over his eyes and his shoulders moved as if he were weeping. His wife held a handkerchief to her nose.

Dr Gelletreau was packing his stethoscope into an ancient medical case. Father Sentout was also there and Bruno spotted the gleam of oil on the eyes and forehead that meant the dead man had been given the last rites. 'Accidental death,' said the doctor. 'Died in the night, dead drunk. No suspicious circumstances.' He sidled up to Bruno and murmured in his ear, 'The poor fellow drowned in his own vomit.'

That was quick, Bruno thought. Gelletreau usually hummed and hawed and left his options open. 'Who found him?'

'I did, this morning. I brought him some breakfast, expecting to find him nursing his usual hangover,' said Victor, turning to Bruno and releasing his wife's hand. He looked stricken as he pointed to a tray on a small side table. It carried a coffee pot, a cup and a glass of orange juice. 'I shook him to wake him up but he was already pretty stiff so I called Dr Gelletreau.'

'The night wasn't cold so I'd put the time of death at around midnight, maybe a bit before or after,' the doctor said. 'I checked the lividity and the body temperature. He died here and hasn't been moved.'

Bruno moved forward to stand beside the lounger and look down on the grey hair and the face of the drunk who had tried to pull Chantal away at the party, before being bustled off by some of the men who stood here. Somebody had cleaned his face and chin but there were drying pools of vomit on his chest and on the lounger where it had trailed down the side of his neck. His name had been Gilbert, Bruno remembered, the air force friend of Victor who, after becoming too old to fly fast jets, had been air attaché in Moscow.

'My condolences on the loss of an old friend.'

Bruno turned from the corpse to face Victor. 'I'm sorry but you'll understand I have to ask a few questions, just for the formal report. I saw you escort him away from the party yesterday afternoon, just before the fly-past for your father. Is this the room where you brought him?'

'Yes, it was convenient and close by, somewhere we could put him down to sleep it off,' Victor replied. 'Gilbert was plastered, staggering drunk. We just wanted him out of the way quickly. I knew the fly-past would be coming and I didn't want that spoiled for my father's sake. He'd been looking forward to it for weeks.'

'I saw Gilbert carried off by someone who didn't look dressed for the party,' Bruno said. 'Who would that have been?'

'That was Fabrice, the gamekeeper,' said Madeleine. 'When I saw what was happening, I asked him to remove Gilbert.'

'Did you look in on him after that?'

'I did, some time after seven, when most of the guests had gone, except for those staying the night,' said Madeleine. 'He was still drunk, snoring, but there was no vomit. I'm sure if he'd been sick I'd have smelled it. I didn't see that flask or I'd have removed it but I put that blanket over him.'

'It was the same at about ten, when I looked in just before I went to bed,' said Victor. 'No sign of vomit and the blanket was still in place, as though he hadn't moved.'

'I heard he was an alcoholic. Is that true?'

'He was always a heavy drinker,' Victor said. 'After Moscow, he was incapable half the time. We got him into a couple of clinics and then into Alcoholics Anonymous. He'd stop drinking for a while but always went back to it. Vodka, mainly. He acquired a taste for the stuff in Russia.'

'Had he been this drunk before, throwing up in his sleep?'

'Not to my knowledge.' He turned to look at the body of his friend and the sadness on Victor's face aged him so that he looked more like Madeleine's father than her husband. 'We didn't often have to put him to bed.'

'Just before I saw him being carried away from the party, he was obviously drunk but still on his feet,' Bruno said. 'Did he go straight to sleep when you brought him in here?'

'Yes, he seemed to crumple when we got him in here and by the time we got his shoes and tie off and laid him down he'd passed out.'

Bruno turned to Dr Gelletreau. 'Alcoholics usually have a fairly high tolerance for booze. Is this sort of reaction unusual in any way?'

'It might have been, if we hadn't found this.' Gelletreau pointed to a large leather-covered hip flask, perhaps twice the size of the one Bruno took when he went hunting.

It lay between Gilbert's chest and his arm. Bruno pulled on a pair of plastic gloves then lifted it to his nose. It was empty, had no cap, and smelled of alcohol. He put it in an evidence bag and found the cap underneath the lounger. There were markings on the bottom of the flask and he squinted in the dim light to make out *Made in England, 12 oz*. He knew about English fluid ounces from whisky bottles and that would be about a third of a litre. Presumably he'd drunk the lot.

'What did he usually drink?'

'A Russian vodka, Stolichnaya Blue,' Victor replied. 'It's a hundred proof, fifty per cent pure alcohol.'

Bruno raised his eyebrows. Gilbert had been stumbling drunk at five in the evening. If the flask had been full, it was more than enough to keep him dead drunk until midnight.

'Do you know if he left a will or where he kept his papers? I should go and take a look.'

'I don't know about a will but he had nothing to leave. Gilbert was usually broke. He lived in a small house on the vineyard and had an old car but with the drinking . . .' Victor ran his hand across his eyes. 'You should have known him before. He was a good man, an amazing pilot, brave as a lion.'

'Gilbert hadn't driven a car for years,' Madeleine interrupted. 'We wouldn't let him. He had a bicycle to get around the estate and if he needed to go into Bergerac, he'd come with us.'

'If there's nothing more for me to do here, I'd better get to the clinic,' said Dr Gelletreau, handing Bruno the signed certificate of death. He'd written, 'Natural causes; alcohol abuse.'

26

'Was it you who called the Mayor?' Bruno asked him. 'I'm surprised you didn't call me as you usually do.' Bruno was more than surprised. He was offended. Wealthy and well-connected people in their grand chateaux so often seemed to think they were above the law, able to sidestep any legal difficulty with a phone call to a friendly politician.

'I called the Mayor first, and then Vincent called the doctor,' said Madeleine, interrupting. 'I'm sorry, with the shock I wasn't thinking straight. Perhaps I should have called the gendarmes.'

'Has Gilbert's family been informed of his death?' Bruno asked Victor as Gelletreau left.

'No family, only divorced wives and abandoned mistresses,' said Madeleine sourly. 'Most of them will probably celebrate at the news.'

'Are there any next of kin that you know of?' Bruno pressed. 'Brothers, sisters, cousins? There's usually some relative.'

'He always wrote down me as next of kin,' said Victor. 'I was his wingman for years, in the same squadron, so we were very close. I think there was a sister who died a few years ago.'

'I'll call the funeral parlour in St Denis and they'll arrange to pick up the body,' said Bruno, thinking this was a sad end for a man gifted enough to be a fighter pilot, one of the lords of the air. He remembered his own youthful dreams of becoming one. 'It looks as though you'll have to decide whether it's to be burial or cremation.'

27

'I can help you with that,' broke in Father Sentout. 'Perhaps I should call later in the day when you've had some time to settle yourselves.'

'Well, that all seems quite straightforward,' said the Mayor briskly, in the way he did at council meetings when the main decision had been taken to his satisfaction. 'It's very sad, of course, and a great loss to you, Victor, an old friend and comrade of your youth. But I'm sure the chief of police here will handle matters with his usual efficiency and discretion.' He gave Bruno a beady look. 'We don't want anything to cast a shadow over the Patriarch's celebrations.'

Bruno nodded amiably, then put his hand beneath the body, found a full pocket and drew out a well-used wallet. Inside was an identity card, one of the old driving licences in pink cardboard, a Carte Bleu credit card, a *carte vitale* medical card and four twenty-euro notes. In a smaller pocket he found an out-of-date ID card for the Foreign Ministry and a membership card for the Air Force Association. He took the cheap mobile phone from the pouch on Gilbert's belt and thumbed through the recent calls, surprised at how few there were. He'd made just one call the previous day, to a number identified as Victor.

'He rang you yesterday morning?'

'I took the call,' said Madeleine. 'It was about what time we'd pick him up to drive here to the chateau.'

'Did you drive home after the party?'

'No, we stayed here last night,' Victor replied patiently. His wife broke in, 'We live at the vineyard but we keep a suite here.'

'Was Gilbert going to stay here as well?'

Victor shrugged and looked at his wife. He seemed to let her take a lot of the decisions, Bruno thought.

'No, the chateau is pretty full with guests so Raoul or somebody would have given him a lift back,' she said. 'In fact, some of them must be getting up about now so I'd better go and check on breakfast.'

'I'm sure the chief of police won't need to disturb your guests,' the Mayor said firmly, and looked pointedly at his watch.

'Just one more thing,' said Bruno. 'I'd better take a look at Gilbert's house in your vineyard. Where do I find it, exactly?'

Madeleine explained, before excusing herself and leaving, swiftly followed by Father Sentout, who muttered that he needed to be at Mass. The Mayor stepped forward, took Victor's hand and shook it solemnly. Then he turned to put his hand on Bruno's back and steer him to the door. It was very neatly done.

'You don't have any reason for doubt about this, do you?' the Mayor asked, when they were outside.

Bruno pondered some non-committal reply. He was about to say that he didn't like being pressured and then ask why the Mayor had been called first instead of him, but his phone began vibrating at his belt. He checked the screen and saw it was Albert, the chief *pompier*.

'There's been another accident on the Rouffignac road, just after the turn-off to the big camping site,' Albert said. 'It's those damn deer again. You'd better bring a gun in case the poor thing is still alive.'

CHAPTER 4

The accident wasn't that serious, at least for the humans involved. A small Berlingo van had hit a deer, which had dented its hood and broken its headlights. Bruno knew the driver, Adèle, a woman in her forties whose husband worked for the milk cooperative. She'd been heading for church with her widowed mother. Adèle was shocked and weeping but the mother was made of sterner stuff, leaning against the van and smoking an unfiltered cigarette as she looked critically at the deer. Both its front legs were broken and it kept trying to rise on its back ones, mewing pitifully. It was painfully thin, its ribs standing out through the light-brown fur, its chest heaving as it panted in terror.

'Not enough meat to make it worth taking back for the freezer,' the old lady said. 'It will be that crazy woman up the hill again.'

Bruno asked her to take her daughter back into the car while he took care of the deer. He pulled a tarpaulin from the back of his police van and asked Albert to hold it to screen the deer from Adèle's sight. He despatched the poor beast with a shot behind the ear. Albert helped him roll it onto the waxed canvas and put it into Bruno's van. Then Bruno drove the women to church in Adèle's car, reckoning she'd be in good enough shape to drive after the service. Albert drove him back to his van and he took the dead deer to the local butcher.

'Hardly worth it,' said Valentin when Bruno laid out the dead deer on the chopping board in the room behind the shop. That was the arrangement in St Denis; deer killed on the roads were given to the butcher, who'd prepare the meat for the old folks' home. 'There's no flesh on it; it must be one of Imogène's. I keep telling you, Bruno, you're going to have to do something about that damn woman.'

'We're doing our best, but we have to go through the legal procedures,' Bruno replied. 'She still has a few weeks to put up that fence the court ordered, and then she might try an appeal.'

'One of these days those deer will kill someone, mark my words,' said Valentin, picking up his big cleaver.

Valentin was right, Bruno reflected as he drove up the hill to the home of Imogène Ducaillou. A rather eccentric widow, she worked as a cashier and caretaker in one of the smaller prehistoric caves that dotted the region. She was a mainstay of the town's literary club, with an inexhaustible appetite for romantic novels and books about animals. She owned and lived on a large tract of mostly forest land that abutted one of the main roads leading to St Denis. A passionate Green and strict vegetarian, she loved all animals and hated hunting. She had posted *Chasse Interdite* notices all around her land, which was surrounded by hunting preserves that were used by the town's hunting clubs. Deer aren't foolish. Given a choice between land stalked by hunters and territory where they were banned, the deer made a refuge of Imogène's property as soon as the hunting season opened.

At first, all was well, although the hunters were unhappy at the scarcity of game in their traditional preserves. But soon the concentration of deer on Imogène's land had become a different kind of problem as their population exploded and destroyed much of her vegetation. As a result, the deer were all painfully thin and becoming desperate enough to risk the hunters' guns in their search for food. Today's accident was the third in the past year to have been caused by deer jumping from her land, despite warning signs and speed limits placed by Bruno on that stretch of road. Imogène had repeatedly rejected pleas by Bruno and the Mayor to allow the deer to be culled. As a last resort, the Prefect had secured a court order that Imogène must within six months fence her land to protect the road. Five months had passed and she hadn't begun. It would be expensive, probably too much for her to afford.

Deer were everywhere as he drove up the

winding, gravel lane that led to Imogène's house, stretching up to nibble the remaining bark on trees, nosing into the earth to see if any shoots remained. There was no undergrowth, just earth and dead trees and Bruno could see, rising ominously at the edges of Imogène's property, the wooden watchtowers where the hunters waited for the deer to risk leaving her land in the search for food. The sight gave him an eerie feeling, stirring memories of newsreels of prison camps guarded by similar towers manned by sharpshooters.

Bruno stopped and climbed out of his vehicle, struck by the sense of standing at some strange frontier between the overgrazed, almost dead land to his left that was Imogène's and the thick, healthy undergrowth to his right. The frontier was not precise but over a belt of some thirty or forty metres the woodland thickened from barren earth and bare trees to the usual fertile jumble of shrubs and ferns. Gazing at this strange contrast, his eyes sensed a sudden movement and he realized that one of the watchtowers was manned. He leaned through his car window and sounded the horn, waving until he saw an answering signal from the distant hide. He walked towards it, moving through the thickening vegetation and into a clearing. The hide stood on its far side, mounted on four sturdy poles. Two men in camouflage jackets, one big and burly and the other shorter and slim, looked down at him curiously.

'Come to check our hunting permits?' asked the bigger man. His flat tweed cap triggered Bruno's memory. This was the gamekeeper at the Patriarch's chateau, the man who had carried Gilbert from the party. The smaller man was hanging back a little, almost as though trying to keep out of Bruno's view.

'I can if you want,' Bruno replied affably. 'But I was going to ask if you knew whether Imogène was at home or if you'd seen her car leave.'

'That crazy bitch,' the big man said. 'No, we've seen no cars coming and going until you arrived. And we've seen no deer close enough for a shot, not even those skinny ones that come from her land.'

'They probably know you're here,' said Bruno. The shorter man lifted a hand to pull his baseball cap further down over his eyes and Bruno recognized him as Guillaume, a bartender at one of the big campsites during summer who signed on as unemployed for the rest of the year. The gendarmes had picked him up a couple of times on suspicion of dealing drugs to campers, but nothing had been proved. Guillaume was a notoriously poor shot but still had the right to hunt his quota. Such men were useful; a keen hunter could go out with Guillaume, shoot in his stead and share the meat. And there were some who just liked extra opportunities to shoot to kill.

'*Bonjour*, Guillaume,' Bruno said. 'Who's your friend?'

'I'm Fabrice, from Bergerac way,' said the game-keeper. 'I'm just spotting for Guillaume.'

'Don't you work for the Patriarch? I saw you at his party, carrying away that drunk.'

'That's right. He was plastered, didn't give me any trouble. Laid him down and he went right off to sleep.'

'Do you know he's dead? Died in his sleep and never woke up. I've just come from the chateau.'

Fabrice shook his head, looking surprised. 'Poor bastard.' Then he shrugged and said, 'There's worse ways to go.'

Bruno considered checking their permits but he needed to see Imogène and so he wished them luck, told them to watch out for his return and headed back. He drove on at a crawl but had to keep stopping as the deer strolled along the track and gazed at him incuriously, somehow knowing that they faced no danger on these lands. He found it rather beguiling, thinking that a real refuge such as this could be a wonderful place, so long as there was sufficient food and water and a rational culling or export plan to prevent overpopulation. Perhaps that could be a solution, and maybe funds could be raised to help Imogène pay for the fence and the food. But she was unlikely to accept the culling. Bruno knew he'd have to try, pointing out the desperate thinness of the deer and the weakness of the young fawns he'd seen.

As he parked the van and climbed out, looking at her run-down house with its missing tiles and sagging shutters, deer came up to nuzzle Bruno, doubtless hoping for food. She must feed them herself with what little money she has, he thought. He knocked on the door, which badly needed repainting, and got no reply. But her old Renault 4 was parked beside the house and her bicycle was on the porch. He knocked again and called her name, saying it was Bruno.

'What do you want?' she said, from behind the closed door.

'There's been another accident on the road. One of your deer had its legs broken.'

'So what did you do, kill it? That's all you know to do. Kill, hunt, kill; why can't you leave the animals in peace?'

'Because they're starving, Imogène. The fawns are dying. The deer are desperate so they come onto the roads. This cannot go on. Open the door and let's talk about this. I have an idea that might help.'

The door opened and Imogène eyed him suspiciously. 'What sort of idea?' She looked normal enough, short grey hair neatly brushed, wearing brown corduroy slacks and a bulky sweater, and neither make-up nor jewellery. The sound of a piano concerto came from the room within.

'You only have a few weeks to put up this fence, and you can't afford it. That means you either pay a stiff fine, which might entail having to sell your property, or you let us organize a cull of the deer. You're now a bigger danger to these poor starving deer than the hunters.'

37

'You've said that before. I'm trying to raise funds from other animal lovers. I'll find a way. But what's this idea of yours?'

'I was thinking as I drove up here how pleasant it could be to have a real refuge, properly fenced and with sufficient food, allow schoolchildren to come and walk here among the deer, no cars. Maybe some tourists in the season could pay enough of an entrance fee to help feed them. It would mean fencing the whole property but I think there may be ways to raise funds for that.'

'There has to be a catch,' Imogène said. 'Of course it would be a wonderful place for children. Come in and have some tea. We can talk about it.'

He entered a large sitting room that took up half the house. A kitchen stood at the far end, where Imogène put a kettle on the old-fashioned wood stove. The piano music gave way to a voice on the radio he recognized; it was tuned to France Musique. Three cats occupied an old sofa that looked comfortable. There was a big round table covered in sketch pads, magazines and photographs of deer. More photos of deer filled the spaces on the walls that were not occupied by bookcases. Some of the deer were so thin he assumed Imogène must have taken the photographs in these woods. He was surprised to see Raquelle, the Patriarch's daughter, in one of the photos, feeding a fawn.

'That's one of my Green Party friends,' said

38

Imogène, joining him. 'We worked on the campaign together.' She handed him a cracked mug of what smelled like mint tea. 'I know everybody in town thinks I'm mad, but I'm perfectly rational. I know the deer are hungry and my land can't support them.'

Imogène went on to explain that she'd been promised some funds from animal rights groups, but not nearly enough. She'd been quoted 14,000 euros to have the fence built and that wouldn't be for the whole property, just the stretch by the road and a couple of hundred metres more on each side.

'I've already got a mortgage on this property that I can barely afford, although heaven knows I've got nobody to leave it to,' she said. 'I can't afford a fence and I can't afford to buy any more fodder for the deer. I'm at my wits' end. So I'm ready to consider anything that won't involve hunting them or killing them.'

Bruno wondered if any compromise would be possible. When she spoke of her deer, Imogène had an almost religious fervour. It would be hard to shake her conviction but he had to try. 'We'd need to assess how many deer your land could maintain, but looking at it now, that won't be many. Your woods are dying from the animals chewing the bark and the shoots.'

'And what happens to the deer you'd call excess?' she countered.

'We could try zoos, other refuges, perhaps release

them elsewhere in national parks . . .' It sounded feeble, even to Bruno.

'You think I haven't tried that?' she demanded. 'All the animal refuges in France have the same problem. Some of them are even using contraception to stop them breeding. And most of the national parks permit hunting these days, to their shame. No, Bruno, thanks for trying. I appreciate that you want to help but we both know that your solution would mean culling the herd every year and I couldn't permit that.'

'The choice seems very clear, Imogène. Either you have the refuge and give a lot of your deer a good life, or you lose the lot, whether to the courts or to starvation. You could lose your house and land as well. It will just need one of your deer to cause an accident that kills or injures somebody and you'll be sued for every penny you've got.'

'I understand what you say but I think the choice is even simpler. Either the deer live or they get slaughtered.' She put her mug of tea down firmly on the table and sat up straight with her hand on her heart, as if striking a pose. 'Whatever the cost, I will do everything I can to ensure that they live.'

It was like watching a bad actress, Bruno thought, convinced that Imogène had imagined this scene, rehearsed it in her mind, and now at last had the chance to play the role. It suggested that he was dealing with a woman entranced by her own self-image as a crusader, a woman who might seek to become a martyr for her cause. Still, he talked on, throwing out argument after argument about the needs of the deer and the demands of ecological balance until at last Imogène promised, perhaps out of sheer boredom, to consider what he'd said. But as he left, picking his way slowly through the hungry deer on the track, he suspected that his efforts had failed.

CHAPTER 5

Gilbert's house was not easy to find and in the end Bruno had to go back to the vineyard office for directions. When he finally found the place, a small cottage that might once have belonged to a shepherd, an almost new Range Rover was parked outside. There were two small windows on each side of the open front door. Through it, he could see Victor and Madeleine sifting through papers at a desk in what seemed to be the sitting room. Neither one offered the usual polite smile of welcome nor seemed surprised to see him. Victor vaguely waved an arm to invite Bruno in.

The room was about four metres square. A single armchair stood beneath the window. Beside the desk was the kind of bentwood chair that might have come from a café. An old-fashioned cast-iron stove occupied the chimney, a neat pile of chopped logs beside it, and Bruno caught a faint, not unpleasant smell of woodsmoke. Against the far wall was a kitchen area with a sink and a two-burner cooking stove of the kind fed by bottled gas. A kitchen table, only large enough for two, was covered by a red plastic tablecloth with a glass bowl that held apples on top.

'There's no will that we could find, no personal papers, just a lot of bills, and bank statements that suggest Gilbert's only income was his military pension,' Victor said from his place at the desk. Dressed in sagging jeans and an ancient sweater, Victor look considerably older than he had at the party. Bruno noticed that his hands carried old scars and scratches, suggesting he did much of his own work in the vineyard. Victor turned from the desk to pass some recent bank statements to Bruno, who saw there was not quite a thousand euros in Gilbert's current account with the Crédit Agricole.

'I remember him saying once that he'd never bothered with a will since he didn't have anything worth leaving,' Madeleine said. She ran a hand over her eyes as if tired, but her complexion was as clear as a young girl's.

Looking at the individual credits, Bruno saw a monthly payment of 3,400. *Mon Dieu*, he thought, that's some pension, a lot more than his own salary. The account was in the name of Colonel Gilbert Clamartin and the address was the vineyard.

'Not much to show for a lifetime in the service,' added Madeleine. Bruno raised an eyebrow; it was a damn sight more than his own time in the army appeared to be worth. 'We thought you might have got here earlier. Anyway, we started trying to sort through the mess Gilbert left. We're short of housing for the estate workers so we want to get this place cleared and made ready for someone else as soon as we can.'

By the door was a cardboard box filled with empty vodka bottles. Beside it a big black plastic bag stood open containing some dead flowers, overripe bananas and half a baguette. In one of the large yellow plastic bags that the local communes distributed for recycling Bruno saw old newspapers, yoghurt pots and empty tins of tuna and processed meat.

When Bruno explained that he'd been delayed by the situation with Imogène, Madeleine's mouth tightened in disapproval. 'That sort of Green bunny-hugger drives me mad. She doesn't know the first thing about the environment she claims to love so much. You ought to arrest her for cruelty to animals.'

'My wife has been a keen huntress since childhood,' added Victor. He gave her an affectionate smile, more the look of an indulgent father than of a husband, Bruno thought.

'Sometimes I wonder if we're hunting the wrong species,' said Madeleine, and then smiled as if to take any menace from her words.

Her long blonde hair, which at yesterday's party had been worn down, was today pulled into a loose ponytail. She was wearing well-cut jeans, ankle boots and a flannel shirt in some tartan of greens and blues. Her only jewellery was a pair of simple gold earrings and on her wrist she wore a masculine-looking watch. She was perched casually on a corner of the desk on which Gilbert's papers were strewn. Even without make-up she looked too young to have a daughter old enough to make her a grandmother.

'I like to hunt as well, but mainly *bécasses* because they're so cunning and I enjoy eating them,' Bruno said.

'I haven't the patience for that, waiting all day until your dog finds one and then it flutters away too low to shoot,' she said, looking at him with interest now that she knew he was a fellow hunter. 'Besides, there's no danger in it. That's why I like hunting wild boar; you never know when they might start hunting you. It seems to make it more fair.'

Bruno gave a neutral nod, thinking how a woman could get away with a remark like that. A man would be mocked in any hunting club for a remark so vainglorious. He looked around the room. There was an old TV set opposite the big armchair and several framed photographs on the walls of warplanes and young men in cockpits. He spotted a framed certificate that seemed to be in English. Bruno went across and read that Gilbert had been through the Top Gun course in Nevada with the US Air Force.

'We did that together,' said Victor, proudly. 'We flew our own Mirages. The Americans hadn't seen them before so we could give them a few surprises. It was the nearest we ever got to combat.' He paused.

'I'd known him forty years. It's a wrench to think I'll never see him again.'

Bruno broke the ensuing silence. 'As you knew him best, do you have any idea what he was trying to do yesterday when he was bothering your daughter?'

Victor shrugged. 'He said he had to talk to her urgently about something private and she said it would have to wait. Gilbert was her godfather and when she was younger they were very close. When she realized he was an alcoholic, she began avoiding him. Apparently he said it was too important for that and tried to pull her aside. She objected, tried to free her arm, but he persisted. I've no idea what he had in mind.'

'Was he disturbed, or angry, or behaving at all unusually before the party began, when you drove him over there?'

'Not at all,' Madeleine replied. 'He was his usual self, freshly showered and shaved, beautifully dressed. Clothes were his one extravagance, other than the booze. You had to know him to realize he was already quite drunk. He concealed it well. Chantal said she wasn't even sure he was drunk, and he was certainly not angry with her, just very determined to haul her off.'

'Did you find anything interesting here among his papers, anything that might explain what he wanted to tell your daughter?'

'Not really. Gilbert wasn't one for keeping records or souvenirs, beyond his logbooks and other stuff to do with flying, and they're all here in his desk. No letters, no photos beyond the ones on the wall, not even an address book. I suppose he kept them all on his phone, and you found that on his body.'

'He had no laptop?'

'No computer of his own,' said Victor. 'He'd sometimes come up and use the office desktop at the vineyard if he had to look something up or send an email. People at Alcoholics Anonymous were always trying to get him back to the meetings. Well, not so much people, just one man, a chap called Larignac from somewhere near Bordeaux, one of our former mechanics in the air force. He always thought the world of Gilbert and he'd been helped by AA so he kept trying to get Gilbert to dry out again.'

'Decent of him to try,' said Bruno. 'Talking of the air force, will it be a military funeral?'

Victor looked startled. 'I hadn't even thought of that. Perhaps I should call the old squadron or the Air Force Association.'

'With a colonel, I think it would be customary.'

'Of course. I'll make enquiries.'

'Have you looked at the other rooms yet?'

'There's just the bedroom and bathroom – take a look,' said Madeleine, slipping down from the desk. 'I'd better clear out whatever he left in the fridge and store cupboards, although heaven knows the man hardly ever seemed to eat. He got most of his calories from vodka.'

The bedroom was monastic in its sparseness. A metal-framed single bed stood against the wall, made up military style, the blankets stretched so tight Bruno could have bounced a coin off them. The bedside table carried only a pitcher of water, a glass and a book in Russian of what looked like poetry. Beneath the bed was a pair of white flannel bathroom slippers of the kind provided to guests by expensive hotels. These carried some sort of heraldic device on the toe and the words *Grand Hotel, Vaduz*. Bruno had no idea where that might be.

There were more books in Russian on a small bookshelf, along with some French classics, a few of the garishly covered SAS spy novels by Gérard de Villiers, a French–Russian dictionary and a pile of *Aviation Weekly* magazines in English. On top of the bookcase was a plastic cigarette lighter and an ashtray with several white cardboard tubes that seemed to contain tobacco. They looked like the remains of joints. He slipped one into a small evidence bag and put it in his pocket.

He took the poetry book and the ashtray back into the main room. 'Does either of you read Russian?' he asked, holding out the book.

'I do, a bit,' said Madeleine. 'That's Akhmatova, a poet; she was Gilbert's favourite. Her husband went to the Gulag under Stalin.'

'And did he use marijuana?' he asked, showing her the ashtray.

'They're *papirosi*, Russian cigarettes,' she said,

smiling in a way that made Bruno say to himself, *mon Dieu,* this is a beautiful woman. 'They come like that with those little tubes instead of filters. He always smoked them when he could get them. It's a brand called Belomorkanal, White Sea Canal.'

'Where did you learn your Russian?' he asked.

'I studied it at university and then went to Moscow during a long holiday,' she said casually. 'I got a job as an intern in our Embassy's commercial office.'

She took the ashtray and emptied it into the rubbish bag. He thanked her and returned to the bedroom. The handsome wooden armoire was almost filled with neatly hung clothes, and the shelves down one side contained folded shirts from Chauvet. He checked the pockets and then looked to see where Gilbert bought his suits. The labels said London; the names meant nothing to him. In the dressing table, Bruno found drawers in which socks and underwear had been rolled and carefully arranged, something Bruno had never seen a man do before.

He found no papers or notebooks in the pockets and the suitcase atop the armoire was empty. Gilbert's shoes looked expensive, of beautiful rich leather, and Bruno guessed they had been hand-made. There were four pairs, two of classic black dress shoes with toecaps and laces, and two of brown brogues. They were neatly aligned on the floor of the armoire, each with its own wooden stretcher inside.

In the bathroom, a military washbag stood on a glass shelf alongside folded towels. Above the sink, a razor, shaving brush, toothbrush and toothpaste and a pair of silver-backed hairbrushes were lined up precisely, as if on parade. There was no cologne and the soap seemed to be a standard white *savon de Marseille*. The sink, shower and toilet bowl all gleamed as if freshly scrubbed. Even the underside of the seat had been cleaned. This orderliness was unlike any drunk Bruno had ever known. Maybe they instilled a stricter discipline in the air force; he doubted it. Automatically, Bruno plucked some hairs from one of the brushes and put them in an evidence bag.

There was something odd here, but he couldn't identify quite what. Dr Gelletreau had signed off the certificate for accidental death with unusual speed. Well, he was the family's doctor and so must know the background. The Mayor had made it clear he wanted the matter wrapped up, Bruno recalled the exact words, 'with his usual efficiency and discretion'. That was understandable; nobody would want the Patriarch's big day to be overshadowed by death. But Chantal had not been sure Gilbert was drunk when he tried to haul her away. No, Bruno told himself, he couldn't count that; he had instantly assumed that Gilbert was drunk when looking at him from the balcony. It had been something about his movements, the way he set his feet, the cock of his head as he pulled Chantal towards him.

Bruno had never known such a tidy drunk as Gilbert appeared to have been, nor any human being with so empty a paper trail. Usually there were notes, letters, old bills and address books, all the pocket litter of modern life. He wasn't hearing alarm bells, just some tinklings that triggered curiosity rather than suspicion. But like the way they had called the Mayor rather than the police, it was odd. Gelletreau and Father Sentout would usually have called Bruno first as a matter of course.

'Nothing of interest in there, so I'll leave you to it,' he said, stepping out into the main room and heading for the door. He paused, turned to them and asked, 'Either of you heard of a place called Vaduz?'

'It's the capital of Liechtenstein, a small duchy on the Swiss–Austrian border that used to be known as the false teeth capital of the world, when they were made from porcelain,' said Victor.

Bruno gazed at him, astonished. 'How on earth do you know that?'

'Playing Trivial Pursuit with the children.'

'It sounds like a useful game, maybe I should take it up,' Bruno said with a smile as he turned to go. 'Thanks for your help, and again, I'm sorry for the loss of your friend.'

'I'll phone you at the Mairie, about that lunch we discussed with Marco and the Countess,' Madeleine called after him.

CHAPTER 6

Bruno went home to change out of his uniform and pick up his dog. This was supposed to be his day off duty, but Gilbert's death and the accident with the deer had taken well into the afternoon. If he ever charged St Denis for all the off-duty time he spent working, he'd be almost as rich as the late Colonel Gilbert. At least he was alive and well to enjoy a fine day with the bracing nip of autumn in the air and the trees flooding the valley with colour. It was a perfect afternoon for a ride.

He called Pamela to see if she'd like to join him. He knew that she'd already been out today, automatically taking the horses for morning exercise whenever Bruno failed to turn up by seven-thirty. She would know it was police work that delayed him. There was no reply. She must be out of range or have her phone switched off. When he reached her house, he saw her car had gone. In the stables, his own horse, Hector, was evidently infected with the same urge to run. He tossed his head eagerly and pawed at the ground until Balzac trotted forward to greet the great horse, with whom he often slept, tucked up in a nest of warm hay in a corner of Hector's stall. The elderly mare, Victoria, ignored Bruno and the young basset hound, keeping her attention on the hay in her manger, as if to demonstrate that she'd had quite enough exercise already.

With Balzac at his horse's heels, Bruno trotted up the lane and then slowed to a walk as they went up the slope to the ridge. Pamela had returned a few days earlier from another trip to Scotland for the sale of her late mother's house. They'd shared several rides but not slept together for some weeks now, unusual even for their off-again, on-again affair. A woman who carefully guarded her privacy, Pamela always seemed delighted to see him but somehow matters had been arranged that when she invited him to dinner they were never alone. She would bid him an affectionate goodnight with the other guests. Bruno felt he could read the signs. Perhaps she was right, seeking a gentle way to end the affair that ensured they could remain friends and riding partners. Not for the first time, he chided himself for breaking his usual rule of never getting romantically involved with a woman who lived in the commune of St Denis. It meant their relationship was constantly observed by the other townsfolk, which would make ending their affair more than usually deli-cate. Bruno was never quite sure if continuing the relationship was what Pamela had in mind. She could go for days without seeing or contacting him and then suddenly greet him with passionate affection. It was disconcerting and over the months Bruno had come to the conclusion that it was deliberate, not because Pamela was cruel but as a way to reassure herself that she was in charge of this affair.

But now he suspected that she was signalling that it was ending. Pamela had said often enough that it had no future, that she was determined never to marry again. Bruno knew he would flounder in any attempt to relate to a woman who chose suddenly to become a kind of stranger after a year of sharing her bed. Courtesy required that he make it clear that he still found her desirable, even when they both knew their intimacies were over. Indeed, it was graven deep into the bones of any true Frenchman that every woman from sixteen into old age had still to be treated as possessing sensual charm and allure.

And Bruno knew that he was a romantic at heart, incapable of involving himself with a woman if he was not at least a little in love, sufficient to sweeten the precious time after lovemaking and to make him eager to spend time with her outside the bedroom. He felt a deep and enduring affection for Pamela and so told himself that to safeguard their friendship and allow her to retain her self-respect he should let her decide the future course of their affair. If she sought to wind it down with kindness, so be it. That meant that, whatever his own inclinations, he resolved to go along with Pamela's wishes.

It would be his role to convey sadness along with a resigned acceptance, the impression of a man bearing up despite a broken heart.

As his horse topped the rise and he could see down into the valley, he felt a certain satisfaction that he had reached a decision that he had too long delayed. He bent forward to pat Hector's neck, reflecting how much more clearly he seemed to think when out riding. He then tapped his heels gently and let Hector stride out into a canter and then into a pounding, thrilling gallop along the ridge. He glanced back to see Balzac running bravely behind, his long ears flapping as he tried in vain to keep up. But at least now his dog was big enough to keep his master in sight. As they reached the trees, Bruno reined in and steered Hector along the trail down to the quarry and to the long hunters' track that led back towards St Denis.

As he was trotting back up the lane to Pamela's house, he saw her ancient Citroën *deux chevaux* parked in the courtyard. The car was older than he was, and Pamela was proud of the fact that its vintage status meant it was worth considerably more now than when she'd first bought it. She came out from the kitchen door when she heard Hector's hooves on the gravel, bent to greet Balzac and then followed him to the stables, hugging Bruno when he dismounted. He took off the saddle and then each of them automatically picked up a rag to rub Hector down, one on each side.

'Is it your Sunday off tomorrow?' she asked as they brushed Hector. Bruno said it was. 'There's a riding stables that I know near Meyrals,' she went on. 'It's up for sale. Some of the horses are first-rate and I thought you might want to help me pick one out. Poor Victoria is getting too old for the kind of riding I enjoy.'

'You know more about horses than I do, but I'd like to come along,' he said, giving the horse his after-ride apple and draping a blanket over his long back. Pamela had taught him to ride and was a much better rider. He'd noticed that she had become more cautious since her accident on Bess, her favourite horse. The animal had broken a leg in a rabbit hole and had had to be put down. Bruno sometimes wondered if Pamela had ever forgiven him for doing that, necessary as it had been.

'I had a text from Fabiola,' Pamela went on. 'She and Gilles get back this evening so I went shopping for dinner and got a shoulder of lamb. I was hoping you might make that dish of yours with Monbazillac.'

'Not enough time to do it properly,' he said, thinking that there was rosemary and mint in the garden. 'The traditional version takes twelve hours but I'll see what I can do.'

'I've got some smoked trout and horseradish to begin and I'll make an apple tart. You know where the wine is. There's an open bottle of Monbazillac in the fridge if you need that for the lamb.'

Pamela kept her wines in a small *cave* Bruno had helped her make beneath the stone steps that led up to her pigeon tower. He brought back a 2011 white from Chateau Monestier La Tour to go with the fish, and a bottle of Pécharmant from Chateau Tiregand for the lamb. He went back to the garden for the herbs and then he and Pamela worked together in contented silence as they so often had before, each with their own work surface on opposite sides of the sink.

'What time did Fabiola say they'd get here?' he asked, putting the white wine into the fridge. He began to decant the red.

'In time for drinks before dinner, about seven or so. I'm assuming we'll eat some time after eight.'

So Bruno had not much more than two hours for the cooking. He turned Pamela's sometimes temperamental oven to mark 6, about 200 degrees, and began by wiping the lamb with kitchen paper until it was completely dry. He cut some rough slashes into the fat side of the meat and then used the knife to poke a series of deep holes in the flesh and inserted a clove of garlic in each one. He stripped a couple of twigs of rosemary of their spiky green leaves and used a pinch of them to top off each hole. Next he poured half a glass of the Monbazillac over the lamb, enough to moisten the surface. He'd already mixed together sea salt and cayenne pepper and he patted its surface with the mixture.

He glanced across to watch Pamela make the

pastry, wondering at that gift some people have of making perfect pastry every time. His pies usually turned out well enough, but even when he copied her trick of plunging his hands into iced water to cool them before working the dough, his pies never had the lovely, light touch that made Pamela such a peerless pastry cook. She put the pastry into the fridge to chill and began peeling the big green apples from her garden.

Bruno put two generous tablespoons of duck fat into the roasting pan and lit one of the burners on top of the oven to melt it. Then he browned the lamb on all sides and removed it. He laid down half a dozen sprigs of rosemary, replaced the lamb, surrounded it with heads of garlic and then added the rest of the Monbazillac. He was about to place the roasting pan into the oven when Pamela put a hand on his arm.

'Trust me,' she said. 'I know this will work. I remember my mother doing it when she cooked lamb with a Sauterne.'

He watched, intrigued, as she took a bottle of Worcestershire sauce, filled a tablespoon with the rich, dark juice and drizzled it over the meat. Bruno raised his eyebrows but Pamela's cooking instincts were good and he was always game for an experiment. He put the pan back in the oven and checked his watch. He'd baste the lamb every fifteen minutes or so and it should be done by eight. That would give time for the meat to rest while they had the smoked fish. He was looking forward to that. Pamela's blend of cream and horseradish went perfectly with the trout.

Looking round for the next task, he began to peel potatoes while relating the events of the day. He'd expected Pamela to be more interested in Imogène and her deer than in Gilbert's death.

He was wrong. She looked startled. 'But that was the man I met, good-looking in a raffish, ravaged kind of way. He's an old friend of Jack Crimson's; apparently they were at their respective embassies in Moscow in Gorbachev's time, when the Cold War was ending. He came up, embraced Jack and chatted with us for a while and then steered Jack away for a moment to talk privately. Later I saw him being led stumbling away, and I thought he must suddenly have hit the booze hard because he seemed pretty sober when talking to us.'

'Are you sure?' Bruno asked sharply. His tone was so aggressive it surprised him. 'Sorry,' he went on. 'I didn't mean to sound that way, it's just that everybody else has been making a point of telling me he was an alcoholic, a total wreck. And now you say he was sober. I suppose that if he was an alcoholic maybe he could disguise his drunkenness for a while.'

'No,' said Pamela firmly. 'He was switching back and forth between French and English, talking to me and Jack and to that minister from Paris. When the Russian Ambassador joined us, he and Jack began talking with him in fluent Russian. I was most impressed. Juggling three languages and being coherent enough to talk to a foreign minister and an ambassador tells me that he can't have been that drunk.'

'He had a flask with him, full of super-proof vodka,' Bruno said thoughtfully. 'Maybe that was what put him over the top.'

'I didn't see him use it and it wasn't that long after he'd left us that I saw him being led away. But tell me about this woman with the deer. Why can't the court just order her to accept a cull to control the numbers?'

'Politics. Neither the Prefect nor the judges want to become hate figures for the animal rights brigade, so that would be a last resort. By ordering her to build a fence, they're trying to force Imogène to agree to a cull.'

'And then we'd all be eating venison for weeks.'

'There are worse fates,' he replied, putting the potatoes into a pan of water and the peelings into a plastic bag, planning to take them home for his chickens. 'How did Fabiola sound?'

'Very happy. I think it's all worked out for them.'

'Let's hope so.' Fabiola Stern, the young doctor who had arrived in St Denis the previous year to work at the medical clinic, had been renting one of Pamela's *gîtes*. She'd become a good friend and a regular riding partner for them both. She spent much of her free time volunteering at a shelter in Bergerac for abused women and seemed to take no interest in the opposite sex. Then Gilles had arrived, a journalist from *Paris Match* whom Bruno had first met when serving with the UN peace-keepers in Bosnia. Bruno and Pamela had watched fondly as the two of them had begun falling in love, but their affair had been blighted by Fabiola's inability to consummate the relationship and her refusal to explain why. Some mysterious trauma in her life had blocked her. Bruno, along with Pamela and Yveline, the head of the local gendarmerie post, had tracked down Fabiola's old professor at medical school and found that Fabiola had been sexually assaulted by another teacher at the school and the incident hushed up. Bruno had managed to identify the man who had raped her, and he was now in prison. With that symbolic act of closure, Fabiola had been able, slowly and gingerly, to rebuild her emotional and physical life with Gilles.

Fabiola disliked big cities and wanted to stay in the Périgord so Gilles's own commitment to her had been important. He had accepted a redundancy deal and given up his staff job at *Paris Match* to move down to St Denis but still wrote for them from time to time on a freelance contract. He had signed a lucrative contract for his book on the notorious Afghan bomb-maker known as the Engineer, who turned out to be an autistic youth of Arab background who had grown up in St Denis. His first draft finished and sent off to his publishers, Gilles had taken Fabiola to the coast at Arcachon for a holiday together to celebrate.

When they arrived at Pamela's door hand in hand, it was plain that their time away together had been a success. Fabiola was glowing and Gilles wore that dazed, enchanted smile of a man utterly in love. Bruno found himself chuckling to see their happiness and saw that Pamela was beaming at him, similarly enchanted by the sight of their friends.

But over supper, the question of Gilbert's death nagged at him and he asked Fabiola if an alcoholic could go from apparent sobriety to being stumbling drunk within a few minutes. Everyone reacted differently to alcohol, she replied, but since alcohol had to be absorbed into the bloodstream there was usually no sudden tipping point from one state to the next. Bruno's case sounded unusual but her colleague Dr Gelletreau was an experienced medical man. If he had signed off on the death certificate, she was reluctant to take matters further, unless Bruno saw some clear motive for the death being unnatural. He shook his head at her implied question. As yet he saw no such motive, but even as he praised Pamela's addition of the Worcestershire sauce to the lamb, Bruno knew he could not let the matter drop.

CHAPTER 7

The riding school sprawled for about 400 metres along the side of a minor road. To the left there was a large riding ring filled with sand and surrounded by a wooden fence. To the right were two rows of stables for about twenty horses and directly ahead stood a large barn with a cottage attached that seemed to be the office. A sign above the door said *Acceuil*, welcome. Behind the barn, a generous paddock sprawled back up a gentle slope to a manor house atop the hill. A handsome nineteenth-century building with a porch supported by two stone pillars, it was flanked on each side by two smaller buildings of the same stone that might have been wings to the house or separate cottages. Altogether it made an impressive ensemble, and Bruno saw a diving board behind the house that suggested a swimming pool. But overall it appeared run-down and almost deserted. The paint of the stables was peeling and the windows of the offices had not been washed for months. There were no riders to be seen and only a few horses poking their heads curiously above their stable doors.

'It must once have been a good-looking place but it hardly looks like a going concern. Do you know why it's for sale?' Bruno asked Pamela as they climbed out of his Land Rover. She told him that two women had been running the place and the one with the reputation as a champion horse-woman had died nearly a year earlier. The other, Marguerite, had found the upkeep too difficult with a big bank loan to be paid off.

The door to the office was locked and there was no reply when they rang the bell. They strolled to the stables, looking at the horses, and then saw a woman in a headscarf half trotting, half walking down towards them from the big house. She was wearing jodhpurs and a quilted riding jacket and looked to be well into her sixties. She was panting when she arrived and took a moment to collect herself before she greeted Pamela by name, shook hands and said she was Marguerite. Bruno introduced himself and she must have recognized him, since she instantly said, 'Ah, the policeman from St Denis. I hear you ride, too.'

The place had been up for sale for several months but had attracted no potential buyers, Marguerite told them. She was selling off the horses one by one to raise money. She shrugged her shoulders, muttering, '*La crise,*' the standard French term for the recession that had gripped the country for more than half a decade.

'I can't keep the place up on my own and I can't really afford stable hands,' she went on. 'So I'm prepared to be flexible on the sale price. For the right owner, of course.'

'It was just one of the horses that I came to see,' Pamela said, sympathy in her voice. 'It's a lovely spot. You've evidently made a very handsome estate of it all.'

'We were happy here for a long time. It was valued at well over a million a few years ago but I know I'll never get that now. It's heartbreaking to think that Dominique and I put more than thirty years of our lives into building this up and now . . .' She bit her lip and seemed to brace herself. 'If I must, I'll sell it off bit by bit, the horses, the land, the *gîtes*, the house. I suppose that's the only way.'

'Perhaps we'd better go and look at the horses,' Pamela said kindly. 'It was your Selle Français that we spoke of on the phone. I've always liked that breed. A mare, five years old, you said?'

'Yes, we call her Primrose. She was born here, although she's not one of the foals descended from Duchesse, the horse Dominique rode at the Olympics. I had to sell all those.'

Marguerite led the way across to the stable block, pointing out the various horses by name. Bruno noticed that all the stable doors needed painting and some looked beyond repair. Tiles were missing from the roof. But the stables that contained horses had clean straw and full buckets of water and the stable yard was still damp from that morning's cleaning.

'And there's a Dutch Warmblood gelding you might also want to look at if you want a good strong horse,' Marguerite said. She was leading out Primrose for Pamela but she was addressing Bruno. 'We call him Rudi. I'll bring him out if you like, then you can ride them together. Rudi can do with a bit of exercise but he's very good-natured so you won't find him difficult.'

She walked the two horses in turn around the stable yard. Pamela and Bruno began by making friends, offering each horse a carrot and then stroking their long necks. Pamela checked the teeth and legs and shoes with a practised eye. Then they saddled each of them and took them to the ring, trotting gently. Marguerite kept the gate open and she signalled to them to take the horses out into the paddock for a canter. They rode up to the house and then around the back, pausing to take in the weeds that were beginning to attack the all-weather tennis court that stood beside the empty pool. There was another paddock with half a dozen rather battered jumps that needed a fresh coat of paint. Pamela took Primrose over two of the smaller jumps and then stopped beside a fine-looking orchard and asked Bruno to change horses.

'What does she want for the Selle?' he asked.

'Seven thousand but I think she'll have to come down. She's a good horse but there's not much of a pedigree so I won't pay more than four. What do you think of the Warmblood?'

'I hadn't heard of that breed but the name suits

66

him,' said Bruno, stroking Rudi's neck. 'He's certainly strong with lots of energy, keeps wanting to break into a gallop, but he's not difficult to handle.'

Pamela gestured at something hanging in the apple trees. 'What's that?' They led the horses across to look and found each tree had a small plastic net containing crushed eggshells hanging in its branches. Baffled, they exchanged horses to ride back to the stable yard, where Marguerite waited, a hopeful expression on her face.

'I think seven thousand is a lot more than I can afford, even considering what you told me of the pedigree, and I'm not planning to ride her in competitions,' Pamela began. 'But before we get into that, tell me about the *gîtes*. Do you rent them out?'

'Every summer. That's what's kept me going after Dominique died.'

'So your *gîtes* haven't been full?' Pamela asked. She was speaking casually but there was an alertness to her posture that Bruno recognized, a little tilting of her head that meant she was getting her teeth into something.

Marguerite shook her head. 'Not this summer. There was a leak in the swimming pool that I didn't have the money to repair. That's why I have to sell Primrose. I'll never be able to rent the *gîtes* if I can't offer the guests a swimming pool.'

'I'll give you four thousand for the Selle, and we can complete the sale this week, subject to a check-up by my vet. I don't want to bargain,' Pamela said firmly. 'But if you let me look through your books, I've got a friend who might be interested in buying the whole estate, if the price is right.'

'I've got some other people coming to look at the horses and then a riding class. If you came back this afternoon, we could go through the books then. Could you go to five for the horse? I really don't want to let Primrose go for four thousand. She's my favourite.'

'In that case we might not have a deal. But let's look at the books together and then we can talk. By the way,' Pamela added, 'why do you have those eggshells hanging in the apple trees?'

'It's an old local remedy to stop leaf curl and pests. I'm not sure it's very scientific but it seems to work. Dominique was born in the countryside so she was full of old remedies like that.'

Soon after leaving the riding school, Pamela and Bruno were sitting on the terrace at Laugérie Basse, whose great cliff loomed above the cave shelters of prehistoric people with their carvings of giant auroch bulls. The restaurant was a local favourite, family run and serving lavish meals at low prices. In the hunting season, Bruno came here once a week with his hunting club, dining inside the same overhanging cave where people had lived over 15,000 years ago.

'If I get all those *gîtes* running properly, I could bring in a hundred thousand a year,' said Pamela, showing him the notebook in which she had been calculating possible rental income.

'Less taxes, cleaning costs, repainting and upkeep, and then there's the marketing,' said Bruno. 'You might clear forty thousand if you fill them all every week from Easter to the end of October, but that's unlikely. And the place needs a fortune spending on it. You'd need a couple of stable hands at least, and somebody else to help with the riding school and with the cleaning in the summer. There goes your revenue from the *gîtes* and that's without thinking of the costs of fodder and the vet's bills.'

'I like running my own business and I'm good at it,' she replied, sipping at her glass of rosé. 'Unlike Marguerite. I can't believe what a bad businesswoman she was, telling us all about what she can't afford to do. Every time she spoke, I mentally knocked a few more thousand off the price.'

'She struck me as overworked, tired and depressed, and still mourning her dead partner,' said Bruno. He didn't add that he'd been even more struck by Pamela's uncompromising business style.

'I'd get a good price for my own place,' Pamela went on. 'And with the money from my mother's estate I'd have the cash flow I need plus a healthy cushion. I'd have to buy some new horses and a couple of ponies for children. The horses we didn't examine seemed quite old and a bit run-down, like the whole place.'

'Well, you know the risks and the hard work involved.' Bruno sat back as the plates of *rillettes de canard* were served along with a basket of bread and a bowl of cornichons.

'The risk might not be all mine,' she said, serving herself some *rillettes*. She paused, reaching to pour each of them some water. 'It was Jack Crimson who told me the place was up for sale. He said if I was interested in running it, he'd be ready to take a share in the venture. I'd have to set it up as a company and it would be useful to have a second shareholder.'

Bruno put down his knife and looked at her, about to remind her that there was a reason why riding schools in the region were going out of business. He caught himself before he spoke. After all, it was her affair, her inheritance. Pamela raised her eyes to look at him and her voice seemed deliberately offhand when she added, 'Jack thought it could be a good investment.'

This was a surprise. Bruno liked Jack and counted him as a friend, even though he'd been surprised when he'd first learned that the retired civil servant had spent his career in British Intelligence. They had become friends after sharing an adventure that had begun with Jack's home being burgled and Bruno then being lucky enough to track down his stolen possessions and restore them. A handsome man in his late sixties, Crimson was a widower whose wife had died shortly after they had bought their house near St Denis. He seemed very comfortably off and was always generous to local charities. If he'd already spoken to her about an investment, it was not just to look at the horse that was for sale that had inspired Pamela to visit the riding school.

'He's a decent man and very smart. If he thinks it's a good investment, it probably is,' Bruno said, recalling that he'd introduced Jack to Pamela at one of his own dinner parties. 'I didn't know you knew him that well.'

'Both being British, I suppose,' she said vaguely, looking away again and then starting to eat. 'He knew I was looking for a horse so he emailed me about the place and said it looked like being a bargain. We talked about it over dinner in London with his daughter, Miranda. I think Jack wants to get her involved, help her make a new start with the children. She's just been through what sounds like a very unpleasant divorce so I can sympathize.'

Bruno digested this. It was the first he'd heard of their meeting for dinner in London. 'Would Jack be involved in running the place or is he just planning to invest some money?'

'Too early to say, but he's no horseman.' She put down her knife and fork and paused before looking Bruno in the eye. 'I think he recognized that I was ready for a new challenge, something I could get my teeth into. I've been vegetating rather, with just the two *gîtes* to run once Fabiola started renting one of them. When Mother died, I began

71

asking myself if I was really happy with my very pleasant but predictable life, and I realized that I want to do something really ambitious while I still have the energy. This seems like a worthwhile project. I know *gîtes* and I love horses and this way I can combine the two while building a real business.'

'It sounds as though you've already made up your mind,' he said, beginning to eat. If Pamela was intent on making such an important change in this aspect of her life, she was probably ready for something different in her romantic life, too. He'd expected this, and while he felt some sadness he was also aware of a small but distinct sense of relief.

'I'm certainly determined to do something different,' Pamela said. 'I think I told you I'd spoken with Florence about giving English conversation classes to the senior class at the *collège*. But I'd rather do something involved with horses. I always have.'

'It sounds as though the riding school is what you want to do. I'm sure you'll make a great success of it.'

'Do you really think so?' she asked, her eyes shining. Their empty plates were whisked away and replaced with generous portions of roast chicken and *petits pois* with carrots. 'It won't leave me much time to spend with you.'

'I understand, but I'll still have to come along to exercise the horses, morning and evening. But if you're going into business, I'd better start paying stable fees for Hector.'

'Don't be silly,' she said. 'But morning exercise will be different if we're taking out a long string of horses behind us.'

'You'll just have to ensure you have so many pupils at your riding school that they'll do most of the exercising for you,' he said. 'Then you might not even need Fabiola and me.'

'That reminds me,' she said, sitting up in her chair. 'Fabiola was raving about the lamb this morning when we had coffee together before we took the horses out. It's good to see her and Gilles so happy.'

Bruno smiled his agreement. Fabiola, the gifted doctor, and Gilles, the writer, were well-matched, his passionate interest in national politics tempered by a warm good humour and a dry wit that Bruno appreciated. Bruno's own interest in politics was mainly confined the affairs of his commune and the *Département*, but he liked to listen to Gilles's views. It was something new for Bruno to have a close male friend who didn't hunt, had little interest in rugby or any kind of sports, and spent most of his time reading or attached to his laptop. It made him a good partner for Fabiola, whose radio was always tuned to France-Culture and whose favourite reading, apart from medical journals, seemed to be *Le Monde Diplomatique*. Other than the Mayor, Bruno supposed they were the first intellectuals he'd known.

The *crème brûlée* finished, they ordered coffee and enjoyed the view down the cliff and over the River Vézère. Bruno wondered if this would be the last time this year he'd be able to lunch in the open air.

'Would you like me to drive you back to the riding school?' he asked.

She shook her head. 'I'll probably be there some time, poring over account books and getting a sense of just how far the place has run down and how much it's going to cost me to put it back in order. If you drop me off at home, I'll drive myself over there. I want a good look around inside the *gîtes* and the big house. From the outside it seemed rather too big for me but maybe I could live in one of the *gîtes* and rent it out. There's always a good market for big manor houses like that in the summer. I'll let you know what I find out.'

CHAPTER 8

Even though he knew the place well, Bruno paused at the end of the gravel drive, looking down the avenue of fruit trees to admire Jack Crimson's home. It was a small manor house of the kind that was these days called a *gentilhommerie*, a gentleman's residence. Crimson said he'd chosen it because it reminded him of the Georgian country houses in England, albeit in miniature form. A handsome front porch was flanked by stone pillars, two sets of French windows on each side of the door with five mansard windows on the upper floor. The effect was pleasingly symmetrical and it looked comfortable and inviting with its roof of old tiles and the warmth of the honey-coloured stone. Some hardy late roses provided a splash of pinks and yellows.

Balzac gave a cheerful bark and scampered down the drive, stopping to sniff at the various trees before deciding that a cherry tree was the most suitable for him to lift his leg against. Then he ran onto the porch just as Crimson opened the front door and bent to caress the basset hound he'd known since Balzac was a puppy.

'My dear Bruno and Balzac, a pleasure to see you both, and you're just in time for a *p'tit apéro*,' said Crimson with a wide smile. As usual, he looked as if he'd not just taken care over his dress but as if he was ready to be photographed for a glossy English lifestyle magazine. His grey hair was neatly brushed and there were precise creases in his khaki slacks. His checked shirt was open at the neck and a yellow cashmere sweater was slung with casual elegance around his shoulders. His brown brogues were highly polished.

'A glass of Scotch? A Ricard? Some wine? I think it's still warm enough to enjoy it in the open air while Balzac renews his acquaintance with the garden.'

Installed on the terrace with its view across a well-kept lawn to the ridge that led down to the River Vézère, Bruno accepted a small glass of Scotch. He recognized Crimson's usual bottle of Balvenie and his host added a splash of water, murmuring something about the need to liberate the bouquet. Crimson clinked their glasses together and said, '*Slange!*' and Bruno replied, '*Chin!*' in the French way.

'This isn't entirely a social call,' Bruno began. 'You may have heard that one of the guests at the Patriarch's party died later that evening, Gilbert Clamartin.'

Crimson's glass jerked as he was raising it to his lips. 'Gilbert, dead? I had no idea. What happened?' His surprise looked genuine.

76

'He died in his sleep, very drunk, and never woke up. Apparently he threw up when he was passed out. No suspicious circumstances, the doctor said.'

'Old Gilbert . . . I knew he was hitting the bottle pretty hard but he seemed fine when I saw him at the party, not drunk at all.'

'You're sure of that?'

'Quite sure. He was bouncing back and forth between French, English, Russian, making a lot of sense and being amusing. He could be one of the most charming people you'd ever hope to meet and he was certainly on form at the party. He died that evening, you say? Do you know about the funeral arrangements?'

'Not yet, but once I hear I'll let you know. Did you notice a small disturbance at the party, a sudden drop in the conversation and a flurry of people?'

'Can't say I did. I was having too good a time, at least until those damn planes came over. I thought there were rules about how low they were allowed to fly. What was this disturbance about?'

'Gilbert was apparently bothering a young woman, Victor's daughter, trying to pull her away, and then Victor and some others intervened and escorted him off. I saw it and he was stumbling drunk by then. But a short while before that I saw him with you and Pamela and the Foreign Minister. It didn't seem long enough to get so drunk.'

'I see what you mean,' said Crimson. 'But I lost track of Gilbert after we were joined by our mutual chum, the Brigadier.'

Bruno would not have put it like that. The Brigadier was a senior official in French Intelligence, attached to the staff of the Minister of the Interior but with a remit that seemed to run across the range of France's police and security forces. He sometimes roped Bruno in to help with problems, political or diplomatic, that emerged in the Périgord. A thought struck Bruno: the Brigadier also drank Balvenie. Perhaps Crimson had introduced him to it.

'Did the Brigadier know Gilbert?' Even as he put the question, Bruno felt a sinking feeling. Whenever the Brigadier became involved, it spelled trouble, usually in the form of a letter from the Minister to the Mayor, asking for Bruno to be seconded temporarily to the Brigadier's staff. Since he was still officially on the reserve list of the French Army, Bruno could always be conscripted if he tried to refuse the request.

'Of course. You don't get to be military attaché in Moscow without getting to know people in the intelligence community.' That was where he had met Gilbert, Crimson explained. That might explain why Gilbert's military records had been sealed, thought Bruno.

Crimson had been attached to the British Embassy in that twilight of the Cold War when Gorbachev was in the Kremlin. Gilbert had been very well informed with lots of good contacts in the Soviet Air Force, so Crimson had made a point of befriending him. It was also through Gilbert that

Crimson had met the Patriarch. Gilbert had introduced them at one of his celebrated parties in his apartment in the old Arbat, the most desirable district of Moscow. It had been a great deal grander than the usual places the Soviets assigned to one of Gilbert's rank; Crimson assumed that the Patriarch's influence had helped.

'Of course, the Patriarch was like a god to the Soviet military, fighting alongside them all the way to Berlin,' Crimson went on. Marshal Akhromeyev had been the Patriarch's bosom friend; he was the chief of staff of the Soviet armed forces, and the last serving Soviet soldier to have fought his tank into the heart of Berlin in 1945. So the Patriarch had smoothed Gilbert's way in Moscow, introducing him to the Marshal as a fellow fighter pilot and a close friend of his son.

'Moscow was an extraordinary place back then,' Crimson went on. 'Gorbachev dismantling the old Soviet system, his glasnost bringing amazing revelations in the press every day, people speaking out on TV and in public meetings like never before.'

Most of the Western diplomats were fascinated by it all, Crimson related, even as the security people were issuing dire warnings about remaining on guard. And most Westerners were still sufficiently in Cold War mode to stick together. Not that Gilbert took much notice, said Crimson, which was one of the many reasons he'd liked him.

'Gilbert was a man of great charm, made friends

easily and he probably had more Russian connections than almost any other Western diplomat in Moscow,' Crimson continued. 'The Patriarch's Russian son, Yevgeny, was doing some set designs for the Chaika Theatre at the time. He introduced Gilbert around the artists and theatre people, who were all having a glorious time with the new freedom. It gave him a way into the Soviet elite.'

'How was that?' Bruno asked. 'I'd have thought those worlds would be quite separate, particularly in Moscow.'

Crimson grinned. 'First rule of diplomacy, Bruno. The ruling classes in any society, the Communist bloc included, feel it part of their duty to cultivate the arts, the opera and ballet, symphony concerts and the theatre. At least their wives do; they like to think they're part of the cultured classes, members of the intelligentsia. Get yourself invited to the artists' parties and their weekend dachas and pretty soon you'd start running into the sons and daughters of the *nomenklatura*.'

'What's that?'

'The *nomenklatura* were the party elite, the Communist Party central committee and their staff, government ministers and their top advisers, newspaper editors, directors of the big state enterprises. Gilbert already knew a lot of the top military men, and pretty soon he was uniquely well connected, hearing all the top-level gossip. I just rode along on his coat-tails and I did pretty well out of it, even though Gilbert was very discreet, particularly about his dalliances with influential wives. As I said, he was a very charming man, handsome and with that fighter pilot's dash about him. It wasn't just the women that he bowled over, he was also the kind of chap who also got on well with men.'

'So you and Gilbert stayed friends after Moscow?'

'Indeed, even though we didn't see one another that often. But that sort of time in that sort of place, it creates a lasting bond.' Crimson refilled the glasses. 'I knew he'd become a bit of a drunk but he could still hold his liquor pretty well when he wanted to. And for the Patriarch's birthday party, I'd have thought Gilbert would have wanted to stay in control. It seems a bit odd.'

'You mean there wasn't enough time between your seeing him and his being led away to get that drunk?'

'That's not quite what I mean. Since I didn't see him carried off I couldn't say how long it might have been.'

'That incident took place very shortly before the Patriarch announced the fly-past.'

'In that case I'd say maybe ten minutes, fifteen at the maximum. But he'd have to have been drinking very hard and very fast.'

'He had a large flask with him, made in England, twice the size of a usual hip flask.'

'Heavens,' said Crimson, breaking into a smile. 'I bought him that as a Christmas present when we were in Moscow. I'm touched that he still kept the old thing. It held half a bottle, I remember, because naturally I filled it before I gave it to him. If that's what carried him off, I suppose that makes me an accessory. A bloody shame, he was a good man.'

'Did you see him after you bought your house here?'

'Off and on, the occasional lunch, but he always came to my garden parties, including the one you were at last year. I could never turn him onto Pimm's, unlike you. Gilbert was a vodka man.' He paused. 'Where are you going with this, Bruno? Do you think there was something fishy about his death?'

'I don't know.' Bruno shook his head. 'I saw him drunk and I saw the body and it was pretty clear how he died. It's just the timing I can't fathom, how he got so drunk so quickly.'

Crimson shrugged. 'Alcoholics can be like that, one moment fine and then the next drink tips them over the top.'

'I suppose so,' Bruno said, wondering why Crimson seemed so dismissive of his friend's death. Knowing Crimson's background, Bruno speculated to himself as to whether he might have another motive for his lack of concern. He took a last sip of his drink, debating with himself whether to ask the next question that troubled him. Then he plunged in. 'I didn't know you were interested in horses,' he began. 'Pamela told me of your interest in the riding school.'

Crimson's eyes crinkled into a smile. 'I was wondering if you'd bring that up. Are you intending to ask me if my intentions toward your Pamela are honourable?'

'She's not my Pamela, as you put it. She's her own woman,' Bruno said, more curtly than he'd intended. He softened his tone. 'And no, I'm not asking that. I'd simply like to hear why you think Pamela could make a success of the place when those other two women didn't, and one of them was a well-known horsewoman, an Olympic rider.'

'Two reasons; the first is that Pamela understands that such a place is best run as a tourist rental business which happens to have a riding school attached. So she won't be investing far too much money in very expensive horses. The second reason is that I've got a daughter, recently divorced, who has always dreamed of running a riding school. She was mad about horses as a girl and worked in some stables before she got married. It would mean a new start for her and her children.'

'Have she and Pamela discussed it?' Bruno was beginning to see just how advanced Pamela's plans were. He'd assumed she was interested in a horse and had only then begun to think about the stables. He felt surprised that she had not taken him more into her confidence.

'Yes, we all had dinner together in London when she was on her way up to Scotland. They got on well and Miranda, that's my daughter, likes the idea of living in France. The children are five and

83

seven, a boy and a girl, a good age to put them in school and make them bilingual. And I'd see more of them since I'm planning to spend a lot more time here in the Périgord.'

'It sounds as though you've all worked it out quite thoroughly. Has your daughter been over here yet to see the place?'

'No, but she's coming over this weekend, if Pamela still wants to go ahead with the plan after going through the accounts. I'm planning a dinner party for her and of course you'll be invited, along with Fabiola and Gilles.' He held up the bottle. 'Another drink before you go? And talking of dinner, I've got a lasagne in the oven that's far too much for me. Would you like to share it or do you have other plans?'

'That's kind of you. I was planning a quiet night with an omelette and a novel but a bachelors' evening sounds more fun.'

'I'll go and set the table and perhaps you'd go down to the cellar and pick out a really good couple of bottles to go with the meal. After all, if you hadn't got my wines and furniture back from those damn burglars, I'd have nothing to drink.'

After some agreeable minutes admiring the collection in Crimson's cellar, Bruno turned his back on the classic Bordeaux and Burgundies and focused on the Bergeracs. It was partly regional loyalty, but also he was impressed by Crimson's knowledge. Bruno climbed from the cellar carrying two bottles that he'd heard of but never tasted and could not choose between. One was a 2005 Côtes de Bergerac red from Les Verdots, made by a young *vigneron* with a stellar reputation, David Fourtout. The other was a 2009 cuvée made only in exceptional years by Chateau Montdoyen. His friend Hubert de Montignac, the local wine merchant, had told him this was his favourite of all the white wines produced in south-western France. Hubert had organized a blind tasting among sommeliers at the last VinExpo wine fair in Bordeaux and the Divine had tied with the great whites of Chateau Haut-Brion and Chateau Margaux.

'You pick,' said Bruno, joining Crimson in the kitchen. 'I can't choose between these two.'

'That's easy,' said Crimson, taking a corkscrew to the Divine. 'We'll open both. If you could decant the red into that carafe, I'll serve the smoked salmon, which should go well with the white.'

He poured them each a glass of the Divine, swirled his own and sniffed. 'Nectar. So we'll have no lemons with the smoked salmon. And when it comes to red wine, I can't think when a humble lasagne has been so honoured.'

CHAPTER 9

Bruno always enjoyed visiting Le Thot, the companion site to the famous Lascaux cave. It appealed to him as a place that tried to give modern relevance and meaning to the prehistoric cave art that had been painted 17,000 years ago. It was an unusual mix, part museum, part education centre and part zoo. As he always did, he started by walking round the park filled with animals that had been bred to resemble as closely as possible the giant auroch bulls and primitive shaggy horses, the deer and goats that had shared this valley with the Cro-Magnon people who had painted the caves. He grinned at the life-size model of a woolly mammoth that towered over him and thought of the courage, or perhaps the desperate hunger, of those remote ancestors who had taken on the massive aurochs, now placidly grazing like domestic cows.

He stopped off at a place he'd never seen before, a small stone building with three walls and a throng of children busy inside. The interior walls had been painted white and, with tools and pigments like those the cave painters had used, the kids were happily painting aurochs, horses and deer on the walls. The clamour of their voices testified to their enthusiasm as they ran back and forth from wall to table with the pigments. Bruno smiled at the cheerful patience of the artist in residence who was draping the young painters in leather smocks to protect their clothes and showing them how to make their first outlines in charcoal. Museums had never been like this when Bruno had been taken on school trips.

Bruno strolled back past the woolly mammoth, seeing a spindly new fence around a deep pit at the edge of the woodland. He glanced in, wondering whether they were mining for flints or planning to recreate a mammoth trap, possibly with models of prehistoric hunters attacking the trapped beast. There was a prehistoric park at Tursac that specialized in such scenes.

He didn't linger in the museum since he'd already seen the first copies of the paintings in the original Lascaux cave, made by Monique Peytral and other local painters who had then produced the exact copy of the cave that tourists could now visit. The original, its paintings damaged by the bacteria brought in by hundreds of thousands of visitors, has been closed to the public for fifty years. But Bruno always liked the exhibition that showed how the cave people had used moss and animal fur as paint brushes on the white chalk walls, and tiny blowpipes to apply the paints they made from crushing minerals. He knew they had used manganese for the black pigment, ochre for the yellows and a brown clay that turned red when baked in a fire. And he always marvelled at the tiny stone lamps they had used, with deer fat and juniper twigs as wicks, the only combination that would burn with a clear and smokeless flame which would neither asphyxiate the painters nor darken the chalk with smoke.

'*Bonjour*, Bruno,' came a voice at his elbow and he turned to kiss Clothilde on both cheeks and to shake the hand of her companion, Horst, a German archaeologist attached to the prehistory museum in Les Eyzies, who had become a friend. Bruno was surprised to see that Clothilde, an expert on the cave artists who had helped design Le Thot's original exhibits, was still curious enough to visit it yet again.

'Have you seen this new twist?' she asked, pointing at the tiny blue glows that helped illuminate the life-size models of Cro-Magnon people. Some were using flints to scrape out the bowls of stone lamps or to cut the pelts of reindeer, and others were attaching tufts of fur from reindeer tails onto sticks to make paint brushes. Bruno had to crane and peer to see what they were doing since the museum tried to recreate the dim lamplight the cave painters would have used.

'They're using ultraviolet light to pick out the flint; it makes it easier to understand the various tasks they're performing,' Clothilde said. 'But that's not what we're here to see.'

She led the way down the corridor and into a large room where Raquelle was waiting for them, an iPad in her hands, using it to control the images on a giant screen that covered one entire wall. She lifted one hand to wave a greeting and then pointed at the screen where Bruno saw himself, Clothilde and Horst standing by Raquelle. He raised one arm and saw his onscreen image do the same.

'Don't expect too much,' said Raquelle. 'We're still working out a few bugs, but here goes. Pick a prehistoric animal: your choice: cave bear, mammoth, giant stag.

'Cave bear,' Clothilde replied.

Raquelle pressed some buttons and suddenly Bruno saw a giant bear appear before them, apparently sleeping, the sound of its snores coming from some speakers he could not see. Inside the room, there was no bear, only the astonishingly real image on the screen. He bent to try to touch the fur where the bear ought to be but felt nothing. And yet as soon as he stretched out his hand, the bear onscreen appeared to stir and then to wake. It rose to stand and stretched its arms out and opened its jaws wide as if yawning, its great height overawing the puny human figures onscreen. Then it went to the image of a cave wall and began to scrape with its giant claws. To Bruno's delight, the sounds of nails on rock came over the speakers and the image of claw marks appeared on the rock wall to match the movement of the claws. He knew that what he saw onscreen was an illusion but it seemed extraordinarily real.

The bear sidled off, to be replaced by a miniature woolly mammoth, apparently a baby, taking hesitant steps and making feeble sounds that were quickly drowned out by the trumpeting sound of a full-grown adult as a giant beast with great tusks came onscreen to steer the baby away. Then came a cave lion, creeping with feline grace as if tracking the humans who were its prey before leaping onto a cliff.

'That's incredible,' said Bruno, whose knowledge of computers did not go much beyond emails and Google searches.

'It took a lot of computer time to create the beasts and then to make them move in lifelike ways,' said Raquelle. 'We're using actors to train our guides to get the children involved in this virtual reality in a positive way. The last thing we want to do is frighten them.'

'This is just the beginning,' Clothilde added, turning to Raquelle. 'But perhaps I'm speaking out of turn. Do you want to talk about the new project yet?'

'It's early days,' Raquelle said. 'So far we've got an auroch built and working after a fashion, although the movements are still jerky.'

She touched some more buttons on her iPad and the screen went dark as the lights in the room came up. She led the way out of the museum and across to the building that housed her studio and workshop and introduced them to the two young men and the young woman who sat at giant computers. On one screen, Bruno saw a giant stag with enormous antlers, its body criss-crossed with a grid of green lines. On another was an auroch bull standing over a cow that was being suckled by a calf.

Raquelle opened a door and led them into the workshop, where they were confronted by a giant bull, not onscreen but standing in the middle of the floor and dominating the space with its huge, curved horns. Bruno stepped back, awed by the sheer bulk and the air of menace of this prehistoric beast. The skin, made of some material he'd never seen before, seemed to glow with a sheen of health over what looked like bunching muscle. Raquelle slipped into a seat before another computer and as she tapped the keyboard and began to manipulate a control stick the bull raised and then lowered its great head and turned it from side to side. Its eyes seemed to remain fixed menacingly on Bruno.

'This is my own project, not yet official, but we're working with a robotics company in Boston and with the robotics group at the national research agency in Grenoble,' she explained as the great bull began to back jerkily away towards the open double doors at the rear of the workshop. The Americans were already producing robot animals that could carry munitions and supplies and evacuate casualties for the American military, and the

French had a similar project. 'At first we had trouble getting him to walk on uneven ground but I think we've fixed that now. What we don't know is how the real bulls will react to him. If they try to fight him, we could be left with some very expensive junk.'

'It's amazing, frighteningly lifelike. You could terrify the kids with this,' Bruno said. 'May I touch it?' When Raquelle told him to go ahead, he reached forward and touched the horns and then stoked the great neck, jumping back when Raquelle laughed and made the neck shift towards him.

'Are you going to try to make similar robots of the bears and cave lions?' Bruno asked.

'Eventually, if we can get the funding. My dream would be to recreate the whole landscape and fauna of prehistoric man, the bulls and giant stags, the mammoths and cave bears. Maybe one day we could even build some Cro-Magnon people and try to re-enact hunting scenes, the way they looked and how they dressed and lived and even the way they painted their caves.'

She brought the robotic auroch back to stillness. 'But all that's a long way off and I'm getting hungry. We're having lunch at my place and the other guests will be arriving on the doorstep any minute. It's just family. They were going to join us to see the computer-generated animals but something came up.'

★　　★　　★

Raquelle lived in the heart of Montignac, the small town nearest to the Lascaux cave, in a terraced house of stone that nestled against the old city wall, just before the bridge. She led him through the sitting room and kitchen to a small paved garden tucked against the medieval wall, at least ten metres high. Somehow her garden still managed to capture the sun. A long and narrow pool, apparently designed for swimming laps, took up part of the space, and a dining table and six chairs stood on a terrace by a small cave or tunnel that had been cut into the wall.

Raquelle came out with a tray containing plates, cutlery and glasses, a chilled bottle of white wine from Chateau Thénac and a corkscrew. He opened the wine and set the table and then looked into the cave. It was only a couple of metres deep with a pool of clear water at the bottom. Raquelle had rigged a small fountain and a lighting system that would doubtless look striking in the evenings. The walls and shelter made the place a suntrap and Bruno took off his uniform jacket and sat back, closing his eyes and enjoying the feel of the autumn sun on his face.

'I'm glad you've made yourself comfortable. I love this spot; the colour of the stone reminds me a little of the part of Jerusalem where I grew up,' Raquelle said, coming out with another tray, full of food. 'It's a very simple lunch, *salade Niçoise*, bread, cheese and fruit.'

Bruno heard footsteps inside the house and then

Clothilde and Horst emerged with Yevgeny, the Patriarch's Russian son, whom they had met on the doorstep. That made five, thought Bruno, wondering who might be the sixth at lunch. Raquelle asked him to pour out the wine and said, 'My sister-in law, Madeleine, will be joining us, but a little later.'

'She drove Victor home after the cremation,' said Yevgeny. He was taller than Bruno, broader than Horst, and had a clumsy way of moving that occupied so much space he seemed to dominate the terrace. 'Victor was very upset, his oldest friend dying in such a way.'

'Cremation?' asked Bruno, startled. 'You mean Gilbert?' That was fast work, Bruno thought, wondering why Victor hadn't taken his advice about contacting the air force to arrange the military funeral that was Gilbert's due.

Clothilde sat down abruptly in one of the chairs and gasped, 'Gilbert, dead? But there was nothing in the newspaper.'

Bruno began to count in his head. The Patriarch's party had been on Friday, Gilbert died that evening and today was Monday. That made three days, traditionally the minimum waiting time for burial or cremation. And that meant there would be no possibility of an autopsy, even if he had a shred of evidence to question Dr Gelletreau's verdict of natural death, or anything to suggest somebody might have had a motive to tamper with Gilbert's drinks.

'Yes, Gilbert, he wanted to be cremated,' Yevgeny replied. 'He used to joke about it, saying he'd spent his life as a pilot but never been shot down in flames nor exploded in a crash landing, so it was only fair that the fire should get him in the end. He had a strange sense of humour, very dark, very Russian. Maybe that was why we all liked him so much.'

'You knew him in Moscow?' Bruno asked.

'Of course, he was one of my best customers,' Yevgeny replied. 'He'd bring distinguished visitors from Paris to my studio. Since in those days the state wouldn't give me an exit visa I was obviously some kind of dissident, so that was an extra thrill for them. I was even quite fashionable for a short while.'

'How did it happen?' asked Clothilde. She looked stunned. Horst put his arm around her shoulders.

'He killed himself with vodka,' said Yevgeny, raising his hands in a gesture that was half resignation, half blessing.

'He died in his sleep after the Patriarch's party,' Bruno said. 'Did you know Gilbert well?'

'We were very close at one time, not long after he came here,' she replied, with a sad smile. 'It was not long after he came back from Moscow. He'd just retired, or rather he'd been pushed out. He was very bitter about it. I wish I'd known, I'd have liked to attend the funeral.'

Into the silence that then fell, Raquelle changed the subject, talking of her recent trip to Chicago to help launch the new travelling exhibition of the Lascaux cave, which she and Clothilde had helped design. It was a topic that drew Clothilde back into the conversation and lasted until the sound of stiletto heels on Raquelle's tile floor signalled the arrival of the final guest.

Victor's wife, Madeleine, strode into the walled garden with an apology for her lateness and air kisses for all except Bruno, to whom she stretched out her hand and held his for just a heartbeat too long. She was wearing tight jeans and a loose white cotton sweater that revealed one smooth, tanned shoulder, and announced, 'I just had to get out of those depressing funeral clothes. Didn't I hear you talking about your work on Lascaux, Clothilde? I'm so sorry to interrupt, do go on.'

'I'd finished,' said Clothilde, stiffly. There was evidently little love lost between the two women. But then Clothilde, as a scholar with an impressive reputation in France and abroad, was accustomed to dominating any gathering by force of her personality as well as her academic renown. Madeleine could achieve the same effect by her looks alone. Raquelle, Bruno noted, was watching both women with a cocked eyebrow and a slightly mocking smile, enjoying the subtle rivalry between them. Horst and Yevgeny had their eyes on Madeleine, as would any man in his senses, Bruno thought, as he shifted his eyes back to her and caught her examining him, perhaps wondering why his gaze had been elsewhere.

'Where does the exhibition go after Chicago?' he asked Clothilde.

'Montreal, then Tokyo; after that I'm not sure. Perhaps China.'

'I hope not,' said Horst. 'Lascaux is crowded enough without millions of Chinese coming to see it. They've already made the Louvre impossible and driven up the price of Bordeaux wines to the point where I can barely afford them.'

'Drink our good Bergerac instead; it's a lot cheaper and often better than the wine made by those hidebound snobs in the Médoc,' said Madeleine, picking up the bottle on the table and pretending to be shocked. 'Shame on you, Raquelle, serving a Bergerac that hasn't come from the family vineyard.'

'Rest assured, Madeleine, the next bottle is one of ours,' said Raquelle, guiding them to take their places around the table. She began slicing a fat *pain* and told them to help themselves to the salad. She took the head of the table and Yevgeny took the foot. Bruno sat beside Clothilde, facing Horst and Madeleine.

'Do you know you're quoted in the paper today?' Madeleine asked Bruno. She pulled a folded copy of *Sud Ouest* from her bag and passed it to him. The paper was opened to a page about Imogène and her deer, with a photo of Adèle standing by her battered car and another of an emaciated fawn. Bruno was quoted as saying that unless Imogène built the fence the court had required the next step

97

would be for the Prefect to seek a court order for the deer to be culled. But perhaps an agreement might be reached to establish a proper refuge.

'It sounds like you're on the side of this crazy woman,' Madeleine said. 'You ought to stick up for your fellow hunters.'

'I don't think there's much hope of raising the funds for a refuge but any form of amicable agreement is usually better than going to court,' he replied. 'And I don't think she's crazy, just obsessed with saving her deer. I went to see her. She obviously loves animals and has taken some very impressive photos of them. I was thinking an exhibition of them might raise some money.'

'A lot of us are getting very fed up with the way these animal rights people and the Greens are getting more and more powerful,' Madeleine said firmly. 'This is the Périgord. Hunting is in our blood; we're carnivores, just like our ancestors. Any ecology needs predators to stay in balance and that's the problem with this stupid woman. I often think we hunters are the real protectors of the environment, because we know that.'

Bruno nodded politely. It was an argument he'd heard before, usually at election times when the Pêche-Chasseurs Party fielded a candidate, but the attempt to build a political alliance of hunters and anglers had faltered. They had once got fifteen per cent of the vote in the *département* of the Dordogne but now they had just a few scattered councillors in rural communes.

'I think the most likely outcome will be a cull,' he said amiably. 'But it's my job to try to find an acceptable compromise.'

'Good for you,' said Raquelle. 'I know Imogène a bit through the Green Party and I used some of her photos when we put the computer models together. I like her and respect her commitment but she can be infuriating.'

Raquelle poured out the rest of the wine and asked Bruno to open the next bottle. It carried the label *Domaine du Patriarche*, the vineyard run by Victor and Madeleine. Bruno knew it as a decent everyday wine with few pretensions. It was not a wine he bought himself, despite his reverence for the man for whom it was named. A drawing of the Patriarch, wearing an old fashioned flying helmet, dominated the label.

'You're being diplomatic, Bruno,' said Madeleine, smiling at him but with a challenging look in her expression. 'Tell me what you think of our wine.'

'Very agreeable,' he said politely. 'I'm only sorry that having to drive back means I can only drink half a glass.'

She studied him coolly for a moment, then looked at the others before addressing him. 'We all know this wine is nothing special, but perhaps all of you ought to come out to the vineyard and taste the surprise we're preparing.'

'A special cuvée?' Clothilde enquired.

'Very special,' Madeleine replied. 'We've assigned a separate part of the vineyard, brought in a new

99

winemaker from St Emilion, bought new oak barrels to age it and to the white wine we're adding about eight per cent Muscadelle grapes that we planted five years ago.'

She leaned across the table and tapped the back of Bruno's hand with an elegant finger that looked as though it had never worked in a garden, far less in a vineyard. 'We've been planning this for years. And it will be a completely organic wine, fully certified. We're going for a different market entirely, a real quality wine with a much higher price point. And the new red wine we're making also has something special to it.'

'It sounds like a wine worthy of the Patriarch,' Bruno said politely.

'The Patriarch's Reserve, that's what we're calling it. He's going to lead the marketing drive himself.'

'I wish you every success,' he said. 'It must involve a lot of investment.'

'*Tolko dyengi*, we say in Russia,' Yevgeny broke in, laughing. 'It's only money. Seriously, the new wine is very good, we've all tasted it. There's something about time in the barrel, and the Muscadelle in the Bergerac Sec really adds something.'

'When do you launch it?'

'At the end of the month, aiming at the Christmas market,' said Madeleine.

'When can we buy some?' asked Horst.

'We're doing a tasting for the trade tomorrow morning at eleven and there's a buffet lunch afterwards. Come to the vineyard about noon.

100

The Patriarch will be there, and he'd like to see you.' Madeleine waved her arm to include Horst and Clothilde but her eyes were on Bruno.

Bruno looked at Horst and Clothilde, who were eagerly nodding their heads. 'It looks like that's settled. I can't wait to try it and I'm certainly honoured to be invited. Here's to its success,' said Bruno, raising his glass in a toast. 'To the Patriarch's Reserve.'

CHAPTER 10

In his office the next day, Bruno found atop his pile of mail a letter with no stamp that must have been delivered by hand. The envelope was thick, the paper creamy and his name and address had been written with a fountain pen. Inside was a handwritten letter of invitation to join the Confrérie du Pâté de Périgueux, a body whose members were sworn to uphold the traditions and quality of this delicacy. Each winter, dressed in medieval robes, the Confrérie awarded prizes for the best duck and goose pâtés of the year after a morning of tastings, followed by a lunch whose lavishness had become a local legend.

The *pâté de Périgueux* itself was a very special dish that dated back to medieval times, not easy to make but one of Bruno's favourites. At its heart were foie gras and truffles, which had to be the unique black truffles of the region. These were then surrounded by a pâté made of pork, and sometimes with a crust of pastry. That had been the traditional way to store it in the centuries before the invention of canning. Like many of his friends, Bruno made a point each year of going to the old town square in Périgueux where the name of that year's winner, usually a local farmer or a *charcutier*, was announced by the members of the Confrérie, wearing their red and green robes and bonnets. He would buy an example of the winner's product to be eaten at a lunch on the first day of the new year.

Bruno was surprised and extraordinarily pleased to be invited. It was a considerable honour, and he wondered what had inspired them to include him. There was a second letter inside the envelope, on similarly heavy paper but written in a different hand and headed with the engraved name and address of the Patriarch.

My dear Bruno, he read.

It was a pleasure to make your acquaintance on the occasion of my birthday. My dear friend the Countess has informed me of your services to her. And as the honorary president of the Confrérie du Pâté de Périgueux, I have also recently learned from the Mayor of St Denis and our mutual friend Maurice Soulier of your fortitude in defending the interests of our local producers of foie gras against its critics. It would give me great pleasure and add greatly to the talents of our Confrérie if you could join our ranks. Be assured, my dear chef de police, of my most distinguished sentiments.

It was signed, simply, 'Marco'.

Bruno at once wrote two letters of acceptance, one to the Patriarch and the other to the Confrérie itself. Then, feeling almost childish in his pride, he went out from the Mairie and down the Rue de Paris to the *maison de la presse* and bought a small picture frame to fit the Patriarch's letter. Once back in his office, he inserted the letter, took a hammer and nail from the caretaker's room and hung the frame on his wall. He sat back in his chair and was admiring it when the Mayor walked in through the open door and said, 'I heard the hammering.'

Bruno rose in respect and shook hands, as he always did for the elderly man who had become his friend as well as his mentor, and gestured at the framed letter. The Mayor smiled as he read it, murmured something about it being well deserved and then perched on the corner of Bruno's desk.

'Is there any realistic prospect of Imogène raising the funds to make a refuge for those wretched deer of hers?' the Mayor asked.

Bruno shook his head sadly and recounted the conversation he'd had with her. Given the recession and the budget cuts, the Mayor replied, there was no chance of any public money being forthcoming. Bruno suggested an exhibition and sale of Imogène's photos but admitted this would hardly raise more than a fraction of the funds required. It would at least show that the Mairie was trying to help.

'I don't think some of the councillors would stand for it, and if we mounted an exhibition for her I think it might well get wrecked,' the Mayor said. 'Feelings are running pretty high against Imogène. Some of the shopkeepers and the stall-holders in the market have already told me they'll refuse to serve her. I suspect some of our hothead friends in the hunting club might be tempted to take the law into their own hands. Perhaps you should have a word with them, try to calm them down, at least until the time runs out for Imogène to build that fence. I've spoken to the Prefect this morning and the moment she's in breach of the court order, he'll apply to the judge for authority to cull her herd. You'll have to arrange that and keep Imogène out of the way while it happens.'

Bruno nodded, thinking how often he was given tasks that had never been thought of at the police academy he'd attended after coming out of the army. And that reminded him of the news he'd heard at Raquelle's lunch.

'That man who died after the Patriarch's party – I found out by chance that he was cremated this morning,' he said. 'They certainly didn't waste any time.'

The Mayor shrugged. 'It was an unpleasant business so probably best to get it all out of the way quickly. Why not?'

'There are one or two aspects of it that trouble me,' Bruno replied. 'I've been told Gilbert was quite sober just a few minutes before the incident with the girl when we all thought he was so drunk. Then I went to his house and it was impeccably neat. I don't know about you but I've never known a drunk like that. If Gelletreau hadn't already signed the death certificate, I'd have been tempted to suggest an autopsy.'

'That's pretty thin. And I was there, don't forget. It was blindingly obvious how he'd died. I watched Gelletreau make a thorough examination of the body. It's sad, but there we are. These things happen.' He turned to leave. 'Don't forget to have a few words with the hunters, you know the ones I mean.'

When the Mayor left, Bruno dealt with the rest of his paperwork and then called the regional crematorium and asked them fax him a copy of the legal certificate of disposal for Gilbert's remains. While he waited for it, he called Annette, a friend who was a magistrate in the Procureur's office in Sarlat to ask about procedures in the event of someone dying without leaving a will.

'Have you checked the *fichier central*?' Annette asked. When he said he'd never heard of it, she explained that it was the central depository of wills in France, and all legal wills drawn up by a notary had to be filed there. She offered to do the search for him and he gave her Gilbert's name. She asked if he had any special interest in the affair and he told her about Gilbert's death and his surprise at the speed of the cremation.

'If a doctor signed the death certificate and said

no suspicious causes, then that's all they need, unless the death was in a public place. In that case we'd have to issue it. If you know the doctor, it all sounds pretty straightforward. I'll let you know about the will.'

He thanked Annette and turned to the fax machine, where the crematorium had sent their reply. It cited the date and number of the death certificate, noted that the death was the result of natural causes and in the section for next of kin it gave Victor's name, identifying him as 'landlord and oldest friend'. Bruno had never heard of such a designation, but then he'd never known anybody die without any living kinsfolk. Even he, an orphan, listed his aunt in Bergerac and her children, his cousins, as next of kin in the Mairie employment records. That made him think about Imogène, who'd told him she had no heirs to her property. He'd have to check whether she had any friends or distant relatives she might be persuaded to stay with when the cull eventually took place. The only person she'd mentioned had been Raquelle, the Patriarch's daughter by the Israeli wife. He took out the card she'd given him and called her.

'I'm probably as close to her as anyone,' Raquelle replied. 'She's something of a loner and even among the Greens she's got a reputation of being a bit batty. She's got a good heart but you can never rely on her to do anything much beyond stuffing envelopes at election time. But I came to respect her when we worked together on those photos, and I remember she told me she had no family.'

Bruno explained that a cull of Imogène's deer was beginning to look inevitable and he wanted to be sure she wasn't there when it happened. Was Raquelle close enough to her to take her in for a day or two? As she reluctantly agreed, Bruno was thinking it might be longer than that.

He began to draft some notes on what he'd have to do to organize the cull. He began by making a list of the reliable hunters he'd need. Then he sat back to reflect. What could he do with all the dead deer? Bruno tried to think how many deer he'd seen as he drove up to Imogène's house. At least fifty to the hectare, he estimated, maybe more. There could be a thousand deer to be disposed of. He called the nearest abattoir and asked to speak to the director, a man he knew from the rugby club. He replied that he was sorry, but there was no way he could process or store that many deer. Even if he rounded up some other abattoirs to help, they would need to check the quality of the meat. Culled deer were usually too thin for consumption. Quite often after a cull the dead deer were simply piled into heaps with a bulldozer and then burned in situ.

He went to inform the Mayor that they would need everyone in the district with a hunting permit to volunteer in exchange for the meat, and get the Prefect to authorize raising the limit beyond one deer per hunter for this season. The Mayor rolled his eyes at the scale of the operation they would have to mount. There would be a lot of venison on the menu this winter.

'By the way,' the Mayor said, 'what's happening with you and Pamela? I was surprised to see her with Crimson at the Patriarch's party.'

'I had to escort the Countess in her wheelchair,' Bruno said. He left quickly, feeling uncomfortable at this intrusion into a part of his life that he felt was private.

Back in his office, there was an email from Annette. She had traced a will for Gilbert, registered by a notary in the Cantal district of Auvergne, with an address near Riom-ès-Montagne deep in the Massif Central. Bruno knew this region of ancient volcanoes mainly for its splendid cheese and the aperitif made from the roots of the local gentian flower. He dimly recalled seeing signposts for the place once, when taking some of the schoolchildren on a skiing trip. He called the notary's number and was surprised when a voice answered, 'Mairie.' The notary, he learned, was also the mayor. Bruno introduced himself and asked if the notary was aware that his client, retired Colonel Gilbert Clamartin, had died and been cremated.

'*Mon Dieu*, no, not Gilbert. Oh, God rest his poor soul.' Bruno could hear the shock in the man's voice.

'I'm sorry to be the bearer of sad news but although we made a thorough search we couldn't find any will among his effects and a local magistrate found you had registered one in his name,' he said.

'You say you are the chief of police in St Denis in the Périgord?' the notaire replied, sounding suspicious. 'I don't know of any connection he had in that town. Let me check your credentials with the St Denis Mairie and I'll call you back. Can I reach you through their switchboard?'

Within minutes, Bruno's phone rang and the mayor-notaire, apparently satisfied, was back on the line, asking if Bruno could fax him a copy of the death certificate. He took down the fax number, sent it over with the cremation document and waited again.

'This is very depressing news,' said the mayor-notaire a few minutes later. He gave his name as Amédée Rouard, an old-fashioned Christian name Bruno hadn't heard for years. 'Gilbert was a childhood friend from school and we were quite close until he left for the air force. The death certificate says he died of natural causes when drunk. It's very sad but I can believe it. I know he was certainly hitting the bottle when I last saw him, just as he was when he came back from Moscow. He was never the same man again after that.'

'When was it that you saw him last?' Bruno asked.

'Four years ago, when his sister died, Gilbert's last remaining relative. That's when he made his will. It's going to take some time to sort out but in the meantime I'll have to arrange a meeting with his heir for the formal reading of the will.'

'I didn't know he had one,' said Bruno, surprised. 'I thought you said his sister had been his last remaining relative.'

'She was the last one I knew of, not even any cousins remaining, certainly none around these parts. It was only when Gilbert made the will that I learned of another heir.'

'I presume there's not much in the estate,' Bruno said, half expecting Rouard to tell him to mind his own business. He recalled Madeleine saying that Gilbert had left a trail of ex-wives and mistresses but nothing about children. Surely his friend Victor would have known.

'It's complicated,' said Rouard. 'But as you'll see when you read the will, there's some property near here, the family farm. It must be worth a hundred thousand or more, maybe a lot more now that they're building ski chalets for Puy Mary. It's all been rented out since his sister died, house and land separately. And then there's some kind of trust fund that Gilbert set up but I've no idea what's in it.'

'The people he was living with near here told me Gilbert was broke, spending his pension on clothes and vodka,' Bruno responded, thinking that this Gilbert was full of surprises.

'I don't know why they should say that,' Rouard replied. 'Gilbert wasn't rich but he was comfortable enough and a very generous man. The rent was paid directly to a charity, along with other donations he made from time to time, always to the same one.'

'What was the charity?' Bruno asked, expecting something like the air force widows' fund.

'The children of Chernobyl, a fund to bring the sick kids to France for summer vacations. You remember that nuclear accident?'

'Of course.' Bruno sat back in his chair, thinking that this was suddenly becoming complicated and wondering how much more the notary might be prepared to tell him. 'Is there anything I can do from St Denis that would help you settle Gilbert's affairs?'

'Not really. I'll have to write to the bank where the trust fund is based and send them copies of the death certificate. I can't say I've ever dealt with anything like it. The bank is somewhere in Liechtenstein, for tax reasons, Gilbert said. Then I'll have to trace his heir, but it's a delicate matter. If I should need your help, I have your email address and your number.' Rouard hung up.

Bruno emailed Annette to ask her to send him a full copy of Gilbert's will, since he'd learned it contained some interesting new information. That would ensure she'd read it and she'd certainly take a look at the fiscal aspects of this trust fund. Tax evasion had become a serious issue and French citizens were required to register any foreign holdings. But did it have any impact on Bruno's own curiosity about the death? Probably not, unless this mysterious heir was somehow involved in it. Even then, there was no evidence of foul play and no longer any remains that could be autopsied.

He knew something of the way military pensions worked from his own case; the wound he'd received in Bosnia entitled him to an invalidity pension after thirteen years' service. But there was a sizeable difference between his pension as a *sergent-chef* and that of a colonel; moreover, he had no idea how long Gilbert had served. He called a contact in military records who had proved helpful before and gave him Gilbert's details, and was told it would take a few hours. The moment he put his phone down it rang again. It was Annette.

'This case is getting interesting,' she said. 'I've tipped off my colleagues in the *fisc* and they're going to look into it, check Colonel Clamartin's bank and tax records and see whether this Liechtenstein account was ever registered. Depending on what's in this trust, there could be some heavy death duties. Who's the heir?'

'I don't know. The *notaire* said it was in a separate codicil.'

'We'll find out after the will is read and it goes to probate,' she said. 'It looks like there could be more to this death than meets the eye. I should know better than to dismiss your hunches.'

'I'm not sure I'd even call it a hunch, more curiosity,' he said. 'Whatever it is, the trail seems to have gone cold.'

'Except for the money,' she said.

Bruno called the clinic and learned it was Dr Gelletreau's day off but he was on call and could be found at home. He drove out to the village of

Bigaroque, on the road to Sarlat. He parked off the road and climbed up the steps to the house, one of a group of old buildings nestled into the hillside, where the doctor lived with his wife, who worked as a pharmacist in St Denis. Their son, Richard, was at university in Paris. He found Gelletreau dozing in the autumn sun in his small walled garden, a copy of that day's *Le Figaro* on his lap. Bruno accepted a glass of apple juice and the doctor took a small Ricard.

'I presume this isn't a social visit,' Gelletreau said.

'Not exactly. Did you know that Gilbert has been cremated already?'

'No, and I'm surprised I wasn't invited to the funeral. I was his doctor for nearly twenty years.'

'Since he came back from Moscow?' Bruno asked.

'That's right. I liked him when he was sober, which wasn't often. We tried getting him into various clinics to dry out but it never lasted. I can't say I was greatly surprised at the way he died.'

'Something odd has cropped up about his will, so I need to ask you if there was anything at all unusual about his death.'

Gelletreau spluttered into his drink. 'Unusual? You mean foul play? Not in the least. Dead drunk and drowned in his own vomit. I've seen it before, although usually with people who've taken barbiturates.'

'So is it common with drunks?'

114

'The amount of alcohol taken is what matters and you saw the size of that flask. He was already stumbling drunk when we took him away from the party. He passed out when we put him on that couch. I made sure he was lying on his side, just in case he did throw up, and I told Victor to keep checking him.'

'Was he in the same position when you pronounced him dead?' Bruno asked.

'No. When we found him dead, he was lying on his back, his mouth completely blocked. He must have woken up at some point to empty that damn flask we found, so he probably changed position after that.'

'In retrospect, don't you think an autopsy might have been justified?'

Gelletreau shook his head and looked Bruno in the eye. 'I didn't then and I don't now. I knew Gilbert and his drinking so I simply wasn't surprised by the manner of his death. There was nothing suspicious about it, no bruising round the nose and mouth that you might have seen if somebody helped him along, no sign of chest constriction or of any flailing of the limbs you might expect if he had resisted. The coverlet was neatly in place.'

Bruno took a deep breath. 'Okay, I understand. But I had to be sure.'

'So what's this funny business with the will?'

'There was no will among the papers at his house but now one has turned up with a notary; that's all I can say.'

'I'm surprised he had anything to leave, other than his pension,' Gelletreau said. 'He'll probably have left anything he had to Victor. I remember when we first checked him into a clinic, there was a form to be filled in and he wrote in Victor's name as next of kin.'

'Did you know Gilbert before he went to Moscow?'

'Just a bit. He was at the christening for Victor's son, Raoul, by his first wife, so I'd met him and we chatted. He seemed a nice fellow, a bit bouncy, like most fighter pilots. I took him on because I've been Victor's doctor since he came out of the air force, long before you came to St Denis. Not long after Gilbert arrived to live at Victor's place, I was called in to treat him for bronchitis. The silly bastard had been too drunk to get the key into the door of his house and he'd fallen asleep in the rain on the doorstep. It was a cold night, too. I tried to take him in hand, get him to stop drinking, but you know how it is, Bruno. At the end of the day, it has to be up to them; they've got to want to stop.'

'So you look after the whole family?'

'No, just Victor and the children. Madeleine has some fancy doctor in Paris; that's where she went to have her baby. But for the usual childhood ailments they'd call on me, not that I see them often. Perfect physical specimens, both of them, and a very pretty girl, that Chantal. Don't tell me you haven't noticed.'

'And how's your boy Richard doing in Paris?' Bruno asked, rising to take his leave.

'Fine, fine. I'll tell him you asked.'

When Bruno got back to his office, he found a message on his phone from his friend in military records. The file on Colonel Gilbert Clamartin was unusually thin. It gave his date and place of birth, the date eighteen years later when he'd joined the air force and of his subsequent commission and his decorations and promotions. It also listed his honourable discharge in 1993 with full pension after twenty-five years' service. The rest of the record had been sealed.

CHAPTER 11

As Bruno drove along the river road that led to Victor's vineyard, he felt troubled. He knew that he should be looking forward to seeing once again his childhood hero and thanking him for the invitation to the Confrérie and also to this wine tasting. But he was nagged by the growing mystery about Gilbert and his hunch that something was not quite right about the accepted version of his death. And Bruno suspected that the Patriarch's family had an agenda in suddenly welcoming him into their world, a much more privileged one than he usually knew. Was he being drawn in so that as a policeman he would feel a sense of obligation to such an eminent family and to help the Patriarch's heirs protect their secrets? Perhaps that was why that decent man Dr Gelletreau had been so quick to sign off on Gilbert's death and why the Mayor had used that phrase about 'efficiency and discretion'.

On the whole, Bruno enjoyed his work and took pride being a country policeman, known to everyone and welcome in almost every home in his commune. But every so often he felt himself standing slightly to one side, observing events with a different eye. It was not that Bruno looked for the worst in people's behaviour and their motives but he was aware that his profession had over the years kindled a subtle change in his thinking. When anything unusual occurred, his natural curiosity could swiftly evolve into suspicion. It was partly a sense of duty to the uniform he wore, but he knew that there was something deeper in his own character, a need to get to the root of the matter, to learn not just what had happened but how. Above all, he needed to know why, to understand the human dynamics behind the choices and decisions that had been made. So as he slowed to cross the bridge at Lalinde, glancing at the fleet of swans who always seemed to gather at this stretch of the river, Bruno felt himself going on alert. He would taste the Patriarch's wine and enjoy the company but he would remain watchful.

The entrance to the vineyard was guarded by two tall stone pillars but the barred iron gates were open and balloons of red, white and blue floated above them as if signalling a children's party. After a hundred metres, with vineyards on each side of the road, came a fork. The sign to the left was marked *Privée*; that way presumably led to the family house. More balloons danced above the sign to the right that said *Dégustation*. It pointed the way to the tasting room, a modern single-storey building of glass and wood. Before it was a large, cobbled courtyard framed on each side by stone walls covered with Virginia creeper, the green leaves just turning to a reddish-brown, where some long wooden tables stood. Behind the tasting room loomed the big stone barns where the wine was made and stored. At least a score of cars filled the car park lot and Bruno drove on, looking for a place to leave his car, and found himself at a modern tennis court.

Two young people in white were playing and from the sound of the ball being hit and the brisk pace of the exchanges he could tell that they were good. He climbed out of the Land Rover, replacing his uniform jacket with a sports coat, and went closer, to see Chantal and her brother, Raoul, hitting the ball hard and deep. Two professional tennis bags stood at the side of the court, each capable of holding four or five rackets and the balls they were using looked brand new.

They made a handsome couple, slim, tanned and athletic. Chantal's blonde hair was pulled back into a ponytail and like her brother she wore a white headband. They were not knocking up; the ball was being driven into alternate corners and each of them was racing back and forth along the baseline to make the return. Suddenly, after one particularly hard drive to her brother's backhand, Chantal raced for the net, ready to volley. Her brother scrambled to reach it and returned a lob, trying to get the ball over her head, but it was a little short. The girl smashed it hard into the forecourt so it bounced high, way beyond Raoul's reach.

Bruno was tempted to applaud; this was tennis of a quality he seldom saw at the club in St Denis. But he didn't want to interrupt, and waited to see Chantal serve. Her first attempt was just out; if it had been in, Bruno knew he would never have been able to return it himself. Her second was almost as hard, but with a spin that made it kick unexpectedly high. Raoul waited and then drove it hard back over the net and the two of them were back at their powerful baseline game, topspin sending the ball fast and low from the bounce until Chantal played a perfect drop shot with enough backspin to make it die and then roll backwards into the net. But at the next point, to save the game, Raoul defeated his sister with a well-judged passing shot, too fast for her to reach as she rushed to the net. They were well matched but Bruno thought Chantal might be the better player, varying her strokes rather than relying on sheer power like her brother.

The tasting room was full when he entered and noisy with boisterous chatter. Most of those inside were men with wine glasses and notebooks in hand, gathered in front of a long counter covered with opened bottles and large spittoons. They filled the tasting room and spilled out into the *chai* behind. Bruno saw Victor standing behind the counter, looking harassed as he poured out wine, a fixed smile on his face. Yevgeny and Raquelle were helping him serve the throng of *négociants* from Bordeaux, wine critics and journalists and buyers from the big wine chains. Raquelle noticed his arrival and gave him a quick wave.

Bruno looked around and spotted Horst and Clothilde, chatting with a man he recognized, the wine writer for *Sud Ouest*. As Bruno joined them, he heard Clothilde saying, '. . . and so Victor married into the vineyard.' After the usual greetings, Bruno asked what she had meant. The vineyard and much of the land around had belonged to Madeleine's family for centuries, Clothilde explained, but over the years most of it had been sold. By the time Madeleine married Victor, the vineyard, the family house and the ruined chateau on the far side of the hill were all that were left, along with an ancient name that dated back to the medieval dukes of Aquitaine.

'The title has gone, of course, but that's why Madeleine claims to be a descendant of Eleanor of Aquitaine,' said Clothilde, rolling her eyes as if to mock Madeleine's claim. 'She once told a friend of mine that she only married Victor so the Patriarch's money could save what was left of the family estate.'

Bruno raised his eyebrows, surprised. Clothilde was not usually so waspish about another woman. 'You sound as if you don't approve,' he said.

'We aren't friends,' Clothilde replied. 'She's an arrogant woman, of the kind who reserves her charm for men. And I don't like her politics, about as far to the right as you can go without joining the Front National. It runs in the family. During the war, they were collaborators. Her uncle was an out-and-out Nazi, anti-Semite, a follower of Charles Maurras in the thirties. He shot himself in nineteen forty-four after the Liberation before he could be arrested. What was left of the lands and title went to his brother, Madeleine's father, a naval officer who stayed loyal to Vichy until almost the last moment. Around here, these things aren't forgotten.'

Bruno nodded slowly before changing the subject and turning to the wine writer. 'Tell me about this new wine they're making,' he said, and was told it was very good indeed, a class above the usual wines the vineyard had produced. The new white was charming, crisp but with a touch of sweetness that lingered pleasantly in the mouth. The new red was even better; the writer planned to make it his *coup de coeur* for his next column, recommending it as a personal favourite.

Bruno said he'd better try some, excused himself and headed for the counter, looking for a route through the crowd. At one end of the counter Bruno saw a flash of pale-blue silk and golden hair surrounded by a knot of attentive men. Then their ranks parted and Madeleine, looking elegant and lovely in a cream linen suit with a blue Hermès scarf at her throat, sailed through them smiling, her eyes on the newcomer.

'Welcome, Bruno,' she said, greeting him with a kiss on both cheeks. He was surprised that she seemed to be wearing no scent. Of course, he told himself; it might interfere with the bouquet of the wines. 'Marco asked to see you the moment you arrived.'

She led the way into the *chai* and pointed him to the steps that led down into the dimly lit *cave*, where the Patriarch was standing between long rows of large oak barrels. Hubert, from the St Denis wine shop, was with him along with two middle-aged men in dark suits. The bung from the nearest barrel had been removed and a plank had been stretched across two more barrels to hold some wine glasses and a silver spittoon.

The Patriarch plunged a dipper into the opened barrel and poured some of the fresh wine into a clean glass. Before handing it to Bruno, he put the glass on the plank of wood, shook hands and introduced him to the two strangers, one from the Hachette wine guide, the other an English buyer. Hubert then explained that Bruno was one of his partners in the St Denis vineyard, which was stretching the reality of Bruno's modest investment as a shareholder but gave him a status the two men seemed to find acceptable. He wondered how they might have reacted if he'd arrived dressed as a policeman.

'It's a very promising wine indeed, lots of fruit but unusual depth for a Bergerac and for a wine so young,' said the man from Hachette. 'But there's something in here I'm trying to identify beyond the usual Merlot and Cabernet.'

'What do you think, Bruno?' asked the Patriarch, handing him the glass. Bruno raised the glass to assess the colour, holding it against the glow of a candle that had been placed on a nearby barrel. It was clear, but slightly darker than he'd expected. He swirled the glass a little to see the healthy crown as the liquid trickled back down the sides of the glass. He swirled it more and then sniffed, cocking his head as he'd been taught to give each nostril a chance to savour the bouquet. He smelled dark fruit, a fresh earthiness like a ploughed field after rain; that would be the Merlot. It might have been a young St Emilion but there was something else, elusive and slightly unusual. He swirled the glass again and sniffed once more, recognizing the freshness of the Cabernet Sauvignon. He took a sip, let it settle in his mouth to reach those less-used taste buds at the back of his tongue. He detected something mineral in the flavour, like that hint of iron he found in a good Pécharmant.

'I'll give you a clue,' said the Patriarch, with an almost sly smile. 'In the *chai*, we have a private nickname for this cuvée: Eleanor. That should help you.'

Bruno was no great connoisseur of wine. He could tell the Gamay grape of a Beaujolais from a Syrah that came from the Rhône, and he could usually distinguish between a Médoc and a Pomerol. He could tell a fresh young wine from one that had matured but the individual estates and vintages were far beyond him. But for this unexpected test of the Patriarch's, Bruno knew that Clothilde had given him the essential clue.

'You've added some *Cot*,' said Bruno, suddenly understanding the darkness of the colour and the elusive taste he couldn't quite identify. 'The wine that was served at the wedding of Eleanor of Aquitaine, to whom this vineyard can trace its family origins.'

'Absolutely right,' said the Patriarch, looking delighted. 'The black wine of Cahors, gentlemen, usually known as Malbec but round here the local name is *Cot*. It was the traditional wine of Aquitaine, served at the great royal wedding in Bordeaux in the year 1152, when Eleanor, Duchess of Aquitaine, married one of her two husbands. She was the only woman ever to have married both a king of England and a king of France, and she was an ancestor of my daughter-in-law. This cuvée is sixty per cent Merlot, thirty per cent Cabernet and the rest is Malbec.'

'Eleanor of Aquitaine was also the only queen to have gone on crusade to the Holy Land,' said the English buyer. 'She was the mother of our Richard Lionheart and of his wicked brother, King John, the one who gave us Magna Carta. Our clients do love a wine that comes with a legend; it gives them something to talk about. Are you selling this *en primeur*?'

'If you're buying, we're selling, even in the

barrel,' replied the Patriarch, with a smile. He was wearing corduroy slacks and a checked tweed jacket over a roll-neck sweater that looked to Bruno like cashmere. 'We plan to taste it again in the spring, see if it's ready for bottling.' He poured another glass for Bruno, this time from a bottle that carried the familiar label with a drawing of the Patriarch's face. 'Now try this, the new Réserve du Patriarche.'

Bruno sniffed carefully and tasted. It was a much more serious wine than the standard product of this vineyard that he'd been given at Raquelle's lunch party. He found it to be a straightforward Merlot-Cabernet blend but beautifully balanced. It was deep and rich, full of fruit but with a slight hint of spice, almost peppery in the aftertaste, the flavour he always relished in a good Pomerol.

He said so, and added, 'It's very drinkable now. But after five years it should be something very special. When does it go on sale?'

'As of today,' the Patriarch replied. 'This is the coming-out party; it's the wine I always wanted to make and to drink before I die. Since I'm ninety years old, I probably don't have long so I'm glad we agree it's drinkable already.'

'All the same, I'll look forward to opening a bottle with you in five years time,' said Bruno.

The Patriarch laughed and addressed the two men in suits. 'One thing I learned in my years in the military was always listen to the sergeants. They always know more than the officers, and

127

usually drink better wine, and Bruno was a very good sergeant. He and I have something very unusual in common. We were each awarded the Croix de Guerre while serving under non-French command, me with the Red Army on the Eastern Front and Bruno with the United Nations peacekeepers in Bosnia.'

Hubert replaced the bung in the barrel, tapping it home with a rubber-tipped mallet, and the Patriarch led the way from the cellar back to the tasting room, where people had now spilled out onto the cobbled courtyard to enjoy the sun and attack the plates of cheese and pâté, ham and smoked fish that now covered the long tables. There were no spittoons here, Bruno noticed, just ranks of opened bottles. The tasting was over and the guests were now entitled to drink with their lunch. From the smiles and friendliness of the chatter and the way Victor was being clapped on the back, the event had evidently been a success.

Madeleine seemed to be everywhere, charming the guests with warm smiles and tinkling laughter, a fond squeeze of this one's arm, an attentive hand on that one's back as she steered him to the food. She was the star of the show, the ringmaster of this circus, at least until the Patriarch climbed up some stone steps and tapped a spoon on a glass to silence his guests. Curious, thought Bruno, that Madeleine's equally attractive daughter had been allowed to duck out of this family event to play tennis. But perhaps Madeleine was the kind of

128

woman who preferred to shine alone in such an assembly.

'Thank you all for coming and for drinking such impressive amounts of this new wine of ours,' the Patriarch began, pausing with accustomed skill for the inevitable laugh. 'I recall my old friend de Gaulle saying how impossible it was to govern a country with over three hundred different cheeses. I often wondered why he never spoke of the even greater number of different wines we are lucky enough to make in this beautiful land of ours. And I'm only sorry that I did not have this vineyard when de Gaulle was alive to treat him to a glass of this wine that I'm sure he would have enjoyed. But I'm delighted that you are all here today and that you enjoyed our wine and now I hope that you all enjoy your lunch while you contemplate those large orders I'm sure you'll be placing.'

Bruno joined in the applause, thinking what an accomplished performer the Patriarch had become. His speech had been short, amiable and the reference to his old friend de Gaulle, now dead for nearly four decades, had subtly reminded his guests that in his presence they were standing close to a heroic part of France's history. As a piece of marketing it was masterly. Bruno could imagine the buyers going home to their wives and friends and recounting what the Patriarch had told them over lunch about de Gaulle and what a fine wine the old boy was making these days.

Bruno was about to get a plate and some food

when his phone vibrated. It was Albert, the *pompier*, to tell him of another accident, a serious one this time with at least one person reported killed. Could Bruno get to the road by Imogène's property as quickly as possible? Several cars had been involved, a crowd was gathering and it was likely there would be trouble.

CHAPTER 12

His blue light flashing, Bruno drove as fast as his Land Rover could manage, using the earphone attached to his mobile so that he could drive and talk at the same time. Sergeant Jules of the gendarmerie had just arrived on the scene, and told him that the *pompiers* were using their heavy equipment to cut open the side of a crashed car to free the injured children trapped inside. Their mother at the wheel was dead, and so was the young stag that had crashed through her windscreen and into her lap. One of the coaches being used to replace the local trains while the railway line was being upgraded was tilted perilously against a tree on the far side of the road, with its wheels in a ditch and two more deer trapped beneath the coach. Another car had run into the back of the coach.

By the time Bruno reached the spot, the firemen had freed the two children and an ambulance was racing them to hospital along with the driver of the coach. The passengers, mostly unhurt except for a few cuts and bruises, were being ferried to the clinic in St Denis by the gendarmerie van and

131

Dr Gelletreau was working on the minor injuries. Fabiola had gone with the children in the ambulance.

A lane had been cleared, sufficient for one car at a time to pass, but a carelessly parked line of cars was pulled off the road; some of them he recognized, belonging to people from St Denis who had come to the scene to help. A knot of perhaps a dozen of them were arguing angrily with a lone gendarme who stood at the entrance to the lane that led to Imogène's house. He had one arm outstretched as if to bar their passage. Bruno went to help him, asking one of his friends in the crowd to find out where the various coach passengers were heading. Then Bruno joined the gendarme. He called for silence and said he needed volunteers to drive the various passengers to their destinations. The coach had a sign on the windscreen saying *Sarlat* so most of them would be heading there or to Le Buisson or St Cyprien, the two main towns on the route.

'*Putain*, Bruno, they'll send another bus,' shouted Hervé, a hotheaded young man recently laid off from his summer job as a bartender at a campsite. 'We want to go and sort out that daft cow Imogène.'

'Imogène can wait,' Bruno said firmly. 'I have to get in touch with the guy who's just been made a widower and get him to the hospital to see his kids. Don't stand in my way, Hervé, or you'll regret it. Now go and see if you can help those poor people from the coach while I try to track this

132

man down and give him the news that's going to break his heart. His wife's dead and his two children are in hospital and he needs to be with them. He's the priority now.'

'Justin,' he went on, turning to a hunting-club friend. 'I can count on you to find out who's prepared to drive people to Le Buisson, and which ones will go on to St Cyprien and Sarlat. You can use my Land Rover since I'll be stuck here for a while.'

Bruno turned his back on them, aware that they were dispersing and some volunteering to Justin, as he began dialling the car registry to get a name and address for the owner of the wrecked Peugeot. The *pompiers* were still trying to free the dead woman trapped inside by the stag. The licence plate carried the digits 24 so he knew it was local. Within minutes he was calling a man named Michel Peyrefitte, a name he faintly recognized, and found him on a golf course near Périgueux. When he heard the clipped voice, familiar from the local Bleu Périgord radio station, he knew he was talking to the lawyer who was campaigning to be the candidate for the UMP conservatives at the National Assembly. There was silence on the other end of the phone when Bruno gave him the terrible news. Bruno was about to ask if he was still on the line when he heard a long moaning sigh that ended in '*Mon Dieu, non*'.

'Your children are being taken to the Périgueux hospital by ambulance, *monsieur*,' Bruno went on.

'Do you need me to arrange a car to pick you up and take you there?'

Somebody else, one of his golf partners, came on the line and said Peyrefitte had collapsed. Bruno explained and repeated his question. 'We have our own cars here, thanks, and we'll leave now,' came the reply. 'I'm his law partner. Can you tell me what happened?'

'It is not altogether clear since other vehicles were involved but Madame Peyrefitte's car was hit by a deer. She's dead and the two children are being taken to hospital.' Bruno did not say that an antler had pierced the woman's chest. The stag was so emaciated that it had almost certainly come from Imogène's land.

Bruno could hear a flurry of agitated conversation, then a familiar voice returned. 'Is this something to do with the crazy woman with the deer who was in the paper this week?' Peyrefitte's voice demanded.

'I can't say for sure, *monsieur*. It's near her land but this is a hunting area; hers aren't the only deer around here. Shall I tell the hospital that you are on the way? And is there anyone else you'd like me to call on your behalf, perhaps your wife's family?'

Saying briskly that he'd make his own calls and go directly to the hospital, Peyrefitte gave a distracted word of thanks and hung up. Bruno let out a long breath. This meant trouble: a prominent politician with a dead wife and injured children in a high-profile accident in a region where most people were already hostile to Imogène. He called the Mayor to inform him and was still speaking when he saw the first of several flashes from a camera. Philippe Delaron now worked full-time as a newsman for *Sud Ouest*. His family's camera shop had been forced to close, a victim of modern technology, but he still did portraits and weddings on his days off. Philippe approached Bruno, notebook at the ready. Bruno gave cautious replies to Philippe's questions as another ambulance arrived to take the dead woman away. It was followed by Lespinasse's breakdown truck, which slowly began to haul the crumpled Peugeot from the ditch.

'Have you got a name yet for the dead woman?' Philippe asked.

There was no reason for Bruno to delay; the next of kin had been informed. 'Madame Monique Peyrefitte,' he said. 'I just spoke to her husband, Michel. He's heading to the hospital to see his kids.'

'The political guy?' Philippe asked. Bruno nodded and Philippe whistled softly in surprise before turning away to phone his newsdesk.

Bruno went over to Lespinasse, who said a special vehicle would be needed to haul the coach from the ditch. His own truck simply wouldn't have the power. Bruno clambered into the empty coach, bracing himself against the slope, and checked behind and under the seats to ensure that all the passengers were out. Then he leafed through

135

the sheaf of papers in the compartment by the driver's side, found the number of the coach operator and called them with the news. A young woman on the switchboard said she'd have to call her boss but she knew of no spare coaches available. The key was still in the ignition so Bruno took it, checked that the luggage compartment was locked and called the operator's number again to say he had the keys but he wanted the coach towed away forthwith. He left his mobile number and climbed gingerly from the vehicle to see that the Mayor had arrived and Julien had returned with Bruno's Land Rover.

'Philippe just told me it's Peyrefitte's wife and kids,' the Mayor said. 'He's putting out the news on Bleu Périgord right now so I'd better call the Prefect. Anything else you can tell me?'

Bruno explained about the coach, the shuttle service he was organizing for the passengers, and that he should get to the clinic to see what he could do for the people being patched up by Dr Gelletreau. He'd learned from the firemen that there had been a couple of broken limbs and several cracked ribs.

'And there was a nasty moment when a group of hotheads seemed to want to march up the hill to confront Imogène,' Bruno went on. 'I managed to deflect them for the moment but that won't be the end of it.'

'Can't say I blame them,' said the Mayor. 'If I weren't the mayor, I'd be tempted to join them.'

'You might be tempted but you wouldn't do it. You know we can't have people taking the law into their own hands,' said Bruno. 'But we can't leave her alone up there; we'll have to try to get her out before night falls. Once people get into the bars and start drinking, they're likely to talk themselves into going up that hill with cans of petrol and burn her out.'

'It's the deer they want, not her. I'm a bit surprised we haven't heard volleys of gunshots already.'

'Everybody's still a bit chastened by the crash but that won't last,' said Bruno. 'I'd better go up to see her while you talk to the Prefect.'

'And what do you do if Imogène refuses to leave?'

Bruno shrugged. 'I'll have to be very persuasive.'

'That won't work and you know it. I'm not having you sitting up there trying to stop a mob,' said the Mayor. 'There is another way. Dr Gelletreau could declare her insane and a danger to herself. Then we could legally take her to hospital overnight for observation and get a court order in the morning. It's not pleasant but it could save her life. Have you got a better idea?'

Bruno shook his head. 'You'd better clear it with the Prefect. If you go to the clinic and arrange matters with Gelletreau, I'll go up to the house and talk to Imogène.'

As Bruno drove up to her house, there seemed to be even more deer in the woods and standing

137

in the lane than there had been at his last visit. They were probably shunning the area by the road because of the noise and people. Imogène opened the door and gave him a challenging look. He heard classical music from the radio in the room behind her.

'*Bonjour*, Imogène. You might want to tune that to the local news,' Bruno began. 'You and your deer are making headlines. They just killed a woman on the road below your house. Her two children and a coach driver were injured in the crash and are on their way to hospital.'

'Oh, no.' Imogène's face was stricken. She brought a hand to her mouth. 'Can I go down and help?'

'It's all under control. And there are people down there who want to tear you limb from limb. You're in danger.'

'Nonsense, Bruno. Were any of my deer hurt?'

'Three dead, one of them with his antler in the heart of the dead woman. She's the wife of an important man, a politician. You can't stay here; people are out for your blood. Do you have any relatives or friends you can stay with?'

'I'm not leaving. Is this just a trick to get me out of here so you can send the guns in to slaughter my deer?'

Bruno shook his head in despair. 'Listen to the radio, Imogène. I'm not fooling here and nor are the people down on the road. I've already talked one lot out of coming up here and it wasn't easy.

There will be more and they are angry. For your own safety, I need to get you out of here.'

She gazed at him levelly for a moment and then said, 'I don't have anywhere to go and even if I did, I'm not leaving my deer.' She went back into the house, leaving the door open, and began tuning the radio to listen to Bleu Périgord. Bruno knew of only one friend who might be prepared to take Imogène in. He looked up Raquelle's number on his mobile, called her and explained the situation. She agreed to put Imogène up for a few days.

'All right, I believe you,' said Imogène, turning away from the excited news reports on the radio. 'This is tragic news but you can't blame the deer. People have to learn to live with them, to share this lovely land with the animals. They have just as much right to be here as we do. People must learn to drive more slowly, give up their cars, walk.'

Bruno grimaced in frustration; Imogène lived on a different planet. His phone vibrated and the Mayor told him that Dr Gelletreau had signed the authorization for Imogène to be taken into custody for compulsory psychiatric evaluation. Gelletreau had added that he'd be the first to volunteer for a culling party.

'That phone call was to tell me that we now have legal authority to arrest you and take you to a psychiatric clinic to be examined,' Bruno said, trying to sound calmer than he felt. Imogène half sat, half collapsed onto the chair behind her, hand to her mouth in shock.

'You wouldn't . . .'

'You leave us no option, Imogène. The order is legal and it has been signed. But you do have a choice and it's simple. You can come with me of your own accord and I'll take you to your friend Raquelle's house in Montignac. She's agreed to take you in for a few days until tempers cool. Otherwise, I'll arrest you and take you to the Gendarmerie cells until the psychiatric ambulance can come to collect you, and you'll be put under restraint and taken to the psychiatric wing in Périgueux. Which is it to be?'

She glared at him. 'You have no right to do this. I won't cooperate.'

Hating himself for doing this, Bruno caught her arm, and, applying a half nelson, he frogmarched Imogène out of her house, bundled her into the back of his Land Rover and locked the door. He climbed into the driver's seat, looked at her and said, 'Last chance. Raquelle's place or the strait jacket?'

'Raquelle,' she said. 'But I'll need a bag, some clothes, toiletries, my purse.'

'I'll give you five minutes and if you try to run, I'll put you in handcuffs and take you straight to the Gendarmerie. Understood?'

She gave him a venomous look and then spat something that might have been agreement so he let her out of the vehicle. With a firm grip on her arm, he led her back into the house and stood in the doorway of the bedroom while she threw some clothes into a bag. He told her to take any valuables, important documents and anything she particularly treasured, some of her deer photos, perhaps.

'What on earth for?' she said fiercely, glaring at Bruno as if he were the enemy. 'I'll be back tomorrow when this stupid fuss dies down.'

'No, Imogène. I'm not even sure this house will be standing by tomorrow. I honestly fear they might burn it down.' Bruno was already working out a safe route to take that would avoid the crowd at the accident site.

He wasn't sure if Imogène was being defiant or just trying to bluster through her own sense of uncertainty, or whether she simply could not recognize the danger she was in, far less her own responsibility for the accidents. He doubted that she'd ever admit to feeling guilt. She braced herself, as if she'd come to some kind of decision, and took some photos from her walls and put them into a file that had been lying on her desk. In little more than a minute, they were in his Land Rover, Imogène's bag and purse and the folder of photos in the rear.

Bruno's car radio was tuned to Bleu Périgord. They had sent a reporter to the hospital and she had managed to snatch an interview with Peyrefitte as he arrived. He said only that this was no time for politics, that he was thinking now of his children and his grief for the death of his wife. But the reporter concluded by reminding listeners that

Peyrefitte had in the past been an outspoken critic of people he called 'Green extremists'. A hospital spokesman said that the surgeons were fighting to save the life of one Peyrefitte's two children.

Imogène was stone-faced as Bruno took a hunters' track through the woods and concentrated on navigating the narrow trail. The news gave way to a talk show which began with a caller denouncing 'that deer woman' as a murderer. He heard Imogène give something like a sob and then she bent over and began to retch. Bruno stopped his vehicle, leaned across her to open her door and helped her lean out to be sick. He switched off the radio and gave her a bottle of water and a towel that he kept in his sports bag. While he waited for her to finish, he texted the Mayor: 'Imogène out. En route to safe house.'

He took the back roads through St Chamassy and Meyrals all the way to Raquelle's home in Montignac. Once in the small car park lot outside her house, he called her and asked if it was convenient for Imogène to arrive now or did she have visitors? She was alone. Bruno escorted Imogène inside, dropped her bag in the sitting room and faced Raquelle.

'I know you'll be discreet,' he said.

'I've been listening to the radio. I understand.'

'Even your family . . .' Bruno began.

'Particularly my family, and most especially Madeleine,' Raquelle said with a grim smile. 'For this issue, we're on different sides. You know she's campaigning to be the UMP candidate for the European Parliament?'

Bruno raised his eyebrows. He hadn't known but the news came as little surprise. Madeleine was a woman of firm opinions and the current socialist government was struggling in the opinion polls. It was a seat she could win. He thought back to the Patriarch's party and the politicians who had been there, doubtless invited to help her cause. And he remembered how tirelessly Madeleine had worked the crowd and how she had done the same at the wine tasting earlier in the day.

'She's been building support among the wine growers, the hunting clubs,' said Raquelle. 'She wants to be sure there's no Pêche-Chasseurs Party candidate taking votes from her. So my dear sister-in-law is the last person I'd let know that Imogène has taken refuge here.'

'I'm grateful, Raquelle. You're a good woman.'

'Don't worry, I'll take good care of Imogène even though I don't agree with her stubborn insistence on saving those deer of hers.'

'If she'd only agree to keep the numbers in balance, I think we could get some kind of refuge status for her land.'

'Maybe I can talk her into it.'

CHAPTER 13

The prefects of France date from Napoleon's time, have a quasi-military uniform and are the direct representatives of the central government in the regions. There is one for each *département* and they have a staff of up to a thousand people, mostly issuing driving licences, passports, car registrations and the like. But the prefects also ensure that the various layers of local government follow national policy and they have particular responsibility for law and order and the different bodies of police.

These include the gendarmes, traditionally a paramilitary force under the Defence Ministry, and the Police Nationale, a body with several different functions. It is first a nationwide police force under the Interior Ministry, responsible for public security, border guards, SWAT teams and the much-feared CRS riot police. It also runs the DCRI, the Directorate of Internal Intelligence, which brings together the counter-espionage service and the old police intelligence network, the Renseignements Généraux. In its second function, the Police Nationale also runs the Police

Judiciaire, a nationwide force of detectives and specialist scientific investigators similar to the Federal Bureau of Investigation in the United States. These elite crime investigators usually work under the direction of a magistrate, who is assigned by the local *procureur*, or prosecutor, to assess whether there is sufficient evidence for a trial. If so, the investigating magistrate takes the case to court.

Along with all these bodies, the Prefect must also seek to coordinate the dozens of separate municipal forces in different towns and communes, among them Bruno's one-man operation in St Denis. So when the Mayor called Bruno as he was leaving Raquelle's house to tell him to drive directly to Périgueux to join him there for an urgent meeting at the Prefect's office, Bruno sighed. He was not greatly impressed by the current Prefect, appointed by the socialist government, which had the support in parliament of the Green Party. The political affiliations did not bother Bruno, but he had learned that their particular Prefect was unusually sensitive to any issue touching on the cherished values of the socialists or the Greens. In the case of Imogène and her deer, the Prefect would be torn between the two. To appease the Greens, he would want to protect the deer and Imogène, which would probably mean deploying a lot of police to protect her property. But the socialists were also traditionally wary of the powers and often ruthless tactics of the police. The deer-related death of the wife of a leading conservative politician made the issue even more complex. The result, Bruno feared, would be that the Prefect would dither, try to please both sides and end up making a mess of things.

As a former soldier, Bruno knew that nothing was worse than a hesitant commander and uncertain orders. When a state deployed force, it had to know what the objectives were and make sure the troops knew them, too. In the case of Imogène, a choice had to be made whether to protect her and her property and thus her deer from a potential mob or to protect the road-using public from the overpopulation of her deer. Since Imogène was now safe, the only things at risk were the deer, which would have to be culled anyway, and Imogène's ramshackle house.

As soon as Bruno arrived at the grandiose Préfecture, he found himself redirected to the Prefect's home. Bruno knew what this meant: a meeting that was not quite official. It could thus, in the event of political embarrassment, be said never to have taken place. Once there, Bruno was invited not to the Prefect's office nor his study but to a long verandah at the rear of the imposing house, where he found the Prefect, the Mayor and the general in charge of the gendarmes, wearing civilian clothes, all drinking coffee and mineral water. A TV set was tuned to the twenty-four-hour news channel but with its sound off, and a radio was giving local news from Bleu Périgord. While driving, Bruno had been listening to its reporter's account of scores of hunters from across the *département* gathering at St Denis, planning to start their cull before dusk fell.

'Ah, Bruno,' said the Mayor as Bruno shook hands with the others. 'We're just waiting for the Commissaire de Police and then we can begin. Anything to report? Imogène is safely stashed away?'

'She's safe for a few days,' he replied. The Prefect waved him vaguely to the drinks table and Bruno helped himself to some mineral water.

'It will be far too dangerous once night falls to send my gendarmes into wooded country full of armed men,' the general was saying. Bruno was relieved to hear it. 'I'm seriously worried that there could be a bloodbath. And I don't have nearly enough men to control the perimeter of this property. Even if you authorize me to call for reinforcements from Limoges and Bordeaux, they won't be here before morning.'

A fifth man, also in civilian clothes, was shown into their presence by a white-jacketed steward, who bowed and backed away. This new man, Pascal Prunier, the Police Commissioner for the *département*, was young for the job, just a few years older than Bruno, but with a sound reputation from his last responsibility in Paris. And he'd won the grudging respect of J-J, the *département* chief of detectives and Bruno's friend. J-J had described Prunier as ambitious, political, tough but trustworthy and always ready to back his men. That was good enough for Bruno. When he'd been younger, Pascal had played rugby for Clermont-Ferrand, one of the best clubs in France. Bruno also had a more personal memory. He played against Prunier in a police versus army match just before he'd been deployed to Bosnia. Being tackled by Prunier was like being hit by a truck. He still looked very fit.

Like his Mayor, Bruno rose to shake hands and noted that both the general and the Prefect stayed in their seats. Prunier shook their hands anyway and then turned to Bruno.

'Glad to see you again, Courrèges. The last time we met you were the man who stopped me getting an otherwise certain try and winning the game. It's been what, ten or twelve years?'

'A good twelve years, Commissaire,' Bruno replied, trying to conceal his pleasure at being remembered.

'Call me Pascal. Is it true you've managed to take this deer woman to a place of safety?'

'Yes, but word from St Denis is that things are hotting up.'

'Gentlemen, let's begin,' said the Prefect. 'The general has just been telling me he doesn't want to deploy his gendarmes at night.'

'He's right,' said Prunier. 'I have my CRS and intervention teams deployed nearby and ready to intervene, as you ordered. But I have to warn you of the very dangerous risks of sending them into the woods after dark. It's not an order I would give, sir.'

'So we permit an armed mob to take the law into their own hands, destroy property and slaughter deer way beyond the limits of their quota?' the Prefect asked. 'That's not what Paris wants. The Deputy Minister is counting on us to keep order here in the Périgord.'

'In that case, he can issue the orders himself,' Prunier replied. 'But has he done so?'

'Only a suggestion. Not an order,' the Prefect replied, looking worried. 'And it was made verbally.'

'I've had no orders from Paris beyond consulting with you, Monsieur le Préfet. So he's leaving us to take responsibility.' Prunier turned to the General. 'What about your gendarmes?'

'I've had no orders from Paris, neither from the Defence Ministry nor from the Interior Ministry. But I agree with you. Sending gendarmes into those woods at night would be insane.'

'You're the man on the ground, Bruno. What do you think?' Prunier asked. It was striking how fast he'd taken command of the meeting, Bruno thought.

'We did a lot of training in night-fighting when I was in the military and even then it was full of risks, despite the night-vision goggles,' said Bruno. 'If you decide to send untrained men at night into those woods, we could have a real disaster on our hands. And even if you ordered us to do so and everything worked as planned, we'd still face the problem of the deer.'

'The question of the deer is now in the hands

of the courts,' the Prefect said, waving a dismissive hand.

'Legally, sir, that's true,' Bruno acknowledged. 'In practice, tonight, those deer are in the hands of those hunters that the radio says are gathering and I don't see how we can stop them.'

'Wait,' said the Prefect, leaning back to turn up the sound on the radio. Peyrefitte was being interviewed at the hospital after seeing his children. One was out of danger, the other was in intensive care.

'I just hope no other families ever have to go through this kind of tragedy and grief,' Peyrefitte was saying in a choked voice. 'And all for the sake of a crazed Green woman and her deer. Have they all gone mad in Paris? Have they no idea up there what our life here in the countryside is like?'

'You say "a crazed woman"; do you hold her responsible for the death of your wife?' the radio reporter asked him.

'Of course, and I shall be pressing the Procureur to bring charges against her for manslaughter. If he refuses, I shall myself file civil charges against this woman, although if I were her lawyer, I'd be tempted to advise that she plead insanity. But people cannot be allowed to make our country roads into killing grounds when we already have so many deer that they're a menace. Cannot we agree that human beings must come first?'

The news moved on to the Middle East and the Prefect turned the sound back down and said, 'I'll have to talk to the Procureur.'

150

'Peyrefitte just gave him a perfect excuse to duck it,' said the Mayor, with an assurance that came from years of experience. 'He'll let Peyrefitte go ahead with his civil suit.'

The Prefect nodded sagely and then said, 'We have to consider the political dimension.'

'If Peyrefitte runs, he'll win by a landslide after this,' said Prunier.

'Why do you say *if* he runs?' the Prefect asked. 'He's running already.'

'He's lost his wife and now has to look after his two children, one of them in critical condition, which means convalescing for quite some time,' the Mayor replied. 'I know Peyrefitte. He's a decent man and he'll put his children first. He'll decide to back out of politics and stay at home with the kids. Quite right, too.'

'Which means the government might not lose the seat,' the Prefect said, looking distinctly more cheerful.

'Possibly, but it depends on the candidate the UMP finds to replace him and they have one in Bergerac, ready to hand, who could be hard to beat,' the Mayor said. 'I'm thinking of Madeleine Desaix. She's good-looking, happily married, a mother, runs a vineyard and the Patriarch is her father-in-law. If the old man campaigns for her, and I expect he will, she's got a very good chance.'

Bruno raised his eyebrows. Madeleine's political prospects seemed even grander than he'd thought. The Prefect sank down a little deeper into his chair and looked out at the sky. Dusk was on the way. He glanced at his watch, evidently wavering as the men around him added their own discreet pressure for him to make a decision, looking at their own watches, glancing at their mobile phones.

'By the way, Monsieur le Maire, I finished those estimates,' Bruno said, thinking that now was a good time to drop another factor into the Prefect's thinking. 'If and when the judge authorizes the cull of Imogène's deer, it's going to cost between twenty and thirty thousand euros.'

'We could try to get the money back from her,' said the Mayor, picking up on Bruno's tactic. 'But that would mean forcing her into selling her home and that would provoke a scandal. The Greens would be furious. So we'd probably have to apply to you, Monsieur le Préfet, for emergency funding.'

The Prefect switched his gaze suspiciously from Bruno to the Mayor and back again, and then looked at Prunier and the general of gendarmes. He suspected that he was being manipulated but he also knew that these men were right about the dangers of sending armed men into the woods at night. If anything went wrong, it would be the end of his career.

'Any news from your men in place, general?' he asked. The general was thumbing through messages on his mobile phone.

'No, sir. There was a report of some scattered gunshots a few minutes ago but there are legal hunting grounds all around there. There's no sign of any organized march onto her property.'

'I'd better stand down the CRS before we get into overtime pay,' said Prunier. 'I can have them on standby to return there in the morning.'

'I'll keep a couple of mobile units on the outskirts of St Denis doing alcohol checks,' said the general. 'We'll have a vehicle, lights blazing, at the entrance to her property and I'll make sure they patrol up to this woman's house throughout the night. Just one thing, Monsieur le Préfet, do you have any orders for my men if they hear shooting break out?'

'Not unless it's World War Three,' said the Prefect with a practised smile. He rose from his seat. 'Very well, we'll just keep a watching brief overnight and not put any of your men at risk. I'll inform the Deputy Minister that your advice was unanimous. Thank you, gentlemen, for your reports and your very helpful counsel. I imagine all this will be settled tomorrow, one way or another.'

CHAPTER 14

As they left the Prefect's home, the Mayor put his hand on Prunier's arm. 'I'm delighted to learn that you and Bruno are old acquaintances. I was about to invite Bruno to dine with me here in Périgueux and perhaps we can tempt you to join us? Since you're both policemen I thought we might try the Hercule Poirot; I've always like the idea of naming a restaurant after a detective.'

'Monsieur le Maire, I really ought to get back to see if I can help the gendarmes keep watch at Imogène's house,' Bruno protested.

'No, Bruno. You're staying with me. You leave this business to the gendarmes, and that's an order. Well, Prunier?'

'I'd like to, but I see my wife and kids little enough as it is,' Prunier replied. 'Why not come back with me and dine with us? My wife's from Alsace and can always rustle up a quick *Flammküchen*. She's used to me turning up with unexpected guests.'

All three of them were parked in the Prefect's courtyard and as they began to follow Prunier towards his home, Bruno's phone vibrated. He looked at the screen and saw the telltale green light that signalled someone from the special security circuit was calling. It was a phone Bruno had been given on a previous mission by the Brigadier, the Interior Ministry official whose calls always spelled trouble.

'Bruno, why are you making enquiries into Colonel Gilbert Clamartin?' said the Brigadier by way of greeting.

'*Bonjour, mon général*,' Bruno said, taking a moment to collect himself. 'He died the night of the Patriarch's party with no will in sight and I was trying to track down his heirs. I was also curious about his death, apparently from drink, but a very early cremation took care of the available evidence. Why?'

'Clamartin's name is on a special list. My office is alerted when somebody enquires into his military file.'

'Is that routine for people who did his Moscow job?' Bruno asked.

'None of your business, Bruno.'

'Did you know he'd died?'

'Not until you told me, which is a little worrying. Our systems need to be more efficient. Do you think there was anything odd about his death?'

'A little, and there seems to be some unusual trust fund in Liechtenstein, although the people he was living with down here thought he was broke. One of our magistrates tipped off the *fisc* and they're looking into it.'

'Very well, I'll take care of that. If you learn anything more, let me know.' The Brigadier hung up.

Bruno followed dutifully behind the Mayor's car to Prunier's house in the comfortable suburb by the Périgueux golf course. Prunier's two daughters, aged five and seven, were briefly introduced in their pyjamas before being taken off to bed. Bruno and the Mayor chatted with Monique while Prunier read the girls their bedtime story, learning that she had been the daughter of the local police chief in Colmar, where Prunier had been posted. She had been a primary school teacher, but sometimes helped out at her aunt's restaurant on busy evenings, which was where she had first met Pascal. Monique said proudly that she had done the repainting of this house herself, so much more room than the apartment in Paris, and with a big garden for the children. The next step, she said, was to get them a dog.

'I think you'd better leave that to us,' said the Mayor. 'Bruno and I know a lot about dogs and we know just the breed you need, a basset. I had them for years, Bruno has one now and there's no better dog for children. Descendants of my last female are all over the valley, and most of the others were fathered by Bruno's last dog, Gigi. There's bound to be someone with a new litter.'

Bruno glanced admiringly around the large room, which ran the full width of the house with a series of glass doors opening onto a terrace and garden. A round dining table, their places already set for dinner, stood between the kitchen and the TV corner. It was all comfortable and inviting, a room where the family could be together. As Prunier came back downstairs to join them, Bruno thrust aside the touch of envy he felt and the concern that he might never have a family of his own to fill a room such as this.

Soon they were sipping Riesling and munching their way through the Alsace speciality which the French call *tarte flambée*. Bruno always thought of it as a Teutonic form of pizza. The thin crust of pastry was covered in *crème fraîche*, thinly sliced onions and bacon. Monique served it with two side salads, one of tomatoes and basil and the other of lettuce and chives.

'Are you still playing at all, Bruno, or have you hung up your boots?' Prunier asked as he opened the second bottle of Riesling and his wife served a second *Flammküchen*, this one bedecked with thinly sliced leeks and sun-dried tomatoes.

'He's the star of our over-thirty team,' said the Mayor. 'And he trains the children's teams. He's a long way from retired, and I heard you're refereeing now?'

'That's right, when I can get the time,' replied Prunier. 'I cursed referees so hard when I was playing I thought it only fair to see the game from the other side of the whistle. But I want to talk about this situation in St Denis. I know our Prefect; he'll want me to go in strong tomorrow and try to make some arrests as a way to appease the Greens.'

'They aren't fools, they'll have all gone by then,' said Bruno. 'And what's the charge? You can't even charge them with hunting out of season. The most you can do is charge individuals with shooting more than their quota and you'll have to prove every case. The guns will all have been cleaned by the time you arrive and there'll be no witnesses.'

'There'll be bullets. We can round up the rifles, run ballistic tests. We can get convictions,' Prunier insisted.

'Say you get some convictions. You might get their hunting permits confiscated and fine them,' the Mayor broke in. 'But in this *département* nearly a third of adult males have a permit and a lot of the women, too. That's a lot of votes. Do you think this Prefect will be foolish enough to stir up that kind of political opposition with Peyrefitte all over the radio and an election on the way? I'll certainly try to talk him out of it and I won't be the only one. At some point he'll drop it and you'll be left to take the blame.'

Prunier nodded glumly. 'When I came to this job, my predecessor warned me that there were two kinds of prefect and this one was the type from whom you wanted to get your orders in writing.'

They drove home slowly, the Mayor following in his own car to ensure that Bruno did not defy his orders and break off to head for Imogène's place. Bruno felt a deep anger at being ordered to drive directly home and stay away from the

158

scene of the action. He understood the Mayor's motives and while he trusted the Mayor's political instincts, he hated the idea of failing in his duty. St Denis was his town and he was its policeman; he knew he should be on the scene. Bruno was surprised that there was nothing new on the radio, no reports of a house being burned to the ground nor of constant volleys of gunfire in the night. As he took the rise from Mortemart to the brow of the hill, he tapped his brakes several times to signal to the Mayor behind, slowed and pulled off the road. He saw the Mayor pull in behind him and they each climbed out, listening. There was no sound of rifle shots and no red glow on the skyline.

'It's all quiet,' said the Mayor, joining him. He sounded relieved. Bruno pulled out his mobile and called Sergeant Jules of the gendarmes, who had been put in charge of the roadblock at the end of the lane that led to Imogène's house. Bruno and the Mayor drove down to join him. There had been a flurry of gunshots lasting for about thirty minutes before dusk, Jules reported. So many deer were fleeing that he'd had to close the road. After that, silence. The gendarmes *mobiles* arrested half a dozen drivers with too much alcohol in their bloodstreams, but each of them had his rifle locked away in a case according to regulations.

'No attempt on her house?' Bruno asked.

'No, it was all too well organized and disciplined for that,' Jules replied. 'And I hear there was a lot of exchanging of rifles going on at the hunters' cabin on the track that leads to St Cirq. So anybody trying to run ballistics tests will have trouble matching the guns to anyone around here.'

Bruno smiled to himself and felt a small glow of pride in the cunning of his fellow hunters, wondering whose had been the brain behind it. He wouldn't be in the least surprised to learn it had been Sergeant Jules, but that was a thought best kept to himself. He should have expected something like this. The people in this valley and its surrounding hills had organized some of the most effective Resistance groups in France during the Second World War. Bruno's neighbours knew almost instinctively how to frustrate the intrusions of outsiders, whether it be an enemy occupation or their own governments in distant Paris.

'Don't tell me you're surprised, Bruno,' the Mayor said. 'You know these people and you're their friend. They took good care that whatever they did wouldn't embarrass you.' The Mayor clapped him on the shoulder. 'Go on home, Bruno, and get some sleep. I'll see you at Fauquet's café when it opens tomorrow morning and I want it confirmed from Pamela that you've already exercised the horses. I don't want you out in those woods at dawn. Goodnight. Remember, go straight home and sleep well.'

Bruno drove home and found Balzac waiting for him at the end of the lane and greeting him with a cheerful bark. He petted his dog and felt the warmth of a body that had not spent a long evening standing and waiting. He checked the outdoor kennel where Balzac slept in summer and the blanket that lined it was warm beneath his hand. Clever Balzac, he must have stayed inside it and only risen when he heard the familiar sound of his master's Land Rover approaching.

Bruno let himself in, Balzac following and looking expectant. His intelligent eyes followed Bruno into the rear hallway, where he kept his boots and the big plastic bin containing his home-made dog biscuits. Balzac wolfed down a bowlful along with a sliver of ham that Bruno cut from the smoked haunch that hung from the kitchen beam. He lapped at his bowl of water and then went to the rear door, turning to look at his master.

It was a ritual, their final round of the property before turning in. Balzac leading the way, they made a circuit of the garden, pausing when they emerged from the shadow of the white oak trees Bruno had planted to start his own truffle planta-tion. As Balzac snuffled his way around the slope where rabbits had once been daring enough to build a warren, Bruno gazed up at the vast bowl of stars in the sky, wishing as he always did that he knew the names of more of the constellations. They skirted the vegetable garden and went up the steps to the giant chicken run. The birds were all asleep and Bruno secured the door to their coop while Balzac sniffed suspiciously around the outside, checking for any recent evidence of fox. All was well. Bruno went back inside, washed and brushed his teeth, donned the old rugby shirt he liked to sleep in and waited until Balzac had settled on the cushion in the corner of the kitchen before giving him a final pat goodnight.

Too tired to read, Bruno turned off the light and snuggled down under his duvet. Just before he drifted off to sleep, he couldn't help smiling as he wondered whether it had been Sergeant Jules who had so thoughtfully organized the cull. Or perhaps it had been the wily old Mayor himself, once he knew that Bruno had managed to spirit Imogène out of harm's way.

CHAPTER 15

Five minutes after opening and Fauquet's café was already full. The espresso machine was working non-stop and the trays of fresh croissants coming from the ovens below were swiftly emptied. The enticing morning scents of butter and baking and fresh coffee greeted Bruno as he entered with the Mayor. The mood was triumphant, reminding Bruno of the time when the town rugby team had won the regional championship. Friends and neighbours came up to slap Bruno and the Mayor on the back. They made jokes about who needed Paris or Périgueux when St Denis could solve its own problems with the deer? The only reporter present was Philippe Delaron, himself a keen hunter, who told Bruno with a grin that anonymous donors had left six neatly gutted deer carcasses outside the old peoples' homes in every town within twenty kilometres.

'Let's hope we don't end up with every hunter in town being arrested,' Bruno said. 'I hope nobody's been foolish enough to put any fresh venison in their freezers.'

Philippe showed them the front page of *Sud Ouest*, with a photo of three unidentified hunters, taken from behind, standing by a heap of dead deer. The headline read: 'St Denis – the law of the hunter'. The second headline read: 'Deer Cause a Family Tragedy', with a picture of Peyrefitte, the lawyer, as he left the hospital after visiting his children, another portrait beside it of his dead wife. On the inside page was a photo Philippe had taken of Imogène at some point in the past, looking furtive and guilty as she tried to avoid his camera. The story said that the St Denis policeman, Bruno Courrèges, had driven her to a place of safety long before the shooting had started.

The Mayor had already alerted the Mairie's maintenance team and two trucks loaded with petrol cans followed Bruno's Land Rover and the car of Achille Veltrier, the town vet, up the track to Imogène's house. Bruno had taken his side arm in case there were any wounded deer to be shot but saw not a single one. The hunters had been efficient. There were no live deer to be seen and few deer carcasses left, most of them having been taken away by the hunters. But in clearings and in the open space around Imogène's cabin they found piles of guts, already swarming with flies. Some of Imogène's cats scurried away from the heaps as the men approached. They sloshed petrol onto the guts and added dead branches to keep the fires burning, then tossed in matches. Bruno wondered how many of the workmen doing the clean-up had been out with their guns the previous evening.

'A strange sight, this wood, and rather sad,' said the Mayor, gesturing at the almost naked landscape. There was no ground vegetation and hardly any bark left on the trees. Some of them had already died. Between their naked trunks Bruno could see for a hundred metres or more. It was indeed strange; usually the thick undergrowth of the Périgord blocked the view after a few paces. There was no birdsong, no scuttering sounds from the hordes of tiny creatures that usually inhabited the woodlands. The sheer numbers of Imogène's deer had killed this wood, but Bruno knew that nature would recover and within a year or two it would return to normal.

'It won't be long before deer start coming back here,' the vet said. 'Once there are green shoots again next spring, you'll see the first of them return. A lot of them were born here and they'll have the urge to come back. And then, after another few years with Imogène protecting them, they'll breed and breed and the whole problem will return.'

'Maybe she's learned her lesson,' said the Mayor. He didn't sound hopeful. 'But I suppose we'll have to see what happens when Peyrefitte brings charges against her. She might have to sell up to pay for her defence.'

'I imagine the Greens will want to make a show trial of it,' said Bruno. 'They'll milk it for publicity, probably mount a campaign to raise money for some good lawyers who'll try to put St Denis on trial instead of Imogène.'

The smell of burning meat was in the air, but not the appetizing odours that come from a barbecue. This was something much cruder and unpleasant, like animal manure mixed with petrol. Some of the workmen had donned masks as they fed the fires with more branches, standing upwind to avoid the dark, oily smoke. Bruno, the vet and the Mayor headed for Imogène's house. It seemed not to have been touched, although the hunters had left one token of their presence. To the porch railing had been tied a young fawn. It lay still and silent on the ground, quivering with fear, its feet tucked beneath its thin body. Its eyes seemed enormous as they watched the three men approach.

'It's only a day or so old,' said the vet. He took care of the farm animals and his partner looked after the domestic pets of St Denis. 'Its mother must have been shot and the fawn wouldn't leave her. The hunters will have brought it here to be sure we'd find it. There's nothing else for me to do here so I'll take it down to the surgery, we can take care of it there.'

'I'll look after the bill,' said Bruno, bending down and trying to stroke some reassurance into the tiny creature, wondering what its future might be without its mother. 'How long before it can feed on its own?'

'We can feed it as long as you like but that's not

the point,' Achille replied. 'The problem will be finding a herd that won't drive it away. It might get lucky. Some of the deer from these woods will have got through the cordon and it might meet up with some of them. Otherwise it faces a lonely life and probably a short one. At least it's not a male; they're always harder to integrate into a new herd.'

'What about humans, keeping it as a pet?' Bruno was thinking this might help soften the blow for Imogène.

'It's possible, but the sooner you get the human keeper to them, the better. They need to imprint them young, and make sure the fawn sleeps with something that smells of the keeper. Are you thinking of this for yourself?'

'No, for Imogène.' Bruno saw the Mayor roll his eyes, whether in amusement or exasperation Bruno could not tell.

Achille nodded his understanding. 'That's not a bad idea; it might help that silly woman get over the shock, give her something to care for. Get her to come to my surgery later today. I can show her what to do.'

Back in his office at the Mairie, Bruno called Raquelle at le Thot but was told she was at home. He called her there, asked after Imogène and was told Raquelle's doctor had her on a course of tranquillizers. Another one, thought Bruno, knowing that France consumed more of the things than any other country in Europe. He told Raquelle about the fawn and she said it was an excellent idea and she'd take Imogène to the vet for the feeding. Then in his emails Bruno found a message from Gilbert's notary, asking him to call.

'Thank you for getting back to me,' said Rouard. 'I hope I can count on your discretion but I might need your help in tracking down the heir. Do you know if Gilbert had any dealings with a family called Desaix?'

'Yes, he lived with them. Victor Desaix was an old friend from the air force; they learned to fly together. He has a wife, Madeleine, and two children, Raoul and Chantal. Victor's father is *the* Desaix, the Patriarch. In fact, it was just after the Patriarch's birthday party that Gilbert died.'

'*Mon Dieu*, I had no idea he was attached to that family. Do you have an address?'

Bruno gave him the address of the vineyard, saying that was the most likely place to reach Victor. Well, he thought as he put down the phone, that was one mystery solved. Gilbert's estate was going to his old friend Victor, the man he always listed as his next of kin. He wondered if the inquiry by the *fisc* into Gilbert's mysterious trust fund in Liechtenstein would cause Victor any problems with the tax authorities. Another thought struck him: it might also hurt Madeleine's political career.

He put her name into the internet search engine on his computer along with the initials UMP, the Union for a Popular Majority, which had become the main political grouping of the conservatives. Several pages came up, mainly citing news stories in *Sud Ouest* and *Dordogne Libre* but with some from wine journals and one from *Gala*, a glossy celebrity magazine. He looked at that one first, a long story with photographs of the Patriarch and the restoration of the chateau. Madeleine was pictured several times, described as his daughter-in-law who acted as his hostess. There was one family group with the Patriarch, Victor, Madeleine and the children, flanked by Yevgeny and Raquelle.

The news stories traced her political career, first as a member of the welcoming party for Sarkozy's visit to Bergerac during his 2007 presidential campaign. She'd already been elected to the Bergerac city council and to the executive committee of the UMP women's section. Sarkozy had then appointed her to the party's agricultural policy committee and she'd been one of the French delegates to some global conference of women in Beijing. That story was topped by a photo of Madeleine chatting with Hillary Clinton.

There were more photos of Madeleine speaking on behalf of mayoral candidates and other conservatives around the region. She was described as a brilliant speaker, a popular campaigner and rising star of the party, almost certain to be elected to the European Parliament in Brussels. Every story had made the point that she was the Patriarch's daughter-in-law.

So that was how it was done, thought Bruno,

climbing through the committees and policy bodies of the party and becoming known to the party leaders. Given her looks, once met they weren't likely to forget her. Bruno took little interest in party politics so it was no surprise that he hadn't heard of Madeleine in this context. But then he saw a reference to an article on marketing the wines of Bergerac that she'd written for the opinion page of *Sud Ouest* and he recalled reading and agreeing with it at the time. There was another, on women in the military, and it also made sense to him.

He clicked back to the full-page picture in *Gala* of her standing with the Patriarch, looking coolly elegant, effortlessly lovely. Victor was a lucky man. And now she faced the choice of accepting a safe seat in the European Parliament or taking the chance of replacing Peyrefitte as UMP candidate for Périgueux in the National Assembly. Bruno had never heard of any individual member of the European Parliament, but maybe she'd prefer the international arena. He was looking again at the bland pose of the photo when the Mayor walked in.

'What brings her to your screen?' he asked.

Bruno explained the potential complications of Gilbert's will for her political career. One minister in Paris had just been forced to resign after admitting to having an undisclosed foreign bank account.

'If somebody leaves something to her husband in a will, I don't see how that can hurt her so long as it's all duly reported to the tax authorities. But if you're interested, come along with me tomorrow evening. Madeleine is speaking at a public meeting in Bergerac, debating with one of the Greens from the European Parliament and I bet she speaks about Imogène's deer.'

'Are you interested in her or the topic?' Bruno asked, smiling.

'Both, of course. I just had a chat with an old political colleague. Peyrefitte has told the party chairman that he's going to step down for the sake of his kids. So the seat looks like being Madeleine's, so long as she does well tonight. A lot of senior party figures will be there, and more of them will be watching.'

Bruno raised an eyebrow. 'A political star is born.'

'Not necessarily,' said the Mayor. 'She has a significant family hurdle to overcome.'

'You mean her own family's links to Vichy? Won't the Patriarch's war record squash that problem?'

'Even with his support, it's not altogether certain that she'll get the Peyrefitte seat. She has to do well in this debate. She can probably count on getting most of the usual conservative votes and she'll have the wine trade behind her. But if she can also bring in the hunting vote, she'll win.'

'I wouldn't miss this debate for worlds,' said Bruno. 'Heaven help that poor Green.'

CHAPTER 16

Yevgeny's converted farmhouse was perched atop the first of several low ridges that rise above the village of Siorac, its terrace facing south and his studio at the other side of the building to catch the subtle light from the north. There was little land attached to the house and no vegetable garden, only some scattered stone urns with straggling geraniums and a lawn that needed mowing. Built of the local stone, the house itself was of modest size, square-shaped with two storeys, and would traditionally have had four rooms to each floor. To the west stood a large old barn that had been used to dry tobacco, now transformed into a white-walled art gallery with some partitions providing extra hanging space for his paintings.

Most of them were not to Bruno's taste, images that sprawled over the borders between fantasy landscapes and science fiction. They reminded him of old album covers from the seventies. In some of Yevgeny's unearthly scenes with unfamiliar vegetation, blue and green women with vastly elongated bodies, enormous eyes and swollen, hairless heads struck artistic poses. Despite the distortions, their faces were evidently painted to be beautiful. Bruno could feel Pamela struggling to make polite comments as she strolled through the gallery, Yevgeny attentive at her side. Bruno's eyes widened as he glanced at the catalogue and saw that the prices ranged from 4,000 to 9,000 euros.

He turned a corner around a partition and came across a series of street scenes in winter that he assumed were Russian from the fur hats and the Cyrillic letters above the shops. Burly women used sharpened iron bars to break up the ice on the pavements. Others plodded uphill, weighed down by children and large string bags. Three men in an alley were sharing a bottle of vodka while a policeman in big felt boots and a grey coat looked the other way. Bruno found them charming, simple and yet conveying an atmosphere of human life defying the drabness of the city with its grimy snow and iron-dark sky. They were priced at 1,000 to 1,200 euros, still well beyond Bruno's pocket.

'I like these,' he said, and Pamela echoed his thoughts. 'Much more to my taste,' she said, leaning forward a little and putting on her reading glasses to examine them more closely. 'Wonderful expressions you have given to the children's faces. They seem very real.'

Earlier that day, Yevgeny had called Bruno at the Mairie and said he'd be at home that evening and would Bruno like to bring a friend for an aperitif and to look at his paintings. He'd called Pamela, a little tentatively since he was less and less sure of their relationship. She had hesitated at first and he was sure she was about to decline. But then she said if it were just for drinks and they could ride the horses first, she'd heard of Yevgeny's work and would like to see it. They'd arrived late, Pamela taking rather longer than usual to shower and change after riding. She had emerged looking particularly appealing in a simple black dress belted with a green scarf that set off the colour in her eyes and the bronze of her hair. Bruno loved her hair, thick and glossy and always seeming to glow with health. He wondered if she'd dressed up for him or for Yevgeny, before telling himself not to be so foolish: women dressed to delight themselves, or perhaps to impress other women. He'd never been sure which.

Yevgeny led them across the courtyard and into his studio, where some canvases with conventional Périgord landscapes leaned against the walls. On one easel was a large head-and-shoulders portrait of a dark-haired young woman draped only in a colourfully striped blanket. The background looked unfinished, the end of a bed and a small table just sketched in. Her expression was solemn but her skin was flushed and her eyes seemed to dance with mischief. One arm was raised, smoothing back her hair, the other hand clutched the blanket around herself, and somehow the artist had made it clear that this was for warmth rather than modesty.

174

'That's very good indeed,' said Pamela. 'Is she from around here?'

'No,' said Yevgeny, looking pleased and a little abashed at the same time. 'She's Laroshka, a girl I knew in Moscow, a wonderful muse of mine. I painted it from memory, a loving memory. It was a long time ago, *Brezhnyevshina* in the seventies, the time of Brezhnev in the Kremlin. Her name is Lara but I called her little Laroshka. She wanted to be an actress but life got in the way. Lara is a grandmother now, very plump with grey hair and thick spectacles, but I always think of her like this.'

On the other easel was an unfinished painting of the aged Patriarch looking entranced up into the sky where three fast fighter jets were approaching. His face was almost complete, the flowing white hair only half done. The warplanes were no more than sketched lines, somehow conveying an inhuman speed and contrasting with the ageing former pilot who watched them with hungry eyes.

'I've been working on this since his birthday party,' said Yevgeny. 'I was watching him when the jets came over, the memories he had and the excitement he still felt. It says something about old age, that the inner passions never die. I try to give him the eyes of a young man but they aren't coming yet as I want them to be. It's difficult.'

He led them into a passage that seemed to run the length of the house to a staircase. The walls were lined with portraits of various members of the Patriarch's family. Bruno stopped to admire the individual paintings of Raquelle and Victor, Raoul, Chantal and the Patriarch, but the only images of Madeleine that he saw were in paintings of several members of the family together. Yevgeny's sitting room was small but comfortable, two sofas at either side of the large chimney, where a wood stove stood with its glass doors open ready to be lit. On the wall opposite the French windows that led to the terrace was a large portrait of the Red Countess wearing an enormous wide-brimmed hat and holding a black walking cane. She was beautifully posed, slender and elegant, like some Vogue model from the fifties.

'Wine, vodka, champagne?' asked Yevgeny, hovering by the door that led to his kitchen. They chose champagne and he handed Bruno a bottle of Gosset, asking him to open it while he brought the glasses. He came back within moments carrying a tray on which stood three champagne glasses of a kind Bruno hadn't seen in years, wide-rimmed and low. Yevgeny passed out small plates and forks and then pointed to the remaining plates loaded with hunks of dark bread and smoked fish, a bowl of cream and pickled mushrooms, slices of ham and cornichons. A bottle of vodka, so cold that the glass had become clouded with ice, remained on the tray.

'*Zakuski*,' he said. 'Russian snacks. We never drink in Russia without eating a little something.' He pointed to a small bowl where a silver teaspoon rested on what Bruno thought might be blackcurrant

176

jam. But Yevgeny said, 'And a little caviare, not Russian, I'm afraid, but from our own River Vézère. Have you been to that place near Les Eyzies where they make it? I think it's very good.'

'If a Russian thinks so, I must try it,' said Pamela, and began praising the portraits they had seen and saying how different they were from the other-worldly landscapes in his gallery.

'That is what Russian customers like to buy.' Yevgeny shrugged. 'When I have an exhibition in Moscow, I double the prices so that the buyers can bargain me down. Russians love to think they are getting the better of a deal.' He finished his champagne and refilled the glass with vodka.

'They are more than I can afford but I'm glad to have seen them,' said Bruno, shaking his head in refusal when Yevgeny offered him the vodka bottle. 'How long does a painting take to do?'

'The new-world landscapes for the Russians take two or three days and the Moscow street scenes you liked about the same. The portraits take longer, but I enjoy them more. My father's portrait will take as long as I need to get the eyes right. The portrait of Laroshka could take for ever. I have been working on her for more than a year but she keeps turning into someone else, another woman who lives in my head.' He laughed and then solemnly raised his glass to them. 'Here's to the tricks that memory plays on us.'

'That's a wonderful painting of the Red Countess,' said Bruno, looking at the canvas on the wall.

He wondered how an artist so talented could make himself churn out the fanciful album covers they had first seen. 'Has she ever seen it?' He put his hand over his glass when Yevgeny tried to pour him more champagne but Pamela accepted a second drink.

'Not that one, but one very like it, which she first saw in Moscow. My father has it now in the chateau, in his bedroom, and I painted this one just for me. It's how I remember first seeing her, when she gave me wonderful chocolates from Paris. I think it was when my father had just fallen in love with her. My mother hated her, naturally, refused ever to go to her films although they were very popular. She was the one who called her *Parizhanka*, the woman from Paris. You can make it sound like a curse in Russian, or you can make it sound like a love song; a very flexible language.'

He raised his glass again. 'Here's to the memory of Gilbert, who was a good Russian in his soul. He spoke our language so beautifully and loved us so well that he almost became one of us, just like the Patriarch.'

'Do you miss Russia?' Pamela asked, while Bruno was struck by how important Gilbert still seemed to this family, and how crucial the Moscow posting had been to Gilbert's life. Bruno had a hunch that he'd have liked the man.

'Do I miss it? The Russia of today, not much.' Yevgeny shook his head fiercely. 'The Russia of my memories, of my imagination, yes, I miss it deeply, so in a sense I'm in exile here, just as Gilbert was when he came back here from Moscow. He left his soul there. But in my head I can always go back, as least some of the way. Perhaps that is why I paint so many scenes of imaginary worlds.'

'Did you see much of Gilbert here in the Périgord?' Bruno asked.

'Yes, there were some nights we drank vodka together, recited Blok and Akhmatova and sang Vysotsky songs. You should have heard Gilbert sing his 'Wolfhunt', it could have been Volodya's gravel voice. I could have been back in Volodya's apartment on Malaya Gruzinskaya.'

'Was Vysotsky the one that married the French actress?' Bruno asked. The other names meant nothing to him.

Yevgeny nodded. 'A great actor, a great poet, a great Russian, and Vysotsky inspired the only Kremlin story I know with a happy ending. All the party bosses like Suslov hated Vysotsky and wanted to ban him from writing and singing and send him to the Gulag. But Brezhnev was the leader and he loved his songs about soldiers. Brezhnev was ill at his dacha one day when the phone rang. It was his daughter, Galina, who'd heard that Suslov had ordered Vysotsky to be arrested while Brezhnev was out of action. She had Vysotsky in her apartment and she got him to sing down the phone line to her father and the old man made sure Vysotsky stayed free.'

Yevgeny paused and raised to them his champagne

glass, newly refilled with vodka. 'I told that story to Gilbert in this very room and he said he'd forgive Brezhnev a lot for that.' Yevgeny wiped his hand over his face. 'We had very Russian evenings but made the mistake of not eating enough as we drank. We'd end up passing out on these sofas.'

'Is there anyone now who can share such evenings with you? Your father?' Bruno asked.

'It's never the same, drinking with your father,' said Yevgeny and poured himself another vodka. 'It's like kissing your sister; your heart isn't in it.'

'Well, thank you so much for letting us see your paintings and for the drink but we mustn't impose on your hospitality,' Pamela said, rising to her feet. Bruno, who had noticed before the way Pamela used politeness whenever she felt embarrassed, followed suit. 'If I might use your bathroom before we go?' she asked.

'Down the corridor, opposite the door to my studio.'

'Me too,' said Bruno.

'There's another one upstairs, at the end of the passage.'

Having climbed the stairs, Bruno found three doors that could fit Yevgeny's vague description. He opened the one on the right and found himself in Yevgeny's bedroom, as large as the living room below. A giant bed was flanked by two windows giving views over the ridges to the south. Facing the bed on the longest wall hung a lavishly framed life-size painting of a young blonde woman lying nude on a single bed. An icon of the Virgin and Child stared down at the naked woman from the wall above her. On a small bedside table was a glass encased in a silver stand with a handle, containing what might have been tea. The nipples were the red of young strawberries and a carefully placed hand did not quite cover her pubic triangle, just a little darker than the hair tumbling loosely from her head.

It was only then that Bruno recognized this woman as the young Madeleine. Well, well, he thought. The only portrait of her Yevgeny seemed to have done was kept in the privacy of this room. Somehow he assumed the painting had been set in a Moscow bedroom, if not painted there. Perhaps Yevgeny had an unusually accomplished imagination, or perhaps Madeleine had posed as his model. But there was something intimate in her gaze that made Bruno think, with more than a touch of envy, that the artist was this woman's lover.

Bruno took a last, admiring look at her and retreated, closing the bedroom door quietly and then finding the bathroom. While peeing, he could not help but grin at the small self-portrait of Yevgeny that winked wickedly at him from above the loo. The shower curtain was clear plastic overlaid with a giant transparency, a photo of Moscow's Red Square taken as the guard was being changed at Lenin's Tomb, and behind them the colourful riot of spires that was St Basil's Cathedral. Back downstairs, he found Pamela at the door, thanking Yevgeny and ready to leave.

'Could you drop me in Trémolat?' Pamela asked as they were driving down the hill to the main road that ran alongside the river.

'How will you get back from there?' he asked.

'Somebody will give me a lift,' she said casually, then went on, deliberately changing the subject, 'I was struck by what he had to say about Gilbert. Perhaps I should say I noticed what he didn't say about him. I had the impression Yevgeny was trying to drop you a hint, as if wanting to reveal something but not sure whether or how to do it. Are you still making your discreet enquiries into Gilbert's death?'

'Not much point,' he replied, not sure whether Pamela was trying not to talk about her plans in Trémolat or was genuinely intrigued by Yevgeny's remarks. 'Even if there was something odd about it, there's no evidence to justify an inquiry.'

'Have you talked to Jack Crimson about it? He and Gilbert seemed to be friends and Gilbert took him to one side at one point for a private chat.'

Bruno's ears pricked up. Crimson had not seen fit to reveal that interesting nugget during their conversation. Bruno made a mental note to pursue it.

'What did you think Yevgeny might have been trying to tell us?' he asked.

'No idea. It may have been a male thing. Perhaps if I hadn't been there he might have said more.'

Bruno threw her a fond and knowing glance. Pamela always seemed to assume that men shared intimate conversations just as she did with her women friends. In Bruno's experience, men seldom did so, except perhaps in variants of those drunken, Moscow-style nights that Yevgeny had described spending with Gilbert. And while Bruno enjoyed a glass of Scotch, it had been many years since he had spent an entire evening drinking spirits. The idea of a vodka-fuelled night with Yevgeny did not appeal.

'Just here is fine, thanks,' Pamela said as he passed the Mairie in Trémolat. He stopped the car and she pecked him on the cheek before climbing out, saying, 'See you in the stables tomorrow morning.'

Bruno turned around in the car park and saw Pamela standing in front of an estate agent's window, looking at photos of houses for sale. He assumed she was killing time, waiting for him to drive away before heading for her destination. He wasn't going to spy on her but as he drove quickly past the car park of the Vieux Logis, the best restaurant in the region, he caught a glimpse of the Jaguar that belonged to his English friend, Jack Crimson.

CHAPTER 17

The next morning in the grey light just after dawn, once they had saddled the horses and ridden up to the ridge that overlooked St Denis, Pamela reined in. She glanced briefly at Bruno and then looked away over the landscape where the sun was about to rise over the woodlands to the east. The air was cool rather than chill, a light breeze stirring the leaves that were just turning gold and red on the trees below. The birds, which fell silent as their horses snorted when they halted, broke out in song, at first a few scattered notes and then a full chorus. Balzac had stopped at Hector's side, one paw up, and was poised, his tail standing proud and high, ears cocked and nose and eyes alert as he sniffed for game. Bruno leaned forward to stroke Hector's neck and then sat up straight in the saddle, breathed in deeply and braced himself. He had wondered what time and place Pamela would choose for this declaration.

'I've been thinking about how to say this and where, Bruno, and I think this is best. I love you a great deal . . .' She paused and Bruno waited

184

for the inevitable 'but'. Pamela surprised him by continuing '. . . and I always shall, even though we both know that this affair of ours has no future. And while that has been lovely for me, it's not fair on you.

'I know you want someone to settle down and have a family with and so you should. But I can't do that and I can't be that. The longer you and I go on, the more it will delay things for you. That's not a responsibility I want to bear any longer, however selfishly I may enjoy our times together. I feel guilty about you, Bruno. So if the only way to set you free is to tell you to get out of my life, well, that's what I shall say.'

A silence fell until finally Bruno was aware, even though, like her, he was gazing over the long, lazy bends of the River Vézère, that she'd turned to look at him. Expecting this, he'd even tried to rehearse some phrases to say, and in a deep and private place in his heart he welcomed it. But he was stunned by the sadness that gripped him now that it had finally happened, the sense of finality when Pamela with such determination hauled down the curtain on a year of his and her life. In the corner of his eye he caught movement and glanced down to see that Balzac had turned and was looking up at him uncertainly. The scent of rabbits was forgotten as the basset hound sensed that something had shifted in his master's mood.

Suddenly aware of the heaviness in his throat, Bruno didn't want to speak. He did not quite trust himself not to burst out with some phrase of anguish or recrimination that reflected the hurt he felt. He had felt the tiny, spiteful curl of jealousy unfolding in his mind the previous evening when he had seen Crimson's car in the car park of the restaurant and understood how Pamela intended to spend her evening. How could her dinner be innocent, he'd asked himself, if she did not want to tell him she'd been dining with a man he thought of as his friend?

'We'll always be friends, of course,' she was saying. 'And we'll still ride together and look after Hector and Balzac, and cook and spend evenings with Fabiola and Gilles, but I'm closing the bedroom door, Bruno,' she went on. Her voice was very clear and firm and her back straight, a woman in command of herself and her emotions. 'You have to move on, for your own sake.'

Slowly he nodded, still not able to look at her. 'I understand,' he said, turning Hector's head so that his horse faced a different direction. He would not spoil this dignified scene of farewell that she had planned with some spiteful retort.

'Thank you. It has been a wonderful time,' he said. 'I think you know that there will always be a part of my heart that's yours. But I'd better ride on alone. I'll bring Hector back.'

'Just put him in the stable, take off his saddle and then go. I'll take care of him. Fabiola and I will exercise the horses tonight but we'll see you tomorrow.' Her voice was kind but final.

He walked Hector to the edge of the woods and then along the bridle path where the hill began to slope down and the trees closed in so that he was not tempted to turn in the saddle for a final look back. Bruno knew that thoughts of Pamela would trouble his nights for some time to come; memories of her murmured endearments and her gentle cries of pleasure echoing from the walls of his bedroom. Some scent of her would linger on his pillow, some yearning for the touch of her and the welcome of her arms would send him searching in his bed for that familiar soft shape. Even now he could feel certain memories sealing themselves into his mind: Pamela sitting up in his bed and raising her hands to her hair in the moonlight; Pamela pulling him urgently to her; Pamela waking him in the morning with a warm kiss and insistent touch. *Mon Dieu*, how a woman leaves her mark on a man, he thought, and what a wonderful gift it is.

At last his horse came to the firebreak that ran across the slope for the full length of these woods. Finally he gave Hector his head, feeling the strength in his steed as that familiar rhythm began to build, the trot becoming within a few strides a canter and then a steady run, just short of a full gallop. He loosened the reins a fraction and bent lower in the saddle, shifting his weight forward so Hector took the signal and picked up an extra burst of pace until Bruno was aware only of the thunder of hooves, the wind in his face narrowing his eyes, the power of the horse beneath him and the blur of the trees they raced past.

Bruno gave a whoop of joy at the sheer exhilaration of this ride, as fast as he and Hector had ever gone together. Their speed, he sensed, was leaving far behind the meanness that had stolen into his thoughts, and the shared pleasure of horse and rider in this headlong dash left no room for sadness. It was past, swept away beneath Hector's pounding hooves, carried off in the wind of their passage. And he was free, untrammelled, no sense of guilt if he looked at another woman with something more than appreciation. His world was opening with possibilities, with new directions . . .

But even as he thought this he saw the firebreak narrowing ahead, the trees thinning out, this glorious run reaching its end. He began to sit back in the saddle, give a gentle pressure on the reins, but Hector had already seen the changing landscape ahead. His pace was slowing, until they reached the open stretch of parkland that led to the quarry and the road to Les Eyzies. It was time to head back. Bruno slowed to a walk and turned in the saddle to see his basset hound thundering towards him, his ears flapping like wings, his tongue out and his tail stretched straight back. Already, Bruno could almost taste the coffee and croissant that awaited him at Fauquet's café. Perhaps two croissants this morning, he thought, since after a run like that Balzac deserved at least half of one to himself.

'Have you heard about this debate in Bergerac tonight?' Fauquet asked, handing the bowl of warm croissants and the first of two coffees to Bruno. It was a new trick he'd learned from some colleague in the trade. Two fresh single coffees always somehow tasted better than pouring them both into the same cup. 'It's going to be on TV. They'll be bound to talk about Imogène's deer. When do you plan to bring her back here?'

'When I think it's safe and the hotheads have calmed down,' said Bruno, tearing off a corner of his first croissant to give to Balzac. 'You know the people around here. Pretty soon they'll start feeling guilty about her and tell each other she may be batty but her heart's in the right place.'

Bruno's phone vibrated and the screen showed that Rollo was calling, the *collège* headmaster. He sounded furious, insisting that Bruno come to his home at once to view the scene of the crime.

'What crime?' Bruno asked, and groaned inwardly when Rollo replied, 'My garden. It's been sabotaged.'

Rollo's garden was his pride and joy. He lived in a modern house above the road to Limeuil and the rockery he'd installed on the slope down to the road was an explosion of colour each spring and summer. He'd planted fruit trees on either side of the house and on the flat land behind was the finest lawn in the district, weeded, rolled and watered to a perfect green velvet. This lawn was flanked by frames and arches for Rollo's roses, which won all the prizes at the garden show each year. Beyond the lawn lay his carefully tended vegetable garden.

Each Sunday morning, Rollo ran a very popular call-in radio show on Bleu Périgord, giving gardening tips and answering listeners' questions. Like almost everyone he knew, Bruno usually listened as he did his washing and ironing and cleaned the house and he followed Rollo's tips about dealing with slugs and snails and other threats to his lettuces and vegetables. He'd have to tell Rollo about the riding school tip, hanging eggshells in trees.

Bruno found Rollo with tears in his eyes standing beside one of the tumbled arches, roses scattered over the once-perfect lawn, which itself had been torn and heaved up as if by a some crazed and vengeful ploughman. The vegetable garden beyond reminded Bruno of photographs he'd seen of battlefields of the 1914–18 war, crumbled trenches and pits like shell holes. Bruno's heart sank; he'd seen this sort of damage before. Other than artillery, only a troop of *sangliers* could cause such devastation. These wild boar roamed the woods and even electric fences were not proof against their determined aggression when they were hungry.

'There's been all this fuss about a bunch of damn

deer but what are you going to do about these wild boar?' Rollo demanded. 'Just look at the damage they've done.'

'My deepest commiserations,' said Bruno, knowing this was inadequate for the grief and anger Rollo must feel at the destruction of years of work. He was tempted to say this was the price one paid for living in the country, but that was not what Rollo wanted to hear right now and Rollo was a friend. But what did he expect Bruno to do? He could hardly arrest a troop of wild boar. Instead, he asked, 'How did the boar get in?'

Rollo led him through the remains of the vegetables to the tumbled fence posts and loops of broken wire. Bruno recalled a brief thunderstorm overnight; there must have been a local power cut that knocked out the electric fence. But nobody else had complained of losing power. He looked down the hill to the Domaine and saw that some lights were on. To the left, at the Domaine's wine barn, he could see workmen using power tools on the big sliding door.

'You have a separate circuit for the garden?' Bruno asked. Rollo nodded, saying that the fuse had blown in the night. Possibly the boar just blundered into the fence and rather than reeling back from the shock had somehow trampled wires together and made a short circuit. Or perhaps some tree branch had fallen on the fence in the storm. There was one likely candidate: a rotten branch about two metres long and as thick as Bruno's arm lay atop some of the tangled wires. Bruno looked up the slope at the woods, trying to assess distances and wind strengths but he could see no tree near enough from which it might have fallen.

Feeling baffled, he stooped to look at the wires and was surprised to see fresh metal gleaming at one broken end, as if the wire had recently been cut. He strolled up to the edge of the woods, about twenty or thirty metres from the broken fence, and pushed through the undergrowth and the first belt of trees to where he knew a hunters' trail ran along the ridge. He saw wide tyre marks in the rough grass. Some saplings in the wood had been crushed, as if a big vehicle had recently come through. The tyre tracks did not continue to the edge of Rollo's property but there were tracks of something smaller, perhaps a bicycle with very fat tyres. They were too narrow for a wheelbarrow. Bruno measured them and took a photograph with his phone, crouching low to the ground so the shadows of the marks stood out in the rising sun. Maybe they were the tracks of mountain bikes.

'Did you hear any vehicles in the night or see any torches in the woods?' Bruno asked when he returned. Rollo shook his head.

'Any gunshots?' Again Rollo said not.

Poachers and some unscrupulous hunters liked to work by night, using flashlights taped to their rifles to locate and then shoot the game. Some hunters could have been working the woods and driven the panicked boar onto Rollo's land. But that wouldn't explain the severed wire or the appearance of that rotten branch when there was no tree from which it might have fallen. Could somebody have brought that branch? He remembered something he'd read about a court case against a group of hunters in Burgundy who'd tranquillized some boar and left them to wake up in the garden of an anti-hunt campaigner they disliked. Could that have happened here? It would have taken two or even four strong men to carry even a single drugged boar from the woods to Rollo's garden. But one or more could have been draped across a mountain bike and moved that way.

'Have you made any enemies lately among the hunters?'

Rollo looked startled. 'Not that I know of. I'm not a hunter but I've nothing against them. We used to get venison and pheasants from them often enough, in return for letting the Limeuil club hunt my land. It's my property all the way back through those woods. But we asked them to stop last year when our daughter-in-law said the gunshots were frightening the baby. Why do you ask?'

'Just wondering. You know what happened to Imogène's deer.' Bruno decided against mentioning his suspicions to Rollo, at least until he had more to go on than a freshly cut wire. 'I thought maybe some of the hotheads might have been in the woods last night and panicked the boar into running this way. But usually they're careful not to drive boar towards houses, particularly if they belong to friends.'

'More power to the hunters, if you ask me. After what those boar have done to my garden I wish they'd wipe out every damn boar in the *département*. I'm tempted to sign up to join them and start hunting the *sangliers* myself.'

CHAPTER 18

Bruno promised to file a report for Rollo's insurance, stayed for a cup of coffee and some further commiseration but kept his suspicions to himself until he got back to his office. He searched on his computer for the case in Burgundy he'd vaguely recalled and found the reference. As he read the account, he realized it had stuck in his mind because it had triggered some new rules in France over the ownership and storage of tranquillizer guns. On the whole they were restricted to zoos, nature reserves and licensed veterinary surgeons. But in certain circumstances where usually protected animals were becoming a menace, they could be used by a registered hunting club.

He called the Préfecture and they emailed to him a list of the registered tranquillizer guns in the *département*. There were only a dozen or so places on the list, among them the prehistoric wildlife park at Le Thot. The only unusual listing was for a fish farm that was suffering losses from a family of otters and had been approved to use the gun to tranquillize them and move them much further upriver. The guns looked like conventional rifles but were powered by compressed air and fired a small dart. The precise tranquillizer to be used and the dose had to be approved by a vet and the weapon securely stored when not in use.

He called first at the St Denis surgery, where Veltrier showed him the dart gun stowed in a locked cabinet, and similar precautions had been taken at the new wildlife park at St Félix. But the director of the fish farm said he'd never seen their gun; it was in the care of the part-time gamekeeper they had hired to solve the otter problem. The director did not know where the darts were kept, nor did he have on file the vet's certificate for the tranquillizer to be used. Bruno asked to see where the gamekeeper stored his gear and was taken to a corner of a storage barn, mostly filled with fish meal, and was shown a metal locker. It was unlocked and empty except for a pair of rubber boots, a camouflage jacket and an almost empty bottle of cheap cognac.

'I checked his hunting licence and his membership card from the Lalinde club,' said the fish farm director. 'And he had a lockable chest in the back of his truck where he kept his weapons. Fabrice usually works at night, when we've all gone for the day. He's done a good job so far, catching one breeding pair and taking them back upriver into the next *département*.'

'Fabrice?' Bruno said, his ears pricking up. This

was also the name of the gamekeeper at the Patriarch's chateau. 'What's his surname?'

'Daubert, Fabrice Daubert. I think he's from Bergerac.'

That triggered a memory. A man called Daubert had been suspended for a year from one of the regional rugby clubs for dirty play.

Bruno gave the fish farm director a warning and said he'd better have the paperwork up to date and the storage of the dart gun secured for Bruno's next visit. He then called his colleague Quatremer, the municipal policeman at Lalinde, to get a number for the secretary of the hunt club, and mentioned his interest in Fabrice.

'Damn good shot and knows his hunting,' Bruno was told. 'Not very popular, though. Fabrice is a bit too keen to get the first shot in and the biggest bag of the day. That's why the Bergerac club asked him to leave, that and getting suspended from the rugby team. But he seems well settled now; game-keeping suits him and it's a steady job, or rather two jobs.'

'I know about the fish farm,' said Bruno. 'What's the other job?'

'I don't know about any fish farm,' Quatremer replied. 'His first job is over your way with that famous pilot, the Patriarch, and the second one is working for the son at the vineyard near here. They know him through the hunt club. He's fallen on his feet there because the job comes with a cottage on the estate. Apparently there's some problem with the pheasants. Don't ask me what that means, it's just what I heard.'

'How long has he been with the Lalinde club?' Bruno asked. 'I know some of the guys there but I hadn't heard that Fabrice was a member. And after he was banned from rugby, I'd probably have heard.'

'Just a few months. After he left the Bergerac club someone at the vineyard put in a good word for him. It was probably Victor, the owner; his wife Madeleine is the club secretary.'

Wary of trespassing on Quatremer's turf, Bruno asked if Quatremer would like to check on Fabrice's dart gun, whether it was secured and if it had been used recently. Quatremer pleaded pressure of work and said Bruno should feel free to make the checks himself. So he took the now familiar road to the vineyard and was not surprised to learn that Fabrice was installed in what had been Gilbert's home but that he was working at the Patriarch's place that day. He got Fabrice's mobile phone number and left a message asking him to call urgently and also scribbled a note for him, which he left with the secretary who ran the vineyard office. With that, he drove home, showered and changed, selected half a dozen of his duck eggs, since he knew the Countess loved them, and drove on up the valley to the Red Chateau for the promised lunch.

The maid led Bruno through the familiar great hall to the wing that had been the Countess's invalid room when he had first been here. Now it was a light-filled sitting room with comfortable armchairs covered in chintz and it led to the sunny terrace, from which he heard the sound of women's voices. He was the third guest to arrive after Chantal and her brother, Raoul, the one the Countess was hoping would wed her great-granddaughter. Chantal and Marie-Françoise were sitting either side of the Countess, who was gingerly holding a modern mobile phone. They were showing her how it worked. Raoul was sitting facing her, his own phone in his hand, chuckling as he sent her text messages.

'I'm far too old for this texting nonsense, Bruno, and my fingers are far too big,' said the old lady as he bent to kiss her cheeks. In contrast to the solemn black skirt and jacket she had worn to the Patriarch's party, the Countess was dressed in a light-grey trouser suit over a high-necked white blouse that seemed to have been copied from a man's pleated dress shirt. There were two canes by her side but no wheelchair.

'What would I want with the internet?' she went on. 'I've never liked the telephone. If it's important, then it ought to be important enough to visit somebody and see them face to face, or write a letter. I never seem to get any letters these days, except for that lovely card you sent, Bruno. I should have written to thank you for wheeling me around Marco's place, not the other way around.'

Raoul rose to shake hands and the two young women kissed Bruno and asked for all the gory details of Imogène and her deer. Had he really spirited her away amid a volley of gunshots from angry hunters? Had he stayed to see the slaughter? Would she really be put on trial for murder? Or was it manslaughter? He held up his hands and explained his own modest role in the events.

'I had a meeting with the Prefect,' he said. 'Almost anybody else in St Denis will know more about what happened than I do.'

'You deserve a drink anyway,' said the Countess and told him to help himself from a well-stocked trolley. The others were drinking white wine and he joined them, noting it was the new Réserve du Patriarche that he'd been offered at the tasting. Raoul rose and craned his neck to see whatever sports car produced the fierce, mechanical growl that suddenly came from the lane, its volume increasing as it reached the courtyard. A few moments later the Patriarch came in, bowing as he held open the door for Fabiola. She was instantly embraced by Marie-Françoise. Fabiola had been the first doctor to tend to her after the nightmare in the cave and had then recommended the right dentist to repair her battered jaw as well as good language tutors to help make the transition from California.

'I presume that ghastly sound was your car, Marco,' said the Countess, rising to her feet with a single cane and an act of will as the Patriarch came forward to kiss her and then greet the others before turning back to her.

'My little Ferrari is older than our grandchildren,

ma belle, but the car and I would both be honoured if we could take you motoring again. You always loved driving with the hood down.'

'That was so I could leap out before you killed me, my dear.'

Bruno saw the two of them exchange a look of complete understanding and great affection. It must have been almost sixty years ago that they had become lovers and they still shared a deep fondness for one another. Bruno could only hope that if he ever reached a similar age he'd be able to exchange a glance like that with an old love. With a pang, he realized he had not given a thought to Pamela since their parting early this morning. The Patriarch, he was sure, would have been far more gallant. Bruno glanced across at the young people clustered now around Fabiola, noting that despite the Countess's plans no chemistry seemed to be developing between Raoul and Marie-Françoise. Instead, he and his sister had their arms around one another as they listened to Marie-Françoise describe how Fabiola had helped her settle into her new life in France.

The Patriarch poured himself some wine and turned to Bruno. 'We'll be meeting again at the Confrérie on the first Saturday of next month. A dozen duck pâtés for us to taste and pick the best, I believe, and five or six of goose. Then we march in procession to the old square, I make a speech about your virtues, you take the oath as a *chevalier* and then we tap you on each shoulder with a duck and present you with your seal of office. After that, we go to lunch, which usually goes on very agreeably until the early evening. Take my tip: either make sure you have somebody sober to drive you home or take the train.'

'Thanks for the advice. How are your pheasants? I heard you're having trouble with them.'

'*Tiens*, you're well informed. Yes, we've got a few foxes to get rid of and I've hired a gamekeeper to get the woods back in proper shape. Even before the incident with that poor woman and her deer got me thinking about getting the game back into balance. They need predators and we humans are the last ones left. Victor and Raoul seldom hunt and now that Gilbert's dead there's only me and Madeleine left to keep the numbers down. Hunting was about the only thing that kept poor Gilbert sober; he was always good around guns. I hear you're quite keen. Where do you go?'

Bruno explained that he had honorary membership of all three hunt clubs based around St Denis but that he usually went to the woods around St Cirq and Audrix. 'At least you can usually get the compensation of mushrooms even if the dogs can't raise a single *bécasse*,' he said.

A gong sounded, a maid appeared further down the terrace and stood by some double doors. Limping determinedly, the Countess led them to lunch, declaring that this was to be a California-style modern meal as proposed by her great-granddaughter.

'That means very little food indeed by our Périgord standards, Marco, just a little *salade Périgourdine* and cold vegetable soup and for us carnivores there's some smoked ham as a special treat,' the Countess said. Bruno saw her hand quivering with the effort of walking with the single cane. 'Marie-Françoise initially wanted to serve only fruit juice and mineral water but I put my foot down over that.'

The banter continued and the Patriarch's wine was praised until he tapped his glass and asked to hear the full story of the rescue of the Countess and Marie-Françoise's ordeal in the cave. Bruno protested that the real heroes of the incident weren't present, his friends J-J and Sergeant Jules. J-J, chief of detectives for the *département*, had fired the crucial bullet and Jules had hauled Marie-Françoise from the underground lake. He turned to Fabiola, saying that she had been the one who saved the Countess by discovering and exposing the false diagnosis.

'That's not the way Marie-Françoise tells it,' said Chantal. 'And it's not the version that appeared in *Paris Match*.'

'Things never really happened the way they get written down as history or as journalism,' said the Patriarch. 'In retrospect, events have to make sense and take place in order, one thing leading logically to another. It's never that way at the time. Still, all the different accounts agree that it ended happily. And now I'd like some coffee, please, before going home to hear my daughter-in-law rehearse her speech yet again.'

'Is that for this evening's debate in Bergerac?' Bruno asked, as Chantal served the coffee.

'More than that, it's the event that will shape her political future,' the Patriarch replied. 'Madeleine's a very ambitious woman, and of course related to you,' he said to the Countess.

'She goes back to Eleanor of Aquitaine through Eleanor's daughter Alix of Blois, while my ancestor was Eleanor's daughter Joan, who became Queen of Sicily and mother to a line of dukes of Toulouse,' said the Countess. 'And we're related all over again through the de Rohans and through the Rochechouarts, which is the connection to Madame de Montespan.'

'So much of France's history has been made by a long line of extraordinary women,' said the Patriarch, turning to Bruno. 'It serves to put us men in our place.'

'But it's usually you men who write the history,' said the Countess, drily. She took a final sip of her coffee, crumpled her napkin and left it beside her empty plate. 'Marie-Françoise, would you look after our guests, please? Marco and I need a moment to ourselves.'

It seemed like a signal that lunch was over but Marie-Françoise led them into the formal garden, an old-fashioned affair of gravel paths and trimmed topiary, and then down some stone steps to where an obviously new swimming pool had been installed. At the far end, a series of glass arches seemed to pile on top of one another. It took a moment for Bruno to realize that these could be extended to cover the pool so it could be used year round. Marie-Françoise pointed to a large poolhouse covered with solar panels.

'Men to the left, girls to the right and there are costumes and towels if anyone wants to swim,' she said. 'This was Granny's welcome gift to me. She said since I'm from California, I must miss having a pool. It's heated so you can use it any time.'

Raoul and Chantal went straight to the changing room, Bruno and Fabiola accepted Marie-Françoise's offer of another coffee and she went to the central door of the poolhouse. Inside was a kitchen with cupboards of plastic glasses and crockery. She plugged in an espresso machine that stood on a counter beside a large refrigerator and put cups and saucers onto a tray.

'I've been meaning to ask you,' Bruno said. 'At the Patriarch's party, were you with Chantal when that drunk tried to pull her away?'

'Yes, but he wasn't being aggressive,' Marie-Françoise replied. 'He excused himself to me and said he really needed to talk to her. They obviously knew each other and at first I didn't even realize he was drunk. I thought he had some sort of speech impediment. It was only later that Chantal told me he was her godfather and he was an alcoholic.'

Raoul and Chantal emerged from the poolhouse, dived in and began swimming fast the length of the pool. Bruno thought they might have been racing until Chantal suddenly swerved and with a cry of triumph clambered atop Raoul's shoulders to duck him. Marie-Françoise laughed at their antics as she served the coffee, probably wishing she could join her friends in the pool. But Bruno wanted some answers.

'Did you hear what her godfather wanted to talk to Chantal about?' Bruno went on, sipping his coffee, aware of Fabiola watching him curiously.

'I don't remember exactly, just something about the family that he thought she needed to know,' Marie-Françoise said. 'Apparently he'd lived with them for years and was like an honorary family member. Anyway, Chantal and I were talking about something private and she didn't want to be interrupted so she pulled herself away and he sort of stumbled and dropped his glass and grabbed her to keep his balance. That's when I knew he was drunk, and then Raoul and Victor came to take him away.'

'Do you remember what he was drinking?'

'Yes, it was odd. He had a tall glass that looked to be filled with orange juice. I remember because it slopped when he stumbled and went over my feet and then he dropped it. I tried to wipe it off but it ruined one of my shoes. I had to spend the rest of the party with this sticky stuff sloshing round my toes.'

'Do you still have that shoe?' Bruno asked.

'It's in my room. I was going to chuck it but I

thought maybe I'd take it to a specialist cleaner in Bordeaux, see if they could fix it.'

'Let me take care of it,' said Bruno, thinking that the forensics guys might be able to tell just what Gilbert had been drinking. 'I know an expert.'

In the pool, Raoul was now ducking Chantal, who squirmed out of his grip and swam away, as fast and supple as an eel. Marie-Françoise grinned as she watched and then turned to Fabiola. 'Granny keeps trying to pair me off with Raoul. She's not very subtle.'

'Don't you like him?' Fabiola replied.

'He's great as a friend, as Chantal's brother, but we're not interested in each other and it's far too soon for me even to think of settling down with someone. Anyway, those two are so close there wouldn't be much room for anyone else.'

CHAPTER 19

Although it would hold 150 or more, the Salle de l'Orangérie was already filling fast when Bruno and the Mayor arrived. They made their way through the chanting Green demonstrators who lined the paths of approach through Bergerac's Parc Jean Jaurès. Some space had been taken at the back of the hall for a small dais, where a TV reporter was holding a white card before the lens so his cameraman could get the right colour balance. There was a buzz of conversation and the large room was full. Bruno recognized several local politicians scanning each new arrival to see who might be important or useful.

He spotted the Patriarch standing with Raoul and Chantal in the front row, chatting with three men, one of whom was Peyrefitte, the lawyer from Périgueux who had lost his wife. The Patriarch waved him over and Bruno shook hands all round as he was introduced. Peyrefitte evidently knew of Bruno from the press reports and murmured a word of appreciation for his efforts. Bruno asked after Peyrefitte's children. One was fine, the other still in intensive care, he was told. The Mayor of St Denis came to join them, shaking hands en route to right and left with political colleagues from around the region.

The thought had never previously struck Bruno, but he suddenly understood that politicians are not just members of a common profession but a tribe, with common customs and concerns, a shared vocabulary and a fondness for one another's company. He never normally saw his Mayor as a politician since Gérard Mangin reckoned that running St Denis was more about getting the garbage collected on time than partisan struggles between parties. But here the Mayor seemed to be in his element, knowing almost everybody and seeming to have friends from all across the political spectrum. He was sharing a joke and then squeezing someone's arm here and murmuring something into an ear there, nodding and scribbling a note on a business card as someone whispered to him, an arm on the Mayor's shoulder. Finally, he and Bruno returned to the third row, where Fauquet had installed himself earlier and was guarding two places for them.

'The Greens have made a big mistake,' said Fauquet gleefully. 'They're all demonstrating outside but we've got most of the places inside so we can cheer her and whistle at him.'

'Don't you have to be inside to vote?' the Mayor asked.

Fauquet nodded. 'But they're also doing a phone-in vote; you text one number for the Greens, another for Madeleine. That will take a while so we'll be able to claim the first vote and try to be sure that's the one that gets reported. And we've got people lined up all over the *département*.'

As well as running the St Denis café, Fauquet was a veteran of small-town politics and knew all the tricks of local elections. When drinking one evening at a rugby club dinner, he'd confided to Bruno his three rules to win council races. The first was to recruit candidates from the largest families in the commune since they'd usually all vote for a relative, even if a family feud meant they hadn't spoken for years. The second was to work hard to win over the members of the town's tennis, rugby and hunting clubs, which explained the generous subsidies the Mairie usually provided to the town's sports. The third was always to recruit a doctor, a pharmacist or a schoolteacher to be the candidate, since they came in contact with hundreds of potential electors and people always preferred to vote for someone they knew.

'They all know me, too,' Bruno had observed.

'People never vote for a policeman unless they're scared stiff,' Fauquet had replied. Bruno had then argued that the Mayor kept getting re-elected even though he did not come from a large family nor had he been a member of one of the chosen professions.

'The Mayor's different,' Fauquet had grumbled and turned away.

The contrast when the two debaters came on stage to shake hands was striking. The Green politician, a former teacher named Georges Luchan, was tall, very thin and wore jeans and a blazer with an open-necked striped shirt. His thinning grey hair was gathered in a ponytail and Bruno couldn't tell whether the man was trying to grow a beard or was aiming for the stubble that had become fashionable among younger men. He sported a large Green campaign button in his lapel. Madeleine had dressed conservatively in a plain dress of dark blue with a light-blue silk scarf at her throat. Her fair hair was piled into a neat bun and she wore minimal make-up, seeking to appear businesslike and even severe. Yet her classic features and graceful posture ensured that her looks still captivated most of the men in the room, Bruno included. Even as he braced himself to pay attention to a serious discussion, he could not prevent the image of the painting he had seen at Yevgeny's from leaping into his mind.

Each speaker had a podium and the moderator, the Mayor of Bergerac, sat at a small table in the centre. The debate had originally been his idea, to test local opinion on the issue of using fracking technology to exploit the natural gas reserves deep underground in much of south-western France. The socialist government with their Green allies were against it and the conservatives were divided, but more and more mayors of all political parties were becoming interested in what this could mean for local jobs and prosperity. The huge publicity following the death of Peyrefitte's wife and the fate of Imogène's deer had widened the focus of the debate and it quickly became clear that Madeleine was going to make this her main theme.

The rules for the debate gave each speaker fifteen minutes for opening remarks, then twenty minutes to respond to questions from the floor and a closing statement of five minutes each. The event was timed to last exactly one hour, for the convenience of the local radio stations that would be broadcasting it live. The Mayor had tossed a coin to see which of the speakers would go first and the Green won. He gave a competent opening speech on the threat of climate change, the dangers of fracking and the need to build wind and solar farms to replace fossil fuels. Bruno was sympathetic to the theme, but the speaker was lacklustre; it sounded as though he'd given the same speech many times before. He closed with a brief word of condolence to Peyrefitte for the loss of his wife.

'While I oppose the slaughter of those helpless deer at St Denis, I agree we must take precautions against their becoming a danger to road users. We want no more such sad and terrible accidents. What this tragedy teaches us is the need for constant discussion and debate among all citizens over how best we can balance the needs of the environment and the economy, wildlife and people, to ensure such tragedies never happen again and that our children can inherit a safe and sustainable planet.'

Madeleine rose as Luchan sat to polite but restrained applause. She thanked the Mayor for moderating, thanked the Green speaker for his remarks and began by saying, 'I'm glad the Green Party exists and I've even thought very seriously about voting for them in the past. But I wonder if they are not headed for extinction, doomed by the evolution that has made every other political party aware of the need to protect our environment. The Greens have scored a huge political victory. They have fulfilled their historic role and won this big argument.

'But they are becoming an irrelevant and querulous sect, opposed to everything but wind and solar farms with no thought of what we do when the wind doesn't blow and the sun doesn't shine. They are against nuclear power, against exploring for natural gas, against coal and oil, against foie gras and even against the use of genetic science in food when it can prevent famines and ensure that children even in the poorest countries can get the right vitamins in their diet. Many of them don't even want us to eat meat.'

Madeleine gave a thoughtful and balanced assessment of the benefits and problems of fracking, the cost to France of importing natural gas and the danger of depending on importing energy from Russia. Greens should support fracking, she added, since power stations fuelled by natural gas produced less than half the emissions of those fuelled by coal.

Of course, she went on with a smile, not all the Greens are against everything. Monsieur Luchan here is no extremist but a sensible man. She gave her opponent a friendly nod. She was persuaded he had no qualms about hunting animals or shooting deer. From a folder on the podium before her she pulled a page of newspaper and held it up.

'I have here,' she said, 'the report from *Sud Ouest* of the anniversary dinner of the town of Nontron in the north of our *département*, at which Monsieur Luchan gave the formal speech. Quite right, too; it is in his constituency. And what a fine dinner it was. I have here the menu. It started with a fine vegetarian dish, a cream of mushroom soup. It was followed by *foie gras de Périgord* and then by *médaillons de chevreuil*, kindly provided by the hunting club of Nontron.'

She turned to Luchan. 'I congratulate you, sir, on your taste. *Médaillons de chevreuil* is one of my own favourite dishes. There is nothing quite like a fine roast of venison. But, *monsieur*, if you are prepared to eat and enjoy the flesh of deer that have been shot by hunters, how on earth can you oppose using the same method to control their numbers when they become a danger to themselves as well as to humans?

'So I close with three questions for my colleague

214

in this debate. The first question is this: should we seek to maintain an ecological balance between wildlife and the local environment that can sustain the deer without suffering or starvation? If so, and I'm sure a sensible man like Monsieur Luchan would agree, my second question is this: which method do we use – culling or contraception?'

She paused for the scattered chuckles that spread into general laughter. She held up a hand to quiet the audience and Bruno realized she now had the hall in the palm of her hand. Everyone seemed to be smiling, looking up at her expectantly.

'I leave it to your imaginations to ponder how we persuade each doe in our woods to take her contraceptive pill every day,' she said, and the room rocked once more with laughter. She held up her hand again, and then paused with the timing of a natural actress before gazing around the audience with a smile.

'Or perhaps our Green friends think we can persuade each stag to take steps to fulfil his own responsibility for family planning? They might even volunteer to help with the fitting.'

She paused again and this time it took a moment for the mental image she had evoked to take hold and then the room erupted in guffaws and cheers. Beside Bruno, Fauquet and the Mayor were wiping tears of laughter from their eyes and so was the moderator on stage. Even her opponent, Luchan, had a sickly sort of grin on his face. When the hall finally stilled again, Madeleine said, 'My third and final question for Monsieur Luchan, to whom I offer a belated *bon appetit* for those *médaillons de chevreuil*, is this: which comes first – deer or people?'

She stepped back from the podium and inclined her head to Luchan and the moderator and the room broke into a storm of applause. Peyrefitte was the first to rise to his feet, clapping his hands together above his head, and he was followed by the Patriarch and then by Fauquet and most of the hall. Bruno considered for a moment and then rose as well, thinking Madeleine deserved a standing ovation for the most effective and amusing political speech he'd heard in years.

The remainder of the evening was an anticlimax. Luchan stumbled through his questions and closing remarks and then hurried from the stage, leaving the field of battle to the victor. Madeleine remained on stage and nodded her head sweetly as her gaze swept the audience, her glance seeming briefly to meet the eyes of every man in the room. And not a man there was immune to her charms, and even the few women in the crowd were smiling broadly at the triumph of a member of their own sex in such a traditionally masculine preserve.

'You have just seen the selection of the next deputy to the National Assembly,' the Mayor said to Bruno. 'And probably a future minister.'

'That was really something. I pity that poor Green at the next meeting of his executive committee,' said Fauquet. 'She crushed him, chewed him up and spat him out.'

'But she did it all with the utmost respect and courtesy,' the Mayor said. 'And yet maybe she was a little too ruthless. That business with the menu was pretty close to the line. There's an unwritten rule that we don't make politics with people's families or personal matters. And heaven knows a politician can't choose what the menu is going to be at an official dinner. Still, she did it beautifully and I'm very glad I don't have to run against her.'

Fauquet burst into renewed laughter. 'I'm just thinking of that silly bastard Luchan. From now on at every lunch or dinner he goes to, the poor sap is going to have to ask for the vegetarian option or the fruit plate. He'll never be able to eat a decent meal in public again.'

Bruno was thinking that Madeleine was a most remarkable and somewhat terrifying woman. She was equipped with every possible advantage for a political career. She had beauty, brains, acting skills and a mesmerizing style in public speaking that included a natural sense of humour and a way of winning audiences onto her side. She was a wife and mother but she was also a business-woman, helping to run the family vineyard. There can be few professions dearer to the heart of a French voter than someone who combines a family farm with producing a decent bottle of wine. And she also had the inestimable advantage of being the daughter-in-law of one of the best-known and most respected figures in France.

More than that, Bruno mused, she had a subtle but deeply effective charm, a discreet but possibly unconscious way of seducing every man in the audience. Bruno was not sure whether this was deliberate on her part or simply an inevitable result of her beauty. Having never come across anyone quite like her before, he was prepared to give Madeleine the benefit of the doubt. She was the kind of woman whose every look seemed to carry some flirtatious signal and yet she was no flirt. There was nothing overt about her manner and the other women did not seem to resent her; they had applauded and cheered as sincerely as the men.

'Come along,' said the Mayor, breaking into his reverie. 'My counterpart has invited us to the Mairie for a post-debate reception. Apparently Luchan has cried off, probably terrified of being cornered by some aggrieved local Greens. But we can enjoy mingling with all the political king-makers celebrating the launch of their new star.'

The reception turned out to be a scrum, too many people and too much alcohol in too small a room, and all of them trying to cluster around Madeleine. She had managed to secure some space around her by standing behind a small table on which stood her handbag, a vase filled with flowers and a stack of campaign leaflets which carried a photograph of her with her family and the Patriarch.

The caption read 'Madeleine Desaix, mother, wine-maker and a powerful voice for our Périgord'. She was signing them as souvenirs. Bruno felt absurdly pleased when she spotted him, called out his name and beckoned him to struggle through the crowd to be kissed on both cheeks.

CHAPTER 20

As always when he slept alone, Bruno came at once to full consciousness, aware of his familiar bedroom despite the darkness. The firmness of Pamela's decision came back to him, along with happy memories of amorous awakenings. He would be waking alone for the foreseeable future, he reflected. Rather than brood, he threw back the duvet and turned on the light. He rose and opened the door to greet Balzac, who slept in the kitchen and somehow always seemed to wake a moment or so before his master. Bruno ran through the morning exercises he remembered from the army, drank a small glass of water and then donned his tracksuit and running shoes.

With Balzac at his heels, he checked the chicken run and then set off into the familiar woods for the morning jog that cleared his head and allowed him to think about the day ahead. There was Hector to exercise, then breakfast at Fauquet's before the market began and he should check that all was well with Imogène. That meant he'd have to make some discreet enquiries in the Procureur's office to see if he planned to prosecute her.

He also needed to see Fabrice to ask what he'd been doing the night that Rollo's garden had been destroyed.

He was in the café just before eight. Now that the summer rush had ended, only the regulars remained in the market. They all knew each other, and in the space behind their stalls they prepared and ate their *casse-croûte* together at around ten when the morning rush was over. Over his coffee, Bruno scanned the headlines in *Sud Ouest*, lingering only over the photo of Rollo looking sadly over his demolished garden. The story took up most of an inside page.

Bruno waited until the stroke of eight before calling his colleague Quatremer in Lalinde to ask if Fabrice had a regular girlfriend. He got a name, Véronique Ferreira, and asked what car she drove. A small red Peugeot, he was told. The name Ferreira meant she came from one of the Portuguese families who had come to the Périgord in the twenties and thirties to work as fruit and grape pickers. Hard-workers, most had stayed and prospered. Bruno finished his croissant and second coffee and went out to the market to see José, who ran the stall that sold work clothes, flannel shirts and cheap boots. He was also a Ferreira and Bruno asked him if he knew Véronique, who turned out to be a cousin.

'Why do you want to know?' José asked, some suspicion in his voice. He knew Bruno well, but family is family. Bruno explained that it was her boyfriend, Fabrice, who interested him and he needed to check with Véronique whether she had been with him on Wednesday evening. Bruno was so accustomed to young men citing their girl-friends as their alibis that he'd learned to check with the girlfriends first.

'She can't have been with him,' said José. 'It was my aunt's birthday. We were all there until well after midnight, the whole family, and there was no young man with Véronique. She left with her parents so I don't think she'd have gone out after that, not on a week night. She works in the dentist's surgery in Lalinde and they start at eight. What's this Fabrice like? Is he in trouble?'

Bruno shrugged and said the young man seemed to have a job but suggested that José check with the rugby club about Fabrice's suspension. He thanked José, then rang Fabrice and found him in his car, heading to work on the Patriarch's estate. He sounded nervous but agreed to meet Bruno at nine in the barn behind the chateau where the estate offices were located. Bruno had seen Fabrice play and knew him to be a large and brawny young man, fit but not very fast, with his head shaved to a stubble and tattoos on his neck and arms. In his gamekeeping gear, they weren't visible.

Outside the barn was a battered open-bed truck, the bonnet still warm. If there were any doubt about Fabrice being the owner, one bumper sticker said *Rugby Men Do It Without Armour* and the other read *Hunters Are the Real Ecolos*. Bruno began by asking about the rifle that fired the tranquillizer darts and Fabrice unlocked the chest inside his truck and brought it out. It was clean and well cared for, recently oiled.

'You know the regulations say it has to be stored in the place where it's registered, the fish farm,' Bruno said.

'I know, but this is more secure.'

'Not if your truck gets stolen. Where's the vet's certificate and the inventory for the darts and tranquillizers?' Bruno checked through the papers and asked, 'When did you last use the gun?'

'Last weekend and then I stayed up all Monday night, watching for those otters. I got one on Sunday evening, the male, and then we put him in a trap by the fish pond. Sure enough his mate came up after midnight. She was very quiet, very careful, but I got her as well and now they've both been shipped way back upstream.'

'You haven't filled in the number of darts fired. You know you have to do that. And where are the doses of tranquillizer?'

'In the fridge at home. I fired several darts, some missed.'

'Are you trying to tell me that you fired and missed and an otter still stayed around to be hit by a second dart? Or maybe a third? That's hard to believe.' Bruno was now convinced that Fabrice was lying.

Fabrice shrugged, saying nothing.

Bruno tried another tack. 'I heard you're pretty keen on mountain biking, is that right?'

'What, mountain bikes? Me? No way, you must be thinking of some other bloke. I like motors.'

'Where were you Wednesday evening and night?'

'With my girlfriend, Véronique.'

'Are you sure about that? A truck that sounds a bit like yours was seen late at night near Limeuil, we were told, hunting wild boar.'

'Nothing to do with me,' said Fabrice, shaking his head. 'I was with Véronique all night. She's quite a girl; you know these passionate Portuguese.' He gave Bruno a wink, one guy to another.

'Right, we'll draw up a statement and you sign it. You have to be sure it's right because it will go to the Procureur's office.' Bruno had no qualms about trapping the young man. He didn't like dirty play on the rugby field, didn't like men talking about their girlfriends that way and didn't like people misusing weapons. And he did like Rollo and his garden.

Fabrice took Bruno into the small room in the barn that was his office to draft the statement. There was a calendar on the wall featuring naked photos of big-bosomed girls.

'Let's be absolutely sure about the date, Wednesday evening and night, the day before yesterday,' Bruno said, handing Fabrice his pen.

'That's right, no doubt about it,' said Fabrice and signed. Bruno witnessed the signature and then used his official stamp to make the document formal. Fabrice looked relieved when Bruno turned as if to go.

'I'll just go and check your story with the girl-friend, Véronique Ferreira, I believe her name is. Am I right in thinking I'll find her at the dentist's in Lalinde?' Bruno asked.

'You know her?' Fabrice looked startled.

'I know her well enough to tell you she was at her aunt's birthday party on Wednesday evening and then went home late with her mum and dad and was still on time at the dentist's office the next morning,' Bruno said. 'You weren't with her all night even though you just signed a sworn statement that you were. That's perjury. Making a false statement is a criminal offence.'

Fabrice swallowed. 'I made a mistake, I confused the day.'

'Tell it to the magistrate. You'd better tell your boss you won't be working today. You're going to be in the Gendarmerie cells. In fact, you'll probably be there all weekend. I doubt the magistrate will get around to questioning you until Monday morning.'

'*Putain*, you can't do this to me when I just got the date confused.' Bruno simply stared at him. 'I can't afford to lose this job,' Fabrice added.

'So tell me what really happened Wednesday night. And don't bother to lie. I know most of it, tranquillizing the wild boar, short-circuiting the fence around that garden, putting the boar in.'

Fabrice's face seemed to collapse. He ran his

225

hand over the stubble on his head and sat down heavily beside the table where he had just signed the false statement. He breathed out noisily and looked first at Bruno and then at the door as if thinking of making a run for it.

'Now it's been stamped and sealed it's an official legal document,' said Bruno, picking up the statement and putting it in his shirt pocket. 'It won't go away, Fabrice. Why not tell me the full story of what happened that night? You weren't alone so who was with you? Did some friend talk you into it after a few beers, a bit of a joke that went too far? Was that the way it happened? Maybe there are mitigating circumstances, but I can't know until you tell me.'

Fabrice remained silent. He had closed his eyes, clenched the fists he was too ready to use on the rugby field and his face was turning red, as if he were holding his breath. Bruno waited, knowing that silence was one of an interrogator's best weapons. Finally, Fabrice blew out his breath, almost like a horse snorting. Half expecting violence, Bruno automatically thought how to react. Fabrice was bigger, younger and probably stronger but the only rule for that kind of fight was to deliver the first, decisive blow. Fabrice would be handicapped by having to rise, his body still half bent.

Fabrice shook his head, as if to clear it. Then his shoulders slumped. This was not a man preparing to fight. A few moments ago he'd had no troubles in the world. Now he looked defeated, but he still had not spoken. Bruno would have to bluff the story out of him. He had no handcuffs with him but he saw leather straps hanging from the wall, the kind hunters used to haul deer from deep woods. They would do.

'The next stop is the Gendarmerie, Fabrice. We'll take your fingerprints, of course,' Bruno said. 'We'll also do a swab for your DNA; you'll know about that from the TV shows. The forensics experts will test that against the wire on the fence in that garden your boars destroyed. There's no arguing with that. So that's criminal damage, and Rollo is a popular guy with that radio programme, so that will be two, maybe three years. Then there's the misuse of a official gun, that could be another year on top. You'll never get a hunting licence again and you can forget about Véronique. And then when you get out of jail there'll be the civil damages to pay to Rollo for the loss of his garden.

'That's not much of a future,' Bruno went on, his voice sympathetic, but privately he was starting to worry. Unless Fabrice started talking he had very little on the man. Swearing a false statement was hardly a serious charge, simply the kind the police used as a lever to extract more information. The Procureur's office would probably laugh at Bruno if he tried to file it.

'Anything you can tell me that might help? It's just that I can't work out why you did it, what you had against Rollo and his garden. You didn't even go to his school. Do you know who he is?'

'That gardening guy on the radio,' Fabrice said.

Bruno felt a wave of relief. At last he'd broken his silence; it should be easier now. 'So why did you do it? Why risk your job, your freedom?'

'I was told . . . I was asked to do it, like a favour.'

Bruno felt even more relief; he had an admission. 'Who asked you to do it?'

Fabrice shook his head and refused to say another word. Bruno felt more baffled than frustrated until he finally went outside to phone Sergeant Jules at the Gendarmerie to say he'd be bringing Fabrice to spend the day in the cells while the petty charge was filed. Bruno could almost hear Jules's surprise down the phone but he agreed to take a DNA swab. He and Bruno both knew that the swab would never be examined. Police budgets didn't stretch to a full DNA test on something as minor as this.

Bruno felt rather ashamed of himself as he informed the estate office manager that Fabrice was being taken into *garde à vue* in an inquiry over false statements and then set off to drive Fabrice to St Denis. His interrogator's tricks had not worked, his threats were going to prove empty and he still had no idea what lay behind the destruction of Rollo's garden. Who could be the person for whom Fabrice was doing the favour? It had to be someone or some group in a position to reward Fabrice very handsomely indeed or to punish him with something greater than Bruno's threat of

228

prison. It could be a close member of Fabrice's family or perhaps someone he loved.

Once he had started, Bruno knew he had to carry through this charade with Fabrice and marched him into the Gendarmerie to be processed. Sergeant Jules solemnly entered Fabrice's details in the big day book, gave him the usual warnings and told him of his rights. Fabrice's belt and boot-laces were confiscated, his fingerprints and a mouth swab taken, and then he was led downstairs. Bruno tried one last time to get Fabrice to talk but he just shook his head stubbornly, sat on the cell bench and lowered his head to stare at his laceless boots.

As Bruno turned to go, Fabrice asked, 'When do I get my phone call? The gendarme upstairs said I had a right to see a lawyer and to telephone someone. When does that happen?'

'As soon as the desk sergeant has a free moment. I'll tell him you asked. Anything else?'

Fabrice shook his head and Bruno left, the cell door locking itself automatically behind him. Upstairs, he checked the *annuaire* for the number of the dentist's surgery in Lalinde, called and spoke to Véronique, who confirmed that she had indeed spent Wednesday evening at a family celebration. She'd not seen Fabrice since the previous weekend and added that she didn't intend to see him again.

'Is he in trouble again?' she asked, not sounding too concerned about the answer.

'Just a routine enquiry,' Bruno replied.

Bruno waited in a side room until Fabrice had been allowed to make his call and been taken back to his cell. Bruno dialled the code that brought up the last number called on the Gendarmerie phone. It seemed familiar. He checked the special directory that indentified subscribers by their number and found that Fabrice had called the office at the Patriarch's vineyard, even though he knew Bruno had already informed them of his arrest. Why on earth would Fabrice do that? And why had Madeleine put in a good word for him to join the Lalinde club? He'd have to call her.

'You'll be interested in this,' said Sergeant Jules. 'I called it up on the computer after you phoned.' He handed Bruno a printout of Fabrice's criminal record. He had done a stint in juvenile reform school for repeated car theft, one six-month suspension for drunken driving and he was still serving out a year of probation for putting another man in hospital in a fight in a Bergerac bar.

'Nasty young bugger,' said Jules. 'He belongs inside if you ask me so we'll keep him here over-night. I heard what happened to Rollo's garden. Do you reckon Fabrice was behind that?'

Bruno nodded. 'I'm surprised it was just proba-tion with a record like that.'

Jules pointed to the name of the gendarme who'd arrested Fabrice after the bar fight. 'You know Ducas. He and Fabrice played rugby together so he probably went easy on him in the report.'

★   ★   ★

230

As he climbed the stairs in the Mairie, heading for his office, Bruno's mobile began to vibrate. He looked at the screen and saw it was Pamela calling.

'Jack Crimson's daughter has arrived,' she began in a businesslike tone that served to remind him of the change in their relationship. 'We're all going out to the riding school this afternoon to look it over if you'd like to join us, but in any event you're invited to join us for dinner at Jack's house this evening. Jack particularly asked that you come; I think he wants to show off his daughter's cooking. He's obviously very proud of her. Her children are still back in London with the other grandparents.'

'Have you decided whether you want to go ahead?' he asked.

'She hasn't seen the place yet but even if she doesn't like it, I think I might buy it anyway. There's some rather good furniture in the big house and a lovely antique armoire in the barn so I might offer to buy, furniture included. The barn is full of useful stuff, garden furniture, some of those handsome old-fashioned canvas loungers for the pool. I've been through the books and even being badly run it was making a modest profit. I know I can do better.'

Bruno didn't doubt it. Even beyond his affection for her, he had a firm appreciation of Pamela's talents. And it would be interesting to see Jack in the company of his daughter. One of the many things he had learned in his decade as a policeman was that one can learn a great deal about a person from the way they relate to their grown-up children.

But one of her remarks had reminded Bruno of something. She had mentioned a canvas lounger, which reminded him of the dimly lit room in the Patriarch's chateau where Gilbert had died. Some of his vomit had pooled on the lounger. If he could get that analysed, thought Bruno, it might tell us something. He drove back to the Patriarch's estate and was greeted at the main door by the house-keeper, who noted his uniform but also remembered him from the party. She raised no objection when he said he needed to visit again the room where Gilbert had died. She led the way and when his eyes had grown accustomed to the gloom inside, he looked around the half-familiar room but saw no lounger. He asked if it had been moved.

'We burned it, she said. 'It was ruined anyway, even without the fact that he'd died on it.'

'Did you do that?'

'No, the new gamekeeper did it earlier this week. I think Victor may have told him to do so. Fabrice just said it was someone in the family.'

CHAPTER 21

Bruno was so used to wearing uniform, or disguising it slightly by putting a civilian jacket over his dark-blue trousers and light-blue shirt, that he felt slightly odd in his khaki slacks and checked shirt and blazer as he presented himself at Crimson's front door just after seven. Wearing brown leather loafers rather than the customary black boots, his feet felt unusually light. In one hand he carried a jar of his home-made raspberry jam and in the other a bottle of his *vin de noix*. The door was opened by a plump, pretty woman in her early thirties with a hesitant smile and something in her eyes that suggested she felt bruised by life. Her dark-brown hair fell in natural curls to her shoulders and over a simple dress of light blue she was wearing a *Vins de Bergerac* apron that Crimson must have found in the wine shop.

She held out her hand to greet him and asked, 'Are you Monsieur Bruno?' She spoke in that stolid, English-accented French that made native speakers wonder if the English had any ear for rhythm or the musical tones of the French language. 'I'm Miranda and you're very welcome. Do come in.

I have to thank you for getting my father's paint-ings and furniture back after the burglary.'

'I think he was especially pleased that we were able to recover most of the wine that was stolen,' Bruno said with a smile. He kept hold of her hand and kissed her lightly on each cheek before releasing it. She may have wanted to maintain the ridiculous English habit that men and women should just shake hands as if they were the same sex, but Crimson's daughter was in the Périgord now. 'And as someone who's sometimes allowed to share his wines, I was almost as pleased as your father.'

Looking slightly flustered at being kissed, she thanked him for the jam and bottle and led him through the house to the terrace, where her father and Pamela were watching the sunset and drinking Scotch. A thin file of papers that looked like accounts was open before Crimson and in front of Pamela was one of the notebooks she liked to use. It was open at a page filled with figures and notes in her neat handwriting. Bruno felt a flash of something that might have been jealousy at this new intimacy between Crimson and the woman whose bed Bruno had been sharing for the past year. Their affair might be over, thought Bruno, but some of the ties that accompanied it never really go away. Miranda excused herself to return to the kitchen.

'Are you going to buy the riding school?' he asked, careful to kiss Pamela on the cheeks rather than her lips. He shook hands with Crimson, who poured him a generous helping of Balvenie and left Bruno to add a splash of water.

'Well, we're making an offer,' said Crimson. 'If she accepts it, we're going to divide the property. Pamela buys the main house and the *gîtes* and the garden and runs them separately, and then we all jointly buy the riding school and stables. And the paddock, of course.'

'If this all goes ahead, Fabiola and Gilles are going to buy my property,' said Pamela. 'They'll live in my house and rent out the *gîtes* just like I do. Fabiola continues working at the clinic and Gilles writes his books and runs the *gîtes*. Fabiola likes riding my old mare so Victoria goes with the deal, and Gilles will be our first new pupil at the riding school.

'We're a bit on tenterhooks,' she added. 'Marguerite said she'd call us this evening to let us know if she accepts our offer. Jack has a bottle of champagne in the fridge so we can celebrate if she says yes.'

'In that case we must talk of something else until she calls,' said Bruno.

'That's good, because I've just remembered something,' Crimson said. 'When you were asking about Gilbert, it had slipped my mind. A waiter came up to us with a tray that had a large glass of orange juice, murmured something to Gilbert and he took it. He hadn't finished his champagne, I recall, hardly even sipped it. But he gave it to the waiter.'

'One of the waiters dressed in air force uniform?' Bruno asked.

'That's right. I'd assumed Gilbert had asked for it, so he wouldn't be tempted to drink too much and disgrace himself.'

'And that was all?' Bruno asked, and he felt a sudden frisson as he realized that Crimson may have had the opportunity to slip something into Gilbert's drink. And who knew what motives might have been in play among old acquaintances in that strange, warped world of Cold War intelligence? It was an uncomfortable thought to nurture while enjoying the man's hospitality but Bruno realized that if his hunch about Gilbert's death was correct then Crimson had just become a suspect.

'Then your chum the Brigadier joined us and Gilbert sort of drifted away, you know how it is at parties,' Crimson said. 'I never saw him again.'

The doorbell rang and Fabiola and Gilles were shown in by Miranda and moments later Pamela's mobile rang. She rose and turned away to answer it, gesturing at them with her fingers crossed for luck, and then turned back with a grin on her face and the crossed fingers had become a thumbs-up.

'That's wonderful, Marguerite,' she said into the phone. 'We'll meet at the *notaire*'s tomorrow to sign the initial contract.' She rang off and beamed at them as she declared, 'Time to open that champagne: we've got it!'

Fabiola and Gilles kissed one another, announcing

that this meant they were now to become joint householders of Pamela's property, Pamela kissed Miranda as Crimson went for the champagne and then once it was poured and the glasses were clinked, toasts were proposed and everyone kissed everyone else.

Miranda led them into the dining room and Bruno was able to appreciate the furniture and paintings he had recovered after Crimson's burglary. On the longest wall were two large oil paintings, each of food. One showed birds and animals after a hunt, game birds, duck and hares all displayed on a wooden table, with two deer hanging from pegs in a stone wall behind them. The other painting showed fruit and vegetables heaped up in generous bounty on what looked to be the same wooden table, an old-fashioned bulbous wine bottle and small glass in the foreground. Bruno recalled the inventory Crimson had made of the stolen goods. The two paintings were French, eighteenth century. He'd forgotten the name of the artist but they had been valued at 60,000 euros.

On the wall to Bruno's right was a nineteenth-century English oil painting of a landscape with hills and sheep and a sky with a mixture of cloud and light that Bruno thought was wonderful. Again he had forgotten the artist's name but recalled that it had been valued at 30,000 euros. The painting stood above a handsome chest of drawers in dark wood that was also valuable, although Bruno had forgotten how much it was supposed to be worth.

The antique silver cutlery at the place settings had been valued at 12,000 and Bruno knew the stolen wine was worth even more.

All this meant a degree of wealth that Bruno could hardly begin to comprehend. But this was not like the Red Countess's home, where Bruno had somehow expected the furniture and possessions that went with the chateau's history and her aristocratic heritage. Crimson's was a different kind of comfort, more modest and far more personal, reflecting Crimson's own taste as a collector rather than the Countess's inheritance from centuries of noble forebears. Bruno recalled Crimson telling him that he'd been most distressed by the theft of two charming English watercolours that he and his wife had bought one another early in their marriage.

The arrival of Miranda with the soup tureen brought Bruno out of his reverie; she had evidently been cooking for hours. They began with a carrot soup flavoured with ginger and the main course was a dish that Bruno recognized as one of Pamela's favourites: a fish pie topped with mashed potato and dusted with cheese to make a crisp, brown *gratin*. Miranda had used salmon where Pamela made it with cod, but they both used smoked mackerel, shrimps and slices of hard-boiled egg atop the creamy sauce. Bruno thought he detected a pleasing hint of nutmeg in the sauce that he didn't recall Pamela ever using. Miranda had cooked *petits pois* to accompany it and her father served a dry white Bergerac from Chateau Thénac.

Toasts were drunk to Miranda and her cooking. The salad and cheese were served and then Crimson brought a bottle of Clos l'Envège Monbazillac to accompany what he described as his favourite dessert. Miranda brought out what looked at first like a cream cake, but on close examination Bruno saw it was a large and almost brown meringue, sliced in half and filled with cream and raspberries. Only as he took his first mouthful did he realize that the meringue had been flavoured with hazelnuts.

'This is wonderful,' he told Miranda, who blushed prettily as the rest of the table chorused their praise. 'I'd very much like to have the recipe,' he added.

Bruno knew only that Crimson's daughter had just gone through a difficult divorce and for the past several years she had known her father as a widower. Seeing him in this quite different environment, with new friends, speaking a different language and embarking on a new business venture, must be something of a shock to her. And he suspected she'd felt under a certain pressure when her father had asked her to produce a dinner for French guests in the culinary heartland of France.

Crimson lifted the bottle to pour out more Monbazillac and asked Bruno whether he expected any further developments over Gilbert's death. Bruno put his hand over his glass and shook his head. This wasn't something he wanted to discuss with Gilles present. Good friend though he was, Gilles was also a journalist, still with some freelance connection to *Paris Match* although he'd accepted the magazine's buyout when he'd got his first book contract.

Crimson seemed to understand Bruno's reluctance. He turned to Gilles and asked, 'Can we go completely off the record here?' Gilles nodded and said he was off duty.

'Come on, Bruno, tell us what you can,' Crimson said. 'You know Gilbert was a friend of mine. Some of your questions left me wondering if there was something suspicious about the way he died.'

'We'll have to wait for the reading of the will,' Bruno said, wondering if Crimson's determination to probe was itself suspicious. 'That sometimes throws up surprises. But now that he's been cremated, we'll probably never know.'

'So it could have been a perfect crime,' Crimson said. 'An alcoholic dies in a drunken stupor. End of story.'

Bruno shrugged. 'Who had a motive to kill him? And why would they need to take the risk of murdering him when Gilbert was already killing himself with the booze.'

'Well, a bit of history goes with him,' said Crimson. 'He probably knew better than any other non-Russian why that coup against Gorbachev failed, and how Gorbachev was so easily replaced by Yeltsin. I remember him telling me on the first day that the coup was doomed, that maybe the generals agreed to overthrow Gorbachev but the captains and majors didn't and nor did the troops.'

'He was that close to the military?' Bruno asked.

'Very much so. When he wasn't at the Yeltsin White House, the Russian parliament building, he was at the Defence Ministry on the Frunze Embankment. He told me that orders from the generals were piling up unsent; the signallers just refused to send them, screwed up the coding and disabled their teleprinters.'

'Is that widely known these days?' Gilles asked.

'Yes, there were stories about it in the Russian media after the coup failed. Old Marshal Akhromeyev and his generals were drafting orders but nothing happened. I was able to tip off London that the coup might not be a sure thing but poor Gilbert had trouble with his Ambassador, who simply refused to believe him. I heard they had a screaming match in the Ambassador's study and Gilbert was thrown out of the Embassy and the diplomats tried to get Paris to recall him. Since he was a military attaché, under Defence Ministry orders, the diplomats couldn't do it. And within a couple of days Gilbert was proved right, of course.'

'It's almost unbelievable that a French officer could get into the Soviet Defence Ministry in the middle of a *coup d'état*,' said Gilles. Picking up on his tone, Fabiola turned to look at him and the three women stopped their conversation to listen.

'Quite right, but Gilbert had these amazing contacts and, above all, by day two of the coup he was going in and out with the Patriarch. The

241

old man had just flown in from Paris at Mitterrand's request. His was one of the few planes they allowed into Soviet airspace. The Patriarch and Akhromeyev were old friends and the Marshal wanted a private channel to the Western leaders, just to reassure them that the coup was a purely internal matter and there'd be no need for any military alerts. Akhromeyev arranged for the Patriarch to fly into one of the military bases and they took him to Moscow by chopper.'

'I don't think that is publicly known,' said Gilles. 'I knew he'd acted as de Gaulle's private emissary to the Kremlin but not that he did the same for Mitterrand, nor that he was in touch with the coup leaders.'

'He must have been one of the last people to see Akhromeyev alive. The old man killed himself when it was clear the coup had failed.' Crimson sipped at his Monbazillac. 'It's all history now, a long time ago. And I've just remembered something one of our own generals told me after he'd had a meeting with Akhromeyev. The fellow had two words of English, both of them from the Second World War. The first was Spam, that tinned American meat, and the second was Studebaker, the name of an American truck. Akhromeyev said the Red Army could never have got to Berlin without the Spam to eat and the Studebakers to bring up the troops and the supplies. He talked of that Spam with such nostalgia that we arranged to bring him in some cans of the stuff. He'd open one and eat it straight away.'

'It sounds like Proust's madeleine, that little cake brought back all his memories of childhood when he tasted it,' said Miranda. 'And now, who would like coffee?'

'Do you think the Patriarch might give me an interview?' Gilles asked. 'A last, unwritten chapter of the French role in ending the Cold War.'

'You can always ask,' said Crimson, rising from the table and inviting them to take their coffee in the sitting room.

Bruno followed, wondering at his growing suspicion of Crimson, a man he'd thought of as a friend. It was all circumstantial, of course, but if he was right in thinking Gilbert's death had not been natural, the roots of his death most likely went back to his years in Moscow, a period in which Crimson had been closely involved. And Crimson had not only had the opportunity to spike Gilbert's drink, he'd also given Gilbert the very flask from which the doomed Colonel had taken his final drink. Had it really been the original flask from twenty years ago? Or had Crimson obtained a new one, just the same, to fill with super-proof vodka and give to Gilbert at the Patriarch's party?

But what would his motive have been for Gilbert's death? Were there still any secrets of importance from that Moscow of two decades ago? Or was the motive connected to Gilbert's trust fund? If so, would Crimson be among those who might know of the fund's existence?

CHAPTER 22

Imogène looked beatifically happy, sitting beside the animal cages at the rear of the veterinary clinic, feeding the fawn on her lap from a baby's bottle. She looked up as Bruno entered and smiled a welcome which broadened when she saw Balzac potter in behind his master, sniffing curiously at the mingled scents of deer, dog and cat, disinfectant and fresh straw that filled the long room. Then Balzac saw the fawn and stopped, adopting the classic stance, one paw raised, head cocked, tail straight out and flat behind him, a pose he'd inherited from generations of bassets.

'Some good news,' Bruno said, crouching to stroke Balzac's neck and hold his collar. He didn't want his dog leaping playfully at the fawn and terrifying it. Bruno usually listened to the local radio news bulletin as he did his early-morning exercise and there had been two items of interest. The first was that Peyrefitte's son had been declared out of danger and transferred from the intensive care unit. The second was that the Procureur had decided not to bring criminal charges against Imogène. He'd called Raquelle on her mobile and she told him he'd find Imogène at the clinic.

'I think that means you can go back to your home and resume your life,' said Bruno. He did not mention the still pending threat of a private lawsuit by Peyrefitte, hoping that time and the need to help his children move on from the tragedy might soften Peyrefitte's anger at his loss. 'I presume you'll take the fawn with you. And this is Balzac; he's still very young, not much more than a puppy and very friendly.'

'He's a lovely dog,' said Imogène. 'I remember seeing you with your old basset in the market. Was he Balzac's father?'

Bruno shook his head. 'Balzac was a gift. If I hold him, can he come and say hello to your fawn? He's very good with other animals, often sleeps in the stable with my horse.'

Imogene nodded, slightly warily, and Bruno let Balzac creep forward, sniffing delicately until he was at Imogène's feet, his head raised to look at the fawn, which was only a little larger than him. The fawn twitched but stayed in place, apparently reassured by the shelter of Imogène's arms, and slowly turned its head to examine Balzac. The two animals looked curiously at one another and then the fawn stretched out a long neck and delicately advanced its head towards Balzac. The two noses almost touched and then, as though satisfied the dog represented no threat, the fawn curled back into Imogène's embrace. Balzac sat on the ground at her feet and continued to stare.

'Yes, I'll try to take the fawn home but only to see if she'll be accepted by some of the other deer. One or two are already back,' Imogène said. 'Raquelle drove us up to my house on the way here this morning and I was happy to see it was still standing, despite your fears. If the other deer won't take her, Raquelle says she can add her to all the other animals they have at Le Thot and I'll be able to visit her. She's been very kind, and at her suggestion I've applied for a job in the gift shop there.'

'There's some more good news,' Bruno said. The Mayor had agreed to his suggestion of a small exhibition of Imogène's local wildlife photos in the local tourist information office. There was a large room in the building that was regularly used for shows by local artists, mostly amateurs. 'So if you pick out about thirty of your best photos, we'll get them framed. You might want to get some extra prints made so you can sell them. I'll certainly want to buy one.'

'That's wonderful, but I think you're entitled to one as a gift,' Imogène replied. The bottle was empty but the deer stayed calmly in her lap as she caressed its back. 'Raquelle explained how you'd been trying to help so I'd like to say thank you and apologize for being difficult and taking all my anger and frustration out on you.'

'I'm sorry it worked out the way it did, for you

and your deer as well as for Peyrefitte and his family.' Bruno paused and looked around. 'Where is Raquelle? I thought I might find her here with you.'

'She's gone to work. I usually stay on here and help the vet by cleaning out the cages, walking the convalescent dogs and generally try to make myself useful. We picked up my car at the house so I'm independent again. That reminds me, the vet had an idea I'd like you to think about: deer whistles.'

She explained that the vet had wondered if dog whistles, which operate at a frequency too high for humans to hear, might also be used for deer. Imogène had done some research on the internet at Raquelle's house and found that they had become quite common in the United States and Scandinavia, fitted to cars so the passing airstream drove the whistle that warned deer to stay away.

'I never thought of that,' Bruno said. 'It's a great idea.' He thought of Jean-Luc who ran the metal-work class at the *collège*; maybe he could get the students to start making some of the things for sale. They couldn't be that complicated and if demand built up, it could be a useful little business for St Denis.

Back in his office, with Balzac scouting the familiar corridors of the Mairie to see which of his master's colleagues might be offering biscuits today, Bruno scanned his post and emails. There was one from the *notaire* handling Gilbert's will, saying he was having trouble contacting the various heirs and asking Bruno to call him. He tried and got a recording. He left a message and began dealing with other office work, wondering vaguely why he'd been called; *notaires* were supposed to be skilled at tracking down elusive heirs. He'd just finished drafting a note to the Mayor about Imogène's deer-whistle plan when the phone rang. Gilbert's *notaire* was on the line.

'Let's get the easy question out of the way first,' said the *notaire*. Had Bruno heard of anyone named Larignac, for whom there was a bequest? Bruno recalled the name, and told the *notaire* he'd been one of Gilbert's mechanics in the air force who had later tried to get Gilbert into Alcoholics Anonymous. Larignac had lived near Libourne and he might be able to find a phone number.

'Hold on a second.' He took from his cupboard the box in which he'd been collecting various items of potential evidence. He pulled out the plastic bag containing Gilbert's phone, a cheap model with a standard charging socket. He used his own charger and turned it on. It took a moment before the screen came to life. There was no password protecting it and he thumbed through the address book to Larignac and read out the number to the *notaire*.

'Thank you, but that's not it. The will names a woman named Nicole Larignac, not a man.'

'No number for her,' said Bruno.

'We'll put that to one side for a moment. The second one might be impossible, a Russian, Yevgeny Markovitch Garanov?'

'He had a Russian friend called Yevgeny but the other names aren't familiar. It may be the same guy.' Bruno was thinking he could easily call Yevgeny and check the surname, and it was probably listed in the phone book. He was just thumbing through it when the *notaire* spoke again.

'I believe the second name in Russian is a patronymic that indicates his father's name is Marc,' said the *notaire*.

'Marc, Marco,' said Bruno, 'that must be the Patriarch. Yevgeny is his Russian son.' He scrolled through Gilbert's contacts until he came to Garanov, Yevgeny. He gave the number to the *notaire*.

'Thank you. My last question is rather different,' the *notaire* said. 'I need some advice on a rather delicate matter. The main bequest is to a member of the Desaix family and I wrote to the person in question at the address you gave me but I've had no reply.'

'That shouldn't be a problem. Victor Desaix was his oldest friend, a man he listed as next of kin after his sister died,' Bruno said. 'Gilbert was godfather to Victor's children. I'm sure if you call the vineyard, they'll put you through to him.'

'Thank you, that's helpful, but it's also where it becomes delicate. Just one person inherits. Would Chantal Eleanor Rochechouart Desaix be one of Gilbert's godchildren?'

'She would, she's Victor's daughter. But I think he was also godfather to her brother, or half-brother, Raoul. He's Victor's son by his first marriage.'

There was nothing listed in Gilbert's phone for Chantal. There was only the vineyard number and a landline number for the Patriarch, presumably at the chateau, and separate mobile numbers for Victor and for Madeleine.

'In my experience, when one child in a family inherits but not another, problems tend to arise,' the *notaire* said.

Bruno nodded. He could see that might provoke family jealousies but that was hardly his problem, or even the *notaire*'s. He said, 'I understood that it was your job simply to ensure the will is carried out according to the intentions of the deceased.'

'That's right, but Gilbert was a friend from childhood so you'll understand that I don't want to cause any embarrassment. And since I've heard from his bank I'm aware that there's a surprisingly large sum involved in his trust fund, or rather funds.'

'Really? How much?'

'I can't say. But it's a lot more than I've ever handled before. So I'd like you to do me a favour, or at least a service. I'm empowered to employ private investigators to trace beneficiaries to an estate so might I hire you to find this Nicole Larignac and to put me in touch with this Chantal girl? It's all perfectly legal, I've used local policemen

250

before on other enquiries. You'd be paid at the same rate as a *huissier*, a court bailiff, thirty-six euros an hour. I presume you'd have to go to Libourne to track down Nicole Larignac, and we'd pay the standard rates for mileage. For a day's work you could be picking up three hundred euros or so.'

'Not bad,' said Bruno, thinking that he'd be able to treat Pamela to dinner at the Vieux Logis, except that she'd probably see such an invitation as an attempt to worm his way back into her bed. It should be enough for him to go up to Paris for the next two rugby internationals, or even fly over to Twickenham to see France play England. 'I'll just check with the Mayor that he has no objections and call you back.'

The Mayor gave his approval, saying that he might well join Bruno on a weekend jaunt to Twickenham. 'And given all the unpaid overtime you do, you needn't wait until your day off,' the Mayor added.

Bruno told the *notaire* that he'd start right away, and asked the *notaire* to fax him a letter authorizing Bruno to make enquiries on his behalf. He began by calling the number listed for Larignac on Gilbert's phone but it had been disconnected. Then he called a colleague from the Police Municipale in Libourne. There was no Larignac in the current *annuaire*, Bruno was told, but a Laurent Larignac had been listed at a Libourne address two years earlier and another policeman lived on the same street.

Bruno was given the policeman's name and number and called him, only to learn that Laurent Larignac had died over a year ago and his wife, Nicole, had moved to Bordeaux to be nearer her daughter and grandchildren in a suburb called Talence. Directory enquiries had no listing for a Larignac in Talence, which was often the case nowadays, with most people now using mobile phones. Bruno called the Mairie in Talence, introduced himself and asked for a check of the electoral register and failing that of the register for *taxe d'habitation*. They promised to call him back. He checked his fax machine: the *notaire*'s letter had arrived, naming Bruno as his legal representative 'in the matter of the last will and testament of Colonel Gilbert Clamartin'. That would do.

He tried phoning Chantal at the vineyard, only to be told she was back in Bordeaux at the university. Marie-Françoise was also at the university so he called her mobile and got the recording telling him to leave a message. He did so and also texted her, saying he'd have to be in Bordeaux shortly and needed to see Chantal on a legal matter. He checked his watch. He could be in Bordeaux before lunch if he took the autoroute. Needing to check how and why Fabrice had been hired, he called the vineyard, asking for Victor or Madeleine, but neither was there. He left messages, and then rang Sergeant Jules at the Gendarmerie telling him to let Fabrice go but caution him that the file was going to the Procureur and he could expect to be called back for further questioning. Maybe a night in the cells would have taught him a lesson.

The Talence Mairie rang him back with an address for Nicole Larignac. Bruno collected Balzac, knowing there was no better introduction than to be accompanied by a friendly young basset hound, and set off on the road that led to Périgueux and the autoroute. Not for the first time, Bruno was struck by the suburban nature of so much of the Bordeaux wine industry. The vineyards were tucked in between houses and hospitals, and the great estate buildings and chateaux of legendary wines like Haut-Brion and Pape Clément were surrounded by bungalows and small family homes. He found Avenue Candau just off the vineyard-lined road of Mission Haut-Brion and parked outside the pleasant two-storey house that he'd been given as Nicole Larignac's address. Balzac investigated the children's toys in a sandpit in the garden. The door was opened by a handsome woman who looked to be in her fifties with lively blue eyes and blonde streaks in her grey hair. She was wearing jeans, ballet shoes and a black sweat-shirt that did little to conceal a trim and shapely figure. A toddler crawled at her heels, erupting in squeaks of delight at seeing Balzac and racing forward to greet him faster than the woman could grab the child.

'Madame Larignac? Nicole?' Bruno asked, and scooped up the toddler to hand to her before he introduced himself and his dog and stated his business. He showed her the *notaire*'s letter and was invited in for coffee.

'We had a basset when I was a girl,' Nicole said, leading the way into the kitchen and plugging in an electric kettle. She pulled a cafétière from the draining board and filled it with three generous spoons of Ethiopian coffee with a fair trade logo. 'Ours was called Hubert and I remember him being very patient with me and my brothers and sisters, whatever devilment we got up to. Do you think little Patrice will test Balzac's patience?' She put the child down and much to the dog's pleasure he immediately began fondling Balzac's long, velvety ears.

'So Gilbert is dead,' she said, shrugging, not seeming to be greatly moved by the news. 'He didn't long outlive my Laurent. Cirrhosis of the liver was it, like Laurent?'

'He died in his sleep,' said Bruno, diplomatically. 'Would you like to call the *notaire*? He wants to make arrangements for the reading of the will.' He offered his phone but she waved it aside.

'I wouldn't have thought Gilbert would leave much,' Nicole said. 'At least Laurent went on the wagon from time to time. He managed five years one time, three years another, thanks to AA and his job at the airport. I'd have left him otherwise. But Gilbert never seemed to want to stop drinking, however much Laurent tried to persuade him.'

'Did you know him well?'

'That would be telling,' she replied with a playful

smile and looked away, staring through the kitchen window with a fond expression, as though recalling happy if private memories. Bruno thought she must have been a very lovely woman when Gilbert had known her. Nicole was still attractive and she knew it. She put cups and saucers and coffee onto a tray and a jar of honey and handed the tray to Bruno. 'Put it down in the main room, on your left. I'll bring the coffee.'

'I take it Patrice is your grandson,' Bruno said when they were settled on two armchairs that faced each other across the coffee table. On top of the table lay an open magazine about yoga; perhaps that was how Nicole stayed trim. The room was painted white, the furniture was modern and a huge photograph of the New York skyline at dusk dominated the main wall.

'Yes, he's my son's boy. Like his dad, my son was a mechanic in the air force and now works for Air France; so does Patrice's mum, at the airport. I suppose I'd better call the lawyer.'

Bruno called the number, handed her his mobile and sipped at his coffee as she spoke. She gave the *notaire* her own address and mobile number and asked if it would be necessary for her to make the long trip to the Auvergne for the reading of the will. She seemed relieved to hear that it would not and the lawyer could send her a copy of the will once it was done.

Bruno finished his coffee, thanked her and rose to go. 'You might remember Gilbert's fellow pilot

Victor. I think he might be at the reading,' he said.

'Can't say I much want to see him again. Gilbert was twice the man and ten times the pilot that poor Victor was, always living in the shadow of his famous dad. If not for Gilbert, Laurent doubted whether Victor would have made it through training school. How is he, anyway? How's that second marriage of his turning out?'

'He looked after Gilbert for the past few years and was very upset when he died. I think Victor's doing fine, producing some good wines at his vineyard, and his wife seems bent on becoming a politician,' said Bruno. 'He has two fine kids, one from each marriage.'

'I wonder if they take after him,' said Nicole, almost slyly, as Bruno extracted Balzac from Patrice's embrace. Bruno gave a neutral nod and steered Balzac out of the door. 'Sometimes I can still see something of Gilbert in Patrice. What a waste the booze made of a lovely man. That's why I never touch the stuff myself.'

Bruno absorbed that news, which explained why Gilbert had wanted to leave her the money, and gestured at the nearby vineyards.

'Not even the Haut-Brion they make round here?'

'Not even that,' she said. 'Thanks for coming, and for bringing the dog.'

CHAPTER 23

Marie-Françoise had texted Bruno a reply, saying they'd meet him for lunch at a bistro in Pessac called the Boeuf sur le Toit; it was opposite the cinema, he couldn't miss it. On the way there he was again struck by the way the vineyards that produced the lovely Pessac-Léognan were squeezed between suburban settlements. Domestic gardens covered in lawns and cheap swimming pools must be taking up land that could produce grand vintages. Marie-Françoise was at the Montaigne University, an arm of the much larger Bordeaux university system which specialized in the humanities, while Chantal was studying wine at the Segalen University. The two girls shared an apartment in Pessac, and arrived together on bicycles while Bruno was enjoying a *citron pressé* on the terrace in front of the bistro.

Each one was wearing jeans and a sweatshirt. They removed their helmets and shook their heads, laughing as they used fingers to fluff out their long hair and looking ridiculously young. Feeling his age at the sight of them, Bruno rose to greet them, and after studying the menu scrawled on a blackboard they each ordered the *plat du jour* of *bifteck-frites* with a green salad and a glass of Pessac-Léognan.

'It's about your godfather, Gilbert,' Bruno began, and went on to explain the *notaire*'s wish to contact her directly without alerting the rest of the family. Chantal looked stunned, unable to believe that Gilbert had anything worth leaving and even more surprised that it all went to her rather than being shared with her brother. Bruno used his mobile to call the *notaire* once more and handed it to Chantal. After listening for some moments, she pulled a diary from her backpack and suggested the following Monday, when she had no lectures. She looked at Bruno.

'He wants to know if you can escort me up to this place at Riom-ès-Montagne on Monday. I'll get a train to Brive and you could pick me up and drive on from there. Is that all right with you?'

She handed Bruno the phone and the *notaire* told him, 'I don't want to impose on you but there's something that I think you need to see. It would be good if you could come.'

Bruno agreed and closed his phone. Marie-Françoise was huddled over her smart phone. She looked up and said, 'I'm just checking the train schedules. Here's one from Bordeaux St Jean at seven-thirty that gets to Brive just before ten, but you may have to come back from Périgueux.'

'I don't think I want his money,' said Chantal when their food arrived. 'I feel guilty about it. I

258

wasn't very nice to him in the last few years; he always seemed to be drunk. He was different before.'

'How do you mean?' asked Marie-Françoise. 'He wasn't drinking then?'

'He stopped drinking whenever it was time for my treat, the little trips he'd take me on. You know I was sent to boarding school in England when I was twelve, so I'd be fluent in the language? On the first half-term holiday, he took me to London to see all the sights. And then the next time, he took me to Venice, and after that it was Barcelona, then Amsterdam and Florence. And he never touched a drop, just took me to the museums and the sights and good restaurants and treated me like a princess. I adored him then, but then when I came back to the *lycée* and lived at home, seeing him in that grim little cottage and drinking, it became awful for us both, humiliating for him.'

'You have to take the money but you don't have to keep it,' said Bruno, not looking up from the steak on his plate, asking himself why Gilbert would have left everything to this one of his godchildren. Maybe he felt close to her, but there was another, more likely reason. He looked up at her but could see no apparent physical resemblance to Gilbert. It might be useful to check her DNA. He was pondering whether to take away her empty glass or her napkin after the meal when Chantal sneezed into a tissue and tossed it into an empty ashtray. That would do.

'Do what you like with the money,' he said. 'Buy your own vineyard, give it to the poor or to a decent charity. There's a woman in St Denis trying to raise money for a wildlife refuge. Or start your own business, go travelling. Your godfather has given you the freedom to choose. Think of him kindly, I think he earned that money in a very hard way.'

'What do you mean?' Chantal asked, her tone suggesting a challenge rather than a question.

'I'm pretty sure the money was his pension from the intelligence services for the work he did in Moscow during the Cold War. Can you imagine what that must have been like: the secrecy, the pressures, the strain?'

'But he was a diplomat. If the Russians had caught him, they'd have expelled him, not sent him to jail.'

'What about the people he worked with, the Russians who trusted him?' Bruno countered. 'He must have felt responsible for them, knowing what their fate would be if he were caught and deported. That strain must have weighed heavily on him. Isn't that why he started drinking?'

Chantal looked at him solemnly before nodding. 'I see what you mean.'

'If you think it's not fair for Raoul to have none of the money, you can always give him some,' said Marie-Françoise. 'It's not like you're trapped by this. Bruno's right; you're in charge of the money, you can do what you want with it. And it's not as though you or Raoul were poor before this.'

'In that case,' said Bruno, smiling affectionately at the two wealthy young women who could afford luxury but preferred to ride bicycles and share a student lodging, 'you can each pay for your own lunch.'

Not for the first time, Bruno wondered how his life might have been different if he'd had better schools, better teachers and a chance to go to university. It might also, he mused, have meant the chance to meet intelligent and cultured young women like Chantal and Marie-Françoise rather than the hard-faced women who hung around the bars and discos outside the military barracks where he'd spent so much of his youth. Bruno didn't regret his days in the army. He had seen a bit of the world and learned how to lead a group of tough young men and how to take care of them as well as himself. Above all, he'd learned to be self-reliant, with a good sense of his own capabilities and limitations. His education had been basic, but he'd always been curious and had discovered in himself a love of reading, histories and biographies at first, and then the classic French novels.

Women, Bruno knew, had been crucial to awakening this side of himself. Katarina, the Bosnian schoolteacher, had started him reading seriously, Isabelle had introduced him to the poems of Prévert, Pamela to horse-riding and classical music and Fabiola to the cinema. And now Florence, who

261

seemed to think it was Bruno rather than her own qualification who had arranged her teaching job at the *collège*, had encouraged him to try some books on science and the environment. His men friends had also played a role. The Mayor got him reading French history and Hubert had lent him books on wine. His German friend Horst had shared his books on archaeology, immeasurably increasing his appreciation of the wealth of prehistoric paintings and engravings in the caves of Périgord.

As he strolled back to his parked Land Rover, he considered how much he owed to his friends and how he'd changed since arriving in St Denis a decade earlier. His work here was done, Chantal and Nicole had been put in direct touch with the *notaire*, and he had some time to himself. His first action, once in his vehicle, was to label the evidence bag into which he'd put Chantal's used tissue. Then he pondered how to spend the rest of the afternoon before driving home.

He recalled that he'd never visited the contemporary art museum at the Entrepôts Lainé. Built in the 1820s as a vast warehouse for produce from France's colonies, it had been saved from demolition by a popular campaign and now housed what he'd heard was a striking collection of contemporary art. He was just studying the city map when he was interrupted by his mobile phone. It was not a number he recognized but he answered and was surprised to hear Madeleine's voice, saying she was returning his call about Fabrice.

'I'd like to talk to you about him,' said Bruno. 'He's been arrested. It looks like he was responsible for tranquillizing some wild boar and then deliberately letting them loose in a prized garden.'

'I can't meet today, I'm in Bordeaux for a tedious political meeting that lasted all morning and I have another one this evening followed by lunch in the city tomorrow. Maybe sometime tomorrow afternoon? I don't know much about Fabrice. It was my father-in-law who hired him.'

'I'm in Bordeaux myself,' he replied. 'I was about to spend an hour trying to understand modern art at the Entrepôts Lainé before driving back, but perhaps you have some time free?'

'I'm free until dinner and we keep an apartment here, overlooking the Quinconces.' That was the huge square by the river with its statue to the martyred Girondins, the moderate delegates from Bordeaux to the National Assembly whose slaughter launched the Terror that followed the Revolution of 1789. 'It might be one of the last days this year we can enjoy the sun on the balcony.'

She gave him the address and entry code for the street door and within thirty minutes he'd parked, found the place and was installed on the top-floor balcony in his shirtsleeves, a pot of fresh coffee before him. She had greeted him with a real kiss on each cheek, not the brief and contactless pout towards an ear that had become the fashion. And she'd held his hand a moment too long to lead him to the balcony.

Madeleine was barefoot, wearing white capri pants and a white blouse that set off her golden tan. Her hair had been pulled back into a loose ponytail held by a white ribbon. She gave off a faint scent of toilet soap, as if she'd showered after her lunch. Her face was free of make-up but her complexion seemed as clear and youthful as her daughter's. And yet to Bruno she was somehow more beautiful, more self-aware, with something in her eyes that spoke of lessons learned and a life that had known disappointments but still held promise.

Beside the coffee cups were two tall glasses and a bottle of mineral water. The view over the Gironde River was spectacular and the balcony was as large as the ground floor of his own home. A pair of secateurs and gardening gloves lay on the table and a bucket of weeds from the tall pots filled with red geraniums stood by the glass doors that led into the living room.

'I was catching up on the gardening,' she said. 'Thank you for saving me from that chore. You probably know more about it that I do. Do you think it's time to bring the geraniums into the conservatory?'

Madeleine pointed to the glass-covered end of the balcony where he presumed the family could enjoy the view throughout the winter. Even so casual a gesture seemed elegant and poised. She'd have made a wonderful actress, Bruno thought, suddenly recalling a film with the young Catherine Deneuve.

If anything, Madeleine was lovelier, perhaps because she had more animation or more of that toughness he'd seen as she demolished her opponent in the Bergerac debate.

'In Périgord I'd be surprised if we got any frost before December but maybe here in Bordeaux the weather is different.' Bruno felt relieved that he could focus on something as mundane as gardening. 'You need to ask a local, or call Rollo, the expert with the radio programme, the man whose garden was just destroyed.'

'Destroyed by Fabrice, you believe?' She poured the coffee and turned slightly to look at the river, giving Bruno the benefit of her classic profile.

'The evidence points that way but it will be up to the Procureur to decide whether to bring charges. I gather you got to know him through hunting, when he transferred to your club after he was asked to leave his old one. Did you know about that?'

'I heard some gossip, yes, and I know about his being banned from rugby.' She continued to gaze across the river. Was she avoiding his eyes? 'But if we banned every aggressive young man who goes a bit too far, we'd end up living in a world of wimps. You ought to hear Marco on the topic. Fabrice is a fine shot and a good hunter. Marco had been out with him and been impressed so we accepted him to the club and then gave him the job. Marco knew that Fabrice's dad had been a gamekeeper so he knew the life, and it's not easy to find decent ones these days. I think Marco was just trying to do the young man a good turn. You should ask him.'

'I shall.' He sipped his coffee, enjoying its quality, trying to suppress the image of Yevgeny's painting of Madeleine that came creeping into his head as he looked at her. 'Do you know Fabrice well?'

'We chatted a bit when he joined us and naturally we were at the occasional *casse-croûte* after a morning's hunting, and I think I recall a club dinner. But he was a bit shy at first, at least until he'd had a drink or two.'

'He was mainly hunting what, boar and deer?'

'Yes, mostly deer, from one of the hunting stands. I was only out with him once. One of the older guys had complained that Fabrice was too quick on the trigger so I went out to the stand with him. He wouldn't dare shoot before a woman.'

'Did you ever know Fabrice to use a tranquillizer gun?'

She turned back to face him, looking directly into his eyes and nodding pensively. 'Just once, on a pregnant deer with a broken leg. I wanted to save the fawn. We had to take her to the vet and the vet said it would be the best way.'

'Were you there?' He held her gaze but heard his voice sounding a little hoarse, his throat dry. He took a sip of mineral water.

'Not for that. It was a bit too heavy for me, like the boar,' she said with an expression that was half smile, half grimace.

266

'A bit heavy for me, too, on rough ground,' said Bruno, smiling. A couple of times he'd brought boar back from a kill to the trail where the trucks could come. A full-size boar could weigh well over a hundred kilos, a heavy load for two men struggling up and down slopes thick with undergrowth, the boar slung on a pole over their shoulders.

'That's why our club bought one of those new German trolleys with big wheels and a ratchet system to lift the boar clear of the ground,' she said. 'It makes hunting a lot easier.'

Bruno hadn't thought of that, hadn't even heard that such trolleys existed. That must have been what Fabrice had used to take the boar to Rollo's garden. That was the essential piece of evidence against Fabrice he needed to get the Procureur to take the case. But there was something else he had to ask.

'Fabrice told me that he was asked to attack Rollo's garden, apparently by somebody with influence over him or a hold over him, but he won't say who.' Bruno said it casually, looking for some kind of reaction. He was guessing but could think of nobody outside her family with that kind of power over the gamekeeper. So that meant Marco or Victor or Madeleine.

She stared at him levelly, her hands immobile on her coffee cup. 'Maybe his girlfriend,' she said. 'Or some close friend he wants to protect.'

Bruno nodded slowly, watching her but seeing nothing except that cool, self-confident beauty.

There was nothing more to be got from her. 'Well, thank you for your help, and for the coffee,' he said.

'You needn't rush off,' she said amiably, no sign of relief that the interview was over. 'You haven't told me what brings you to Bordeaux, nor what you thought of the debate.'

'Just tracking down a witness on another matter,' he said. 'And you don't need me to confirm that you won that debate. I hear you're now the favourite for the National Assembly seat.'

'You follow politics?' she asked, rising from her chair to go into the main room. She returned with two glasses and a bottle of Balvenie, poured two moderate drinks, splashed in some mineral water, clinked her glass against his and took a sip. Suddenly they were quite close together, each leaning forward over the small table. He felt a stab of sexual tension and found himself wondering how she coped with the impact of her looks. It must become tedious, he thought, always having this effect on men.

'Not really,' he replied. 'But enough to be curious why you decided on the National Assembly rather than the European Parliament.'

'It's a lot easier to commute to Paris than it is to Brussels, let alone Strasbourg,' she said, smiling, and then she turned the tables on him. 'I might ask you why you stay in St Denis when I hear there's a much more significant job waiting for you at the Interior Ministry in Paris.'

'Where did you hear that?' It must have come from the Brigadier, he thought, recalling that he'd been invited to the Patriarch's birthday party.

'At Marco's party. Marco asked Lannes about you, they're old friends, and I overheard the conversation.' She paused and then looked at him roguishly. 'I hadn't known you were so interesting.'

'It's very simple. I love living and working in St Denis and I don't want to move to Paris,' he said. 'I wouldn't be able to keep my dog and my horse. And I don't want to work for Général de Brigade Lannes.'

'I'm told you're wasting your talents while waiting to succeed Gérard Mangin as the next mayor of St Denis.'

Bruno chuckled. 'That's just the mayor's joke. He knows I don't have a political bone in my body except on election day and then I tend to vote one way for the presidency, another for the legislature.' He smiled broadly, teasing her. 'It's a way to keep you politicians under control.'

'Good for you, we need that sometimes,' she said and then added, her eyes twinkling at him, 'just as sometimes we all need to be a little out of control.'

What on earth did she mean by that? Bruno cast around for a safer topic to discuss. 'I very much enjoyed your wine tasting but I was really impressed by the quality of tennis played by Raoul and Chantal. I saw them when I parked and stayed to watch; they must be tournament standard.'

'You must come and join us for a doubles game at the vineyard,' she said. 'You can play with me.'

This time he was in no doubt of the double entendre in her words. Her foot was resting lightly on his beneath the table and she was leaning forward over the small table, her arms pressing her breasts together to deepen her cleavage. Somehow without his noticing she had undone another button on her blouse.

Yevgeny's portrait rushed back into his mind and he could remember the sight of her breasts and the achingly desirable length of her and the ivory skin. The expression on her face in the portrait was the same expression she was wearing now and she stretched out a hand to take his. He felt suddenly flooded, liberated by the sexual tension he had been trying to suppress. Bruno rose eagerly, helpless before this twin assault of her warm and living presence, moving into his arms, her mouth opening with soft urgency beneath his, and the surging power of the painted image becoming a glorious physical reality that was blocking out all the doubts in his mind.

CHAPTER 24

There had been no political dinner she had to attend, she told him as they lay entwined on the long couch in the living room, the twilight gathering in the eastern sky. The night was theirs, she said, and led him into the half-darkness of her bedroom. He felt at once helpless and yet hugely empowered. He had never known a lover so accomplished, so tantalizing in her shifts of mood and pace, so seductive in her murmurings and her soft laughter.

At one point she had asked if he were hungry and he was about to reply that his hunger was only for her when he realized that he felt famished. She wearing his shirt and he in a towel, they explored the kitchen. Bruno found a packet of pre-made pizza dough in the fridge, along with tomatoes, onions, cheese and *lardons*. She opened a bottle of the Réserve du Patriarche, poured each of them a glass and then stood watching him as he fried the onions and *lardons*, set the oven, grated the cheese and slipped the tomatoes into boiling water so he could remove their skins.

'It's very sexy, watching a man cook for me

before taking me back to bed,' she said. Bruno knew he'd remember every moment of this evening, every word that she spoke, every touch and gesture. The sense of hurt over Pamela that had been lurking at the back of his mind was now stilled, which made this new enchantment all the more sweet.

The evening had turned cool so she closed the door to the balcony and they sat on cushions on the floor, Madeleine curled into his arms and feeding him pizza, and he could not take his eyes from her. She ate the way she made love, with appetite, deli cacy and appreciation, suddenly overtaken by a lustful hunger as she took a deep drink of wine. Then she kissed him and let the wine trickle from her mouth into his.

He left not long before midnight, leaving her asleep, his head filled with thoughts of her as he drove back to St Denis. But some of the thoughts became questions as he played back the evening in his mind. Bruno was no fool: he knew that he had been deliberately and delightfully seduced by a woman of extraordinary skill.

But why? Was he a dalliance for an evening's amusement? Was he a potential ally to be bound to her with sweet, erotic chains? Hardly; he had little to offer her in the political world. Or was she winning his allegiance as a way to deflect his probing questions about Fabrice and his scepticism over Gilbert's death? Might she already know that he was in touch with Chantal over Gilbert's will? He had no idea how close she was to Chantal, who might have phoned Madeleine to tell her everything before he arrived at her apartment.

It was one of those few moments when he cursed the way his profession had made him so cynical about people and their motives. His job required him to probe and ask questions, to seek to understand not only what had happened but why. He'd rather have spent the drive in languorous reflection on the evening's delights, remembering the shape and feel of her in his arms, the gleam of her eyes in the darkness and how she had so slowly slipped his shirt from her shoulders after they'd eaten.

But there was no escaping the nagging questions. Each memory of her triggered a demand for an explanation and sparked even more curiosity about this extraordinary family of the Patriarch into whose affairs he'd suddenly been plunged. And at the heart of everything was the Patriarch himself, his boyhood hero, suddenly taking an interest in Bruno, bringing him under his wing and offering his patronage. Again, Bruno wanted to understand why. Already, because of the *notaire*, he was trapped into a kind of deception of the family, keeping the secret of Gilbert's will and of Chantal as its sole heiress.

And what connection did Jack Crimson have to all this? And Yevgeny? So much of this affair seemed to hinge on those historic days in Moscow when the Cold War died and Gorbachev was toppled and the Patriarch's old friend Akhromeyev committed suicide once the coup had failed.

Bruno turned up the lane that led towards his cottage, knowing there would be no welcome from Balzac this night. His dog would be sleeping in Pamela's stables, tucked up in the straw in Hector's stall, and Bruno missed Balzac's familiar presence as he checked on the chicken coop and went to the edge of the woods for a farewell look at the stars. He knew that when he undressed he'd be able to smell a memory of Madeleine on his shirt and know that her scent was lingering on his body and the grip she now had on his senses. Sad, he thought, to spend an evening making love with a woman but then not to sleep with her and wake to her presence in the morning.

Suddenly he sensed something different nearby, knowing these woods and the night sounds so well that he'd been jarred into alertness. He wasn't aware of any movement and his ears had picked up no sound but then he caught it again, just the ghost of a scent, something sour and not natural. Just as he recognized it as stale tobacco, he heard the swish of movement on grass behind him and a harsh intake of breath.

Adrenaline surging through him, Bruno dropped to the ground and rolled away. He used the momentum of the roll to rise into a crouch and saw a dark and burly shape recovering from a powerful swing with some weapon that had missed its target. The figure was still off balance when

Bruno stepped forward and slammed his foot hard into the side of a leg. In the darkness, his aim was off, hitting a thigh rather than the knee, bruising his attacker but not crippling him. The weapon was being backhanded towards him now but without much force behind it as his assailant tried to recover his balance.

Bruno ducked beneath the blow and as the momentum took the man round, Bruno rose to slam a clenched fist into the side of his neck where it joined the shoulder. It should have put the man down but again he must have been off target because his attacker simply grunted, staggered and heaved his weapon clumsily up and back. There was not much force behind the blow but by chance it connected with Bruno's hip at the very point where the bullet had taken him at Sarajevo. Bruno screamed in pain, lost all restraint and using his full weight behind each fist he hammered once, twice, three times into the soft flesh of his attacker's kidneys.

The man sank to his knees and then Bruno clapped the palm of each hand simultaneously against the man's ears, forcing a concussion that should also burst the eardrums. The man fell, heavily, face down, landing so hard his head bounced against the ground and the weapon he'd been holding fell from his hands. It was a smooth and heavy piece of wood, perhaps an axe handle. Bruno picked it up, surprised by the weight, and felt along the handle until he felt the metal head of the axe itself.

The bastard had wanted to kill him!

The man was sprawled, his legs apart. Breathing hard and using the axe to brace his weakened leg, Bruno fought down the pain in his hip. He resolved, slowly and deliberately and taking his time to aim, to kick the man between his legs until his attacker screeched in pain. He couldn't do it; even with the help of the axe handle, Bruno's leg wouldn't support him. Instead he dropped to his knees, with his full weight, onto his attacker's back just below the ribs, aiming to batter the kidneys again. He felt for the man's head and found fabric, wool – and it had holes: a balaclava to hide the wearer's features. Bruno ripped it down and twisted so the wool was stretched tight around the man's neck, throttling the life out of the brute. He could feel only stubble on the man's head and at that moment he realized that his assailant was Fabrice.

A kind of sanity returning, Bruno slackened his grip on Fabrice's throat and rose, limping with the help of the axe, and staggered back to his cottage and groped for the hook behind the door where Balzac's leash hung. He took it back to the immobile Fabrice and used it to lash his hands together behind his back and then went back indoors to turn on the light and call the Gendarmerie. Yveline answered and he reported the assault and said she'd better also bring an ambulance. He had intended it for Fabrice but when he put his hand to the blazing pain in his hip, it came away bloody.

But he couldn't rest now. He took a leather belt

from his bedroom cupboard and went back outside, turning on the porch light, and tied Fabrice's ankles together. He found a plastic bag in his kitchen and used it to cover the head of the axe, smeared with his own blood. No clever defence lawyer would dare claim Bruno had used unreasonable force against an attacker who had slashed him with an axe. He pulled down his trousers and used his phone to take a photo of his bloodied hip, then took another of Fabrice and of the makeshift restraints he'd used to immobilize him.

Yveline and Sergeant Jules from the gendarmes were the first to arrive, followed immediately by the *pompiers* with their floodlights blazing. Ahmed was driving and Albert was first down from the cab with the medical box. He headed straight for Bruno, who was leaning against his door frame, his trousers still down around his thighs and the blood on his hip black in the harsh lights.

'I'm okay,' Bruno grunted. Now that the shock was setting in he could speak only in brief phrases, his breath too short for anything longer. 'Check out Fabrice. I had to hurt him. Eardrums. Kidneys. Had to stop him. He attacked me with axe. My blood's on it.'

The last thing Bruno heard as he crumpled to the ground was the double snick of Yveline's handcuffs going around Fabrice's wrists.

Later, Bruno was slowly aware of a different kind of light, the smell of antiseptic, the sound of running water. He could see white walls and there was an intravenous drip in his arm.

'You have the luck of the devil, Bruno,' said Fabiola's voice from somewhere outside his field of vision. 'Six stitches and a massive bruise. The X-ray shows no damage to your pelvis. He must have got you with the blunt end of the axe.'

She loomed into sight, looking down at him severely. 'Your attacker is being taken to Périgueux. We can't deal with kidney damage here. And what on earth did you do to his eardrums?'

He tried to speak but only a croak emerged. Fabiola lifted his head and put a plastic straw in his mouth. He sucked on it and tasted something hot, sweet and bitter at the same time. It was comforting.

'Hot lemon juice mixed with honey,' she said. 'Don't talk, go back to sleep. You'll be fine.'

When Bruno woke again, only a dim light was on and he was alone. On the cupboard beside the bed was a plastic cup with a straw. He sucked on it and tasted the same mixture. It was cold, sticky but still good. Only a dull ache came from his hip so he knew he must have been given some kind of painkiller. He fumbled for a light switch, blinked against the subsequent fluorescent glare and then rolled down the bedclothes and lifted the smock to see the damage. There was no bandage, simply three broad strips of sticking plaster in the shape of an H just below the hip bone holding down a gauze dressing, and a bright purple bruise that spread from the middle of his thigh up to his ribs. He looked at the bag feeding the drip in his arm: saline solution. He tried moving his leg. It was stiff, but it worked. The knee bent, the foot swivelled and he could wiggle his toes.

Leaning against the chair beside the bed was a pair of crutches, which he assumed had been left ready for him. He levered himself to try and sit upright, felt dizzy and was aware of the stitches pulling. His eyes felt heavy so he let his head fall back onto the pillow, turned out the light and slept again.

He knew that he was dreaming. He was in a gallery looking at canvases of Madeleine, now naked in Yevgeny's portrait, now speaking in the Bergerac debate, now gazing across the river from her balcony in Bordeaux, now walking away from him at the Patriarch's party with Chantal and Marie-Françoise at her side. He knew Madeleine was always on display, invariably and deliberately elegant. He had an insight that in his dream he felt was so important that he must engrave it on his memory: that she never moved as other people move but adopted one studied pose after another, as though expecting each moment and each expression to be immortalized by some artist fortunate enough to be granted the privilege. Satisfied with this, he sank into a deeper doze.

He woke to the smell of coffee and warm croissants and the sound of Fabiola unzipping her leather jacket, evidently having come direct from the café. She helped him to sit up and put a tray on his lap: orange juice and two croissants. She poured coffee from a cafétière, a cup for each of them, and there was another croissant and a *pain au chocolat* for her.

'I'm supposed to call Yveline at the Gendarmerie as soon as you wake up. She wants to get your statement. I imagine from the way you're wolfing your croissant that you're ready for that?'

'Sure, just hungry,' he said. He jiggled his leg and wiggled his toes. The hip was sore but bearable.

'I want you up and walking, keep your muscles moving,' Fabiola said. 'Use the crutches if you must today but you should be all right with a cane tomorrow. Your cut wasn't very deep. Yveline wants me to order you to take a week off but I know you won't do it and you're perfectly capable of light duties, office work and so on.'

Whenever a policeman had been in a fight, the unwritten rule was that injuries should be maximized, that hospital stays should be extended and time off must be taken, all in the interest of gaining public sympathy. It was a rule Bruno had never bothered to observe, partly because it was foolish but also because nobody would believe it; most of the people of St Denis had seen him limping off the rugby field on successive Sundays and still turning up for work as usual.

'I can feel you had me on a painkiller. What was it?'

'Aspirin. It's all you need. Do you want me to

help you into the shower? You'll find a plastic chair in it so you can sit down. Try not to get the spray directly onto the sticking plaster.' She handed him a towel. 'I'll tell Yveline you're ready to give your statement. Do you remember clearly what happened?'

'Clearly enough. I got home late, checked on the chickens and was then aware of someone creeping up to attack me, a big man. I fought back and then realized he had a heavy axe that could kill me if I didn't stop him.'

'That'll do. I already gave her my statement, which says your and his wounds correspond entirely with your account. Your blood on the axe should prove everything. You were lucky he hit you with the blunt side, not the sharp edge.'

There was a plastic chair in the shower but Bruno gritted his teeth and resolved not to use it. If Fabiola thought he could manage with a cane and should start walking, that was good enough for him. He ached whenever he moved and it was awkward trying to wash himself while keeping his sticking plaster dry but he managed, after a fashion.

Fabiola was waiting for him with clean clothes as he limped out and said, 'I've told Pamela you won't be riding for a few days,' she said. 'She's gone off to Bergerac with Jack Crimson.'

'That will mean some changes,' he said and started, clumsily, to dress. 'And now you and Gilles are buying Pamela's property.'

Fabiola nodded and bent down to help him put

his socks on. 'Part of the deal is that I get to keep Victoria since I like riding her and we're used to one another. But I wanted to ask if you'd mind keeping Hector in the stables with her? I don't want Victoria to get lonely. When Gilles can ride well enough to have a horse of his own we can think again.'

'Thank you, I'd like that,' Bruno said. He had already checked the trails and there was a hunter's track that covered most of the distance to the riding school, with a good gallop through a forest ride. He imagined that would become a regular morning ride.

'Pamela told me it was over between the two of you,' Fabiola said, her head bent and her face hidden as she tied his shoelaces. 'You don't seem too distressed over it.'

Bruno thought for a moment before replying. 'She made it sound like she was doing me a favour, setting me free to find a woman with whom I can settle down and raise a family.'

'Funny that you never seem to be attracted to such a woman, even though the Périgord is full of farmers' daughters just yearning to take over a homestead like yours and raise babies,' she said. 'You seem to prefer living dangerously.'

He nodded, knowing there was no malice in her words. 'I'm so pleased that things have worked out for you and Gilles. He's a good man, and a lucky one.'

'He wants to get married,' she said and before

he could offer congratulations, she added, 'but I said we should wait and see whether we decide to have children. That will be time enough to go to the Mairie. One thing I've learned from seeing the abused women in those shelters, it's not the first few happy months that tell you whether you can share your life with a man.'

Bruno nodded. He saw the sense in that.

'There are adjustments,' she said. 'I'm already having to get used to the way Gilles likes to write at night and sleep late in the morning; I like to be up and about soon after daybreak. And I've been spoiled by your and Pamela's cooking. He can barely boil an egg.'

'There's a project for me, teaching Gilles to cook,' Bruno said, smiling.

A gentle knock on the door announced Yveline, who entered with a form to take his statement. Hard on her heels trotted Balzac, who put his head onto Bruno's knee before investigating the crutches Fabiola had left. Yveline had thought to bring him and had even remembered to bring Balzac's leash, which she must have rescued after handcuffing Fabrice.

CHAPTER 25

Bruno was limping through the market with a borrowed walking stick that Balzac kept darting in to bite, assuming this was some interesting new game his master had devised. Bruno was fending off questions about his leg from shoppers and stall holders when his phone vibrated with the special tone. The green light showed it was someone on the Brigadier's secure network.

'Something important has come up so I'm on my way down to St Denis, but it's delicate so I don't want to meet at the Gendarmerie,' said the familiar brisk voice. 'I'll see you at your house some time around noon, and J-J and Prunier will be with me.'

The Brigadier ended the call, leaving Bruno baffled. The presence of J-J and Prunier meant something that involved the Police Nationale. And Bruno would only be included if it involved something or someone connected with the region around St Denis. He shrugged; no point in guessing when he'd find out soon enough. But, like any true Périgourdin, his next thought was that since they were meeting at his place at noon the laws of hospitality required that he offer them lunch. Since J-J was coming, the meal had better be hearty, but because of his leg it would have to be simple. For a working lunch, his guests would be satisfied with bread, cheese, salad and cold cuts.

It was warm enough to eat in the open air and he had lettuce and the last of the cherry tomatoes in his garden. There were cans of his home-made pâté lined up on shelves in his barn and his chickens provided plenty of eggs. He stopped at Stéphane's stall to buy some cheese, a nutty aged Cantal and some creamy Cabécous. Gabrielle at the fish stall had some trout that looked too tempting to pass by. *Mon Dieu*, these were his friends and they deserved better than cold meats. It would be little effort to barbecue them. Knowing her trout were always fresh, he bought eight. Gabrielle took one look at his limp and washed and gutted them herself.

Richard at the vegetable stall had a display of large mushrooms; Bruno bought four, along with some lemons to go with the trout. If he was making a barbecue anyway, the mushrooms would be no extra effort. At Fauquet's, he asked for a litre of their home-made vanilla ice cream to be put into an insulated bag and a large and still warm *pain*. A simple baguette would not be nearly enough for J-J's appetite. Fauquet's wife tried without success to worm out of him the cause of his limp as she drove Bruno home. Until the inquiry into Fabrice's injuries were complete, Bruno knew better than to say anything at all.

In his kitchen, with Balzac looking up at him expectantly, he took a can of *pâté de Périgueux*, a gift from his friend Maurice, the pork neatly surrounding the foie gras and interleaved with slices of black truffle. He checked that he had a bottle of Pierre Desmartis's good Monbazillac and another of his Bergerac Sec in the fridge. Balzac followed him into the *potager*, where Bruno selected his best lettuce and some tomatoes. He prepared knives and forks, plates and glasses on a tray and left it in the kitchen. His friends could carry it out. He then headed for his barn to collect a large bundle of the dried vine twigs he always used to start his barbecue. He could carry the bundle in one hand. He returned to fill a small bucket with the apple-wood charcoal he preferred for cooking fish.

He filled the trout with some crushed garlic and lemon slices. He washed the large mushrooms, put a teaspoon of white wine into the bowl of each mushroom and then inserted a *Cabécou* into each one. He prepared a bowl of honey and some crushed walnuts and then opened one of the jars of blackcurrant *compôte* he'd made when the hedge below his house had been thick with the ripe fruit. He was ready. He washed his face and hands and then jotted down some notes to himself for the briefing the Brigadier would demand.

When Bruno heard J-J's car lumbering its way up the lane, he lit the crumpled newspaper he'd stuffed beneath the grape twigs and charcoal.

Bruno had built his own barbecue of bricks and was proud of one little extra that he'd devised. The charcoal itself rested on a metal plate and he'd arranged the bricks in such a way that he could put the grill at different heights. But beneath the metal plate he'd built an extra shelf, reckoning that the heat from the metal plate above would act as an overhead grill and allow him to make a *gratin*.

'Very good of you to receive us like this, particularly after J-J told me about your injury,' said the Brigadier, handing Bruno a bottle of Balvenie. 'How's the leg?'

'I can stand, walk and cook,' he replied, and thanked the Brigadier and then J-J, who gave Bruno a bottle of Heidsieck Monopole, still chilled. He must have just bought it from the *cave* in town. Having sniffed at their shoes, Balzac realized that he'd met both men before and moved on to greet Prunier, who was looking embarrassed at arriving empty-handed.

'I've put a twenty-four-hour guard on that guy who attacked you but the medics won't let us in to question him,' said Prunier. 'J-J showed me the statement you gave to the gendarmes and we've got the axe. I already talked to the Procureur, so you don't have to worry about an inquiry into excessive force. But as of now, the Brigadier agrees that you're on medical leave until further notice.'

Prunier had arrived in his own car, a policewoman at the wheel. Bruno thanked him and suggested they might ask her to join them, thinking he could make do with a single trout.

'Better not,' said the Brigadier. 'We may need her for courier duties.'

'Champagne first, I think, then we'll eat,' said Bruno. He handed Prunier J-J's bottle and asked him to open it.

'*Mon Dieu*, it's a remarkable view you have here,' said the Brigadier, gazing out across the blackcurrant bushes and fields to the series of wooded ridges that unfolded before him, not another house in sight. '*La belle France*. I wish I woke up to a sight like this each morning.'

'I'll drink to that,' said J-J, holding out his glass to be filled and looking approvingly at the barbecue rather than at the view. 'Is this where it happened, the attack?'

'Just over there.' Bruno pointed with his walking stick. 'I was lucky I sensed something just before I heard him.'

'You're alive and he's under arrest, that's what matters. And we have other business to attend to, national business,' said the Brigadier, topping up his own glass. 'You began this particular panic, Bruno, when you told me of Colonel Clamartin's trust fund and the enquiries being made by the fiscal authorities. We blocked that, of course. But then came the big surprise.'

The trust fund had been set up to receive the pension Clamartin was due from secret funds for the work he'd done for French Intelligence while based in Moscow, the Brigadier went on. The *fisc* had asked the Interior Ministry to let them know the entire amount in the trust fund, now that his pension had been stopped and his heirs could be liable for taxes. This was not easy with a Liechtenstein trust but by chance, in the course of a separate operation, French agents had bought a CD from a disgruntled bank employee in Vaduz that carried details of many such trust accounts.

'The surprise was that Colonel Clamartin had two trust funds, not just the one we knew about,' the Brigadier went on. And every month since 1989, some unknown benefactor had been paying 3,000 US dollars a month into Clamartin's second account. The money had not been touched and the dividends simply reinvested for over two decades in the Vaduz bank's own investment funds, so Clamartin's secret account now contained well over a million dollars.

'We need to find out who was paying him, and paying him more generously than we were. The money has been routed through the Cayman Islands, the Dutch Antilles, banks in Cyprus and Dubai and all the usual shadowy places so our financial sleuths have not yet identified the donor. Above all, we need to know just what he did for them,' the Brigadier concluded.

'So that's why my suggestion that his death might not have been from natural causes has finally caught your interest,' said Bruno, realizing that the prospect of Gilbert's death turning into a murder inquiry explained the Brigadier's decision to bring Prunier and J-J. 'But first, we should eat. The barbecue's ready.'

He asked his guests to bring out the trays he'd prepared with cutlery and the *pâté de Périgueux*, the mushrooms, bread and the bottle of Monbazillac. He put the mushrooms on top of the grill, poured each of his guests a glass of the sweet, golden wine and watched the Brigadier cut fresh bread as J-J sliced the pâté.

'I've never seen this before,' said the Brigadier as J-J cut into the pâté and the foie gras and sliced truffles were revealed. They ate in appreciative silence and as the last of the pâté disappeared, Bruno took the mushrooms from atop the grill and slid them beneath the heated plate and watched until the goat cheese start to bubble. When he judged them done, he took them out, sprinkled the crushed walnuts and then drizzled honey over each one. Bruno then put the trout onto the grill and served the mushrooms. Without needing to be asked, J-J opened the bottle of Bergerac Sec.

Some thirty minutes later, the trout and cheese and salad all demolished, the wine bottles empty and the bowls of ice cream with the blackcurrant *compôte* wiped clean, Bruno served coffee. Then he handed the Brigadier the notes he had made, listing the few people beyond those at the family vineyard whom Gilbert had seen regularly or been in touch with. They were Crimson, Yevgeny, Raquelle, Nicole Larignac in Bordeaux and the *notaire* in the Auvergne. He'd added Clothilde's name, assuming from her reaction to the news of Gilbert's death that they'd had an affair at some time in the past.

He limped across to fetch the carrier bag he'd brought from his office. From it, he took out one large plastic bag that contained Marie-Françoise's shoes and several smaller evidence bags containing Chantal's tissue, Gilbert's phone, his Russian cigarette stubs, his drinking flask and its separate cap and some of the hairs Bruno had taken from the brush in Gilbert's bathroom. A final bag contained the wire samples he'd taken from Rollo's garden.

'You'd have laughed at me before this, J-J, if I'd asked you for a full forensic check but I suspect that somebody put something into Colonel Clamartin's drink at the Patriarch's birthday party,' Bruno said.

He explained that Clamartin had spilled his drink over a young woman's shoes, so the experts might be able to identify it. 'This is the flask he was drinking from when he died, and its cap, supposedly containing just vodka but I'd like to be sure. And here's a hair sample from Gilbert, along with a cigarette he smoked and his mobile phone. I'd like his DNA checked against the owner of the DNA on this tissue in the bag marked "Chantal" to see if they're related. In return, I'd be grateful if forensics could take a look at this wire from a non-related case.'

The Brigadier turned to Prunier. 'Would your driver please take these evidence bags to the forensics lab at Bergerac? Perhaps you could call them to say it's top priority and you want them to put their best people onto it.'

Bruno was struck by the speed with which Prunier rose obediently to take the evidence bags to his driver. The breadth of the Brigadier's influence never ceased to surprise him.

'Anything else?' the Brigadier asked Bruno.

'Perhaps. I'm in touch with Gilbert's *notaire* in the Auvergne, which is how I learned of the trust fund, and I'm supposed to see him tomorrow for the reading of the will. That may bring up something new. You should know that the main heir is his god-daughter, Chantal, Victor's child by his second marriage.'

'You mean the daughter of Madeleine Desaix, this politico who's headed for the National Assembly?' asked J-J.

Bruno nodded. 'She's certainly the mother of Chantal but Victor Desaix may not be the father. The most obvious reason for Gilbert to make Chantal his heir is that he's her real father. That's why I want to check her DNA against Gilbert's.

'There's more,' Bruno went on. 'I've talked to three witnesses who say that Gilbert Clamartin was not drunk just a few minutes before the fuss started. That's when I wondered if something might have been slipped into his drink. Another witness told me that just before he collapsed

Gilbert was having a brief private talk with your old colleague Jack Crimson.'

'That's interesting because earlier this week the *écouteurs* picked up something from an unregistered phone that was briefly connected to a mobile phone mast in St Denis,' said the Brigadier. 'They have automatic voice-print recognition so it was quickly identified as Crimson, telling an old colleague in London that the local police had some doubts about Clamartin's death and suggesting they might want to look into it.'

'He and Clamartin were old friends,' said Bruno. 'Crimson told me they were in Moscow together. And you told me once that men like Crimson never really retire. But I'm surprised he thought he could have a private conversation, even with an unregistered phone. It seems a little careless.'

'Too careless to be true for an old fox like him. I think Crimson was probably sending us a discreet message,' said the Brigadier. 'That's why you and I are going to see him next.'

CHAPTER 26

Armed with an authorization from the Procureur de la République in Périgueux to launch an investigation into Gilbert's death, J-J was heading to the vineyard to make a full search of Gilbert's cottage and the vineyard computer he'd used. Prunier was on the phone to France Télécom to arrange a full review of Gilbert's mobile phone records. Bruno was perched uncomfortably in the back seat of his Land Rover, Balzac nestled in the foot well below him, as the Brigadier drove to Crimson's house.

'Of course, Colonel Clamartin might have been on the British payroll,' the Brigadier said, in response to Bruno's suggestion. 'But the payments seem rather too generous for them.'

What was strange was that the payments into the second trust fund had never stopped, although Gilbert had been retired and presumably out of the intelligence business for two decades. Pensions were usually paid only to defectors who had to be resettled outside their homeland and had no other income.

'I can't think what he might have been doing

down here in the Périgord that was worth that sort of money,' the Brigadier went on. 'As far as we know, he had no access to anything secret, not even commercial technology, since he'd stopped flying. If he was working for the Russians when he was supposed to be working for us, we'll have to backtrack over a lot of stuff and take a very hard look at some of the agents he recruited.'

'He spent a fair amount of time with Yevgeny, the Patriarch's Russian son, who's an artist,' Bruno suggested. 'They spent evenings drinking together, reminiscing about Moscow. Yevgeny also inherits something in the will.'

The Brigadier nodded. 'We'll take a look at him. The Russians have a history of using artists as bankers for operational funds. Who can say if a painting is worth five hundred euros or fifty thousand? Payments can be made in cash and then the artist can pass the money on to local agents. But we need to know what would justify paying Clamartin.

'Are you comfortable back there?' He turned to glance at Bruno, his legs stretched out along the rear seat, his back jammed into the corner made by the seat and door. Bruno grunted that he was okay and the Brigadier spoke again. 'In the car on the way here, J-J was wondering if there might be any connection between all this business and the attack on you. What do you think?'

'I think it was personal,' Bruno replied. 'I pulled him in for another matter entirely, scared him into thinking he might go inside and lose his job.' Bruno explained the coincidence that Fabrice was working for the Patriarch and Victor as their gamekeeper.

'There are too many coincidences in this affair. I don't like it.' The Brigadier turned into Crimson's drive, parked and helped Bruno out.

Crimson opened his front door, eyebrows raised in surprise. 'My dear Vincent, what brings you down here? And Bruno, why on earth are you using a walking stick?'

After brief explanations and the usual pat for Balzac, Crimson led them to the terrace at the back of the house, explained that his daughter and Pamela were at the riding school, offered drinks and brought a stool for Bruno's leg. The Brigadier chose mineral water and Bruno thought it best to follow suit. Balzac trotted off to explore Crimson's garden.

'So you think Gilbert's death was unnatural?' Crimson began, using the intimate '*tu*' form. But the Brigadier held up a hand.

'That's just one part of the problem,' he said. 'We came across a secret trust fund in Liechtenstein. He'd been getting three thousand dollars a month since he left Moscow and we don't know who was paying him or why. Was it you?'

'Not as far as I know, and I probably would have known.'

'The Americans?'

'Unlikely. He'd been out of the game for over twenty years. What would he have to offer?'

'That's what we can't understand,' said the Brigadier. 'Unless he was being paid for his silence.'

Silence about what? Bruno asked himself, as he watched the interplay between the two intelligence men, one retired and the other still active. He wondered how they had come to know each other and be on first name terms. Their relationship seemed too close to be based on the usual formal liaison meetings that took place between officials.

'Is Bruno cleared for this?' Crimson asked.

'If it wasn't for Bruno, I wouldn't be here,' the Brigadier replied. 'Besides, as you know, it never happened.'

'It came damn close.'

The Brigadier turned to Bruno. 'Jack and I met in the course of an operation that was planned but never took place. It was overtaken by events. And it was probably just as well that it didn't happen. It was also an operation that involved Gilbert.'

It had begun in Moscow, in July 1991, when Gilbert had sent a warning to Paris that he had information that a coup was being prepared by hardliners to overthrow Mikhail Gorbachev and reverse his reforms. At almost the same time, Jack Crimson had sent a similar warning to London. Neither of their ambassadors was altogether convinced and the Americans were equally unsure. But President George Bush was sufficiently concerned to call Gorbachev, who refused to believe it and went to his holiday home at Foros in the Crimea on 4 August.

'Enough people in London and Paris took our warnings seriously,' said Crimson. 'Mitterrand spoke with our prime minister, John Major, and said we should start making contingency plans for possible Western responses in case there was a coup. I was flown back to London and put on an Anglo-French team, which is where I met Vincent here. You call him Brigadier but he was just a captain then.'

After Bush's call, Gorbachev had arranged discreet talks with Russian President Boris Yeltsin and Kazakh President Nazurbayev to discuss sacking the hardliners: the KGB Chairman Kryuchkov, Defence Minister Yazov, Interior Minister Pugo, Vice-President Yanayev and Soviet Premier Pavlov. Convinced that the army under Marshal Akhromeyev would remain loyal, Gorbachev decided to wait until after his return from holiday, when he planned to sign into law the new treaty for a much more decentralized Soviet Union. Gorbachev, however, did not know that Kryuchkov had him under close observation and knew of his plan to dismiss the hardliners. The KGB chief arranged to strike first.

On 17 August, Kryuchkov convened a meeting at a KGB guesthouse outside Moscow, read aloud the terms of the new Union treaty and declared it meant the end of the Soviet Union. Then Kryuchkov played them a clandestine recording of Gorbachev's discussion with Yeltsin about sacking the hardliners; at this, the hardliners agreed to move. Gorbachev must either declare a state of emergency and give the hardliners full powers to restore order or he must go. The meeting agreed to send a delegation to the Crimea the next day to give Gorbachev this ultimatum. Gorbachev refused to cooperate and the coup was launched.

Communications to his Crimean dacha were cut off, his KGB guards reinforced. Kryuchkov recalled all KGB personnel from leave and doubled their pay. Three hundred thousand arrest forms were prepared for Moscow and a quarter of a million sets of handcuffs ordered. The Lefortovo Prison was emptied, ready for new prisoners. Yanayev signed the decree for the state of emergency and it was announced at seven in the morning of 19 August.

Even before the coup plotters held their televised press conference that evening, Gilbert had been in the Russian White House, the seat of the Russian Federation Parliament that was Yeltsin's power base. He had heard Yeltsin's statement of defiance and his call for a general strike against the coup. Above all, he had seen Major Evdomikov, chief of staff of a tank battalion from the Tamanskaya Guards, declare his loyalty to the Russian Parliament. On the first day, Gilbert had reported back to Paris that the coup was by no means secure; short of massive bloodshed, it was likely to fail. That evening, the Patriarch flew in to Moscow.

'Gilbert was there at midday when Yeltsin climbed onto that tank, denounced the coup and called on the military to stand by the constitution and refuse any orders from Yanayev and his emergency committee,' said Crimson. 'In London, we watched it on TV. None of us could believe that the plotters hadn't already picked up Yeltsin and dumped him into some distant dungeon. And by now he was protected by tanks and thousands of protesters and TV cameras.'

In Paris and London, with equivocal support from the United States, one of the contingency plans being considered had proposed a possible commando raid on Foros to rescue Gorbachev and bring him to the West. The joint team of British SAS troops and French commandos were to launch from NATO's Incirlik base in Turkey in helicopters and ride through the Black Sea on a French-owned oil tanker until within range of Foros.

'That was where I came in, as a young captain in the First Marine Infantry Parachute Regiment,' said the Brigadier. 'I was brought in to help plan the mission and to take part in it, if it went ahead. And Jack Crimson was one of the British planners.'

'By the time we got started, on the twentieth, the coup was crumbling,' said Crimson. 'It collapsed that night when the KGB's Alfa and Vympel special forces teams said they could only break into the Russian White House and arrest

300

Yeltsin with massive bloodshed. The plotters lost their nerve, the troops began pulling out of Moscow and Gorbachev's communications were restored. He ordered the arrest of the coup plotters and came back to Moscow.'

'That was it,' said the Brigadier. 'Gilbert came back to Paris to a hero's welcome before being sent back again to take advantage of his connections with Yeltsin and the new regime.'

'How long did Gilbert last in Moscow after that?' Bruno asked after a long silence, during which the other two men, their eyes locked, seemed to be staring into a shared but distant past.

'Just over a year,' the Brigadier replied. 'The diplomats hated him for being right and some of our intelligence chiefs who'd questioned his warnings began complaining that he'd gone native.'

'Lesson one in the politics of bureaucracy: never be right about something too soon,' said Crimson, with a bitter laugh. 'Lesson two: it never matters to be in the wrong so long as everybody else is.'

The Brigadier shrugged and said, 'He was drunk most of the time. We called him home, put him in front of a medical board and invalided him out. He never forgave us, and I don't blame him.'

'The same thing might have happened to me if I hadn't been called back just before the coup,' said Crimson. He rose, saying, 'Christ, I need a drink,' and went into the kitchen. He came back with a bottle of Balvenie, three glasses and a small bottle of Evian.

'Nothing ever seemed quite as important after that, nor as simple,' he said, pouring out the Scotch with a heavy hand. 'Sometimes I miss the Cold War.'

The three men drank in silence. Bruno looked out over the view across Crimson's garden to the ridges of trees turning to gold.

'So what did Gilbert know or what did he do that was worth paying for, over all these years?' he asked. Crimson shook his head and shrugged. At that moment the Brigadier's phone rang. He listened, spoke a few words of acknowledgement and said, 'Thank you.'

'That was Prunier,' he said. 'He's got Gilbert's full phone records. No calls to or from Moscow and the only calls to Britain were to his tailor in Savile Row.'

'Could be useful cover,' muttered Crimson.

'Just one thing,' said Bruno. 'Pamela said that at the Pariarch's party you took Gilbert aside for a private chat. What were you discussing?'

'I said it had been too long since I'd seen him and asked him to give me a call and we'd arrange a lunch,' Crimson replied. 'No more than that.'

Almost immediately the phone rang again and once more the Brigadier listened, acknowledged and thanked his caller and said, 'I can leave it to you to report to the Procureur.' Then he hung up.

'That was J-J with the first forensics report,' he said, passing his hand over his eyes. 'They found chloral hydrate mixed with orange juice on those

302

shoes where Gilbert spilled his drink. Knockout drops; I believe the Americans call it a Mickey Finn. Similar traces on the cap of the flask he was carrying. They think the two together would have been a lethal dose. The DNA analysis will take rather longer.'

'So Gilbert was murdered,' Bruno said. 'And we don't know why he was killed nor why he was paid when he was alive.'

'Welcome to the dark world of intelligence,' said Crimson. 'Even if we find out why and how, we may not be able to do a damn thing about it except put it in the files and hope it turns out to be useful some day.'

'That may be your world,' said Bruno. 'It's not mine. This is a time for simple police work. You told me that Gilbert was given that glass of spiked orange juice by one of the waiters in air force uniform. We have to call them all in, hold an identification parade and grill the one you recognize until we find out where he got that orange juice and who told him to give it to Gilbert.'

The Brigadier pulled out his phone again. 'I'll get Prunier onto it.'

CHAPTER 27

Usually on this day Bruno would have been up at dawn with his colleagues from the hunting club, building the fire in the great pit beside their cabin in the woods. Other members with trucks and trailers brought in the rows of tables and benches, borrowed from the rugby club, to fill the barn where Julien Marty would store his hay once this annual feast of the hunt club was over. The kitchens of both tennis and rugby clubs had been raided, as they were every year, to provide the glasses, plates and cutlery for the 200 people who were invited to the autumn feast.

It had begun long ago, before the time of the club's oldest members, as a way to provide a treat for the wives and children of the hunters. Some said it dated back to pagan days, when the Gauls had celebrated the equinox each spring and autumn. The gathering and feast had now become a civic event, a fixture on the St Denis calendar and the kind of occasion that helped turn the town into a community. More than that, the day of preparation and the evening supper were also a way of connecting the townsfolk to the traditions of their region, back to a time before there were supermarkets and frozen food, a time when the people had depended on what they could hunt and what they could grow.

Bruno was sad to have missed the day's rituals, gathering at the cabin for coffee before they started to build the fire, and then bringing out the wild boar they had hunted to impale them on the long spits, stuff their stomach cavities with herbs and then sew them shut with wire. Bruno usually brought branches of bay leaves, armfuls of rosemary, sage and wild garlic. The Baron was always the one to light the fire. Others would bring the pots of honey and litres of wine, the salt and peppers and other spices that would be mixed in buckets to make the marinade. Long twigs of rosemary bound around a wooden pole to make a kind of broom were dipped into the buckets and then used to paint the wild boar as they turned on their spits above the fire.

Once the fire was begun and the wild boar sewn and placed on their spits, there was a new ritual that had been started by Dougal, the Scottish businessman who ran a local rental agency for holiday homes. Before the feast, he brought along a bottle of whisky and each beast was solemnly baptized with a dram of the Scotch before all of those present then finished off the bottle.

The fire blazed in its pit all morning. The huge logs, two and three metres long, needed four men to lift them. They burned furiously until the early afternoon, when the ashes were judged to be sufficiently hot and deep for the roasting. Then the long spits bearing the boar were hoisted onto supports and fitted with the rubber belts that would rotate them once they were attached to the old Peugeot transmission that had belonged to someone's grandfather. It was a makeshift system, but it had worked well enough for years.

There were twenty members in the hunting club, a number established over the years as the right proportion for the area of hills and woodland over which they had hunting rights. Each member was allowed to invite up to ten guests and each one was expected to bring sufficient tins of pâté, vegetables and wine to provide for them. They never ran short, but then they all knew each other and had been doing this for years and their nearby cabin was by now a sophisticated if rather rustic kitchen.

It contained an old cast-iron stove, a refrigerator and freezer, a sink with running water, an old butcher's counter from a shop that had gone out of business and a formidable array of kitchen knives. This was where the hunters cooked for themselves on hunting days: hearty soups and stews, rabbits and hares, roasted ducks and pigeons and grilled venison. It was where they made their pâtés and cooked their raspberries and blackcurrants to make jam in the autumn, a task at which Sergeant Jules was the club expert. And today, Bruno knew, Xavier from the bakery would be bringing huge pots of pastry to be rolled out into squares, blind baked in the big oven and then covered with a *compôte* of that year's apples topped with apple slices and sprinkled with sugar before being slid back into the oven.

The members of the club were as proud of their cooking skills as they were of their hunting and spent enough time together that they knew one another very well indeed. And just as they trusted their fellow members with loaded weapons, they trusted them in other matters as well. In the event of illness, unemployment or family crisis, the club members rallied around without needing to be asked. Their politics varied, of course, from very conservative to staunch communist, but politics were kept in their place; their friendship and mutual loyalty were far more important. Still, Bruno reckoned he could usually make an accurate guess at the outcome of elections, local or national, from what he heard from his friends around the table at the cabin.

And that, Bruno thought as his Land Rover climbed the road from St Cirq leading to the cabin, was why it was so unusual that Fabrice had been asked to leave his old hunting club before joining the one at Lalinde. Bruno recalled the long deliberations on the merits of various candidates that took place in the cabin whenever old age or illness meant there was a vacancy to be filled. Fabrice must have made himself very unpopular, and Madeleine and Victor must have exerted considerable pressure to get him accepted into their club. Perhaps all clubs were not so long established and tight knit as his own, Bruno considered, and if she and her husband owned the land on which their club shot, they could probably get their way easily enough.

Bruno had long since invited his guests: Pamela, of course, Fabiola and Gilles, Crimson and his daughter, Florence from the *collège* and Yveline from the Gendarmerie. So bringing along the Brigadier as a last-minute addition would still not exceed his quota. He'd been planning also to invite Hubert from the wine shop and Julien from the Domaine, two of his partners on the board of the town vineyard, but the Baron had invited them already, along with Philippe Delaron, the reporter, and Dr Gelletreau.

Attracted by the appetizing smell of roasting boar, Bruno and the Brigadier followed Balzac as he trotted ahead to greet the other hunting dogs he'd come to know over the previous months. The dogs were sitting in a loose line, close enough to the fire to enjoy the scent but far enough back to avoid the heat. Their tongues were hanging out and their eyes were fixed on the slowly rotating beasts.

The Baron and Sergeant Jules were brushing marinade onto the boar and giving the brooms to Dougal to plunge back into the buckets of marinade. The three men wore heavy leather gauntlets and aprons against the heat and headbands to catch their sweat. As Bruno and the Brigadier came closer, the heat became intense. Small flames darted up from the ashes beneath as the fat from the boars dripped down.

'They're about done,' said the Baron. 'Another thirty minutes and we'll be taking them off to rest before we start to carve them.'

It was like a scene from another era. The fire pit and the roasting boars and the leathers of the three men would have looked just like this centuries ago, in forest clearings like this one, surrounded by the same trees and following the age-old rituals of the hunt and the feast. Reluctantly, but knowing his injured leg would make it dangerous for him to take his usual place among the men donning the heavy gloves to lift the spits from their supports, Bruno turned away towards the hunters' cabin. It was an unduly modest name, Bruno thought, for a building that was larger than his own house. But any place where the hunters gathered to dress their meat and cook and eat together was always known as *la cabine*.

Bruno limped into the cabin, walking stick in one hand and a bag full of freshly picked lettuces in the other. The Brigadier was at his heels, carrying one bag containing a dozen tins of Bruno's home-made pâté and another full of baking potatoes. But there was one new arrival he hadn't expected to see.

'Ah, Bruno,' the Patriarch called in greeting. He was standing beside the Mayor, who was pouring him a drink; he was obviously the Mayor's guest. 'Gérard here was just telling me how you'd been in the wars so I'm very pleased you could make it. How's the leg?'

'I can hobble around, thank you,' said Bruno, putting down the lettuces to shake hands. 'And I believe you both know Général de Brigade Lannes, one of my guests this evening, who was kind enough to drive me here.'

'That means you can drink your fill this evening,' said the Mayor. 'Although I'd be surprised if Sergeant Jules lets the gendarmes mount any breathalyser patrols this evening. And didn't you say you were also inviting Yveline from the Gendarmerie?'

Bruno's friend Stéphane, the local cheesemaker, waved a greeting from the sink, where he was opening bottle after bottle of wine from the Domaine. Since every member of the hunt club was a shareholder in the town vineyard, they never served anything else. Behind Stéphane were stacked six cases of red and four of white, which the club knew from memory was the usual amount that was drunk at these feasts. There were more cases in the cupboard if needed.

'So what brings the éminence grise of the Interior Ministry down here to the Périgord,' the Patriarch asked the Brigadier in a jovial tone. He finished the wine in his glass and held it out to be refilled. 'What dark plots and dangers to the République are you unearthing?'

310

'Just visiting my friend Bruno,' the Brigadier replied and turned to Bruno. 'Anything I can do to help?'

'We have two hundred baking potatoes to wrap in tinfoil before we put them in the ashes,' said Bruno, 'And then there are the lettuces to wash and drain. But first you have to try our local wine.'

Stéphane poured Bruno and the Brigadier a glass of the Domaine's dry white wine and they set to work, ripping off squares of aluminium foil and wrapping the fat potatoes, one by one. The Mayor and the Patriarch joined them, piling the wrapped potatoes into big metal tubs that had been rescued from the town's communal laundry when it had closed a generation ago. Bruno began opening the cans of pâté he'd brought, slicing each one into six portions and putting them onto a small plate with a handful of cornichons.

'Is your visit connected to that high-ranking policeman who called at the vineyard today to search poor Gilbert's house?' the Patriarch asked.

'If it were, I couldn't tell you,' said the Brigadier. 'But I assume it was police business. Did he say what he was looking for?'

'No idea, I wasn't there,' the Patriarch replied equably and helped himself to more wine. That was his third glass, Bruno noticed. 'But my son said the chap had shown some document signed by the Procureur and naturally they let him go ahead. Lord knows if there was anything to find; the place was cleared out a week ago. And now my new gamekeeper is under arrest in some hospital. So would either of you two be able to tell me what's going on?'

'Your gamekeeper assaulted a police officer with a deadly weapon, namely an axe,' Bruno said, lifting his gaze from the work table to observe the Patriarch's reaction. 'The person he assaulted last night was me.'

'*Mon Dieu*, I had no idea.' The Patriarch looked aghast. 'My dear Bruno, I'm terribly sorry to hear this, but what on earth was behind it?'

Bruno briefly explained the attack on Rollo's garden and Fabrice's arrest. As he finished, they heard the sound of voices and thuds as the boar were heaved onto the big carving tables outside. Stéphane and the Brigadier took the potatoes out to the fire pit, where Dougal was raking some of the ashes onto a wide step that had been dug into the side of the pit. This was where the potatoes would be roasted. Meanwhile Sergeant Jules and the Baron were sliding a boar off its spit before checking how nearly it was done.

Other guests were gathering around the trestle tables that formed the bar and Stéphane took out a case of wine to serve them. Cases of beer were already piled into tubs that had been filled with ice and the bar tables carried bowls of olives, crisps and peanuts. Bruno limped out to help Stéphane serve drinks behind the bar. Everyone he served wanted to know about his leg; word of the attack had spread fast. At least Bruno's own guests had been briefed by Fabiola that his wound was not serious. Still, they all came up to give him a hug and ask how he was or if he needed a chair and Pamela seemed as affectionate as ever.

Inside the barn, Bruno had reserved one of the trestle tables for his guests and the Mayor had the adjoining table. The Patriarch took the head, with Florence and Fabiola on either side, then Bruno and the Brigadier sitting opposite each other, Pamela and Yveline, Crimson and the Mayor, Crimson's daughter and Jacqueline Morgan, the half-French, half-American historian who was the Mayor's friend, Gilles and some more of the Mayor's guests. There were four separate rows of tables in the huge barn, five tables in each row, one table for each member of the hunt club. The benches alongside the tables began to fill as Stéphane and the Baron steered people in from the bar. It took some time as old friends shook hands, kissed cheeks, exchanged greetings and looked for their host's table.

A large plate of pâté and cornichons, a fat *pain*, a half-kilo of butter, a bowl of cherry tomatoes, a bottle each of red and white wine and a jug of water stood on every table. The Baron tapped his spoon against his glass for silence, welcomed the assembled guests and called on Father Sentout, who said a very short grace. Conversation then resumed and grew into a steady, jovial roar as wine was poured, plates and bowls were passed, cutlery clattered and the feast began.

'This is the life, the real France,' declared the Patriarch, holding out his empty glass to be refilled. 'You won't find this in Paris,' he said, addressing the Brigadier. 'Reminds me of those last months of the war, pushing through Poland and Prussia, setting up the field kitchens in huge barns rather like this, building big fires and roasting any pigs or cattle we could find. It made a welcome change from Russian rations.'

'Wouldn't the fires attract German aircraft?' Florence asked.

The Patriarch shook his head. 'They didn't have many planes left, and even less aviation fuel. We didn't see any fighters so we were switched to tactical duties, supporting the advancing troops, shooting up enemy supply columns and artillery. And when the weather was too bad for flying, we went off with our Russian friends, looking for loot.'

Ignoring the startled glances around him, he went on, his voice slurring a little, 'Women and loot, that's what wars are all about, at least for the poor bastards who fight them.'

The Russian troops wanted watches and women, he said, chuckling. But the French pilots had learned that the safety deposit boxes of rural banks in East Prussia, in which the Russians took little interest, provided the richest rewards in jewels, gold coins and paintings. Wealthy Berliners had stored their treasures out in country banks when the Allied bombing campaign made the city's basements and banks unsafe. And Stalin's decision at the war's end to give the new French state forty of the Yak fighters the Normandie-Niemen squadron had been flying gave the Frenchmen a way to bring the loot back home.

'That was how I had the money to buy my Paris apartment,' the Patriarch said. 'The Germans had been looting France for the past four years, so I felt it was only fair. They invaded us, now we and our Russian allies were doing the same to them. That's war. *À la guerre comme à la guerre*. And it's a terrible shame we didn't learn the lesson from those years. The Russians are France's natural allies. The threat of a war on two fronts is the only way we can control the Germans. It was true in nineteen fourteen, true in nineteen forty and it's still true today. Ideologies may come and go but the geopolitics and facts of geography don't change. De Gaulle understood that, even if nobody else did.'

He raised his glass, said, 'Here's to the Russians!' and drained it.

The table fell silent, the women looking stunned, the men exchanging embarrassed glances. The Brigadier looked amused and Bruno was wondering what he might say to steer his boyhood hero onto more congenial ground when there came a rustle of silk, a whiff of perfume and Madeleine swooped down to kiss the Patriarch's cheeks.

'Darling Papa, are you telling your usual old soldier's tales about fighting alongside the Russians?' she said in amused tones, taking the old man's hand as she squeezed herself onto the end of the bench beside Florence.

'I know some of these people haven't heard your war stories, but think of poor me. I've heard them a hundred times and now I really need a drink. And may I pinch some of that delicious-looking pâté? I've just driven all the way from Bordeaux and I'm starving.'

Bruno swiftly handed her his glass of white wine, so far untouched, toasted her with his water glass and introduced Madeleine to those she didn't know. She threw him a grateful glance, one eyelid fluttering in what might be the merest hint of a wink. It was a signal of intimacy that Bruno cherished, hugging it to himself in private pride. Then she turned back, still chattering gaily to her father-in-law as she discreetly moved the wine bottles out of his reach.

Gilles found a spare plate and cutlery on an adjoining table and served her some pâté and then a roar of welcome came from the rest of the barn as Stéphane and the Baron arrived. They were carrying a door that had been lifted from its hinges and had been loaded with a dozen serving dishes, each one piled high with slices of roast boar. Behind them came Dougal with a wheelbarrow loaded with baked potatoes.

CHAPTER 28

The following morning, driving from St Denis to Brive to pick up Chantal, Bruno asked the Brigadier if he'd heard the Patriarch speak that way before about the Russians. Only when the old man had taken more wine than was good for him, came the reply. But he'd been right about de Gaulle, the Brigadier went on. Always suspicious of the Americans and their British allies, de Gaulle had pulled France out of the military wing of NATO and pursued his own policy of détente with the Russians.

'You have to remember that de Gaulle grew up before 1914, when France and Russia were close allies and the Germans were the enemy,' the Brigadier said. De Gaulle had come out of St Cyr as a newly fledged officer and went almost straight to war. He was wounded in the opening battles, and returned to be wounded again in the hand in 1915. The following year, at Verdun, he was bayoneted, lost consciousness from poison gas and was then taken prisoner. He hated being out of the war, tried to escape five times from his prison camp and wrote that being kept from the fighting was like being cuckolded. And then, in 1940, the Germans invaded once more, but this time they defeated the French Army, occupied Paris and forced France to sue for peace. When France was finally liberated by British and American troops, de Gaulle always remembered that the bulk of the German Army had been fighting on the Eastern Front and that the Russians had borne the brunt of the war effort and most of the casualties.

'De Gaulle didn't trust the Anglo-Saxons and he always believed the Russians were France's best guarantee against another German invasion,' the Brigadier concluded. 'The Patriarch feels exactly the same way. That's why he and de Gaulle always got on so well. For de Gaulle, Marco and his Normandie-Niemen squadron embodied the Franco-Russian alliance. De Gaulle never grew out of that 1914 and 1940 mindset. And Marco never forgot his wartime comrades on the Eastern Front.'

'What are you trying to say?' Bruno asked, shocked by the implication that his boyhood hero might not have been the devoted French patriot of legend. 'Do you think he was too close to the Russians? Was he working for them?'

'No, I don't think that and there's no evidence for it, and believe me, people have looked,' the Brigadier said as they pulled into the car park at Brive to wait for Chantal's train. 'There was a full-scale inquiry when the Russians came out with that supersonic airliner that looked uncannily like the Anglo-French Concorde, but Marco was exonerated. He was always too open and honest about his partiality for the Russians. And Marco was never in a position to make policy. At the end of the day, de Gaulle was a realist, knowing that France was part of the West. Whatever his sentimental views of the Russians and his suspicions about the Germans, de Gaulle made the alliance treaty with Adenauer and committed France to an ever closer union with Europe.'

Bruno directed the Brigadier to take the main road from Brive through Argentat and Aurillac to reach the *notaire*'s office, but even so it took two hours to get there through the hills and valleys. Chantal and her brother, Raoul, were squeezed into the front passenger seat while Bruno stretched out his leg in the rear. When they'd met at Brive Station, Bruno hadn't expected Raoul to join them and Chantal hadn't expected the Brigadier. Bruno introduced him simply as a friend who'd volunteered to drive them after the injury to his leg.

'Raoul and I have never had any secrets between us,' Chantal had said as her half-brother stood protectively at her side. Bruno had shrugged and made some friendly remark about seeing them play excellent tennis together, trying to make conversation, but got no reaction. Raoul glared suspiciously around the station forecourt until Chantal took him by the hand and led the way into the cramped front seat.

They drove in near silence, struck by the way

the deceptive smoothness of the hills from a distance became a much more gaunt and jagged landscape as they came closer and began to penetrate the *massif* of old volcanoes that became ski resorts in winter. Finally, when the peak of Puy Mary came in sight ahead, Chantal seemed to respond to the stern splendour of the views around them, saying she'd never been to this part of France before. Raoul said he'd been once, on a school camping trip, and he remembered the Cantal cheese and the imposing viaducts that carried the railway line.

They turned off at Segur-les-Villas and headed for the small village where the *notaire* was also the mayor, passing farmhouses of grey stone with dark-grey slate roofs that seemed to merge into a lowering sky with wisps of cloud swirling around the peaks of the high ridges. The *notaire*'s village was composed of a small, squat church with two buildings on each side of it to form a hollow square. The first building was a private house, separated from the church by a stretch of graveyard. The other had a single entrance, but on one side of the door was a plaque that read *Mairie* and on the other the brass plate of the *notaire*. Behind each building were barns and behind the Mairie stood an empty milking shed. Some cows were lying together in the corner of a distant field.

The door of the Mairie opened and a tall, thin man appeared. In his sixties, with thinning white hair cut very short, he wore a dark suit, white shirt and a very wide tie that might have been fashionable some forty years earlier. He was smoking an old-fashioned pipe with a curved stem.

'Welcome,' said the *notaire*, coming from the doorway to greet them, shaking hands with Bruno and asking what had happened to his leg. Bruno explained briefly and introduced his companions. Raoul and the Brigadier were asked to wait in the Mairie, a grandiose title for what turned out to be a single room with a desk and two hard-backed chairs. The *notaire*'s office was larger and more comfortable, lined with shelves for books and files of legal documents, a heavy wooden desk for the *notaire* and a matching table with six leather-backed chairs around it. A coffee pot and three cups stood on a small silver tray. The *notaire* took the head of the table, gestured for Chantal and Bruno to take a seat and asked Chantal for her identity card. She showed it, the *notaire* sat, asked Bruno to pour coffee for each of them and opened a box of black cardboard labelled 'Clamartin, Gilbert' that rested on the table.

'My condolences on the death of your godfather,' the *notaire* said, and began to read the will. Almost everything went to Chantal. The first exception was that a painting, described as a nude portrait of a young woman, went to Yevgeny, the artist who had painted it and in whose house it was hung. Yevgeny had been informed by telephone and the *notaire* had sent him a formal statement of ownership pending valuation of the painting for tax purposes. The second was an envelope that was to be delivered, unopened, to Nicole Larignac, and the *notaire* was in correspondence with her about how best this was to be done. The third was another sealed envelope, marked, 'To be handed to a responsible officer of the law in the event of my death.'

'I believe that you would be a qualified person to receive this envelope, Chief of Police Courrèges, if you would sign here for its receipt and to confirm that it came to you unopened.'

As Bruno signed the receipt, the *notaire* turned to Chantal. He informed her that he'd asked a local estate agent to value Gilbert's house and property, and passed over a valuation document that estimated it was worth 180,000 euros in current market conditions. The agent would be happy to put it up for sale for her if she so chose. He then turned to Gilbert's trust fund in Vaduz, which was valued at just over 600,000 euros.

Bruno held his breath as the *notaire* began to speak, half expecting him to read out a letter to Chantal from Gilbert revealing that he had been her natural father. But there seemed to be no such personal note; the dry tones of the *notaire* explained only more financial details.

'In correspondence with the Vaduz bank, I have been made aware of a second trust fund in Gilbert's name, of which Gilbert made no mention to me when his will was drafted. It is worth nearly three times as much and also passes to you under the terms of the will. Altogether, *mademoiselle*, you inherit a little more than two million euros after my estimate of the various fees and taxes that will be due.'

Chantal looked stunned and stared at the *notaire* in disbelief. Bruno poured her a second cup of coffee and she sipped at it gratefully. The *notaire* passed her a large, unsealed envelope and asked her to sign a receipt and to give him the details of a bank account into which the final sum could be paid after the fiscal and legal formalities were complete. Chantal took her chequebook from her purse, tore out one of the RIB forms giving account details at the back of the book and handed it across.

'I should add that your godfather was a friend of mine from boyhood and I shall miss him greatly. In his memory, my wife and I have prepared a small and very informal lunch in our house across the square. It's a long way to and from Brive and we'd be honoured if you and your companions would join us and raise a final glass to Gilbert.'

Chantal stammered her thanks and they rose from the table. She asked to use the bathroom and rejoined them looking calm and collected and smelling of toilet soap. Bruno noticed beads of water on her hair and shoulders. They collected Raoul and the Brigadier and strolled across the square to the other house, where a thin woman, who looked like a female version of the *notaire*, opened the door and guided them into a parlour.

She was introduced as the *notaire*'s sister. The parlour had the air of a room that was very seldom used, full of old-fashioned furniture with faded upholstery that seemed never to have known the weight of a human body. Bruno tried to recall the name of the small squares of cloth that hung over the back of each chair; he hadn't seen those for decades.

A trolley on castors stood against one wall, with cold meats, pâtés, cheese, bread rolls and a seedcake on its lower shelf, plates and cutlery, glasses and two bottles on the upper. One bottle was wine, of a colour between rosé and pale red, and the other was Gentiane, the yellow aperitif from the gentian root that grew locally.

A short, plump and rather younger woman entered with a coffee pot and some napkins. This was the *notaire*'s wife and she spoke with an Auvergnat accent so strong that Bruno had to strain to understand her as she asked if he would like pâté or ham. The *notaire* remained standing while urging the others to sit and directed his sister to distribute plates and glasses. Beside each seat was a small, low table, each covered with a lace cloth. Bruno and the Brigadier each took a glass of Gentiane, as did the locals. Raoul and his sister took a glass of wine, and the young man's mouth pursed and his eyes widened when he took a sip.

Bruno and Chantal made rather forced conversation with the *notaire* about his and Gilbert's boyhood in the area. The room that was now his office used to be the schoolroom, the *notaire* said, and he'd had to walk three kilometres each day to and from school. Gilbert had had even further to come from his family's farm. There were no phones and the road to the village hadn't been tarred until the sixties. The eldest sons stayed to run the farms, some sisters stayed to marry the farmers and all the other young people left for Paris, where the Auvergnats were famous for running most of the bistros in the city.

'There were so many of us they even had their own newspaper, *l'Auvergnat de Paris*,' said the sister. 'We used to get copies down here.'

They ate, drank a toast to Gilbert's memory, thanked the *notaire* and his family and left, Bruno edging carefully into the rear seat once more while Raoul and Chantal made do in the front. Taking out his map, Bruno directed the Brigadier back via a different route, aiming to cross the headwaters of the River Dordogne at Bort-les-Orges and taking country roads through Margerides to rejoin the autoroute at Saint-Angel. He hoped it would be faster, but it seemed to make little difference. At least this time there was conversation in the car. Raoul was eager to hear the details of the will but Chantal seemed reluctant to reveal them, diverting him with good-natured jokes about the old-fashioned parlour they had just visited and the thin, rather sour local wine they had been served.

'You should have tried drinking the Gentiane instead,' the Brigadier said. 'Some call it bitter but

I'd say it's sweet and sour, very healthy and good for you; there's quite a cult for it in Paris. My grandmother swore by it as a remedy for indigestion.'

With the map open on his lap, Bruno discreetly opened the envelope the *notaire* had given him and found a handwritten letter and another sealed envelope inside. The letter, addressed 'to whom it may concern', said that this was being entrusted to an officer of the law to be passed on 'to the appropriate authorities in the event of my death'. It was dated three years earlier and signed by Gilbert Clamartin, with his military rank printed below.

Bruno pondered whether Gilbert had intended him or some other law officer to read it before passing it on. There was no doubt that the Brigadier, as a senior official of the Interior Ministry, qualified as an appropriate authority. But knowing the Brigadier, Bruno was far from confident that he'd ever be allowed to see the document again once he handed it over. And he was curious. So he opened the second envelope and began to read Gilbert's neat handwriting.

In June of 1989, serving at the Embassy of France in Moscow, I was informed by the doorman that a Russian had appeared and had asked to see the air attaché. I went down to ask his business and found a young man in his mid-twenties, neatly dressed in jacket and tie and speaking an educated

Russian with a noticeable Siberian accent. He asked to speak to me privately and we went into one of the small side rooms that we used for interviews. He showed me his identity documents. His name was Dmitri Ivanovitch Gromov, born 20 October, 1961, in Novosibirsk, capital of Siberia and Russia's third largest city. He said he wanted me and the French authorities to know the truth about the famous French pilot and Hero of the Soviet Union, Marc Desaix. He had learned it from his father, who had been an aircraft mechanic attached to the Normandie-Niemen squadron. He handed me a letter, in Russian, which he said explained everything. I asked him to tell me in his own words.

His father, Ivan Tomasovitch Gromov, had been born in Leningrad in 1922, gone to technical school there and when called up for military service was assigned to be an aircraft mechanic. After training, he was posted in late 1942 to join the 18th Guards Air Regiment. In April 1944, he was transferred to join the Normandie-Niemen Escadrille at Borovskoiya, near Smolensk, to service the new Yak-9T fighters, equipped with a 37-millimetre 'tank-buster' cannon. This was shortly before the big Red Army offensive that was to liberate Belorussia that summer.

Originally one squadron of a dozen pilots, and serviced mainly by French mechanics, the Normandie-Niemen force had now been expanded to four squadrons but depended increasingly on Soviet mechanics, armourers and other staff, many of them female. In the course of that spring, Ivan Tomasovitch formed a liaison with a very pretty parachute-packer named Oksana, but after the Red Army took Vitebsk and launched an advance that would drive the Germans back 200 kilometres, Ivan was sent to a forward landing strip. Oksana remained at the main base for the Normandie-Niemen, which was in the meantime moved forward to Mikountani, about fifty kilometres from Vilno, in what had been Poland. It was during this period that Lieutenant Desaix began to pay attention to Oksana, who had vowed to remain loyal to her Ivan Tomasovitch.

On his return to the new Mikountani base, Ivan was warned by Lieutenant Desaix to steer clear of Oksana if he knew what was good for him. This warning took place at a popular relaxation spot near the base known as Frenchman's Hill, since it was the mass grave of nearly 200 members of Napoleon's Imperial Guard who had been buried there during the 1812 retreat from Moscow. Ivan told him to get lost and find his own girl. The next day, Ivan was arrested by the unit commissar, Major Vdovine, and handed over to the NKVD internal security force, accused of slandering Stalin. He was sentenced to twenty-five years, and in the course of the brief trial was told that his accuser had been 'a loyal ally', Lieutenant Marco Desaix, who had already been awarded the Order of the Red Banner for downing enemy warplanes.

Ivan was sent to a labour camp in Magadan, in the far east of Siberia, assigned to logging duties. He was released in 1956 when Nikita Khrushchev opened the gates of the Gulag, but was refused permission to return home to Leningrad and was restricted to living in Siberia. He found a job in the Novosibirsk aircraft factories, married and had a son, Dmitri. But Ivan was never in good health after his years in the Gulag and he died in 1970. Dmitri said he had taken advantage of the new freedoms to come to Moscow to seek full rehabilitation for his father, to denounce Marco Desaix as a '*stulyagi*', an informer, and to ask the French authorities to confront Desaix and make him confess his crime.

I took the young man's details and told him I would be in touch when I had contacted the proper authorities. I then read his written account, which added nothing to what I had heard, and filed it pending preliminary checks of dates and place names. In the following week, General Desaix made one of his regular visits to Moscow.

As a close friend of his son Victor, I knew the General well, and took him into Gorky Park for a stroll, where I explained Dmitri's strange accusation. The General told me that he and most of the other French pilots had enjoyed romantic liaisons with Russian servicewomen at the various bases, and their first NKVD officer, Kapitan Kounine, had turned a blind eye. He did not recall the incident reported by the young Russian mechanic. But there had been a young woman called Oksana, who became pregnant and later gave birth to his Russian son, Yevgeny. He never married her but was able, with the help of Kapitan Kounine, to have her posted back to Moscow to have the child, and he supported her and the boy for the rest of Oksana's life.

The General asked me what I intended to do, and I said I would deliberately misfile Dmitri's written report and send a cable to Paris saying that it was evidently a crude blackmail attempt and the basic facts did not check out. He thanked me and we never mentioned the incident again. Knowing Yevgeny, the General's

Russian son, I established that he was born on 2 May, 1945. He was therefore conceived in late July or early August of the previous year, the period when Ivan Tomasovitch was at the forward landing strip, far from the rest of the unit.

About a month later, I received in the post, addressed only to the air force attaché, an envelope containing a news item clipped from a Novosibirsk paper, which reported the death in a hit-and-run accident caused by an unknown driver of a young man, Dmitri Gromov. Across it was scrawled in red ink the Russian word *'ubiyitsa'*, which means murderer. This has been on my conscience for many years.

Marco Desaix is known as a war hero and a great Frenchman. He has been a good friend to me. But he is also an old man and I imagine we shall both be dead by the time this is read. I am aware that this report is based on hearsay, and also aware of the routine use of disinformation by Soviet Intelligence. This may all be a deliberate KGB concoction to confuse us; if so, we would probably have heard more of the matter. Since we did not, I can only assume the KGB did not want to publicize these allegations. I report all this simply because I believe that we have a duty to history. I misfiled Dmitri's statement in a batch of minutes of meetings of the Moscow branch of the Franco-Soviet Friendship Association, 1981–8. They were being shipped back to Paris for storage in the archives. The statement is attached to the entry for January 1985, the meeting at which Marco was elected president of the association.

So much for the hero of my youth, thought Bruno, looking inside the envelope, but there were no pages written in Russian, no scrap of newsprint with its single word of accusation. There was only the hearsay report of a dead man.

CHAPTER 29

They dropped Chantal and her brother at the station in Périgueux, and the Brigadier then called Prunier and J-J to arrange a meeting at the Commissariat of Police on Rue 4 Septembre. He closed his phone and said, 'I'd better take a look at that document you were reading; I presume it's some form of testament from Clamartin.' He made no comment on Bruno's decision to read it, simply held out his hand to receive it and they stayed in the station car park while the Brigadier read it, once quickly, and a second time more carefully.

'At least we have an explanation for Gilbert's money. This suggests he was being paid for his silence,' the Brigadier said when he'd finished. 'What do you make of it, Bruno?'

'The first question is whether it's true. If it is, I imagine the Patriarch would have been disgraced if it had been leaked that he was an informer for the NKVD – I assume that was the wartime version of the KGB.'

'Yes, pretty much the same thing. NKVD stood for the Peoples' Commissariat of Internal Affairs and the KGB was the Committee for State Security. They changed the names after the war. But go on, what would the fallout have been if this had become known?'

'I don't know how the Patriarch would have lived it down if the French press reported that he'd had a man sent to the Gulag over a woman. And then there's the implication that after Gilbert told him about the young man's visit, the Patriarch tipped off the KGB and they arranged his death. That would make the Patriarch an accessory to murder.'

'So your conclusion is that the KGB has had a hold over the Patriarch for all these years?'

'Yes, but is it that simple?' Bruno asked. 'If it's true, others must have known, starting with Oksana, Yevgeny's mother. Did she ever tell her son about it? And then there is Dmitri's mother, presumably the one who sent Gilbert the newspaper clipping with the accusation of murder.'

The Brigadier shrugged and pocketed Gilbert's letter. When Bruno asked what he intended to do with it, the Brigadier threw him a sharp glance. 'What would you do, Bruno?'

'No idea, but I'm not in your shoes,' Bruno replied. 'You're the one who has to make a decision and I can't say I envy you. He's an old man. Whatever damage he did is long past and the Soviet Union doesn't exist any more. If he was a spy, I suppose we need to know the details. But he's such a patriot I find it hard to believe he'd ever do anything against French interests, or at least his view of French interests.'

'I'm not sure it was ever so crude as him being a spy,' the Brigadier replied. 'I suspect it was far more subtle than that, and probably more important. It seems that he was an agent of influence, a sympathetic voice with access to French presidents as well as the Kremlin, a trusted go-between. But not a word of this to Prunier or J-J.'

They drove the short distance to the Commissariat and were shown to Prunier's spacious office, with photos of Prunier in various police units on one wall and in different rugby teams on another. J-J was with him, coffee and mineral water on the conference table. Alongside the drinks lay a laptop and several files; one of them spilled printouts from a telephone log. Bruno took a seat at the head of the table so that he could stretch out his leg. He rested his walking cane against the arm of his chair.

'The DNA results came through,' said J-J, his tie loose and his shirt and trousers rumpled as usual. He was looking pleased with himself and, like Prunier, he'd risen to shake hands with the new arrivals. 'Gilbert was Chantal's biological father, so she's not the Patriarch's granddaughter.'

'And she's just inherited two million from her late father,' said the Brigadier. He pulled his own, specially secured laptop from his bag, put it on top of Prunier's desk, plugged it in and with a cursory '*Vous permettez?*' to Prunier he sat down to log on. Prunier casually nodded his permission for the Brigadier to take over his desk. With approval, Bruno noted that Prunier didn't seem the kind of man to make a fuss over precedence or protocol. He'd known some senior cops who were different.

'Two million euros? She's a lucky girl,' said J-J, and turned to Bruno. 'That guy you put in hospital, Fabrice, we have a trace that links him to the attack on Rollo's garden. The Procureur will file a formal *délit* against him and probably assign Bernard Ardouin as the *juge d'instruction*, since Bernard's also dealing with the assault on you. He wants to see you when you're free.'

'Which *juge* has the Procureur assigned to Gilbert's death?' Bruno asked. The quality of investigating magistrates varied and policemen kept a close watch on their performance, their style of work and their political leanings. Some were good investigators but were seen as bullies by the detectives who had to work with them. Others, usually those with political ambitions, were thought to be partisan for certain causes or too keen to win newspaper headlines. Inevitably, the best cops wanted to work with the best magistrates and were assigned the most interesting cases. Less popular magistrates got the worst cops, or the laziest ones. Bernard Ardouin was a good magistrate; Bruno had worked with him before.

'The Procureur's going to deal with that himself,' said Prunier, giving Bruno a sympathetic glance.

On the one hand, this meant top-level attention with all available resources deployed and no concerns about budgets; on the other, since the Procureur had so much else to do, it meant he could give the case only spasmodic attention.

'Don't worry, Bruno, he asked me to keep an eye on the investigation and I've assigned J-J,' Prunier went on. 'We had detectives at the Mont-de-Marsan and Mérignac airbases today, showing a photo of Gilbert to the waiters. One remembers serving him orange juice but said he'd brought it because Gilbert had asked for it. The waiter got the juice from the barman, so we spoke to him and he said several people were drinking it and he poured out half a dozen glasses from a jug.'

'But nobody else collapsed, only Gilbert,' said Bruno, mystified by this development.

'Right, so if it wasn't in the orange juice, the drug must have been secretly slipped into the drink somehow. So we assigned Inspector Jofflin in Bergerac to start trawling through the guests we could trace from the Patriarch's party to see which of them had been taking photos on their mobile phones. It turns out most of them were. We've gone through hundreds and here are some of the clearest.'

He pressed a button on his laptop and dozens of thumb-sized photos appeared on the screen. He zeroed in on one, clicked twice and up came a selfie of Pamela and Crimson, grinning, with their arms around each other. Gilbert's face was visible behind them, talking to someone out of shot. To their left, standing back so as not to intrude on their photo, was a partial image of a young woman. All that was visible was a bronzed forearm with a silver bracelet on the wrist and some locks of long blonde hair. In her hands was a small bowl containing silver tongs and what looked like ice cubes.

'Ice cubes,' said Bruno, almost to himself. He'd never thought of that. Prunier clicked on the next picture, another of Pamela's selfies, but one in which Crimson had his eyes closed and his hand holding a drink was a blur. But this was a much clearer image of Gilbert behind him, smiling at someone on the other side of Pamela and Crimson. He looked sober, impeccably dressed and was carrying a glass of orange juice.

'It looks like he's smiling at the woman with the ice cubes,' said Prunier. 'These photos were taken one after the other, just instants apart. There's a date and timing feature for the photos on some of these phones.'

'Here she is again,' said Prunier, flicking through to another folder of photos and clicking on one. 'No ice cubes this time. But it's the same bracelet, the same hair.'

This photo had been taken from a different phone, a snatched shot of the Patriarch with one hand on the stone balustrade as he descended the steps from the balcony. He was smiling at a woman in a yellow dress whose back was to the camera. With a start, Bruno remembered Chantal had been wearing yellow. Prunier flicked to another photo

338

that showed the same woman, bowl in one hand and tongs in another, her face obscured by her hair, talking to Madeleine. Now he was almost certain of her identity.

The next photo was another selfie of two people Bruno did not recognize, but behind and above them was a scene on the balcony. He could see the Countess's wheelchair, Bruno himself was standing behind it and smiling at the two young girls. Marie-Françoise was in light blue and Chantal was in the now familiar yellow dress.

'It's Chantal, the girl with the ice cubes,' said Bruno. 'The girl in the DNA report, Gilbert's daughter, I mean, Colonel Clamartin's.'

'So if she was the one who dropped them in his drink, she murdered her own father,' said J-J.

'Only if the ice cubes contained the drug and only if she knew what was in them. And I don't think she knows even now that Gilbert was her father. The *notaire* said nothing about it,' said Bruno. 'Still, congratulations, you've done well. I wouldn't have thought of trawling through people's phones for photos. But do you have any photos of her actually putting them in Gilbert's drink?'

'Not yet, but we're still collecting the damn things and we've got the Paris police trying to collect more photos from guests who came down from the city,' said Prunier. 'I think we've already got more than enough to call her in for questioning. Any idea where she is now, Bruno?'

'We just put her on a train for Bordeaux with her brother. We spent the day with them, hearing Clamartin's will read by the *notaire*.'

J-J reached for the phone with a speed surprising for one of his bulk. 'Do you know what time the train leaves? We could stop it or have it met at the next station, probably Neuvic.'

'Let's not go overboard,' said Prunier. 'There's no indication that she's going to flee and I want to see what extra photos we can get. We haven't even begun to work out where she got the knockout drops. And perhaps you two could share with me what you got from the session with the *notaire*, apart from the girl's two million?'

The Brigadier threw Bruno a stern glance of warning but Bruno ignored it. He had no intention of breaking the Brigadier's order to say nothing about Gilbert's letter.

'On the knockout drops, Chantal is doing a wine course at university that involves some serious chemistry. It would give her access to a sophisticated laboratory,' Bruno said. 'I don't know how easy these drops are to obtain or to make, nor if they can be frozen into ice cubes or if that degrades their effect. We need to get an expert view on that. And while I imagine you can slip someone a precise dose in a drink, how much of that precise dose can be delivered by a slowly melting ice cube?'

'Right, that makes sense,' said Prunier and turned to J-J. 'Get someone in Bordeaux to have

340

a quiet talk with Chantal's chemistry professor, without mentioning her name, and ask forensics whether there's anything in the ice cube theory.' He turned back to Bruno. 'Go on, you were going to tell us about the will.'

'There were two interesting items,' Bruno said. 'The widow of his former mechanic gets a sealed envelope that might be cash. Of course it might be documents, or possibly a safe deposit key. I just don't know. And Yevgeny, the Patriarch's Russian son, was bequeathed a nude portrait he painted of a much younger Madeleine, Chantal's mother. It hangs in Yevgeny's bedroom but it seems it was owned by Gilbert.'

Given Chantal's age, Bruno explained, she would almost certainly have been conceived in Moscow, when Gilbert was at the Embassy and Madeleine was doing her summer internship at the commercial office. The Brigadier got up from Prunier's desk and went to the bookcase, filled with legal tomes and works of reference. He pulled out *Qui est qui?*, the French equivalent of *Who's Who*, and looked up the reference to Marco Desaix.

'Grandchildren,' he read aloud. 'Raoul, born in Paris, 1986, son of Victor and first wife, Marie-Dominique. Chantal, born 18 May, 1991, in Périgueux, daughter of Victor and second wife, Madeleine.

'What's the date of Victor's second marriage?' Bruno asked, thinking Chantal had been conceived in August of 1990.

'Fifteenth of November, nineteen ninety, in Paris,' the Brigadier read out. 'She'd have known she was pregnant by Gilbert when she married Victor. I wonder if Victor knew?'

'Victor obviously accepted Chantal as his child but if he learned that she was Gilbert's daughter, who knows how he might react? He's a proud man,' said Bruno.

'Cuckolded by his best friend,' said J-J, shaking his head. 'If Victor found out, that gives him a motive to kill Clamartin.'

'If he found out and demanded a divorce, that could have an impact on Madeleine's political plans. It would make quite a scandal and she'd probably lose the Patriarch's backing,' said Prunier. 'That gives her a motive to silence him. And then there's the daughter who's just inherited all the money. That gives her a pretty strong motive to bump him off. Half the bloody family has a motive.'

You don't know the half of it, thought Bruno. He was tempted to tell them that the Patriarch may have had the biggest motive of all. But he held his tongue and instead he said, 'There's not the slightest evidence that Chantal knew about the money before his death. I saw her reaction when the *notaire* read the will: she was stunned by it.'

'But it's worth noting that she didn't say anything about it to her brother when they were in the car,' the Brigadier said from Prunier's desk. He'd been huddled over his laptop and Bruno hadn't realized he was paying that much attention to their conversation. Now he looked up and asked Prunier, 'Do you have an old-fashioned photocopying machine? I need one that photographs only what it sees, rather than the modern ones that take an electronic image that somebody else might call up later.'

'I've got one in my office,' said J-J, and the Brigadier picked up his laptop and followed J-J out.

Prunier waited until the door closed behind them and asked Bruno, 'Anything you can tell me about his involvement? A guy like that doesn't usually get interested in wills and murders.'

'It's the connection with the Patriarch, that and the fact that Gilbert Clamartin seems to have had two paymasters.'

'I know that,' Prunier said patiently. 'I think there's something else going on.'

Bruno sighed and held up his hands. He was about to say something like 'I'm sorry, you'll have to ask the Brigadier', which even to him would have seemed both inadequate and offensive. He was saved by the bell, or at least by the vibration of his phone.

He heard a very alarmed female voice. 'Bruno, it's Raquelle. I'm afraid Imogène seems to have gone mad. She's heading to confront Peyrefitte at the hospital to give his son her fawn. I thought I'd talked her out of it, but she's gone and left a note.'

'Where are you?' Bruno asked, and heard the sound of a car horn down the line.

'Driving like a mad thing to Périgueux Hospital but I'm twenty minutes away. Can you get there faster and stop her? The note says she's called the radio and newspapers to witness what she calls her gesture of reconciliation. She got a legal letter from Peyrefitte this morning, accusing her of manslaughter and demanding compensation.'

'On my way,' Bruno said. 'I'll see you at the hospital.' He closed his phone, explained to Prunier and asked if he could borrow a driver to take him to the hospital.'

'We'll take my car and a couple of uniformed cops,' Prunier said. 'We might need them.'

CHAPTER 30

With its blue light flashing and a police van close behind, Prunier's car carved a way through the beginning of the evening rush hour. The two vehicles raced up Avenue Pompidou and into the Centre Hospitalier to find Imogène blocking the doorway with her fawn in her arms. Peyrefitte, eyes blazing, turned to see Prunier emerging from his car and two uniformed policemen following behind. Hampered by his leg and needing to put down his walking stick to use his arms to extract himself from the car, Bruno took longer to join them.

He saw everything unfold as if in slow motion. Imogène stepped forward, her hair wild and her expression unreadable, and tried to thrust the terrified fawn into Peyrefitte's arms. He flinched, stepped back and put up his hands to protect himself. News cameras began to flash.

The fawn wriggled from Imogène's arms and darted for the nearest patch of greenery, a small roundabout covered in grass and small shrubs. An ambulance, its own siren taking over from the silenced police vehicles, braked hard in an attempt to avoid the animal. With a crunch of metal, it skidded into another car that had just pulled away from the car park. Tyres squealed and another car rammed into the rear of the ambulance.

Glass broke. Airbags exploded. Klaxons blared. Imogène screamed and ran towards her stricken fawn.

'Cardiac victim, emergency,' shouted the ambulance driver, jumping from his vehicle and running back to find the rear doors of his ambulance jammed by the car that had crashed into them. 'We've got to get him out and into the emergency room.'

As a shrieking Imogène ran past, Bruno grabbed her with both arms, lifted her off her feet and used his full weight to press her down against the hood of Prunier's car and keep her squirming form from escaping. Uncomfortably close, the blue light on the hood was strobing in a way that was disorienting him and he closed his eyes against the pulsing glare while burrowing his face into the woman's neck, telling her his name and asking her to stop struggling while her heels drummed furiously into his legs.

Time seemed to stretch out. Then a man in a white coat was beside him, injecting something into Imogène's arm, and slowly she stilled. The doctor helped Bruno stand up and two attendants put Imogène onto a stretcher and wheeled her away. Bruno had lost his walking stick and his *képi*.

The cars had been disentangled from the ambulance. Its rear doors were open, the interior empty. Deflated airbags drooped over steering wheels but there was no sign of the drivers. By the roundabout was a small, inert bundle underneath a blanket. Photographers were snapping away around it. Bruno presumed it was the fawn.

'Looks like I got here too late,' came a voice, and Bruno turned to see Raquelle. She bent down, picked up his walking stick from beneath Prunier's car and handed it to him. She looked him up and down, straightened his tie and collar, took a handkerchief from her sleeve and began dabbing at a sore spot on his cheek.

'She scratched you,' she said.

They walked across to the hospital doorway where Peyrefitte, surrounded by reporters, was saying, 'That women is evidently insane. She needs to be locked up for her own protection, let alone that of others.'

He was speaking in tones of cold, controlled fury. 'Can you imagine the effrontery of this crazed woman, demanding I give this wretched deer to my sons, who just saw their mother killed by one of the damn beasts?'

Prunier gave Bruno a friendly nod and then gestured to the two uniformed cops, who began pushing the journalists back. Prunier took Peyrefitte by the arm, smiling sympathetically and guiding him into the hospital. It was smoothly done, thought Bruno. He turned aside, taking Raquelle's arm, and led her away from the press people towards a bench from which he could keep an eye on Prunier's car and on the hospital entrance. As they sat, a tow truck arrived.

'I'm sorry, I should have kept an eye on Imogène and stopped her, but I thought I'd talked her out of it,' Raquelle said, lighting a cigarette. 'She seemed to be fine until she got the letter from Peyrefitte this morning. It seems to have sent her over the edge. He somehow found out she's working at Le Thot.'

'Somebody probably recognized her,' Bruno said. 'She has become quite a local celebrity over the past couple of weeks.'

'I think it might have been my sister-in-law. She visited me at Le Thot the other day and was quite cross when she saw Imogène working with me. And Madeleine knows Peyrefitte.'

Bruno felt a frisson at hearing her name. 'They're political allies; she's going to replace him as candidate for the National Assembly.'

'It's all she talks about, getting out the vote, visiting every town and village to make speeches, calling at all the hunting clubs. She's got no time now for the vineyard so poor Victor is having to do all the work, as if he didn't have enough to put up with from her already.'

'How do you mean?' he asked.

She threw him a sidelong glance. 'An older husband, a much younger and beautiful wife who's never at home; what do you think? That marriage has been a sham for years.'

'Poor Victor,' said Bruno, feeling his face colour as the guilt began to build. It was odd; he'd never been able to control his blushing. It was as if the blood vessels in his face were hard-wired into his conscience.

'My brother is a very unhappy man.' Raquelle shook her head sadly and then looked at Bruno. 'Oh, Bruno, don't say she's got her hooks into you, too.'

He looked down at his feet and said nothing, knowing his face was burning.

Raquelle sighed heavily, and then looked back at the hospital. 'How long will they keep Imogène in there?'

Grateful for the change of subject, Bruno explained the usual procedure. The hospital would contact her doctor, which in Imogène's case was Fabiola. They'd review the police report on the incident and probably agree on a psychological assessment. It was rare these days for anyone to be confined unless they'd been violent or were deemed to be a danger to themselves.

'I'll brief Fabiola on what happened and then we'll see,' he said. 'Once Peyrefitte calms down, he'll probably agree that he can hardly claim to have been assaulted with a baby deer by a woman half his size. People would tell jokes about it and then he'd start losing public sympathy, particularly if he pursues his case against Imogène to the point where she'd be homeless. Peyrefitte's a decent man, a good lawyer with political instincts and

349

he's no fool; for the sake of his boys, he'll realize it's time to move on.'

'What an unusual cop you are,' said Raquelle stubbing out her cigarette. 'Is that how they train you village policemen?'

'It's not what I learned at the Police Academy, no. But it's how the people of St Denis trained me over the years.' Through the hospital's entrance doors Bruno could see Peyrefitte and Prunier still locked in conversation.

'How's your robot bull?' he asked. 'If that got loose around here, it could do a lot more damage than Imogène's fawn.'

'I've got it moving over rough ground, not very gracefully, but it copes. Did you ever hear of BigDog, that American military robot with four legs, designed to carry supplies and the wounded over any terrain? It's a bit like that, except BigDog can run at fifty kilometres a hour. My auroch only manages six or seven.'

'Sounds like just the thing for hunters, carrying game back through the woods,' he said. 'Ah, I think I have to go. That's Prunier, the police commissioner; he's my lift. We'll stay in touch about Imogène.'

Bruno limped across to Prunier, who was shaking hands with Peyrefitte before the lawyer headed back into the hospital. Prunier beckoned to Bruno to join him in his car. Once Bruno had inserted himself gingerly, Prunier told his driver to head for St Denis and began punching numbers into his phone. When it was answered, he handed it to Bruno and said, 'The Brigadier wants to talk to you.'

'Prunier is going to bring you to join us at the Patriarch's chateau,' came the Brigadier's voice. 'On the way, can you brief him on Colonel Clamartin's statement, the one from the *notaire*? He's been cleared to know.'

Bruno handed back the phone and said, 'That was quick. Just an hour or so ago he told me not to tell you anything. How did you change his mind? You had time for no more than a couple of calls.'

'The Brigadier is not the only one with friends in Paris,' said Prunier. 'So what did Clamartin's last testament say?'

'That the Patriarch might have been working under Russian control for many years,' Bruno said, and gave as full a version as he could remember of Gilbert's statement.'

Prunier nodded thoughtfully. 'So Gilbert knew of this since nineteen eighty-nine, but presumably Russian Intelligence would have known of it since nineteen forty-four. However, this is the first we've heard of it, even though people boast that we had some well-placed agents in Moscow over the years.'

'The Brigadier told me that people had taken a close look at the Patriarch over the years and nothing was ever found against him.' Bruno said, feeling some vestigial loyalty to the bold young fighter pilot who had entranced his boyhood.

Bruno was stretched out on the back seat,

Prunier in the front passenger seat, his body turned so he could study Bruno, and his face was neutral. After a long moment, he nodded, as if reaching a decision, and plucked one of the files from the briefcase by his feet.

'I have something for you, on that guy who assaulted you, Fabrice,' he said. 'We wanted to find out how long he'd been waiting for you so we checked his phone. According to the logs of the various phone masts, he'd barely moved for nearly three hours. The signal kept coming from a location around your house. His next connection to a mast came about thirty minutes after you called the emergency services and it tracked him all the way to the hospital here in Périgueux. So he was waiting for you at your place for more than two hours.

'That's not all,' Prunier added. 'He got two calls, both from a disposable phone, not registered, so we don't know who it was but it was a number he'd called earlier that day, in the morning. That number called him back just before three in the afternoon and then again after midnight. It sounds like somebody was telling him your movements.'

'What's the number?' Bruno asked, thinking there was only one person who would have known his movements that afternoon and evening, known them all too well.

Prunier read it out. It meant nothing to Bruno. Prunier added that the phone hadn't been used since that late-night call and there had been no subsequent connection to a mobile phone mast that could give its location.

'What was the phone's last known location? Bruno asked, knowing he could already guess the answer and feeling the stirrings of some emotion he couldn't quite name. There was some shame in it, some humiliation, some self-loathing at having been played for such a dumb, masculine fool.

'Bordeaux,' said Prunier. 'For each of the calls to and from Fabrice, that phone was in central Bordeaux.'

Bruno nodded, aware that his shock must already be plain on his face and that Prunier was watching him closely. Any reputation for competence as a policeman that Bruno had earned over his decade in St Denis was crumbling.

'Your statement said that you had been in Bordeaux all day and had driven back late after dinner with a friend,' Prunier went on. His voice was sympathetic but still implacable. 'Your mobile phone bears out your statement. What's interesting is that while you were in Bordeaux your phone was pinging the same mast as the phone that was in contact with Fabrice. That's quite a coincidence.'

Bruno sighed deeply. 'I'm an idiot. I've been played like a teenage boy.'

'You're saying you were with a woman? A woman who seems to have been briefing the guy who was waiting to brain you with an axe?'

'Pathetic, isn't it?' said Bruno, glumly.

'Oh, I don't know,' said Prunier, a glint of humour in his eyes. 'Think of the jokes when news of this gets around. Screw what's-her-name and die. That'll teach you to take her flowers next time.' Prunier turned to his driver. 'If word of this does get out, Marcel, I'll blame you. And you'll be back in uniform and on night shift for the rest of your days.'

Prunier pulled from his briefcase the political leaflet Bruno had seen at the Bergerac debate, the one where Madeleine tried to coax the elegant beauty of her face into something less intimidating, more like the girl next door.

'Is this her?' he asked. 'I can't say I blame you. She's almost worth a visit from the mad axeman.'

Bruno found himself smiling, briefly, a touch of gallows humour before the gloom returned. 'Do you want my resignation?'

'Apart from the fact that you don't work for me, why on earth would I want that?' Prunier asked. 'It's not a crime. You're not married. It's not even an indiscretion. And she's not a suspect. Or is she?'

'She had a motive to bump off Gilbert,' Bruno said. 'And she went through the same wine course that her daughter is currently attending, which means she knows just as much chemistry. And there's never any shortage of decent laboratories in wine country.'

'Would she have any conceivable motive to have you killed?'

'Only that I was suspicious about Gilbert's death and kept on asking questions,' Bruno said. He was trying to see this from Prunier's point of view. The phone logs meant that Madeleine would have to be questioned. Since she was a rising political star, this was tricky. If charges were brought against her and resulted in a conviction, her political career was over. If not, Prunier would have made a mortal enemy of a future deputy of the National Assembly, who might even rise higher in the future.

'We can't take this much further until we can question your axeman, Fabrice,' said Prunier. 'And surprise, surprise, he's just got himself a very good lawyer. The cop we've stationed at the hospital says nobody was more surprised than Fabrice when this lawyer turned up and started referring to him as "my client".'

'I thought Fabrice wasn't able to hear anything,' Bruno said.

'Apparently the lawyer knew about that. He carried a big notepad to write things on to show Fabrice. The docs reckon it will be a couple of weeks before he gets his hearing back. What did you do to him?'

'Clapped my hands hard over both his ears at the same time. Something they taught us in the army, unarmed combat.'

'I wouldn't say that at the inquiry, if I were you. You know how lawyers like to talk about unreasonable force, even when their clients were using an axe.'

'I think I can guess who hired the lawyer,' said Bruno.

'In this kind of case, Bruno, we have to do better than guesses.'

CHAPTER 31

The housekeeper showed Bruno and Prunier into a large room that she called the library, whose French windows opened onto the terrace where Bruno had stood with the Red Countess. Books lined the walls, an old-fashioned desk faced the windows and at the far end of the room the Patriarch and the Brigadier were sitting amicably in two leather armchairs. Two glasses, a water jug and a bottle of red liquid with a label in Russian stood on the small table between them.

The Patriarch gestured for the new arrivals to draw up two chairs and fetch glasses from the small bar in the corner of the room. Above the bottles were two framed photographs of warplanes that Bruno recalled from ones he'd seen as a boy. One was of a single-engined fighter, a Yak-9, the Soviet-built aircraft the Patriarch had flown. At one point it had been the fastest petrol-driven plane in the world. The other was a Dassault Mystère, the French jet in which he'd broken the sound barrier. The Patriarch began pouring drinks for the newcomers.

'*Pertsovka*,' he said. 'Vodka spiced with red peppers, gives it a bite, and since we have a Russian theme this evening, it's appropriate.'

Bruno took a sip. It was hot and fiery, sharp on the throat but then he felt a warm glow spread down his chest. There was a discreet knock on the door and the housekeeper came in with a tray of salami, smoked fish and black bread. It reminded him of the evening at Yevgeny's place.

'Help yourselves to *zakuski*,' said the Patriarch, using a chunk of bread to pick up a slice of fish. 'It's an old Russian habit, never drink without eating something.'

'General Desaix tells me that neither Colonel Clamartin nor anyone else ever tried to blackmail him over these allegations,' said the Brigadier. 'He flatly denies that there is any truth in them.'

'The one and only time I heard of this was when Gilbert told me about it in Gorky Park,' the Patriarch said. 'Whoever dreamed it up did their homework. As far as I can recall, the dates and place names are right and so are the names of the two NKVD men. But all that stuff is available to anybody who's read my memoirs. The Russian edition sold a lot of copies.'

'When Gilbert came here seeking a place to live, did he make any kind of oblique reference to allegations made by this young man?' asked Prunier.

The Patriarch shook his head. 'Gilbert didn't live here, he lived at the vineyard as the guest of my son. So he never came to me looking for a place to stay. I had nothing to do with it, although I also saw him as a friend – and a damn good pilot. And he never referred to the allegations in any way, other than the one time he told me about them in Moscow.'

'Do you have any idea what might have been behind them, assuming the story is untrue?' the Brigadier asked.

'I haven't really thought about it,' said the Patriarch. 'The obvious possibility is that poor Ivan Tomasovitch invented the story to explain to his son why he'd been sent to the Gulag. It sounds rather better to say he was betrayed by a nasty foreigner than admit that he was criticizing his country's leader in the middle of a war or whatever it was he'd been doing.'

'Did you know that this young man, Dmitri Gromov, was killed in a hit-and-run accident shortly after his visit to our Embassy to make the allegations against you?' asked the Brigadier.

'*Mon Dieu*, no. Is that true?' The Patriarch seemed genuinely surprised.

'We're checking,' the Brigadier replied. 'But Gilbert was sent a news clipping about it with the word "murderer" scrawled across it. That's why he thought there might have been some truth to it all, and why he decided to make sure we knew about it after his own death.'

'So you think I might have been a spy for all these years, blackmailed by the KGB,' the Patriarch said thoughtfully. He leaned forward to pick up some more black bread and then took a long sip of his drink. 'It's plausible, I suppose, except for one thing. They had a far better hold on me than that, if they wanted to use it – my son Yevgeny. They never gave him an exit visa. You might call him a kind of hostage to my good behaviour.'

'And was your behaviour good?'

'It would depend whom you asked. I let my membership of the Party lapse after nineteen fifty-six when they crushed the Hungarian Uprising. They knew that. But I never made it public, never openly criticized them. I always treated them with respect, as former comrades in arms. And I never spied on them, nor for them.'

'But you did have long and regular conversations with senior Kremlin officials,' the Brigadier said. 'You dealt with all of them, from Stalin to Khrushchev, Brezhnev to Gorbachev.'

'I'm not sure I accept your use of the phrase "dealt with". I certainly met them all, was formally received by them, sometimes had private dinners with them, even spent weekends out at the dachas at Usovo and went hunting with Brezhnev at Zavidovo. I gave them my interpretations of French and Western policy, just as I gave our own presidents my interpretations of the thinking in the Kremlin. And yes, we discussed French politics and foreign policy, but I knew nothing that was not in the newspapers.'

'Not quite,' the Brigadier responded. 'We know that you undertook certain missions for de Gaulle, acting as an informal back channel with the Kremlin.'

'I wrote reports on each of those missions and they'll all be in the files at the Elysée, if de Gaulle chose to keep them. And whether you are aware of it or not, I did the same for Pompidou, for Giscard d'Estaing and for Mitterrand, at their request. Sometimes I handed over personal letters, sometimes I gave a verbal briefing. In each case, it was something the president did not want to go through the usual channels.' The Patriarch sniffed, waved a hand airily and said, 'The Quai d'Orsay leaks like a sieve.'

Bruno could not hold back a smile and he heard Prunier chuckle beside him. France's elegant diplomats had long been identified by the address of the Foreign Office on the left bank of the River Seine.

'Could you expand on that?' the Brigadier asked.

'I could but I won't. I was asked to keep those conversations confidential and I have. Both sides were confident that they could trust me. You could ask Giscard if you like; he's still alive.' The Patriarch set his glass down firmly, looked each of the in the eye and went on.

'I don't think you fully understand just how isolated those men were in the Kremlin, how much they feared they were being told only what their advisers wanted them to hear. I was a foreigner but spoke fluent Russian and they all knew I'd fought for them, alongside them, in their own warplanes. They knew I'd shed some blood in their battles. I'd even loved a Russian woman, fathered a Russian son. I'd met Khrushchev and Brezhnev during the war when we were all in uniform. We could use soldiers' slang together, swear like troopers, talk of old times, old battles, men we'd known.'

Bruno felt himself nodding in agreement. He knew the strength of that kind of bond and the depth of trust it could bring. He met the Brigadier's gaze and realized that he too understood.

'And so when we sat naked together on the *banya* out at Zavidovo, beating each other with birch branches until we got so hot we'd go out and roll in the snow, I knew I could believe what they told me. I could take it to my own president and be absolutely sure it was the truth.'

The Patriarch sat back, evidently moved by his memories or perhaps by his own rhetoric, and his head sank onto his chest. 'But if they'd thought for a moment that I was being controlled by the KGB, that I was bought and paid for, I'd have been no use to those lonely old men in the Kremlin. No use at all. They could never have trusted a word I said.'

The Patriarch poured himself another shot of vodka, downed it and went on. 'That's what went wrong with poor Gilbert. It wasn't the KGB, it was your people, fellow Frenchmen playing intelligence games, who just wanted to use him. That's why he was such a mess when he got back from

362

Moscow.' He looked accusingly at the Brigadier. 'Your predecessors worked him too hard. He wasn't built for that kind of life and you didn't even train him for it.'

'He told you of that?' the Brigadier asked, with an intake of breath, and Bruno heard Prunier gasp beside him. *Putain*, Bruno thought, I don't think I should be listening to this.

'That your people told him to accept the KGB's advances so you could feed them false information? Of course he told me, the poor bastard. He had to pretend to be a double agent while being ours all along. Have you any idea of the strain he was under? No wonder he was drinking. Gilbert was at the end of his rope, and then you pulled him out of Moscow and dumped him, with the Légion d'Honneur and a big label round his neck saying *security risk*, so the Russians would never be quite sure whether the stuff he gave them was real or not.'

'He ignored orders, he tried to set policy on his own,' the Brigadier said, in a voice that suggested he didn't entirely believe his own words but felt obliged to speak them.

'The orders were stupid. Gilbert was proved right about Yeltsin,' the Patriarch replied. 'I was there in Moscow, don't forget, seeing my old friend Akhromeyev, something else that Mitterrand asked me to do.'

He poured the last of the vodka and emptied his glass, putting it down hard on the table. 'That's enough for tonight,' he said, almost to himself. Then he looked squarely at the Brigadier. 'Well, you'd better make up your mind, Général de Brigade Lannes. Either arrest me or show yourself and your two witnesses out. I'm ninety years old and I've had enough. I'm going to bed.'

And with that, he picked up a final morsel of black bread and headed for the door. Bruno used his stick to stand in respect as the old man stomped by. Prunier followed suit and then the Brigadier also stood. At the door, the Patriarch paused.

'I've had an interesting request from *Paris Match* to give them an interview on my missions to the Kremlin. I don't suppose it would do any harm and I might remind some people of what I know and whom I served. I'm very tempted to accept.'

As the door closed behind him, the Brigadier shook his head in irritation, looked at his watch and then at Bruno. 'Where can we get something to eat around here at this time?'

'At my place,' said Bruno. 'I can offer home-made pâté, *enchaud de porc* that I made into a *confit* earlier this year, salad and cheese. It will only take ten, fifteen minutes.'

Within the half-hour, the two men plus Prunier's driver were standing at the high counter in Bruno's kitchen and sipping malt Scotch from the bottle of Balvenie the Brigadier had brought the day before. Bruno handed the Brigadier a tin of pâté and a can opener and took his cheese from the fridge. The driver was sent out to pick a couple of lettuces from the garden and Prunier was opening a bottle of the local Domaine red. Bruno took from his freezer a plastic bag that contained a quarter of a *tourte*, the big, round loaf of bread almost as big as the wheel of a small car. He'd sliced it before freezing for impromptu meals such as this and began feeding the slices into his toaster.

Bruno opened the tall glass jar in which he'd preserved the *confit* and scooped out the thick yellow fat that sealed it from the air. From his vegetable basket he took a kilo of potatoes, scrubbed them hard under the tap, sliced them and tossed them into salted boiling water while Prunier and the Brigadier set the table in the dining room. The driver washed and drained the lettuces he'd brought in and Bruno splashed them with hazelnut oil and balsamic vinegar. He took cornichons from a jar in the fridge and all four of them headed for the table to eat his pâté and toast.

Then Bruno went back to the kitchen, sliced the pork, put a spoonful of duck fat into a large skillet and added some garlic. He put more fat into his large frying pan, added three chopped shallots and a splash of white wine. The potatoes were almost done. Bruno rolled them in a towel to dry and then began to sauté them gently in the large pan. He put the slices of pork into the skillet and asked the driver to return to the garden for some parsley. From his freezer he took one of the grey summer truffles, wrapped in tinfoil, that he'd been storing. Once he stirred the potatoes and added some chopped parsley, he turned the pork slices. Already cooked, they only needed to be warmed.

Prunier took the skillet of *enchaud* and the Brigadier emptied the fried potatoes into a serving bowl Bruno had warmed with hot water. And once they were back at the table, Bruno grated the truffle into the *pommes sarladaises*. It should be the real black winter truffle, the famed *diamant noir* of the Périgord, he explained, but it was still too early for them.

He served two healthy slices of pork to each man, told them to help themselves to potatoes, filled his glass with red wine and wished them *bon appétit*. All four men began to eat hungrily. Bruno assumed that the presence of Prunier's driver meant they could not talk in any detail about the meeting with the Patriarch. So when the main course had been finished, the salad and cheese eaten and the second bottle of wine opened, he was surprised when Prunier asked the Brigadier, 'Where do we go from here?'

'We check out everything that can be checked, like the Novosibirsk newspaper in the summer of nineteen eighty-nine for that report of the hit and run,' the Brigadier began. Then they would look for any published records of Ivan Tomasovitch's trial and sentence and subsequent release, review their own files on the Patriarch, draft a report for the Minister of the Interior and leave it up to him.

'He may or may not decide to invite Marco for a friendly chat but I'll be very surprised if anything is done,' the Brigadier said. 'It's all too vague, he's too old, too well connected and there's not a scrap of real evidence. With Colonel Clamartin, it's different. The money in the trust fund makes it different. We'll have to look back over everything he did, but it all took place twenty years ago and we can't question the dead.'

'And too thorough a review would get the Patriarch repeating his criticisms of the way your predecessors handled Clamartin,' said Prunier. 'That could be embarrassing.'

'Indeed it could,' said the Brigadier. 'Which is why it is not very likely to happen. And we shall step back and leave you of the Police Nationale to handle the other difficult aspect of this matter, the murder of Colonel Clamartin.'

CHAPTER 32

The next morning dawned bright and warm, a touch of Indian summer that delighted Bruno as he limped out to greet the day. His hip and leg felt easier and in the shower he saw that his bruises were fading from bright blue to a yellowish violet. For the first time since the attack, he felt capable of driving. He eased himself gingerly into his police van and drove down to St Denis, picked up four fresh, warm croissants and a baguette and then headed for Pamela's place. He was in no condition to ride or even to mount his horse, but he wanted to see both Hector and Balzac and a breakfast with Pamela and Fabiola before they took the horses out would be an extra pleasure.

When he arrived and pulled in by the stables, nobody was stirring except Balzac, who bounded from the stables to greet him. He checked his watch: not quite seven-thirty. The horses would usually be saddled by now but Hector and Victoria were in their stalls. He walked around to the main courtyard, intending to enter by the kitchen door as usual when he saw the stately old Jaguar parked beside Pamela's *deux chevaux*. It was Crimson's car. Feeling embarrassed and a little ashamed of himself, Bruno scanned the upper windows but saw no signs of life. He crept forward and put his hand on the Jaguar's bonnet. It was stone cold, evidently parked all night.

Well, well, he thought, and toyed with the idea of leaving the croissants on the car, or better still on the outdoor table by the kitchen window, as a none-too-subtle message of his visit. He thought better of it. Pamela was a grown woman and their own affair was definitively over. He crept back to his car, taking his croissants and baguette with him, and drove to town, leaving his van in the bank's car park. It was market day and the town square would be filled with stalls. He left the croissants with Stéphane, bought four coffees from Fauquet and asked him to bring them on a tray back to the table behind Stéphane's stall where the stallholders shared a mid-morning *casse-croûte*.

'To what do we owe this honour?' asked Marcel from the vegetable stall. He and Léopold, the big Senegalese who sold belts, T-shirts and African cloth, joined Bruno and Stéphane for an impromptu breakfast. 'Didn't I see you buy these croissants about ten minutes ago and head out as usual towards Pamela's place?'

'You should have been a detective,' said Bruno. 'I'd forgotten that I can't ride with my bad leg so I turned around and came back.'

Marcel raised an eyebrow but gave a token nod, wolfed down his croissant, gulped his coffee and returned to his stall. Léopold thanked Bruno, gave him a sympathetic pat on the shoulder and did the same. Stéphane said nothing but took his private bottle of cognac from the small hatch beneath his stall and poured a tot into his own and Bruno's coffee before turning back to serve his customers.

Bruno gave Balzac the last of his croissant and made his usual tour of the market, feeling he could almost have done so without the walking stick. He was about to go to his office in the Mairie when his name was called. He turned and saw Yevgeny lumbering towards him, an arm outstretched to shake his hand. He insisted on buying Bruno a coffee.

'I wanted to thank you,' he said, once they were settled at a table on Fauquet's terrace. 'The *notaire* said you'd helped him track me down, and I got the document of ownership for the painting.'

'It was yours anyway,' said Bruno. 'You painted it, it was in your possession and nobody knew it had belonged to Gilbert.'

'I knew,' said Yevgeny. 'He helped me out once in Moscow when I badly needed some cash and I was very angry with Madeleine. She'd switched her affections to Gilbert so I gave him the painting and he gave me the cash. If it hadn't been for the money, I might have burned it.'

'That would have been a terrible waste,' said

Bruno, remembering his instant conviction that the artist had been Madeleine's lover.

'So you saw it?' Yevgeny asked, some pride in his tone. Bruno was convinced he'd never have burned it.

'By accident,' he replied. 'I entered the wrong door when looking for the bathroom. I also liked your self-portrait, even though it was a bit strange having it stare at me while I peed.'

'I think I was just Madeleine's bit of Moscow fun, a bit of local colour, an affair with a real Russian artist. I was besotted with her but I think I knew she wasn't at all serious about me,' Yevgeny said as the coffees came. 'Gilbert was the real thing, her grand passion. That's what she said when she left me.'

'This was when, the summer of 'eighty-nine? Not long before she married Victor?' Bruno asked. The grand passion hadn't lasted long, just long enough to get pregnant and then make a cool calculation that the Patriarch's son would make a more suitable husband and father than the drunken ex-fighter pilot.

'I can see you've worked it out, Bruno.'

'Did Victor ever learn he wasn't the father?'

'No, not Victor. He always thinks the best of everyone. I worked it out, and Raquelle had her own suspicions.'

'And your father?'

Yevgeny shrugged. 'You never know what Marco's thinking. He's always enjoyed secrets, little mysteries.'

'Talking of mysteries, did your mother ever mention a man called Ivan Tomasovitch, one of your father's mechanics during the war?' Bruno asked. 'Apparently he was arrested in the summer of 'forty-four, spent a few years in the Gulag. She may have met him.'

Yevgeny shook his head. 'Not that I remember. But there's something I wanted to say. Raquelle called me early this morning to say she left a message on your office phone but you never called back. It's her birthday today and she's having a small party at Le Thot, a picnic lunch. It's closed to the public today. She wants you to come, seems to think highly of you. I said I'd be seeing you at the market and would let you know.'

When Yevgeny left, Bruno called J-J to see if anything more had been learned from the various mobile phone photos that had been collected. They were still checking, he was told, but did he recall another young girl who had been there, wearing a blue dress that looked like silk?

Yes, he replied, it sounded like Marie-Françoise, the Countess's great-granddaughter, the girl who was in the cave. J-J should recognize her.

'How am I supposed to recognize someone who was in shock? We'd just pulled her out of the water and she'd had her face bashed in,' J-J said.

J-J emailed the photo to Bruno's phone and he confirmed it was Marie-Françoise, caught in the background of a shot of a smiling couple. She

372

was spooning ice cubes into a tall glass of orange juice. But with the couple blocking the rest of the scene, Bruno could not see whose glass it was. He called Marie-Françoise's mobile phone and found her just heading into a class at university. Did she recall serving ice cubes to anyone at the Patriarch's party?

'Yes, to Chantal's godfather, the one who died,' she said. 'Chantal was going to do it but her brother called her away and she gave me the bowl and asked me to take care of it. Gilbert always wanted ice in his drinks.'

'Where is Chantal now?'

'She's gone back to the Périgord with Raoul for some family thing she had to attend, a birthday party or something.'

Bruno rang off, called J-J back to relay the news. Then he asked if anybody had yet talked to Chantal's chemistry professor.

Yes, he was told. Chloral hydrate was not difficult to make, a relatively straightforward mixture of chlorine and ethanol in an acid solution. It was used quite often in wine labs in something called Hoyer's mounting medium to prepare specimens for microscope slides. The professor had no knowledge of Chantal ever making the stuff in his lab but in principle she could easily have done so.

'So Chantal is our suspect,' said J-J, 'with two million motives.'

'Let's talk to her first,' said Bruno. 'It might be more complex than that. You might want to call the wine labs in Bergerac and see if they know what Madeleine was up to. She also knows enough chemistry to make the stuff.'

J-J snorted. '*Putain*, what a family.'

Bruno explained he was heading to Le Thot, where he'd see Chantal and probably Madeleine as well.

'The Procureur just had a meeting with the *juge d'instruction*. We're authorized to call them both in for questioning, Chantal for Gilbert and Madeleine for her part in the attack on you. We can pick them up there and bring them back to Périgueux. What time will you get there?'

'About noon; it's a lunch. Maybe a little earlier if I can reach Chantal first to talk to her.'

'Take care. I'll call before we burst in.' J-J hung up.

Bruno called the hospital to ask after Imogène. She'd passed a quiet night and wanted to go home but after Peyrefitte's complaint, the registrar had recommended a psychological review. Bruno then called Fabiola at the clinic but she'd already been informed by the hospital. She'd be going there for a meeting in the afternoon and expected to bring Imogène back with her. The psychological review could be held at any time and there was no reason to detain her.

'I don't think there's much to worry about,' Fabiola said. 'She's never shown any sign of violence and offering someone a fawn may be a little odd but it's hardly outrageous. Imogène has a place to live, a job and friends who're standing

374

by her. I think they only agreed on the psychological review because Peyrefitte was making such a fuss.

'I heard a car this morning,' Fabiola went on. 'Was that you?'

'Yes, with croissants. When I saw Crimson's Jaguar, I thought I'd better forget it.'

'You assumed he was spending the night with Pamela?'

'Wasn't he?'

'No, he spent the night in our spare room and his daughter stayed at Pamela's. They just had too much to drink at dinner last night to drive back. We all did.'

Bruno didn't know what to say. After a moment he said, 'Sorry I missed it, sounds like it must have been fun.'

'How's the leg?'

'A lot better. I can drive.'

'You'd better come in so I can change the dressing and take a look at the stitches. Are you nearby?'

'I'm in the market so I'll hobble across now.'

CHAPTER 33

His dressing was changed and his bruises admired, and Bruno's stitches were pronounced healthy. Cheered by the prospect of getting back on horseback within the week, Bruno headed for Le Thot in his own vehicle. Balzac sat on the rear seat, gazing inquisitively ahead. Bruno was wearing a light blazer over his usual blue shirt and trousers, with his uniform jacket on a hook in the back and his *képi* perched on his sports bag. But he was a worried man.

He suspected J-J and the Procureur were barking up the wrong tree, that Chantal was a most unlikely murderer, even if she had persuaded Marie-Françoise to give Gilbert the fatal ice cubes. She did not know he was her father, had been stunned by the news of the inheritance and even more surprised by the amount of money coming to her.

The Patriarch had to be a suspect. Gilbert had a secret that could destroy the old man's reputation. But Bruno could not begin to explain why that threat had become dangerous now when it had lain dormant for two decades. Then there was

Victor, cuckolded by his best friend, raising in ignorance another man's child as his own. Had he found out the truth and sought his own revenge?

It was possible, Bruno thought, but the more he tried to work out the complex threads of family connections and motives the more sure he felt that Madeleine was at the heart of the mystery. Gilbert could destroy her reputation and quite possibly her marriage and upset her political ambitions just when they seemed to be taking off. An angry divorce would be damaging, the loss of the Patriarch's support even more so.

Above all, Bruno knew her to be ruthless, capable of making love with him before sending him off to be attacked and quite possibly killed by Fabrice. Madeleine had known that Bruno was not taking Gilbert's death at face value, that his suspicions kept him probing for the truth that could explode all her plans. But that was the very reason why for once he felt unable to trust his own hunches. He was too involved, too emotionally caught up with her to have much confidence in his own judgement. He had been enthralled by her. Even now he remembered the intensity of that evening they had spent together, his complete surrender of any critical faculty, his immersion in the delights she seemed so genuinely to give.

It had been, he thought now, like making love to a dream woman rather than to a real one, to some fantasy of his own making. And that was an error of judgement that left him not just ashamed of himself but also doubting his ability to think about her clearly. Piled atop all that was his anger at being toyed with, used and then tossed aside.

She might be a wicked and calculating woman but that did not necessarily make her a murderer. The secret of Chantal's birth had been kept for two decades; why did she fear it would emerge now? Or was it simply the flowering of her political hopes that might have driven her to act, more than twenty years after giving birth to Gilbert's child?

Chateau de Losse came into view on his right, which meant he'd almost reached the turning to Le Thot. Mentally, he gave a salute to its most famous owner, Jean de Losse, an old soldier who had been page to one king, tutor to another, and fought for his kings against the English, the Dutch, the Austrians, the Italians and the Spaniards. He'd been repeatedly wounded and taken prisoner in royal service, fought against Frenchmen in France's religious wars and seen his own son die in battle under his command. He had carved into one of the lintels of his chateau the phrase: 'Man does what he can, Chance does what it will.'

That seemed to sum it up, thought Bruno, and turned off, wondering whether this picnic lunch of Raquelle's would bring any more answers before J-J arrived to haul away two of the guests for questioning. As he climbed from the Land Rover and let Balzac out, he wondered whether he should leave his walking stick behind. He decided to take it. Balzac would doubtless want to romp in the wide parkland where the ground was uneven.

Bruno was not the first to arrive. Yevgeny was standing with Raquelle and Victor on the rear terrace, beside a long table loaded with food, plates and glasses. Bruno saw a whole salmon, a ham, salads and cheeses and a bowl heaped high with lobster tails and claws.

'You could feed an army. How many are you expecting?' he asked Raquelle, wishing her a happy birthday and giving her the cookbook he'd bought in St Denis and had wrapped as a gift.

'It's just the family and some colleagues from here and from Lascaux and Les Eyzies,' she said. 'You'll know most of them and they'll be delighted to see your dog. He's a charmer.' She bent down to pat the basset hound and fondle his ears and then looked up at Bruno. 'I wanted to thank you for everything you've done for Imogène. I just heard from her; she's hoping to go home this afternoon.'

'You're the one who took her in and gave her shelter,' he said. 'How is your robot bull?'

'Take a look,' she said, giving Balzac a final caress and then rising to point to the huge robot auroch she had made. 'He's out beside the fence that keeps in the real bulls. I'm hoping it gets them accustomed to him.'

Bruno thought it looked even more menacing as it stood there, immobile. 'Is it working?'

'It's too soon to tell. They came up one by one

to look at him and sniff him, and then they each backed away looking very confused when he started to move. We're trying to programme him to walk around the fence but it looks like he's frozen in place again. I'll have to go to the control room and see what's wrong. We nearly lost him yesterday in that pit by the woolly mammoth, and he ripped up half the fence.'

Raquelle hurried off and Bruno turned to greet Yevgeny and then Victor, who looked mystified by Bruno's presence but shook his hand politely.

'Have I arrived too soon?' Bruno asked. 'Where are the other guests?'

'Raoul and Chantal are on their way; Clothilde is picking them up from the station at Les Eyzies. And Papa is downstairs looking at the new exhibit,' said Yevgeny. 'Madeleine is out patrolling the grounds, doing what she calls her housekeeping, by which she means keeping down the rabbits. You probably heard the shooting.'

Bruno had not registered any sound of gunshots. Around this part of the world at this time of the year they were commonplace. He was offered a glass of champagne and then Yevgeny steered him away from the terrace towards some low tables, cushions and beach chairs that had been grouped together on the grassy bank that overlooked the enclosure where the cattle grazed. Balzac crept slowly towards the great beasts as if stalking them, his body low, almost touching the ground, his tail down and his long ears trailing.

'This is where Raquelle intends us to eat, down here in the open air,' Yevgeny said, lighting a cigarette, a French Gitane, Bruno noted, rather than the Russian ones Gilbert had smoked. 'I think it's because she doesn't want us to smoke on the terrace by the building. But I wanted to ask you something. Have you ever seen Raoul and Chantal together?'

'Yes, they're obviously very close,' said Bruno, smiling as he recalled them ducking each other like children in the swimming pool at the Countess's chateau.

'They think they're brother and sister, or at least half-brother and sister, but you and I know that they're not,' Yevgeny said. 'They share no blood. Different mothers, different fathers. Gilbert was worried about it.'

'How do you mean?' Bruno asked, uncertain what point Yevgeny was trying to make. He was watching Balzac, close to the fence around the enclosure but immobile, just watching and sniffing at the air.

'I've been thinking. I know Gilbert watched over Chantal closely. He'd spent a lot of time with her when she was younger. And the closeness between Raoul and Chantal is a family joke. We all say they're made for each other and if it weren't for being related they'd be the perfect couple. When she was a little girl, Chantal always said she'd marry him when she grew up.'

'Why did that worry Gilbert? Children say that sort of thing all the time.'

'Because Gilbert believed it. They would be the perfect couple. And he knew they weren't related, there was nothing to stop them from marrying. What really got him worried was Papa's latest little scheme with the Countess.'

'Aah,' said Bruno, suddenly understanding what Yevgeny was driving at. 'You mean the plan to marry Raoul to Marie-Françoise. You know it was as much the idea of the Countess as your father.'

'Yes, and Papa could never refuse anything to his dear *Parizhanka*.'

'So you think that Gilbert wanted to prevent it by telling Chantal the truth, that she was free to marry Raoul if she wished. And Gilbert was then prevented from doing so by his very convenient death.'

'Exactly, *monsieur* detective. And who would want to keep that secret at any price if not my dear sister-in-law?'

'That's the question,' said Bruno, thinking that Yevgeny had never got over Madeleine. He wondered if he would. But, Bruno told himself, at least he wasn't scratching the scab by going to sleep and waking up with her nude portrait every day.

'Talk of the devil,' said Yevgeny. Bruno turned to follow his gaze and saw Madeleine emerging from the trees, a shotgun over one shoulder and two rabbits hanging by their ears from her other hand. The gun was broken open at the breech, the stock in her hand and the two barrels pointing down over her shoulder. Bruno approved. That was the safe way to carry the weapon.

Madeleine raised the arm holding the rabbits in a kind of greeting. He waved back. Yevgeny ignored her, looking instead at the robot bull, which was now moving again but not proceeding as planned to make a circuit of the fence. Instead it was moving a few paces back and then forward again.

'It looks like Raquelle is going to be stuck in the control room for a while,' Yevgeny said. 'I'd better go and get Papa. The others will be here any minute.'

Bruno was about to head back with Yevgeny to the terrace when he saw Madeleine waving again more urgently and then beckoning him to join her. Balzac had seen him move and was trotting to join him. Bruno walked down the gentle slope, the cattle enclosure on his left, where Raquelle's robot bull was now edging sideways and forward as if in some weird bovine dance. Balzac stopped to watch this strange sight, darting forward and then back, baffled by this thing that moved like an animal but smelled altogether different. Bruno smiled and went on, glad he'd brought the walking stick, heading for the edge of the woods where Madeleine stood. Behind her they stretched back and across the hillside and over the far ridge. Another enclosure for the goats was on his right, then the huge, life-size model of the woolly mammoth. He recalled the pit that had been dug near here. He must remember to ask Raquelle why.

'I wanted to apologize,' Madeleine said, smiling at him, and he felt a physical jolt at the sight of her. Or was it his sense of dismay that such beauty could conceal such vicious ruthlessness within? She looked magnificent, her hair pulled back into a loose ponytail, eyes shining and cheeks slightly flushed. She was wearing tight jeans of olive green tucked into knee-high boots and a khaki bush shirt, the sleeves rolled up to her elbows. Around her trim waist was a broad leather belt from which hung a hunting knife and an ammunition pouch. With the gun over her shoulder, she looked like an advertisement for hunting chic.

On an impulse, he pulled out his phone and took a photograph of her standing like that.

'Send me a copy,' she said, laughing. 'That should get me the hunters' vote.'

'Apologize for what?' he asked, half expecting some words of regret for the attack on him by the gamekeeper she'd hired. She must know of Fabrice's fate; who else would have hired him an expensive lawyer?

'I was most discourteous, falling asleep like that, and it was very disappointing waking up alone the next morning,' she said. 'Still, thanks to you it was a marvellous night's sleep.'

Bruno smiled politely as he tried to work out what she was up to. If she had indeed been asleep when he left her bed, she was soon awake enough to phone Fabrice to tell him Bruno was on his way home. Was she so confident of her hold over him that she thought he'd succumb to her smile?

'And I'm sorry I couldn't greet you properly at that supper with the wild boar but Papa was making a bit of a fool of himself.' She smiled again and held out the rabbits. 'Could you take them, please?'

He moved forward and she stepped back down the path through the woodland, beckoning him after her, her eyes dancing as she gave a tinkling, teasing laugh. She gave him the rabbits, threw a swift glance over his shoulder to be sure the fringe of trees gave them cover and then moved close and kissed him on the mouth, the hand that had held the rabbits caressing the back of his neck. When he failed to respond, she teased his lips with her tongue.

'You weren't so shy in Bordeaux,' she breathed. 'I understand; you're thinking the others are just up there on the terrace.'

'No,' he said, stepping back from her, 'I'm thinking of Gilbert and when it was that he informed you he was going to tell Chantal that he was her father.'

'What do you mean, Gilbert was her father?' She almost spat the name and her eyes were blazing. Was it his question or her anger at his rejection? 'That's nonsense.'

'We checked the DNA, his and Chantal's.'

'Gilbert's DNA?' She laughed, mockingly. 'How? From his ashes? Gilbert was cremated.'

'I took samples from his hairbrushes in his cottage when you and Victor were sorting through his papers, looking for the will you didn't find. But I found it, and Chantal inherits everything.'

'You can't prove it's his DNA,' she retorted, and went on coldly, 'We had to wash and clean up after sorting through his empty bottles. Victor used his hairbrush.'

'Nice try, Madeleine. But we got the same DNA from his drinking flask and from those Russian cigarettes he smoked.'

'So she's his daughter. So what?'

'We also know about the chloral hydrate in the orange juice and we know about your unregistered mobile phone, the one you used to get in touch with Fabrice the night he tried to kill me. Fabrice is a weak link and he's going to talk. He'll even tell us why you told him to destroy Rollo's garden, just because you wanted to send a message to people who asked you to stop hunting on their land. The chief of detectives for the Police Nationale is on his way here to arrest you with a warrant signed by the Procureur de la République.'

He turned and was walking the few steps to the edge of the woods when he heard the familiar double click of cartridges being loaded and then the sound of the breech closing. 'Wait,' she called.

'Are you going to shoot me in the back?' he asked, fighting to keep his voice calm. He let the dead rabbits fall from his hand. His only hope was to show no fear, to remain calm and confident. 'It's too late. I'm out of the woods and I can see Yevgeny and the Patriarch. Raoul and Chantal have just arrived. That's a lot of witnesses to the murder of an unarmed policeman.'

Bracing his weak leg with the walking stick he began to wave at the group on the terrace. Chantal and Raoul were carrying trays of food down to the picnic spot. The others were following, Clothilde and Yevgeny, Victor helping his father. Where was Raquelle? Still playing with the controls of her robot?

'Yevgeny just waved back at me,' Bruno said. His throat was dry. 'They're on their way and I'm in plain sight. Raoul and Chantal are coming with the food.'

'You won't live to eat it,' she said, her voice as flat as it was final.

There was more movement ahead. Balzac, who had bounded off to greet Clothilde and to make friends with Chantal, was now trotting down the slope towards Bruno, pausing to investigate the giant mammoth.

'Turn around,' she said. He ignored her and waved again. He heard Chantal's voice calling something to him, too faint to make out the words.

'That's your daughter you can hear, telling us to come and eat,' he said. 'Do you want her to watch you shoot me in the back? Put the gun down, Madeleine.'

'A tragic hunting accident,' she said. He could

hear her stepping off the path behind him and moving through the undergrowth to his left. 'So easy to lose one's footing in this brush.'

Up on the terrace he saw the familiar bulk of J-J, a uniformed policeman at his side, come through the glass doors and stand surveying the impressive table of food.

'The police are here,' he said. 'It's too late, Madeleine.'

'Too late for you, Bruno.'

He saw Balzac backing away from the mammoth, heard the dog growl defiance even as he retreated. And then from behind the mammoth, the bulk of Raquelle's robotic bull emerged, moving jerkily forward and sideways, coming closer. Raoul and Chantal had put down the food trays and were heading down the slope towards him, Yevgeny starting to run as Bruno's waving became desperate.

He refused to look at Madeleine but he heard her, dangerously close, maybe five metres away, almost parallel with him. At this range, the gun would blow his head off.

'Are you going to shoot my dog, too?' he asked.

'As I come out from the trees, they'll see me trip and fall,' she said. 'They'll see the gun hit the ground and fire and see you go down and they'll think it was a tragic accident.'

He glanced across and found himself facing a levelled shotgun and eyes so arctic that it was her chilling smile even more than the gun that

388

froze him. How tragic, he thought, that of all the women whose memory he cherished, this murderer should be the last one with whom he had made love, that her face should be the last one he would ever see.

Bruno closed his eyes and summoned memories: Pamela laughing for joy and bending over her horse's mane as she galloped towards him; Isabelle emerging from his bedclothes, her sweet breasts trembling, laughing as Balzac licked at her ear; Katarina reading Baudelaire to him by the riverbank in Bosnia.

'Goodbye, Bruno, you interfering fool.' Madeleine stepped out of the trees and then Balzac barked. She glanced at the dog, away from the robot bull that was at her shoulder and taking another jerky step forward. In desperation, Bruno hurled himself towards her, his walking stick outstretched like a rapier. But even as he plunged, he knew he'd fall short.

And then she jolted, gasping, her head going back as the robot bull hit her, pushing on with implacable force. She toppled forward and down into the pit at her feet, her gun still in her hands.

Two gunshots came, so close they sounded almost as one. Her scream abruptly ended as the bull toppled into the pit after her.

Bruno crawled forward, smelling the cordite, and peered down. Beneath the jumbled metal of the bull he saw a skein of blonde hair, an arm and hand that were slick with blood, and a leg sticking out at an impossible angle.

Raoul was holding Chantal, keeping her back from the sight inside the pit and then leading her away, her head tucked into his chest. J-J was still lumbering down the slope. Victor let out a long, whining cry of grief and sank to his knees on the far side of the pit. Yevgeny helped Bruno to his feet and gave him his walking stick. Balzac was at his side, body pressed for reassurance against Bruno's leg, peering back and forth from the pit to his master.

'A hunting accident,' said the Patriarch quietly. He gazed impassively at Bruno as if daring him to say anything different.

Bruno pulled his phone from his pocket. He had pressed 'Record' when he put his phone away after taking her photograph. Now he pressed the 'Play' button.

Her voice was faint and tinny and only Yevgeny and the Patriarch were close enough to hear. The key phrase came out clearly enough. 'They'll see me trip and fall. They'll see the gun hit the ground and fire and see you go down and they'll think it was a tragic accident.'

Bruno looked at the Patriarch, thinking of all he had done for France as memories of his boyhood adulation flooded back. They merged with the image of Madeleine melting into his arms. *Mon Dieu*, what a gullible fool he'd been! He looked down at his phone, knowing he'd look again and again at the photo of her he had taken. He glanced at the Patriarch and then back at the 'Record' function on his phone. Sighing to himself, he pressed 'Rewind' and then 'Delete.'

'As you say, Marco, a hunting accident,' he said.